Where Blooms Love

A COLLECTION OF SPRING ROMANCES

Cheryl Rae Johnson

Cynthia L. Simmons

Lane P. Jordan

Linda Wood Rondeau

PeggySue Wells

Sally Jo Pitts

Shelia Stovall

Travis W. Inman

ELK LAKE PUBLISHING INC
PUBLISHING THE POSITIVE
Plymouth, Massachusetts

Copyright Notice

Library Cataloging Data

Names: Johnson, Cheryl Rae; Simmons, Cynthia L.; Jordan, Lane P.; Rondeau, Linda Wood; Wells, PeggySue; Pitts, Sally Jo; Stovall, Shelia; Inman, Travis W. (Cheryl Rae Johnson, Cynthia L. Simmons, Lane P. Jordan, Linda Wood Rondeau, PeggySue Wells, Sally Jo Pitts, Shelia Stovall, Travis W. Inman)

Where Blooms Love: A Collection of Spring Romances / Cheryl Rae Johnson, Cynthia L. Simmons, Lane P. Jordan, Linda Wood Rondeau, PeggySue Wells, Sally Jo Pitts, Shelia Stovall, Travis W. Inman

530 p. 23cm × 15cm (9in × 6 in.)

ISBN-13: 978-1-64949-569-3 (paperback) | 978-1-64949-570-9 (trade paperback) | 978-1-64949-571-6 (e-book)

Key Words: Choices; Small Towns; Short Stories; Contemporary Romance; Inheritance/Legacy; Amish/Mennonite; Historical Fiction; Friendships
Library of Congress Control Number: 2022938126 Fiction

And we know that in all things God works for the good of those who love him, who have been called according to his purpose. (Romans 8:28).

Table of Contents

Nobody Knows Me Like You—Cheryl Rae Johnson.....1

To Love Freedom—Cynthia L. Simmons 77

With Every Step You Take—Lane P. Jordan. 141

My Favorite Leia—Linda Wood Rondeau 201

Tea for Two—PeggySue Wells 275

Color Me Springtime:—Sally Jo Pitts. 349

Welcome Home to Redbird Falls—Shelia Stovall 417

Charity's Shadow—Travis W. Inman 477

Dear Reader,

What better time of year for love to bloom than in the Spring? This collection of stories by our experienced authors has been a labor of love as we arranged a bouquet of romance stories for your enjoyment. We hope that you are enlightened and encouraged as you read these stories. Some are fanciful, some are historical, some overcome tremendous odds for love to happen. But in each of these tales, we pray you discover how God works in every area of our lives, including romance.

Linda Wood Rondeau
Project Manager

Nobody Knows Me Like You

CHERYL RAE JOHNSON

Chapter 1

Arlene counted the times they'd been to the hospital, but the heart monitor's hypnotic beeps interrupted her. *The first time was the end of January right after his birthday. Again in February, I think. Those blasted monitors make my head hurt.*

She scanned the room. *I think we've stayed in this one before.*

Arlene's husband lay motionless on the sterile bed. Her exhaustion meter told her she needed a bed too. Or at least a pillow. The awful ambulance ride. Ten hours in an overcrowded ER. Then, finally, a room. The hospital staff remembered them. Arlene didn't understand why they waited so long in that dungeon of an ER. *We're over ninety years old for crying out loud. Doesn't that mean anything?*

Arlene leaned close to her husband. "The sun is up dear. Another beautiful spring day." Then more to convince herself, she added, "God sends his promises in the spring."

"Miss Arlene, have you eaten today? You don't do your husband any good if you don't eat." Millie arrived for her shift.

Eaten? Arlene wanted to say. *When have I had time to eat?* "I'll get something once we're settled in."

"Miss Arlene, do y'all have anyone living at the house with you? Or is it just you two?"

Arlene understood the implication. How could a couple in their nineties live on their own? *What was so strange about it?* They embraced privacy like a second honeymoon. Each boasted sharp minds. Good health. Until recently, of course. The falls came, the forgetfulness, then the stroke.

"We live alone." Arlene stroked her husband's arm.

With every hospital visit, the clock's hands stopped and held the time. Then like a judge granting a reprieve, the clock wound itself up, and time inched forward. Arlene studied her husband. His stock-still face told her no reprieve would be granted. The clock was winding down.

"Have you called your children? You shouldn't be here alone." Millie and her questions.

"I'm not alone. But, yes, they're on their way."

This satisfied Millie, and she left Arlene in peace.

"The children will be here soon, my dear. They will cheer you."

Children was a misnomer. Wes, the oldest, took after his father in both looks and disposition. Then came the girls, Colleen and April who was named for Arlene's favorite season, spring. They both favored their mother, brown curly hair and hazel eyes. But the children were grandparents, now, and among the three of them, they had enough grandchildren to form a sports team.

Arlene drew her sweater close. "You must be cold, too, my love." She covered him with an additional blanket. "I know you have to go sometime, but I wish you didn't have to go now."

Clouds of loneliness encircled Arlene until she released a flood of tears. She buried her face in his motionless arms. Scents of sawdust and Old Spice soothed her.

"I can't let your last aftershave bottle get thrown away." The smells ferried her to her childhood home of Halford, Texas.

"Remember your blue Ford pickup? You loved that beat up jalopy. So many different paths our lives could have taken." Arlene swirled his gray hair. "You told me you were the one who knew me best. I was afraid I'd lost you forever. What would I have done if you hadn't come back for me?"

Chapter 2

Arlene Hutchins didn't like rising before the sun. But on April 13, 1941, the citizens of Halford, Texas, planned an Easter sunrise service at the town square. Arlene sat on the edge of her bed. Her head ached. *Why do we do this every year?*

"Arlene, you outta bed?" Momma bellowed from the kitchen.

"Yes, Momma. I'm coming." Arlene hoped the hoarseness in her voice didn't give her sleepiness away. She brushed her curls and smiled. *But Jack will be there. He's worth rising early for.*

Arlene dressed and joined her parents downstairs. On their way to town, the family of three stopped at Arlene's aunt's house, where Aunt Jewell joined them as they walked the short distance to the town square. One by one the families of Halford gathered in darkness. Reverend Brock recited from the book of Luke. As if to resurrect Jesus himself, the reverend boomed, "He is not here, he is risen." The sun took its cue. Streaks of yellow, orange, and red burst through the morning clouds. Satisfied parishioners gawked at the grandeur of the moment.

The joyous mood dipped for one small moment at the end of the service when Reverend Brock announced, "Ray Woodard, Kenny Walters, and John Hammond finished their military training and have new base assignments. Remember to pray for them and their families. And pray America stays out of the war."

Talk of war sent the crowd murmuring. Arlene's parents stood next to the Hammonds, their close friends. Arlene's father grabbed Frank Hammond's hand. "We're praying for John. Do you know where he's headed?"

"My boy got lucky. He's shipping out to Hawaii. He said he signed up to see the world, and Hawaii sounds fantastic," Frank said.

"I hear the beaches are beautiful."

"He's training at a base in Pearl Harbor. Not too familiar with it but sounds nice and safe."

"We'll pray the war ends soon and the United States never gets involved."

Mary Hammond piped in. "I can't believe Congress enacted a draft when we're not at war. But at least it's for men twenty-one and older." Mary nodded toward her son. "Thank goodness Jack is only eighteen. Surely, the war will be over before he's twenty-one."

Jack kept staring in Arlene's direction, apparently not listening to his mother. He and Arlene had been standing close enough to each other the entire service that their fingers touched if they swayed right.

The women hugged goodbye. The men shook hands. Jack and Arlene exchanged discreet smiles, an art they'd perfected. The families went their separate ways for the time being. An Easter Sunday sunrise service did not negate the regular Sunday church service. The families would meet again at church in a couple hours.

Arlene couldn't remember a time when she didn't know Jack. The two grew up together in the First Baptist Church where Arlene attended every Sunday morning to make Momma happy. Every Sunday evening, Arlene attended the First United Methodist Church to make Daddy happy. Then one Sunday night, the First United Methodist parishioners warmed their voices with the first hymn. As "and the morning breaks eternal bright and fair" crooned forth, Jack slipped in, crawled over several young men, and planted himself next to Arlene.

"Arlene," her father said when they arrived home. "I know why Jack came tonight. You're too young to date."

"Daddy, girls my age date. Most get married right after high school."

"You're about to graduate. You two can date then."

"Yes, Daddy."

Not long after Easter, the First United Methodists held their annual dessert auction to raise money for missions. Arlene baked an apricot pie made from the apricots grown in the Hutchins's backyard. Her lattice crust adorned the top like a crown jewel.

Jack saved his money, determined to outdo anyone who bid on Arlene's coveted apricot pie. With each auctioneer's cry for bids, Jack held firm until he strolled out carrying the pie on one arm and Arlene on the other. Arlene would graduate in a few short weeks, and Arlene's father didn't stop the pie-crossed sweethearts from seeing each other.

"Jack?" Arlene asked not long after the auction. "Do you want me to bake you another apricot pie? The last one cost you a fortune."

Jack drew her close and held her gaze with mischievous eyes. "I gotta confession to make. I'm not crazy about apricot pies."

Arlene pulled away. "You didn't like my pie? What was wrong with it? Was the crust too tough?"

"Slow down. You didn't hear me. I didn't say that I didn't like your apricot pie. I said I don't like apricot pies. As in I don't eat apricots. Never have. But my dad gobbled it right up. Said it's the best he's ever had."

Arlene's jaw dropped. "If you don't eat apricots, why did you buy my pie?"

Jack leaned toward her. "Because I'm crazy about you. And no one else was walking out of there with your pie."

Arlene squealed and ran back into Jack's arms.

She and Jack spent the summer exploring the countryside. The residents of Halford monitored their coming and going by how much ruckus Jack's old jalopy made.

Chapter 3

Cool autumn breezes replaced the blistering Texas heat. One morning at the breakfast table, Arlene mused over the modern ways of Halford. "Momma, did you know most businesses in Halford have telephone lines? More modern homes have them now too."

"Is that so, dear?"

Arlene studied her father who was busy reading the *Halford Daily News*.

"Daddy, don't you think it's time we installed a phone line? You could call Aunt Jewell any time you wanted to check on her."

Arlene's father peered over the paper. "Aunt Jewell lives down the street. Doesn't take much to check on her."

Arlene sighed and brought her plate to the sink. "Patty is on her way. Telecomm Communications is hiring operators, and we're applying. It'll give us a chance to see each other more."

"How lovely," Momma said. "We don't see Patty much since you two graduated."

"I know. Jack and I are always together, and she's seeing Bill Summers now."

Arlene's father grunted from behind his paper.

"Don't lose your friends because you're dating."

Arlene laughed. "Yes, Daddy."

Patty arrived, and the girls caught up with each other on the way to Telecomm Communications. Both were hired right away.

"We did it, Patty. We're working women." The girls hugged and giggled at their new status. Arlene couldn't wait to tell Jack when he came over later.

She heard Jack's Ford approach as she and Momma finished the supper dishes. She ran to the porch and threw her arms around Jack as he climbed the porch stairs.

Jack laughed. "Hey, I'm glad to see you too. Wanna go for a ride."

"Let me grab my sweater."

They drove through the country with no real destination. Jack reached for Arlene's hand.

"You're about to burst. What is it?" Jack said.

"I have the best news. I got a job today."

Jack slammed his foot on the brake so hard Arlene grabbed the dash to keep from flying through the windshield. "Jack!"

He careened the truck to the side of the road. "You what?"

"I got a job. As an operator at Telecomm Communications."

"Why did you do that?"

"Why? Why not? They were hiring, and Patty and I applied."

"You and Patty, huh?"

"Yes, me and Patty. What is wrong with you?"

Jack thumped the steering wheel with his fingers. "I never thought you'd work. My mother doesn't work, and your mother doesn't work. It never occurred to me you would work."

"Jack, it's 1941. Lots of women work. Women go to college and become professionals."

"College? Professionals? Is that what you want?"

Arlene rolled her eyes. "I'm a telephone operator."

Jack stared off into the field before turning back to Arlene. "You do think I'll be able to support us and a family, don't you? You're not doing this because you think I can't provide?"

Arlene shook her head. "That never crossed my mind. I want to earn my own money. I can't expect Momma and Daddy to give me money every time I want something."

They turned away from each other and stared out their windows. The dark country roads yielded little light, and Arlene didn't like sitting far apart.

She broke their silence. "I had no idea you'd react this way."

"I didn't know you were thinking about getting a job. That's all. You'll be great ..."

They never fought, and Arlene didn't want to start. She inched her way toward Jack, and he slid his arm around her.

"I won't work when we're married. I'll have the house to take care of and kids."

Jack's body relaxed. "How many kids you planning on us having?"

"I hope more than one. I always wanted a brother or sister." Arlene reached for the hand Jack cradled around her neck.

"I'm going to plant a garden too. And we'll have fresh vegetables year 'round. I won't need any apricot trees, though, will I?" Arlene looked toward him with a slight smile.

"Sorry." Jack hugged her. "You can still make your pies. Everyone else loves them."

"Will you teach me to drive? I won't want to be stuck in a house all day."

Jack's muscles tensed. He released Arlene's hand and moved his arm.

"You want me to teach you to drive this old truck?"

"Why not?"

"She'd be hard to maneuver. She always jerks you around." Jack sounded anxious.

"Most girls drive these days."

Jack clutched the steering wheel. "You're Miss Independent tonight. We'll talk about it later."

Jack turned the key, and his truck roared to life. "It's late. I should get you home."

Arlene lay in bed that night and rehashed the evening. Talking to Jack used to be easy and exciting. Lately, conversations with him were like walking barefoot through a field of grass burrs. She prayed life would work itself out.

Arlene and Patty laughed at the ways the residents of Halford reacted to their new phones. Old ladies adopted a sophisticated air. Patty placed her hand on her hip and held out her pinkie to mimic Clara Bedford. "Connect me to Mrs. Smith at 7428. Straight away, please." Both girls bent over in laughter. "Straight away." Patty said. "Does she think she's from England? Nobody says that."

"Then there's the men at Halford Oil where Daddy works." Arlene said. "Hello. Are you there?" Arlene clicked her tongue like a telephone receiver. "Can you hear me? I'm trying to connect."

Between giggles, Arlene said, "I want to reply, 'Yes, and we hear all the times you thump the receiver too.'"

On one of their country drives, Arlene attempted to share these funny stories with Jack.

"You wouldn't believe what happened at work today."

Jack's muscles tensed as soon as she spoke. Instead of finishing the story, she said, "It's not important. Never mind." Why did her having a job bother Jack so much?

Chapter 4

"Arlene, turn on the radio." Momma and Arlene both jumped when Daddy barreled through the door.

"Ed?" Momma said. "Why are you home so early?"

"President Roosevelt is speaking." Daddy rubbed his forehead.

Roosevelt's voice pierced through the crackling airwaves. "Yesterday, December 7th, 1941—a date which will live in infamy—the United States of America was suddenly and deliberately attacked by naval and air forces of the Empire of Japan."

Arlene leaned toward the radio.

Roosevelt continued. "The attack yesterday on the Hawaiian Islands has caused severe damage to American naval and military forces. I regret to tell you that very many American lives have been lost."

Momma buried her hands in her face and mumbled, "Ed, do you think ... John?"

Arlene stared at her father. "What do you mean ... John?"

Daddy rubbed his hands through his hair. "John is stationed there."

Arlene flew out of her chair. "I need to see Jack. Please. Can we go to the Hammonds?"

"Yes, I'll get the car."

Halford didn't need a telephone line for the entire town to know the Hammond's dreadful news. By the time Arlene and her parents arrived at the Hammond house, most of Halford was either there or on its way.

Arlene shot out of the car before Daddy pulled into the Hammond driveway, and she pushed through the crowd. "Jack?" She found Mary Hammond in the kitchen and threw her arms around Mary's neck.

Mary stroked Arlene's hair. "Jack's out back."

Arlene raced to the porch and scanned the backyard. *Where is he?* She sighted his feet first, dangling off his truck's tailgate. Arlene found the rest of Jack sprawled out in the back of his truck. His hands covered his face. He looked asleep.

"Jack?" Arlene whispered in case he had dozed off.

"Aren't you supposed to be at work?" Jack snapped.

Arlene froze. *Is he mad at me? Breathe, Arlene. He's in pain.*

"Patty is covering my shift."

Arlene climbed into the truck bed and pulled Jack's hands off his face. His puffy eyes made her want to cry.

"Jack, does this mean John ..."

"Dad is trying to find out if John is alive or not. It could take weeks."

"We gotta have faith. We have to believe John survived."

A brittle wind brushed over them. Without wanting to, Arlene shivered. Jack grabbed a blanket crumpled in the corner of his truck and wrapped it tightly around her.

Before long, Arlene's father made his way to Jack's truck. "Arlene, we need to go. Jack, we're praying for John's safety. We're praying for you, too."

"Thank you, sir. If it's okay, I'd like Arlene to stay. I'll bring her home later."

Daddy studied her, and then turned to Jack. "I want her home at a decent hour."

"Yes, sir."

Daddy leaned in and kissed Arlene's cheek.

"Thank you, Daddy," she said.

Jack jumped off the truck and grabbed his coat out of the cab. He slipped it around Arlene and said, "Let's go for a walk."

When they were away from the chaos of the house, Jack said, "This isn't the best time, but I want to make plans."

"Of course." Arlene didn't understand what Jack meant by plans, but she would help him get through his grief.

Jack sat on a log and pulled Arlene next to him. "Life will be crazy until we know about John."

Arlene nodded.

"I can't ask your dad yet, but I want to be certain you will marry me."

Arlene's eyes widened at the unexpected turn in conversation. "You know I will."

"I'll ask your father for his blessing after we know John is safe." Jack's voice trailed off. "Or whatever we find out."

Arlene took Jack's hand. "John will come home safely."

"Don't tell anyone about our plans until I talk to your dad. Not even Patty."

"I won't."

"We can get married this summer. What do you say?"

She threw her arms around Jack. "Summer is perfect." Arlene never expected the night to end on a happy note.

Jack shifted his weight. "There's one more thing."

"Yes?"

"I don't want you to work. I can support us."

Arlene stared at him. "You want me to quit now?"

"If Patty weren't working there, would you be here with me now?"

Arlene stiffened. "But I am here with you." Arlene touched Jack's arm. "Let's not fight. Today has been hard. But I'm so happy. If I work until we're married, I can help Daddy with the wedding expenses."

"I suppose." Jack stood up. "I'd better get you home."

Arlene didn't want to leave. She wanted to talk about how she would soon be the future Mrs. Jack Hammond. She'd been excited until Jack expressed once more his disapproval of her working, souring yet another happy moment.

Within a week, Mr. and Mrs. Hammond received word John perished, along with over two thousand other brave men during the attack on Pearl Harbor. Whatever safety net this small Texas town felt lifted when Roosevelt declared America would enter the war.

Chapter 5

After John's funeral, Arlene didn't hear the roar of Jack's truck in her driveway as often. When he did come, his mood was dark, and he hardly said a word.

Arlene attempted to draw him out. "How was work today? Did you have any interesting cars come to the shop?'

"Mr. Jenkins as usual."

"He's gonna keep y'all in business with his old jalopy."

"Yeah."

End of conversation. No more talk of a wedding. Only short answers and vacant stares.

Arlene wanted to talk about John, about how funny he was. She remembered the time in high school when John put a dead frog on the teacher's chair. Instead of screaming, Mrs. Haskins picked up the frog, laid it on a table, and showed the students how to dissect it. John gawked at the scene.

"Jack, do you remember ..."

"Huh?"

"Never mind." *Jack probably doesn't want to hear the story.*

The Friday before Easter, Jack surprised Arlene with a picnic. He spread out a blanket, while Arlene unpacked the sandwiches.

"What a beautiful day. I can't remember the last time we went on a picnic," Arlene said.

"I'm sorry. We should have done this sooner."

They enjoyed their picnic, and Jack reached for Arlene's hands.

"It's time I talked to your father."

Arlene cocked her head. "My father?"

"Yes, asked him for your hand in marriage."

Arlene stared at Jack. Months had passed since they last discussed getting married.

"Arlene?"

Arlene half smiled and half laughed. "We haven't talked about it in so long. I wasn't sure you still wanted to get married."

Jack drew Arlene close and kissed her.

"Of course I do," he said." I'll talk to your dad when I get off work tomorrow."

Arlene clung to Jack and believed they would be as happy as they'd ever been.

Arlene tossed and turned in bed that night. She arrived early for work the next day and barely listened to the calls from her customers. When she arrived home, she found one of her favorite romance novels but put it down to read later. Her thoughts turned to Aunt Jewell. "Momma, how come Aunt Jewell never married," Arlene asked.

Momma didn't look up from darning Daddy's worn-out sock. "She had a beau once."

"What happened?" Arlene asked.

Momma stopped her needlework. "The man went west in search of a dream. They weren't meant to be."

Arlene imagined the many ways her aunt's love story could have ended in tragedy.

How romantic to be the center of an ill-fated love story. As long as it isn't your own love story.

When she tired of remembering her aunt's tragedy, she swept already spotless floors. Her memory flitted back to Mrs. Haskins's English class and Edgar Allan Poe. Arlene recalled her fascination with the author and how she kept reading his works even after graduation. Her favorite work had always been "The Raven"—and the poem still sent chills down her spine, something she knew was not proper for a young lady. She swept while the poem rolled through her mind until she recited it aloud.

"What this grim, ungainly, ghastly, gaunt, and ominous bird of yore/Meant in croaking 'Nevermore.'"

Momma slammed the lid to her sewing box. "In the name of heaven, what are you going on about?"

"It's poetry, Momma."

"Poetry? You think Jack will ever propose if you're spouting Gothic poetry?"

Arlene chuckled. *If Momma only knew.* She took up her sweeping again.

Momma grabbed the broom from Arlene's hands. "My floors are clean enough. Why are you so wound up?"

"Sorry, Momma. Isn't it time for Daddy to come home?"

"He's run late before. Why are you so anxious?"

"No reason."

Arlene decided it would be best for her mother's nerves if she waited for Jack on the porch swing. Arlene heard the truck before he reached the driveway and ran to greet him.

"Hi, Jack. Daddy isn't home yet, but—"

"Let's go for a drive." Jack hopped out and opened her door.

"What? You were going to ask Daddy …"

Jack rubbed the back of his neck. "We need to talk first. Hop in."

Arlene stared at Jack. He motioned for her to get in. She climbed in the truck and Jack sped off.

"Slow down. Where are we going?" Arlene asked.

"I want to get out of town."

"We left town ten minutes ago."

Jack pulled over near the cemetery where John was buried.

"You came to visit John?"

Jack found a bench near a tall oak at the cemetery entrance. "No. Let's sit down. We need to talk."

One dim light pierced the darkness surrounding them. The shadows danced on the oak and reminded Arlene of an Edgar Allan Poe story. Jack's demeanor made her too fidgety to sit.

"I love you. And I am going to marry you," Jack said.

"But?" Arlene paced in front of him.

"I didn't go to work today."

She stopped in front of him. "Why not?"

Jack glanced toward the gravestones. "I went to the army recruiting station."

"You what?"

"I've met with the recruiter a few times. I've been thinking about John. About enlisting and finishing what he started."

"John didn't start anything. You're talking nonsense."

"John fought for our country. You think I can sit here after what happened to him?"

Arlene looked at the shadows in the trees. Her head throbbed. *No, he cannot do this. He isn't thinking straight.*

"You're nineteen. You don't have to register for two more years. The war could be over by then."

"The recruiter says Congress is about to lower the draft age. I'll end up being drafted before I'm twenty-one anyway."

"Then let Congress draft you. Don't do it until you have to." Jack stared—hollow, unmoved. Arlene threw her hands in the air. "How long have you been meeting with this recruiter?"

Jack looked away. "A few weeks."

Arlene resumed her pacing. "What about last night? Are we going to get married this summer and then you go off to war? Are you going to leave me all alone?"

"We can't get married this summer?"

Arlene stopped directly in front of Jack. "Why not?"

"I enlisted today. I leave in two weeks."

"You what? Two weeks? What did your parents say?"

Jack looked at the ground before meeting her gaze. "I haven't told them yet."

Her head swirled. She reached for something to steady herself but still toppled forward. Jack caught her and helped her on to the bench. "Are you okay?"

She closed her eyes. "No. I'm not okay. This isn't okay."

"We can still get married. We can marry before I leave."

She stared at him, her lips tightening.

"Marry you in two weeks?"

"Sure, we can ..."

Arlene put her hand up. "Stop. I don't understand you anymore. Take me home."

"Arlene."

She moved past Jack toward the truck. When they climbed in, Jack reached for her hand. "I shouldn't have mentioned getting married before I leave. We'll wait till I get back. Plan your dream wedding. Pick the church ... Baptist, Methodist ... either one."

Arlene stared out her window. "Pick the church, but don't pick the date because you have no idea when you're coming back. Or if you're coming back."

After Jack left for war, Momma spent many days at the Hammond home consoling Mary. But Momma was always back in time to be with Arlene when she arrived home from work. After supper one night, Arlene knelt beside her mother while she knitted, her head in her mother's lap.

"The Hammonds heard from Jack today. He's in France," Momma said.

"Do you go to the Hammond's every day?"

"Not every day. As often as I can. Mary feels so alone." Momma twisted Arlene's curls. "I'm sure you'll hear from Jack soon."

"It's been months. If he hasn't written by now, he isn't going to." Arlene sat up and straightened her hair. "I pray every day for Jack. I don't want the Hammonds to lose another son. But Jack and I are over."

Momma squeezed Arlene's hand. "Don't give up, sweetheart. All in God's timing."

Arlene gave her mother a peck on the cheek. "I'm tired. Good night."

Arlene crawled into bed and prayed for a night she could fall asleep without crying.

Chapter 6

On Easter Sunday morning, 1943, the Hutchins made their way to the town square for the annual sunrise service. Patty and Arlene chatted about work when a distinct rattling sent goosebumps down Arlene's neck. She turned to see Jack's truck parked on the street. She bolted toward it until her father tugged her back.

"Slow down. That's Mr. Hammond," her father said.

"Why would he drive Jack's truck?" Arlene's stomach churned.

"He needs to feel close to a son today. Nothing wrong with driving his truck."

Arlene stared at the pickup. Her last conversation with Jack played over in her mind like a movie reel. She wished she could rewind it and change the ending. *It's been a year, Arlene. You can't change what happened.*

By summer, Arlene could not blame her restlessness on Jack. She lingered in town one afternoon after work and strolled down Main Street to think. *What I need is a change? But what?*

A warehouse at the end of the street caught her attention. Work trucks parked all around the building.

She moved around the corner to investigate and almost ran into Jack's truck.

Why would Jack's dad be here?

Arlene inched closer. She didn't see Mr. Hammond around, so she tiptoed to the passenger door. The raised windows made it difficult to see inside, but she peered in as best she could. She imagined Jack opening the door for her.

"You admiring Ol' Blue? I'd take you for a spin, but I'm a mess after work." The stranger emerged from nowhere.

"What? Ol' Blue?"

"My truck," the stranger said. "I call her Ol' Blue."

"This isn't your truck."

"Last I checked she was." The stranger threw a toolbox in the bed of the truck.

Arlene studied the man as he wiped a fountain of sweat from his face. "Where did you get this truck? Who sold it to you? You had no business buying this truck."

The man held up his hands. "Whoa, why all the questions? What's the big deal with this truck? I paid cash for her down in Beaumont."

"You bought it in Beaumont?"

"Sure. Hitchhiked my way there for a job. Didn't want to hitchhike back so I saved up and bought her. She's a little rough around the edges but she suits me fine." The man polished the truck with his elbow.

Arlene fell back against the pickup and rubbed her forehead.

"You okay, ma'am?"

"Yes. I ... I saw the truck and confused you with someone else. I'm sorry."

"No harm done. I'm sure lots of fellas drive similar pickups."

Arlene stared at the truck. *You have no idea.* "I need to get home."

The man studied her. "My name is Lon. You seem woozy. Why don't you let me drive you home?"

"No, I need the walk to clear my head."

"Okay, if you're sure?"

Arlene turned her gaze toward the warehouse. "Lon, what's with all the work on this building?"

"It's going to be a new five and dime once we've finished remodeling it."

"I see. Good night."

"Take care, ma'am."

Arlene watched Lon climb into Ol' Blue and then started home. Lon drove the same kind of truck as Jack, but nothing else about the two men seemed similar. Lon stood a bit shorter. Instead of Jack's wavy blond curls, Lon's dark, slick hair highlighted his golden skin. Sun-kissed Momma called it. Arlene observed the slightest gap in his front teeth. Like a motion picture star she'd once seen.

"Motion picture star? Stop carrying on. Jack's the only man you ever viewed as handsome. That man was covered in sweat and grime." Arlene still mumbled to herself as she walked into her house and found Momma folding towels.

"Arlene, what are you prattling on about?" Momma asked.

"Nothing." Arlene collapsed on to the couch and contemplated work, Lon, and two men with the same truck.

"Momma, this town feels small. I'm suffocating."

Momma put the towels in a basket and sat beside Arlene. "Halford is a typical small Texas town. What's bothering you?"

"You weren't born and raised in Halford, were you?"

"No, but I consider Halford home. Been here longer than anywhere. Why?"

"When you were my age, did you ever think of leaving home? You know, seeing places?"

"Back then, girls didn't take off on their own. Are you thinking about leaving?"

"Girls go to college these days. I've always wanted to. I could become a teacher like Mrs. Haskins."

Momma fidgeted with her apron. "What about you and Jack?"

Arlene cocked her head. "There is no me and Jack. I'm only dreaming anyway."

"God gives us dreams for a reason." Momma picked up the laundry basket.

"Momma, did you see Mrs. Hammond today?"

"Yes."

"Jack is okay, right?"

Momma smiled. "Yes, dear. They got a letter from him a few days ago."

Arlene picked up a book and flipped through the pages. Momma put the towels away and came back to the living room.

"Momma, I've been at Telecomm for two years. I might look for another job."

"I see. Any ideas?"

"Not yet."

"God's timing, dear. All in God's timing."

"I know, Momma."

Chapter 7

Arlene monitored the warehouse renovation each day after work. She eyed the transformation from the street opposite the warehouse. Several months had passed since she'd encountered Ol' Blue and Lon, and she didn't want to risk another encounter.

One afternoon, Arlene spotted the bright red and white *DUKE & AYRES 5¢ to $1.00 STORE* sign, announcing to Halford a new shopping experience awaited them. She noticed flyers hung on light posts advertising employment: *Duke & Ayres Hiring All Positions. Apply at 845 Main Street, Office 21.*

That's down the street. I have to try.

Arlene found the office. Her shoulders sagged when she saw the long line of people waiting for an application. She turned to leave when a man said, "You need a Duke and Ayres application?"

"Yes, sir."

The man thrust a clipboard in Arlene's hand. "Fill this out and leave it at the front desk. You'll be notified by mail."

Arlene stared at the application. The process was so different from Telecomm where they hired her on the spot. But she filled out the form and hurried home to tell Momma.

Arlene burst through the front door. "Momma, it's Duke and Ayres."

"Duke and what?"

"Duke and Ayres. The five and dime I told you about. And they're hiring. Anyone interested in a job can fill out an application."

"Is that what you're going to do?"

"No, it's what I've already done."

Arlene came home from work each day and asked, "Did I get a letter?"

"Not today, dear."

After the second week, Momma said, "A letter arrived for you, dear."

Arlene ripped open the envelope. She danced around the house while she read it. "I did it."

Momma shook her head. "Does this mean you got the job?"

"Yes. In fabrics. Can you believe it? I report for training in two weeks." Arlene plopped on the couch and reread the letter. "They'll open to the public after the new year. Momma, 1944 is going to be a good year. I can feel it."

The Duke & Ayres employees trained as deliverymen stockpiled the shelves. Sugary sweets filled the candy bins—circus peanuts, orange slices, haystacks, and candy corn. Merchandise greeted them at every corner ... toys, perfume, even an "unmentionables" department. Arlene had so much to tell Momma when she arrived home.

Arlene met her new coworker, Bessie, and they got busy organizing the department.

"Do you sew?" Arlene asked Bessie as they worked.

"Between my mother and two sisters, we can sew anything."

Arlene sighed. "I would love to have a sister or two. I'm an only child."

Bessie rolled her eyes. "I also got three brothers. I wouldn't mind trading places with you so I could enjoy a little peace and quiet."

"There's six of you? I bet your house gets lively."

The girls moved to a new row of fabric and continued organizing.

"We make quite the ruckus." Bessie said. "Fortunately for Momma, the oldest are married and L.T. floats about on different construction jobs. He worked with the crew on the store. He's the one who told me I could apply for a job."

"Do you live around here? I know most everyone in Halford."

"We live out near Julip. In the country."

"I'm glad we're working together. We'll be great friends."

Arlene and Bessie displayed the fabric as if the finest New York shoppers paraded the aisles. Mrs. Watson came weekly with her two toddlers. Arlene showered them with special attention.

"Mrs. Watson, you will love this fabric for your girls. You could make the most adorable matching outfits with this pattern. Don't you think this material brings out the green in their eyes?"

Bessie had enough. "Arlene, what is it with you and Mrs. Watson's girls? Are they your nieces?"

"I told you. I don't have any siblings."

"So why the extra attention?"

"I adore kids. Aren't they the cutest? I want two little girls like them one day."

Bessie leaned against the fabric bolts. "I see. So no problems in the love department, then? You got a steady?"

"What? You are so bold."

"If you're wanting a pair of girls, you gotta have a steady. Spill it. Who is he?"

"I did, but not anymore."

Bessie leaned in. "What happened?"

Arlene told a curious Bessie about Jack.

"You mean he went off to war without telling you about it first? And you haven't heard from him? What a scoundrel!"

"I cried so many nights. I think Jack losing his brother affected him more than I understood. But what about you? Do you have a man?"

Bessie glowed. "I do. His name is Walt. We've been together over a year. He's shy, but the way he treats me. Ooh … a woman's dream. If he doesn't propose soon, I might do it myself."

Arlene laughed. "I'm sure you will."

Bessie put away patterns scattered by customers and then said, "You need to meet my brother, L.T. He's roamed all over the place during the war, taking odd jobs. Mother would love for him to settle down."

"Don't you dare set me up. I'll meet someone … one day."

"Where? Here in Halford where everyone knows you as Jack's girl?"

"I think by now everyone knows I'm not Jack's girl. Why is your brother rambling all over? Didn't he serve?"

"L.T. signed up but didn't pass his physical, so they wouldn't take him."

"What's wrong with him?"

"Nothing's wrong with him, but they won't put a gun in your hands if they think your peripheral vision is off. L.T.

said it's a bunch of bureaucratic hogwash. He can look down the barrel of a gun just fine during hunting season." Bessie shrugged. "Army wouldn't take him, though, and Mother said God has other plans for him. I don't argue with my mother or God."

Arlene laughed. "No, I wouldn't argue with them, either."

Bessie and Arlene clocked off work promptly at three on Friday. The new friends planned a weekend at Bessie's place. Bessie careened the car through the curvy roads as they drove out to the country.

"I asked Jack to teach me to drive," Arlene said as the spring breeze poured in through the windows. "We see how that worked out."

"L.T. taught me."

"You and L.T. sound close."

"Yes, and we're closest in age. Stairsteps Mother calls us. Besides, Junior didn't have the time or the patience."

Bessie rounded a hill. "Oh, Bess, look at the black-eyed Susans. Aren't they beautiful? And those crimson clovers painting the hillside red. Do you think we'll see any bluebonnets?"

"Not on this stretch. But on the other side of the farm there're fields of them. My little brother has the car tomorrow since I'm not working, or I'd drive us. Walt is working, too, but I'll see what I can do."

A short, stocky woman with a toothy grin met the girls as soon as they arrived at Bessie's house.

"You must be Arlene. Welcome. I'm Bessie's mother, and you can call me Miss Ruth."

"Hi, Miss Ruth. Thank you for having me."

Miss Ruth wrapped her arms around Arlene and squeezed her tight. "I've got hot cookies fresh out of the oven. Supper won't be ready for a couple more hours."

Bessie giggled as she scooped up Arlene's arm. "Mother treats us like a couple of schoolgirls. But if we get hot cookies, who's complaining?"

Arlene giggled, and they bounded toward the kitchen. Walt arrived and joined Bessie along with her younger brother and sister. The noise level escalated to decibels Arlene usually only heard from a barn. She expected Miss Ruth to tell them to simmer down. Instead, she joined in.

The kitchen grew smaller when Bessie's dad and a brother roared in through the back door.

"Goodness," Miss Ruth said. "Did y'all smell the cookies from out back?"

They grunted and grabbed a handful. Arlene assumed the handsome brother must be the mysterious L.T. Her stomach twisted at the idea.

Arlene's stomach untwisted when Bessie asked, "Junior, is L.T. coming home this weekend?"

"Don't think so. Why?"

"I wanted him to drive us out to the bluebonnet fields tomorrow. Walt has to work."

Junior stared at Bessie. Then he turned to Arlene and studied her up and down. He turned back to Bessie. "I think your bluebonnet looking will have to wait. L.T. has to work all weekend."

Bessie sprang from her chair, corralled Arlene, and said, "Okay. Just asking."

They sprinted out the back. Walt followed, and the three collapsed into rockers on the back porch. Arlene could barely breathe. "Bessie. What was that about?"

"Bessie loves to play matchmaker," Walt said. Bessie glared at him. He stuffed his last cookie into his mouth.

"Bess, I did not come here to be set up with one of your brothers," Arlene said.

"Relax. The only one I could set you up with isn't home."

Arlene chewed her lips. "You're missing the point."

"I wanted to see if L.T. could take us to see the bluebonnets. No bluebonnet fields for us this weekend, but we will still have great fun."

L.T. was not mentioned again.

Chapter 8

The morning mob at Duke and Ayres wore Arlene out. She needed Bessie to return from her break. She's late. Where did she run off to?

Between customers, Arlene scanned the store and spotted Bessie. She and a young man stood at the front of the store engaged in an animated conversation. Bessie kept pointing to the fabric department. She'd better be telling him her break is over.

Arlene put up some fabric and then turned back to watch Bessie and the mystery man. *That man looks familiar. Where have I seen him?*

Arlene decided to sneak down an aisle to get a closer look. She rounded a corner and slammed into Bessie.

"You scared me." Arlene said.

"You scared me. Why are you sneaking around?"

Arlene caught her breath and composed herself. "I'm not sneaking around. I'm looking for you. You're late from your break."

Bessie offered no explanation, so Arlene asked, "Who were you talking to?"

Bessie found a box of sewing notions which needed sorting. "L.T."

"Isn't L.T. working?"

"He's on his way home from a job and stopped in for a few supplies."

Arlene stared at Bessie, but she seemed to ignore Arlene's curiosity. She wanted to say, *Those must have been some supplies the way you two were going at it.* But Bessie's conversation was none of Arlene's business, and she had work to do.

Arlene awoke on Friday morning feeling giddy. She had to work the whole day, but she didn't mind because the weekend was here. She never had to work on Saturdays.

Her spirits dampened a bit when she approached the store entrance and spotted Jack's truck parked out front. *I wonder if the Hammonds are here.*

Arlene marched to fabrics determined not to think about the truck, the Hammonds, or Jack. Bessie was busy sprucing up the department.

"Good morning, Bess. I'm surprised to see you here so early."

"L.T. brought me. He came to town, so ..."

"Hi. Remember me?"

A man emerged from nowhere. His clean-shaven face showed off a dark complexion. She'd seen his sun-kissed glow before. His smile brandished a slight gap between his front teeth. *Ahh, yes, his gap.*

"Uhh," Arlene managed.

"We met when I worked on the construction of this store. Remember my blue Ford truck you admired?"

Yes. Lon. And your truck is the one parked out front, not Jack's.

Before Arlene could speak, Bessie said, "This is my brother L.T. He brought me to work." Bessie clasped her hands together. "And since he was here already, there's no harm in you and L.T. meeting."

"L.T.?" Arlene looked at Bessie and then at Lon. "You told me your name is Lon?"

"It is. Lon Taylor. My family calls me L T., but I go by Lon."

Arlene looked at Lon and then Bessie. "Lon is your brother?"

"Don't hold that against me." Lon laughed.

Bessie put her hands on her hips and glared at her brother. "When did you get all fancy and start going by Lon?"

"Since I went to Beaumont and wanted to be taken seriously."

"Junior still goes by Junior."

"Junior works his own ranch. It doesn't matter what the cows call him."

Bessie rolled her eyes. "You're impossible."

Arlene held up her hands. "L.T. or Lon or whatever you're called. It's a pleasure to meet you again, but if you'll excuse us, we have work to do. Come on, Bess."

"What do you mean 'again'? You two have met? Arlene, why didn't you say something?" Bessie pointed at Lon. "I've been going on about introducing you to my brother, and you've already met?"

"You went on about your brother L.T., and I'd met someone named Lon. I didn't know they were the same man." Arlene turned to Lon. "Excuse us, but we have work to do."

Lon gently grabbed Arlene's arm. "I have a few errands to run in town. Can I come by on your break and take you to lunch?"

Arlene stared at him. *Do what?*

Mrs. Watson and her daughters arrived. Bessie steered the trio to a new section of fabric, apparently to give Lon a chance to continue his mission.

Arlene fidgeted with some lace. "Thank you, Lon. But I brought my lunch and plan on eating here."

Lon leaned on the cutting table. "I'll pick up a sandwich from the diner, and we'll enjoy this beautiful day. I'll even grab us a soda."

Bessie finished with Mrs. Watson in time to say, "She takes lunch at 12:30."

Arlene glared at Bessie.

"Good," Lon said. "I'll be outside the front door at 12:30."

Arlene gave a slight nod and watched Lon stroll down the aisle and out the door.

Arlene turned to Bessie who opened a new shipment of lace. "Don't get any ideas. I'll go to lunch with Lon but nothing else. No matchmaking."

Bessie looked up at Arlene. "What's wrong with Lon? Give him a chance. He's a swell guy."

"I'm not ready to date after everything with Jack."

"Jack? You said yourself there is no Jack. He went off to war and hasn't given you the time of day, remember?"

Arlene adjusted the pattern books. Bessie finished the lace and stood beside her. "There's something else. Spill it."

Arlene walked away, and Bessie followed. Arlene waved her hands at an imaginary truck.

"I'm not going anywhere in his old jalopy."

"His truck? You won't go out with him because of Ol' Blue? I never took you for the pretentious type."

"You don't understand. Jack had the exact same truck. Same color even. I have so many memories of Jack's truck. And not all good ones. It's too weird. I'm not doing it."

"Lots of men own pickups."

"Not the exact same. It's taken me too long to get over Jack. I don't need a constant reminder. Besides, I don't want to stay in Halford forever. I want to go to college one day."

Bessie's mouth fell open. "Here's a newsflash. When have you ever talked about college?"

"I've thought about being a teacher one day. Now you know."

"Give Lon a chance." Bessie stared at Arlene with pleading eyes.

Arlene sighed. "I met Lon because I saw his pickup parked outside the store when he was working on the construction team. Jack's dad drives his truck everywhere, and I see it all over town. I even chewed Lon out because I thought somehow he bought Jack's truck."

Bessie chuckled.

Arlene rubbed her eyes. "I'm sure Lon wasn't laughing, getting yelled at by a complete stranger."

"You left a swell impression on him. When he stopped by the store the other day, I wanted him to meet you then. He recognized you but said he was too filthy from work to meet you."

"He looked grimy the first day I saw him too." Arlene laughed.

"He didn't want you to think he always looked so dirty. My brothers don't pay attention to my matchmaking, so I was surprised he said he'd meet you. This explains it."

"I'm serious, Bess. I'm not dating him."

"Uh-huh."

At lunch break, Arlene found Lon outside leaning against the street post. He clutched a brown paper bag from the diner and two cold sodas.

"Hello beautiful," Lon said.

Arlene blushed but did not reply. Jack was cozy like a blanket because they'd always been together. Lon was heart-pounding sensations she'd never experienced.

They found a quiet bench to enjoy lunch. Lon popped a lid off a soda and handed her a bottle. Arlene couldn't remember the last time she'd enjoyed the bubbly concoction. Her nose tingled, and she laughed.

"I didn't notice your dimples when we first met. Your face lights up."

"My goodness. You and Bessie both. You say whatever you think, don't you?"

"Your dimples are beautiful. Like you."

Arlene stared down the street, unable to process the compliment or lunch or feelings she didn't understand.

"I appreciate the soda, but I'm not—"

"Tomorrow would be a great day to see the bluebonnets. Bessie said y'all couldn't go. I'll pick you up in Ol' Blue."

Arlene jumped to her feet. "It's time for me to go back to work. Thank you for the soda."

Lon gazed up at her with a confused expression. "Wait. What did I do?"

"You didn't do anything. It's been lovely. Thank you again."

"If it's been lovely, then let's see the bluebonnets tomorrow." Lon marched in step with Arlene as they walked back to the store.

"I know you're asking me because of Bessie and her matchmaking. You needn't feel obligated," Arlene said.

"Is that what you think? I don't care about Bessie's matchmaking. Then, I realized her scheme involved this beautiful girl I met by my truck one night accusing me of something. What were you accusing me of anyway? Oh yeah, I had someone else's truck, right?" Lon laughed.

Arlene looked away. "I'm so embarrassed."

"Don't be. I'm glad we met. The bluebonnets won't be in bloom much longer. What do you say?"

When they stopped at the store, Arlene stared at it a minute and then looked at Lon. "Okay. We'll just look at the bluebonnets."

Lon climbed into Ol' Blue. He waved and smiled as he drove off. Her knees locked in place, and blood rushed to her face. *What have I done?* When the truck disappeared, she went into the store. Bessie, the interrogator, would be waiting.

On Saturday morning, Arlene decided to wait for Lon on the porch swing. When she heard the rumbling of his truck, she considered running back into the house. When the truck pulled into the driveway, she expected Jack to hop out.

"Hey, beautiful," Lon said as he got out of the truck. "Are you ready to see some bluebonnets?"

Arlene held her purse strap tight. "Lon, I'm sorry. I can't go."

Lon stopped at the porch steps. "Why? What happened?"

Arlene grew quiet and stared at Ol' Blue.

"Arlene?" Arlene still didn't respond. Lon walked to the swing.

His voice softened. "Are you sick? Are your parents all right?"

Arlene turned to Lon and blurted out, "I can't ride in your truck."

Lon's mouth fell open. "What's wrong with Ol' Blue?"

Arlene stared at her hands. Lon sat beside her and rubbed his chin.

"Do you know enough about trucks to have opinions about them?"

Arlene didn't look up. "You wouldn't understand."

"I'm an understanding guy. Try me."

Arlene looked at the truck and then back at Lon. "I've only dated one other fellow. My high school sweetheart,

Jack. We talked marriage, but then he enlisted in the army without telling me. I haven't heard from him since."

"Is Jack alive?"

"Yes. His parents hear from him often."

Lon reached for her hand. Arlene wanted to move her hand away but couldn't for some strange reason. "I can't imagine anyone leaving you. But what does Jack have to do with Ol' Blue?"

"Remember when we met, and I said the truck couldn't be yours?"

"Sure."

"I assumed your truck belonged to Jack. They look exactly the same. I figured Jack's dad drove it into town. He does that. I wanted to get a closer look at the truck because it reminded me of Jack." Arlene closed her eyes. "I'm sorry. Today was a mistake."

Lon leaned back against the swing and rubbed his forehead. "Well, I'll be." Then he turned back to Arlene. "Today isn't a mistake."

"What?"

"Give me today."

Arlene shook her head. "I don't understand."

"You need to make new memories." Lon pointed to Ol' Blue. "We'll drive to the bluebonnets, grab a bite to eat, and whatever else we drum up. If at the end of the day, you don't want anything to do with me or Ol' Blue, you'll never hear from me again. But give me today."

Arlene stared at the truck and then back at Lon. He pulled her up off the swing. "Come on. What do you say?"

Arlene offered a slight smile, and Lon held her hand as they walked to the truck.

Lon made jokes as they drove. He pointed to things along the way that Arlene had never noticed before. Conversation between them flowed as smooth as the country roads they traveled.

Lon careened into a valley where, like magic, bluebonnet fields stretched before them. The blue hues from the flowers merged with the horizon, giving the appearance the clouds and flowers were one.

"Lon, look," Arlene said.

Lon pulled over. He grabbed Arlene's hand, and they hurried to the rolling fields of bluebonnets.

"They go on forever," Arlene said.

"Aren't you glad you didn't miss it?"

Arlene nodded and smiled. "Can we pick them?"

"No law against it."

Arlene ran her hands through the rows of bluebonnets. She picked four and worked her way back to Lon.

Lon admired her flowers. "You didn't pick many."

"I didn't want to disturb their glory. Words can't describe how beautiful this is."

"No, words can't." But Lon wasn't looking at the bluebonnet fields. He brushed a strand of hair out of her eye. She felt the blood rush to her cheeks.

Lon took Arlene's hands. "Life's about chances. I'm not Jack. Having the same truck doesn't make me anything like him."

Arlene observed for the first time this dark-haired, sun-kissed man boasted the most remarkable blue eyes. Everything about Lon surprised her. His eyes. Their conversation. His easygoing manner. But nothing surprised her more than when Lon pulled her close and kissed her.

Chapter 9

Lon and Arlene had been a steady couple for a few weeks when Lon announced, "It's time you learn to drive."

Arlene's eyes widened. "You're going to teach me?"

"Of course. We need to stay on the back roads until you're good enough to take the driving test."

Arlene bolted out the door before Lon changed his mind. She jerked and pulled his blue truck up and down the road. Lon feigned being thrown around the corners of the cab. But by the afternoon's end, Arlene navigated the truck frontward and backward.

"Here's a memory in this truck you've never had," Lon said. "You'll have your license in no time."

"I can't believe it." They hopped out of the truck, and Arlene threw her arms around Lon.

Lon spread a blanket, and they sat down. She opened the picnic basket she'd prepared for their lunch. "I saved you a piece of my apricot pie. You do eat apricots, don't you?"

Lon grabbed his chest in pretend shock. "Who doesn't eat apricots?"

Arlene laughed. "Hmm, some people."

Lon inhaled an extra-large piece of pie. "These would make great fried pies."

"Fried pies? Are you complaining about my apricot pie?"

"No way. Best I've ever eaten." Lon leaned into the dish and grabbed the crumbs. "This crust is crazy good."

"But you want me to fry it?"

"I ate fried pies at the county fair in Warren a few years ago. They were all the rage. As good as your crust and filling are, they'd make amazing fried pies."

"All right," Arlene said. "Next Saturday give me another driving lesson, and then, we'll make fried pies."

"Deal."

When the next driving lesson ended, Arlene and Lon ventured into the kitchen for their fried pie experiment. Arlene prepared the pies, and Lon fried them to a golden brown. Momma, Daddy, and Aunt Jewell couldn't resist the enticing smells flowing from the kitchen.

"I've heard of these," Aunt Jewell said. "But I've never tasted one. Lon, you have introduced us to a delicacy."

"Arlene's recipe is what makes them so good." Lon winked at Arlene.

From then on, Arlene's driving lessons always ended with Lon and Arlene cooking up something in the kitchen, although Arlene observed she did most of the cooking.

"Lon, is this an excuse to get me to cook? I don't see you helping much."

Lon wrapped his arms around Arlene as she set a cobbler on the counter. "It's an excuse to be with you. If I happen to get cobbler out of it, even better."

Arlene turned to face him. "You don't need an excuse to be with me."

Lon kissed her. "I'm glad to hear that." Then he added, "You can take your driving test next week. You're ready."

"What? Are you sure? What if I fail? I'd better wait."

"Don't be silly. You're a great driver. You'll drive around town and show them what I taught you."

Arlene placed a warm piece of cobbler in front of Lon. She watched him eat, and Jack came to mind. She didn't want to compare, but Lon was so different. She never asked Lon to teach her to drive. He volunteered. Lon never complained about her job. And Jack would never think about frying up pies or doing anything else in a kitchen.

Lon caught her staring. "What? Do I have cobbler on my chin?"

Arlene laughed. "No. Thanks for teaching me to drive."

"You were a lot easier to teach than Bessie." Lon laughed.

"I mean it, Lon. You didn't have to teach me. It means everything to me."

Lon took Arlene's hands. "Baby doll. I'm crazy about you. I'll do anything to make you happy."

"Oh, yeah. Except get rid of Ol' Blue?" Arlene raised her eyebrows and laughed.

"You wouldn't want me getting rid of her now would you? After the bluebonnet picking and driving lessons?"

"No, Lon. You and Ol' Blue were meant for each other."

Lon pulled Arlene close. "You and I were meant for each other."

Arlene passed her driving test and enjoyed a new kind of freedom. When Lon worked in town, he left his truck keys under the floor mat in case Arlene needed to borrow the truck. Daddy let her use his car every other Sunday to go to church with Lon and spend the day with his family.

Arlene looked forward to the boisterous family meals. *Momma and Daddy would hate this much noise, but this is exactly what I want one day.*

Lon and Arlene found time alone by taking an afternoon stroll to the family pond. On one of their walks, Lon asked, "You ever think about your future? What dreams do you have?"

His question caught Arlene off guard. *My future? I hope we have a future.* She was cautious. "The usual, I suppose. Get married. Have a family."

"You ever have any big dreams?"

What is he getting at? Arlene looked up at the trees. "Promise not to laugh."

"Why would I laugh?"

"I loved my high school teachers and dreamed about becoming one, but I would have to go to college."

"Dreams may be God's way of nudging us in a certain direction."

"I suppose so." Arlene's stomach hurt, the way it did when Jack took her to the cemetery and told her he'd enlisted.

"We never know what each day holds in store for us. Like the first day we met by my truck. We have to follow God's plan for our lives," Lon said.

Their conversation nagged her as she drove home. *You have to follow God's plan.* Lon's words played over in her mind, like a phonograph stuck on its needle. *What plan was he talking about? I shouldn't have mentioned college. Lon knows I want to marry and have a family. Doesn't he?*

Chapter 10

Momma walked up the porch stairs and joined Arlene on the swing. Cool autumn breezes clipped their hair; and for a while, they swung in silence enjoying the evening air.

Arlene broke the stillness when she asked, "Have you been to the Hammonds?"

"Yes." They swung a little longer.

"Jack is in New York. He'll be home in a few weeks," Momma said.

"Oh? His parents must be beside themselves."

"They are. I wasn't sure how you'd feel about it."

"About Jack coming home?"

"About seeing him after all this time."

Arlene closed her eyes. "I've prayed for him every day. And for the Hammonds. I'm glad he'll be home safe."

"Do you think he'll call on you?"

Arlene stared at her mother. "No, he won't. It's been two years, and I haven't heard from him. Coming home doesn't change anything."

Momma stared off in the yard. "Let's hope it's that simple."

"Is there something you're not telling me?"

"No. We'd better get supper on the table."

Arlene stared at Momma as she walked into the house. *There's definitely something you're not telling me.*

Arlene heard through the Halford rumor mill Jack would be home by Thanksgiving. The fanfare at the train station announced his exact arrival. Momma and Daddy had stood among the crowd of Halford residents to give Jack a hero's welcome home.

"Jack looks older and thinner, but still as handsome as ever," Momma announced at dinner.

Arlene stared at her. "I'm glad Lon is working out of town this week. I'd hate for him to hear this."

"I'm giving you a report, dear. Nothing more."

Momma and Arlene cleaned the dishes, and Daddy retreated to the living room. "Momma, you like Lon, don't you?" Arlene asked.

"Of course, dear."

"Then why are you telling me about Jack?"

Momma pointed to the table. "Let's sit a minute."

Arlene sighed and sat down.

Momma fidgeted with a napkin. "I know this is none of my business, but Mary and I are best friends. You've always been the daughter they never had."

"Momma, I don't think—"

"Let me finish."

Arlene sat back in her chair and crossed her arms.

Momma took a deep breath and continued. "In Jack's last letter to his mother, he said he'd regretted letting you go. He told her he wanted to make things right."

"What does that mean?"

"To start over with you."

Arlene flew out of her chair. "The Hammonds have seen me at church with Lon. Haven't they told Jack?"

Momma scratched her head. "I'm not sure."

Arlene leaned against the counter. "Momma, I know you and Mrs. Hammond are good friends. But I'm with Lon. Both of you need to accept this."

On Friday afternoon, Arlene clocked off work at two. Lon had been working out of town for two weeks and was on his way home. Momma and Daddy agreed to eat at Aunt Jewell's because Arlene planned a special dinner for her and Lon. She wanted to cook Lon's favorites—fried chicken, mashed potatoes and gravy, flaky biscuits, and her famous apricot pie.

Arlene raced to the front door of Duke and Ayres, opened it, and froze.

"Hi, Arlene."

Jack leaned against the hood of his blue Ford truck. Momma was right. A young man replaced the teenager. He was thinner but as handsome as ever. Arlene gawked and then came to her senses. She hugged him and said, "Jack, it's so good to have you home. I know your parents are thrilled."

"It's good to be home. I wasn't sure you'd be happy to see me."

"Of course, I'm happy. I prayed every day for your safe return."

Jack smiled and stepped toward her. "Can we talk a minute?"

"I'm in a hurry. But we'll find a time to catch up. I promise."

"Wait. Where are you headed?"

"I've got to get home. I'm sorry, but I have plans."

"I can take you home. Riding in the truck will sure bring back memories, won't it?" Jack laughed and hit the hood of his truck.

Arlene stared at the blue Ford. If Jack wasn't standing there, she'd think Lon had returned. *How the tables had turned. What a mess.*

"I suppose you can take me home."

"Great."

Arlene wasn't sure how to start a conversation with Jack, so she stared straight ahead as the truck rattled its way down the street. She had questions, but they no longer mattered.

Jack broke the silence first. "I see you gave up the telephone job."

She remembered how much Jack hated her working. *Funny he'd mention this first.* "Yes, the five and dime suits me better."

"You look beautiful."

Arlene played with the strap of her purse. *I should have walked.*

Jack pulled into Arlene's driveway, and she reached for the door handle. Jack stopped her. "Arlene, can we talk a minute?"

"I told you. I have plans, and I don't have much time. We'll catch up later. Thanks for the ride."

"I'm hoping you and I can have a second chance."

Arlene stared at him. She grew up with Jack. But he was a stranger. "Jack, it's been two years. You didn't write one time. Life moves on."

Jack sighed. "I was wrong. I should have written. We've known each other our whole lives. You owe us a second chance."

Her heart pounded. *What did he say? I owe us?*

"Jack, I'm ..."

He reached for Arlene's hand. "No one knows you like I do."

Arlene pulled her hand out of Jack's grasp. "I'm thankful you are home and your parents have their son back. When you first left, I prayed God might give us another chance."

"And here it is."

"No." Arlene grew impatient. "I met someone else." She opened the door. "Goodbye, Jack. I wish you the best."

"Arlene." Jack stepped out of the truck. "Are you engaged? I don't see a ring."

"Not yet, but that doesn't mean anything."

"Means something to me."

Arlene shook her head and walked into the house. She had so much to do before Lon arrived.

Chapter 11

Arlene had supper warming in the oven by five o'clock. This gave her one hour to clean up. Arlene refreshed herself with a lavender bath, then slipped on her favorite dress, a Swiss navy polka dot. The sleeves cascaded into cuffs which ended with a white button clasped at her wrists. These same white buttons flowed down the front from the collar into a point to accentuate her small waist. She put on her best silk stockings and navy heels. Arlene fluffed and sprayed her hair. She powdered her face, applied a pinch of rouge and swirled a hint of lipstick.

She spritzed her perfume in time to hear Lon's knock at the door. One last look in the mirror. Lon hinted tonight would be special. *A proposal is special. Oh stop it, Arlene, and let the man in.*

"Baby doll. You look beautiful." Lon scooped Arlene up and kissed her.

"You know you have to behave." Arlene giggled and took his overcoat. A large envelope fell out. Arlene picked it up and felt how thick it was. *Why would he need that tonight?*

"I'll take that." Lon pulled the envelope out of Arlene's hand. "I want to talk to you about this after supper." Lon pointed the envelope at her to emphasize each word. Then he laid it on the sofa.

Arlene's spirits plunged. *Don't get worked up, Arlene. You shouldn't have gotten your hopes up about a ring. Lon has never mentioned marriage.*

Lon chatted through supper. "This is the best chicken I've ever eaten. I can't wait to get my hands on a piece of pie."

Arlene nibbled at a few crumbs. Her mind floated to the mysterious package on the couch. *Why did I plan a special meal if all we're going to do is discuss a stack of papers?*

She cleared the table and watched Lon sort through the contents of the envelope. She took a deep breath and joined Lon on the couch.

He took her hands. "Arlene, I've been at battle with God, and I can't do it anymore."

"You what?"

"God is calling me to preach. I've told him no, but you can't tell God no."

Arlene stared at Lon. She heard his words, but not their meaning. "You're a carpenter. How are you going to preach? You've never preached."

Lon smiled. "This is the best part. I've been meeting with a mission board recruiter I met on a job a few months ago. The mission board is starting a new program. Pioneer Missions. They need skilled laborers who are also preachers to start churches. I'll be able to preach and use my carpentry skills at the same time."

Lon talked so fast, Arlene had a hard time keeping up. "Slow down. Mission Board? A month ago? Why does Texas need more churches? You've never preached."

"I'm so excited I'm not explaining it right." Lon took Arlene's hands. "I have to go to college first. Then seminary to learn all these things. Once I finish, they'll see where they need me, but it won't be Texas." Lon stopped before continuing. "It might be somewhere like Ohio, or even Pennsylvania."

Arlene sat in silence a few minutes. Then she bolted out of the sofa and buzzed about the room like a bee lost in a field of flowers, unsure where to land.

"Arlene? This is a lot to take in, but come sit back down."

"I've had this conversation before."

"What?"

"With Jack. Out of the blue with no warning." Arlene waved her hands in the air. "'Guess what, Arlene? I talked to a recruiter today. Signed up for the army.' And here you are talking to a recruiter. A kind I've never heard of. But what you're doing is worse."

Lon stood and rubbed his hands through his slick hair. "Worse? How?"

"I've never heard you mention college. I talked about it, and it seemed silly. You going on about dreams. Is this what you meant?" Arlene burst into tears.

Lon put his arms around her. "Arlene, I'm not finished. Let's …"

A loud rap at the door made them both jump.

"Are your parents back already?" Lon asked.

"Of course not."

Arlene wiped her tears and opened the door. "Jack? What are you doing here?"

Without answering, Jack barged in.

"Mind if I come in. You must be Lon. I'm Jack."

Lon approached Jack, but Arlene intervened, this time asking the question even louder. "Jack, what are you doing here?"

"We didn't get to finish our conversation this afternoon."

Lon glared at Arlene. "What conversation?"

"I've heard about you, Lon. And from the ruckus I heard you two making, it appears I came at the right time."

"Jack," Arlene said. "You need to leave."

Jack looked at Lon. "Look, I'm sure you're a swell guy, but Arlene and I have known each other our whole lives."

"What's your point?" Lon asked.

"My point is," Jack glanced at Arlene, "we've always planned to marry. Ever since we were kids."

Lon tensed. "Arlene has moved on."

"You two aren't engaged, right?"

"Not yet. Now if you'll leave us alone." The veins in Lon's neck bulged.

"Then I'm not too late." Jack pulled out a gold ring topped with a single pearl.

Arlene collapsed on the couch and buried her face in her hands.

"I didn't want to do this in front of you, but you left me no choice." Jack moved closer to Arlene.

Lon raised a fist. "Are you out of your mind?"

Arlene hurled herself between the two men. "Lon, stop."

Lon waved his arms, grabbed his envelope, and bolted for the door.

"Lon, wait please," Arlene cried.

But Lon disappeared.

Arlene turned to Jack. "What is wrong with you? How could you do this?"

"I don't want to hurt you, but I'm serious. No one knows you better than me. We never fought like the ruckus I heard from you two."

"What do you mean we never fought? Everything was a fight."

Jack reached for Arlene, but she pulled away. "I can't think, Jack. You came here with a ring?"

"Forget the ring. For tonight. Let's go for a drive tomorrow. In my truck. Think of the memories it'll bring back."

Arlene moaned at the mention of his truck. Then she laughed.

"What's so funny?" Jack asked.

"What I need is a man who drives a different truck. You need to go."

Jack kissed the top of her head. Teenage memories of hayrides and square dances flickered in her mind. She squashed them.

"Please go."

"I love you. I hope to see you tomorrow."

"Leave." She didn't watch Jack go. She crawled into bed and cried herself to sleep.

Chapter 12

On Saturday, Arlene ate lunch at Patty's. She hoped to be showing off an engagement ring but had a horror story to tell instead.

"So Lon didn't propose? And Jack showed up with a ring?"

"A pearl one at that. Who knew Jack had such poor taste?" Arlene gave a halfhearted laugh.

"What are you going to do?"

"What can I do? Lon said he's been fighting with God. I can't stand in his way."

Patty placed a plate of sandwiches on the table. "Lon isn't going to end your relationship."

"We haven't discussed marriage. I assumed too much. What upset me is he never brought this up before." Arlene nibbled on half a sandwich. "And the whole time he was talking, the only thing I heard was 'recruiter.' It reminded me of my last conversation with Jack."

"You know Jack and Lon aren't the same."

"Maybe. But if Lon leaves, Jack will be here. He's made his intentions clear." Arlene covered her face with her hands.

"I can't believe this happened." Patty put her arm around Arlene's shoulder.

Aunt Jewell could be counted on for two things—a fresh perspective and ice-cold sweet tea. Arlene needed both, so she left Patty's and went straight to her aunt's.

"I didn't expect to see you this afternoon. Come in," Aunt Jewell said.

Arlene stepped into the living room. A new quilt stretched out on the quilting rack. "Am I bothering you?"

"Takes a lot to bother me."

Arlene pointed to the quilting rack. "This is a beautiful pattern."

Aunt Jewell pulled another chair over to the rack. "How 'bout I pour us up a couple tall glasses of tea, and you help me work this quilt?"

Aunt Jewell moved toward the kitchen. "I find handiwork clears the mind. Looks like your mind needs clearing. Am I right?"

"Yes, ma'am. My mind is so cluttered I can't think straight."

Aunt Jewell came back with two glasses of tea. "Let's work a bit. Then we'll talk."

Their fingers moved in rhythm, quilting the layers of the hopscotch pattern together.

"You thinking clearly, yet?" Aunt Jewell asked.

"I'm sure you heard Jack is home."

"Yes. I know the Hammonds are relieved."

Arlene stared at the quilt. "I've seen him. Twice."

Aunt Jewell packed away the needles and scissors. "We've done enough for tonight. Let me get you another glass of tea." Aunt Jewell returned with fresh drinks. "You want to tell me about Jack?"

Arlene rehashed the previous day. "The night was as backwards as could be. I wanted Lon to propose, and instead Jack flashed a ring at me. And he did it in front of Lon."

Aunt Jewell took a long breath. "Let me ask you something. If Lon proposed, would you have said yes? Knowing about everything else?"

Arlene raised her eyebrows. "What do you mean?"

"He's going to school, preaching, leaving Texas one day. Which means leaving your family. Would you be able to do that?" Aunt Jewell sipped her tea.

"I'm not sure. It doesn't matter any way. Lon didn't propose."

"And you don't think he ever will?" Aunt Jewell leaned toward Arlene. "I've seen you and Lon together. He's crazy about you."

Arlene fidgeted with the quilt.

Aunt Jewell continued. "You have to decide whether you'd ever leave Halford."

Arlene sipped her tea until the glass was empty again. "I was so upset at the way last night went, I didn't think that far ahead. I could leave for a short time, like college, but I don't think I could move away for good." Arlene looked out the window before turning back to her aunt. "Jack could have come back at the right time. I knew you'd help me see this from a different perspective."

Aunt Jewell moved to the couch and patted the cushion. "Come sit here with me."

Arlene sat next to her aunt.

"I'm going to tell you a story about two women. When faced with marriage proposals, they chose two different paths."

"Are these real women, or did you make them up?" Arlene asked.

Aunt Jewell cocked her head. "Real women."

"Do I know these women?"

"Arlene." Aunt Jewell rubbed her forehead.

"I'm sorry. I'm listening."

Aunt Jewell took a long gulp of tea before starting. "These two women grew up in Tennessee with large, loud families."

Arlene chuckled. "Reminds me of Lon's family."

Aunt Jewell smiled. "The first woman fell madly in love with the most handsome man. He proposed, but there was one problem."

"What?" Arlene leaned in toward her aunt.

"The man wanted to go west to Wyoming right after the wedding. He planned to start a cattle ranch. He asked the young woman to move out there with him. The woman would have to give up her life in Tennessee—her family, her parents, everything."

Arlene interrupted. "Are you sure you're not making this up?"

"I'm sure."

"What happened?"

"The young woman decided she couldn't do it. A new life in Wyoming scared her. The weather was too cold. People didn't have many cars then, so she worried she might not see her family again. She had a million excuses, so she turned him down."

Arlene picked up a couch pillow and hugged it. "What about the other woman. Was she the first woman's sister?"

"No. They hadn't met yet. When World War I started, the second woman wasn't married, but she was happy surrounded by her family."

Arlene tilted her head. "Go on."

"Then a young soldier returned, they met, and fell in love. This young man struggled to find work after the war, and he wouldn't propose without a good job."

Arlene shifted on the couch. "What did he do?"

"He had army friends who could get him a job in Texas. Texas oil offered stable jobs right after the war."

Arlene tossed the pillow to the side. "So this woman wouldn't leave her family either, and you have two tragic women who are left alone? Is this the point you're trying to make?"

"No, it isn't. The second woman learned the lesson from Ruth."

"Who's Ruth? The first woman?"

A small laugh escaped Aunt Jewell. "From the Bible."

"Oh."

"You know the story. One daughter-in-law couldn't leave the comfort of her own family. But Ruth didn't go back to her own people. Ruth followed her mother-in-law to a strange land to live with people she didn't know. She didn't go because of a man." Aunt Jewell let them sit in silence before she continued. "Ruth went with her mother-in-law because she followed God. The Bible is full of people who leave everything they know because God has a better plan."

Aunt Jewell took Arlene's hand. "The point isn't to say 'yes' so you get a man. The point is to find God's will for your life and follow where he leads you. Even if it means leaving your family."

Arlene chewed on her lower lip. "The second woman. It's Momma, isn't it?"

"Yes, she left her whole family and moved here to Halford. She didn't do it to make sure she got married. She did it because marrying your father and moving here was God's plan for her." Aunt Jewell smiled. "And because she loves your father."

Arlene looked away a minute before asking, "Who's the first woman?"

Aunt Jewell shrugged her shoulders. "I was afraid to go to Wyoming. I was shy and unsure. When our parents passed, your father moved me here. You were a baby when I came." Aunt Jewell took Arlene's hand. "But I've been happy in Halford. I believe this was God's plan for me all along."

Arlene threw her arms around her aunt. "Thank you for telling me."

Aunt Jewell held Arlene's gaze. "Promise me, whether it's Lon or Jack or no man at all, you won't accept a marriage proposal unless you're certain it's what God wants."

"I promise."

Arlene rose to go home.

"Arlene?"

"Yes, ma'am?"

"That Lon sure does fry up some good apricot pies."

Arlene smiled. "Yes, ma'am. He sure does."

Arlene walked home and found her father on the front porch swing.

"You stayed at Patty's a long time," Daddy said.

"I decided to visit Aunt Jewell."

"What's my sister up to today?"

"Quilting, as usual." Arlene sat next to her father. "I'm surprised to see you on the swing. I thought you'd be out back with the apricot trees."

"I was, but Jack came by."

"He's persistent." Arlene rubbed her forehead. "Momma thinks I should hear Jack out."

"We've always been good friends with the Hammonds. That doesn't mean you have to marry their son."

"I know."

Daddy clasped his hands together and rested them on his lap. "I want to say one thing. Jack interrupted your conversation with Lon last night, right?"

"Yes."

"Then your conversation with Lon isn't over. You need to let him finish it."

Daddy got up and walked to the front door.

"Daddy?" Arlene stopped him. "Was it hard leaving Tennessee and starting a new life here?"

Daddy stared at the door a minute before turning back to Arlene. "So that's what you and Aunt Jewell talked about?"

"Yes, sir."

"Leaving Tennessee was a mixture of excitement and terror. I hated taking your Momma away from her family. But coming here was the right thing to do."

Arlene nodded. "Thanks, Daddy."

Daddy smiled. His eyes looked sad. She wanted to say something, but Daddy turned and walked in the house.

Arlene loved Sunday mornings. But this morning, she needed a reason to stay home from church. Without Lon, she would have to face Jack alone. She felt her forehead. Cool as the morning breeze. She coughed. Nothing believable.

"Arlene," Momma yelled. "You have a visitor."

Who called this early on a Sunday? Arlene planted her feet on the cold wood floor. Then it hit her. Only Jack would come this early on a Sunday. Jack missed her yesterday. Today, he wanted to strut into church showing Halford he'd won his prize.

She wrapped her robe around her and brushed out her curls. *Jack will have to wait.*

Arlene put on her Sunday dress, stockings, and shoes. She didn't worry about her hair, rouge, or lipstick. She glanced in the mirror. *This will have to do.*

She peeked in the living room. Empty. *Good. I hope he gave up.* She turned to go back to her room.

"He's on the porch." Her father's voice boomed from the kitchen.

Arlene composed herself and headed to the porch ready to face Jack. She swung open the door and gasped.

"Lon?"

Lon leaned against the porch railing, arms crossed. He wore the same suit from Friday night and looked every bit as handsome. He didn't smile when he saw her or take her in his arms. He didn't say, "Baby doll, you look beautiful this morning."

Lon unfolded his clasped arms. He held the same envelope from Friday night. Arlene slumped at the reminder.

"I wasn't sure if I'd see you again after you stormed out the other night."

"I had to leave. I wanted to punch Jack. And if I did you might never speak to me again." Lon studied her for a moment, then continued. "I see you're not wearing the pearl ring he flashed at you."

"I see you're still carrying that envelope." Arlene did not want to fight, so she added, "Look, if God has called you to preach and you need to go to college, I'm not going to stand in your way."

"Arlene, Jack barged in before we could finish talking about this."

"I can't sit around and wait for you, Lon. I waited for Jack. I was lonely and heartbroken. School could take you a long time."

"Arlene."

"Jack says he knows me better than anyone. But—"

Lon clenched his jaw and swatted the envelope on the rail. "Is that so? Does he know you learned how to drive? That you drive everywhere? That you commandeer my truck while I'm at work and go wherever you want to?"

Arlene grew quiet. "No, he has no idea."

"I didn't think so. Does he know you can recite 'The Raven'? The whole entire poem?"

Arlene's eyes widened. "You know I can do that?"

"Sure. When we went to the old cemetery down in Grimes. When you obsessed about finding some old relatives among the tombstones. I sat in the back of Ol' Blue while you roamed through the graveyard reciting it, all however many stanzas it has. Maybe you thought I couldn't hear you, but I could."

Arlene rubbed her face. "I memorized it in high school. I wanted to see if I could still recite it."

"High school, huh? Jack might know about 'The Raven' then."

"No, he doesn't. I never told him. I was too embarrassed."

"Why?"

"I didn't think memorizing a Gothic poem was a very ladylike thing to do."

"I think it's brilliant you learned that. I've never met anyone as smart as you. Always with your nose in a book. Does Jack know about your dream to go to college?"

Arlene shook her head.

Lon loosened his tie. "I don't think Jack knows you at all."

Arlene reached for the swing to steady herself. She fell into the seat. A cool breeze caught her hair. She ached for Lon to be next to her and wrap his arms around her. Instead, he pulled the stack of papers out of the envelope and handed them to her.

"You need to see what's in this envelope."

Arlene studied the top page. "Says college application."

Lon sat beside Arlene. "Keep looking. How many applications are there?"

Arlene shuffled through the papers. "Two. Why are there two?"

Lon cradled Arlene's face in his hands. "Do you think I'm going anywhere without you? One is for you."

Arlene gasped. "You want me to go too?"

"This is what I wanted to talk about the other night. College. Preaching. Moving out of state one day. I can't do any of this without you. I have your father's blessing."

"What? You mean ..." Arlene shook her head and stared at Lon.

"There's one more thing Jack doesn't know about you."

"I can't imagine." She pushed back tears.

"You would never want a pearl engagement ring."

Lon slipped down on one knee and pulled out a glimmering diamond ring—simple but perfect.

"I love you, Arlene. Since the day in the bluebonnets. Come this spring, I want to marry you. Will you be my wife?"

Arlene flew off the swing and into Lon's arms. "I love you. I'll go anywhere with you. Nobody knows me like you."

"You and me, baby doll. Till death do us part."

Chapter 13

Lon's breaths grew shallow. Arlene kissed his unshaven cheeks.

"I know it's your time to go. I wish God would give me a sign of his promise."

The heavy hospital door heaved open announcing Wes, Colleen, and April's arrival.

The three encircled her like armor, ready to pick up their father's protective mantle. Without taking her eyes off Lon, she reached for their hands. Wes placed a bluebonnet in her outstretched hand.

"What?" Arlene asked. She turned to see Wes holding a vase full of her favorite flowers. "Where did you find them? I've never seen any around here."

"Colleen found a spot. We knew they would cheer you, Mom." Wes kissed her forehead.

Arlene closed her eyes and inhaled the fragrance.

"Mom," April said through tears. "Will we always associate spring with sadness?"

"We will be sad, yes. But your father is about to embrace the best promise ever given. Eternal life with Jesus. So we will celebrate this joy."

Arlene put a bluebonnet in Lon's hand.

"The children are here, Lon. No need to worry." Her voice crackled. *Breathe, Arlene. You must tell him.* She kissed Lon one last time.

"You can let go now. It's too hard for you to go on. Our children will take loving care of me. God gave me his promise."

Cheryl Rae Johnson

Cheryl Rae Johnson teaches writing and literature at Lamar University in Beaumont, TX. She enjoys traveling, college football Saturdays with her family, and finding a great estate sale. More than anything, the author enjoys being CeCe to her grandchildren. She is the author of the *Benny the Dachshund* children's book series, based on the antics of her daughter's miniature dachshund. Cheryl Rae Johnson resides in Port Neches, Texas, with her husband, Jim, the one who knows her better than anyone.

https://www.facebook.com/cherylraejohnsonauthor
http://www.cherylraejohnson.com/

To Love Freedom

CYNTHIA L. SIMMONS

Chapter 1

RURAL GEORGIA, OUTSIDE DORCHESTER
DAWN, MARCH 1776

Blinding pain seared through Jason Howard's shoulder from a gunshot wound. However, as a private in the Continental Army, nothing would hamper his mission. He longed for freedom and had agreed to pay liberty's price. Important papers burned in his coat pocket that he must deliver to the courier tomorrow night.

"Father, guide my steps today." He traveled another mile and knelt in a clump of trees overlooking the Moore farm. Before he moved, he gazed left and right for the three Redcoats but saw no one. The farmyard stood deserted, but Mr. Moore would let him rest. While darkness still cloaked him, he inched toward the simple barn and opened the door. He welcomed the scent of animals and straw as he buried himself in the hay. Sleep overtook him.

Streaks of sunshine peaked over the horizon as eighteen-year-old Sara Moore tiptoed downstairs to prepare johnny cakes. The spacious room served as a kitchen and gathering place. An oblong table sat in the center and two rocking chairs occupied the back of the room. Handmade cabinets held the dishes. She opened the cornmeal bin. She could see the wooden bottom. What would she fix for breakfast if they ran out? Ever since her father left to fight with the Continental Army, she worried she and her brother, Benjamin, couldn't keep up the farm.

But Reverend Reynolds would scold her and tell her to trust God. As she measured cornmeal into the mixing bowl, she remembered to be thankful her brother had already brought in milk and lit the fire in the wood stove.

As she stirred the batter, a cry from upstairs made her cringe. She'd hoped Anna, her five-year-old sister, would sleep a little longer rather than wake Mama.

Sara wiped her hands on a towel and hurried up the narrow stairway to the tiny room she shared with her sister. The morning sun bounced off the mirror over the rustic dresser. Anna sat on the edge of the bed rubbing her eyes. Rumpled sheets all around her cascaded to the floor. Sara sat beside her sister and patted her chubby cheek. "Good morning."

"Where's Mama?" Anna pushed Sara away and stuck out her lower lip.

"We must let her rest." Sara smoothed Anna's unruly blonde curls.

Anna's face reddened. "She *rested* yesterday."

Sara swallowed. She couldn't explain Mama's stillborn baby, too much bleeding, and the frowning midwife. Four days seemed forever to a child. "Oh, I want Mama well too. I miss having her around the house. I tell myself to be patient while she gets well."

"I don't like patience." Scowling, Anna folded her arms.

"Remember Reverend Reynold's sermon. He said to be kind to others. It pleases God."

"Why doesn't God want to please me? I want Mama." Anna burst into tears.

Sara gathered Anna into her arms and wished for her father. His quiet voice always calmed her. She could trust him, at least until he deserted them to fight. "I am cooking breakfast. Could you sleep a little longer if I brought in the kitten?"

Anna nodded and smiled. "Buttercup and I will snuggle. She will be in the barn."

Sara headed toward the barn, hoping to find Anna's cat right away. Buttercup often disappeared when you wanted her most. Sara hurried past Mama's blueberry bushes and took a deep breath of the cool morning air, inhaling the smell of hyacinths.

Benjamin must have left the barn door ajar. How careless! Wild animals would love to eat the hay and animal feed. She pulled it open wide and called Buttercup. Where was that cat?

Her foot hit something. *Whack*!

What made her fall? She lay astride something soft but firm.

"Are you going to get off me? That hurts."

The hay to her left parted, and a dirty face with messy brown hair and eyes the color of pecans appeared.

Sara's heart lurched. A huge man appeared out of the hay. She got off his stomach and sat back on her heels. A scream formed in the back of her throat, but he covered her mouth.

"Don't cry out. I won't hurt you. I have no bullets."

"Get out!" She stood and pointed to the door. "Why are you here?"

"I needed a place to sleep." James gazed into her blue eyes and recognized her from his apprenticeship in Dorchester. She belonged to the Moore family.

"Why here?"

"Don't worry. I will not injure you." He winced and reached for his shoulder. His arm had swollen. "I have a gunshot wound."

Her eyes widened. "Is there fighting around here?"

"No. You have nothing to worry about." He tried to stand, but dizziness overtook him.

"What are you doing here?"

He sighed. He was at this lady's mercy, so he'd best tell the truth. "I am avoiding the British."

"Well, this is all your fault, then." She put her hands on her hips.

"What?" He couldn't imagine what she meant.

"Our pastor rides through here for services once or twice a month. He taught us Romans, chapter 13, which says we should be submissive to those in authority over us."

"I have read the book of Romans." Ugh. He thought Mr. Moore's family would welcome him. However, he had chosen to hide in a barn belonging to Loyalists. He might hang if she turned him in.

Her face hardened. "Well, why didn't you obey God's word?"

She was pretty and plucky. But he must try logic. Hiding would do no good if she gave him to the British. "Have you read Daniel? He appealed to authority when he felt those over him didn't understand God's laws."

Her blue eyes blazed "What?"

"Let me show you." He gritted his teeth as he reached

inside his coat and pulled out his small Bible. His left hand didn't work well, so he had to use his right hand to find the passage. "Romans 13, verse 4. The passage refers to the government. It says, 'For he is the minister of God to thee for good.' That means God authorized the government to do good, not evil. If they do evil, we should attempt to change them."

"You think the British have done evil?" She crossed her arms. "Nonsense."

"Don't you believe people have rights?" He could hope. She did not appear ready to defend her position.

"What rights?"

"The Ten Commandments." He pointed to the tools behind him. "I cannot steal your tools."

She shook a finger at him. "And you shouldn't be here without asking."

"I would characterize my actions as borrowing. Not stealing. I was in dire need." If his reasoning didn't work he was in trouble. But with the British chasing him, he expected to die anyway. "Are you going to turn me in?"

Sara gazed into his large brown eyes. He didn't appear evil. Despite being covered with dust and bits of hay clinging to his disheveled queue, he had an attractive face with strong cheek bones. Besides, he read the Bible.

"I frightened you. I apologize." He glanced at his left arm and sighed.

"You are in pain." Dried blood covered his coat and down his sleeve. His swollen fingers made her want to help him. "You'll need some water, medicine, and food."

"That's generous of you." He cleared his throat. "However, the British may be searching for me."

"Poppycock. They seldom come here." He looked as ill as her mother, and the Bible commanded Christians to be kind—even to strangers. Enemies too.

She left for the house. Had she put her family in danger?

Chapter 2

LATER THAT MORNING

Sara served breakfast to her family before sneaking back out to the barn. After Benjamin and Anna ate, she set aside leftovers for her soldier and prepared her mother's meal.

Carrying a tray with milk and corn pudding, Sara entered her parent's simple bedroom which sat just off the main room. The room had a bed, a chest for linens, a wardrobe, and a table beside the bed. After she placed the tray on the rustic bedside table, she pulled open the curtain across from the bed to brighten the room. She winced at her mother's ashen face. "Mama? I brought breakfast." She sat on the bed and shook her mother's shoulder. "You must eat."

Her mother groaned. "Not hungry! Let me sleep."

Sara raised her mother to a sitting position and held a cup to her lips. "Sip some milk. Your throat must be dry."

"That's enough." Her mother pushed the cup away, spitting out milk left in her mouth.

Sara wiped up the spill. She wasn't sure Mama drank anything. However, her mother refused, and Reverend Reynolds always said to obey your parents. Good sense dictated she should keep trying. What should she do?

Father would know, but he said he was fighting for freedom. Whichever ... she was still alone.

Anna, her blonde curls bouncing, ran in the door and jumped on the bed. "Mama, Mama."

The bed creaked under Anna's weight. Dust and feathers flew everywhere. Mama coughed until her face turned blue.

Sara covered her mouth to hide her anxiety from her sister. Mama would only grow weaker without food. Sara couldn't manage her sister's boundless energy. "Anna, I think you can do a grown-up chore. Could you gather up the breakfast dishes while I feed Mama?"

"And I can start washing them too." Anna jumped off the bed and ran from the room.

Mama pushed aside the food. "I want to sleep."

Armed with a basket of provisions, Sara hurried out to her soldier while her sister put away dishes they had washed together. With her brother plowing, she didn't have to worry about being seen. Doubtless, Benjamin would insist they notify the authorities, and Anna would tell mother. She'd have to keep the soldier a secret. When she entered the barn, she didn't see him. She'd call his name, but she'd forgotten to ask him.

A soft sound behind her made her jump.

"Apologies, again."

She turned to find him peeking from a pile of hay behind the door. "Why did you move?"

"Remember? I have to hide. We seldom look behind us when we enter a building."

"Quite true." What a sharp intellect, despite his injury. She walked toward him and set her basket down.

"I brought food and water, but I won't have time to dress your arm right now."

He drained the glass of water she gave him. Rivulets ran down his face, leaving streaks on his dirty skin.

His obvious need gave her confidence she had made the right choice. She thrust a plate of pork toward him.

"Thank you!" He shoved hunks in his mouth, making his cheeks bulge.

When he finished, she handed him a damp cloth. He wiped his face, then said, "Forgive my manners."

As he rubbed his mouth with the towel, he compared his looks to hers. She wore an attractive pink dress and tiny tendrils of blonde hair curled around her face. He hated to think how long since he'd had a bath. He must appear grubby, and he'd rather impress her. "You do not remember me."

"No." She frowned. "Should I?"

"I thought you belonged to the Moore family. When your brother came in here for the plow, I was certain. I made your rocking chair."

"Oh, that's attractive and sturdy." She raised her eyebrows. "Yes, Father let me choose. You worked for Mr. Barker?"

"I apprenticed with him." He liked the smile that warmed her face.

"He was such a fine man." She glanced out the barn door.

"Was?" His throat tightened. "What do you mean?"

"He died." She grabbed her basket. "If you had stayed with him, you could have his business ... and you would not be wounded. I shall come back later."

James gazed at her back as she left. She scolded him, so he must have left a bad impression. A soldier with an important job should not care if a civilian liked him. But he did.

He pictured her lovely face when she sat beside him with the basket, and a strange longing tugged at him. He should push her from his thoughts. Tonight, he would leave again and complete his mission, so he would never see her again.

Except he wanted to.

Sara caught Anna just before she could burst inside the barn. Tears cascaded down her face. "Is something wrong?"

Anna nodded. "Mama. Come quick."

Sara ran, leaving her sister to catch up. Mama's coughing greeted her when she entered the house, and a pungent smell filled the bedroom. Her mother had lost her breakfast all over the bed and soiled her nightgown.

Anna ran in the bedroom behind Sara. "See? She is not well."

"Thank you for coming for me. I am so proud of you." Sara bragged on her sister until her smile returned. However, the whole house would smell unless she washed the sheets, and she still had baking to do. She hoped her soldier hid himself well because her sister had to help with chores. She turned to Anna. "While I work on this mess, could you feed the chickens? Do you recall where I keep their food?"

"But what about Mama?"

Mama rubbed her face. "I must sleep."

"You see. Let her rest." Sara hoped her mother was right. Whatever happened, she must keep Anna calm.

"Once you feed the chickens, bring me the wash bucket. I am so proud of you, my sweet big girl."

"We must tell Benjamin how grown up I am."

Sara nodded and hoped her fourteen-year-old brother praised Anna. But what if she found the soldier?

Chapter 3

EARLY AFTERNOON

The oblivion of sleep disappeared, and a sharp ache radiated through James's shoulder. Someone was shaking him. Groaning, he opened his eyes. Miss Moore peered down at him, and her blue eyes radiated kindness and warmth. "Ouch!"

"Am I hurting you?" Her eyes widened.

"Yes." He could gaze at this beautiful lady forever. "You are squeezing my left shoulder. Gunshot."

"Oh! Sorry." She pulled back. "I brought stew for lunch. I knew I would find you behind the barn door."

The fragrant smell of stew made his stomach growl. This time he must show better manners. "Thank you. I am so dirty."

"Never mind." She turned to her basket, then pulled out a bowl and a small pitcher of water. "You can wash up a bit."

Aware of her gaze, he washed his face and hands even though his left hand was swollen and hard to move. The water turned black as he removed as much grime as he could. "Thanks, Miss Moore."

"Sara. Call me Sara." She smiled as she took the bowl of now-dirty water. "What is your name?"

"James." He took a bite of the savory stew she handed him. What a treat to eat hot food. "James Howard."

"Oh, I recall Father speaking of you. He preferred your work over Mr. Barker's."

"I have not seen him." He almost hated to ask if Mr. Moore was still living.

"He joined up, like you did." She shrugged. "He never spoke of his thoughts—and after listening to our pastor, I was shocked."

Since her father went to war, he might be able to persuade her he was right. "Men feel a heavy responsibility to protect their families."

Her head jerked backward. "Do you have a wife and children?"

"No." Her reaction pleased him. "And my parents are staunch loyalists."

"Oh dear." She looked out the barn door. "Anna's calling my name. I planned on dressing your wound. Stay where you are, and I shall do that tonight."

His heart deflated as she ran out.

Tonight, he would leave and fulfill his duty.

Her heart clenching, Sara ran to Anna who stood beside the house. "You called me?"

"A man came to the door. Mama said to call you."

Sara found a soldier wearing a tri-cornered hat, boots, a brown coat with dark brown facings, and straps crisscrossing his chest. He wore a knife on his belt and carried a musket. "Hello?"

The man saluted. "You must be Miss Moore. I apologize, but I have a message for Mrs. Moore."

Sara tried to swallow, but her throat cramped. The image of her father's body popped into her mind. "Message? For Mama?"

"Yes, Ma'am." He handed her a letter. "Give this to your mother right away, and I express my deepest condolences."

Unwilling to hold the paper, Sara took it by the corner.

He bowed and walked away.

Benjamin, his dark brows furrowed, ran up as the soldier left. "Who was that? I saw him from the field, and I was worried."

"He appears to be a soldier, but he did not give his name. He wanted me to give Mama this." She held up the disgusting missive.

Benjamin's mouth fell open.

She knocked on her mother's door. "Mama, I think you have a letter about Father."

"Come in."

Her mother pulled herself up in the bed and held out her hand. "Please leave."

Sara nodded and walked out. As she shut the door, her mother screamed.

"That means ... " Benjamin ran his hand through his black hair.

"*Sh-Sh!*" Sara couldn't hear the words.

Benjamin crossed his arms. "I want to enlist."

"No! I cannot run the farm. Do you want us to starve?"

As the sun moved lower in the sky, James sat up. The sweetness of Sara's face made him want to stay, but he must go. He would die a patriot. He crept along close to the ground, moving as fast as he could around the barn.

93

Once he reached the clump of trees overlooking the Moore farm, he stopped and glanced back. He breathed a prayer for Sara and left with a heavy heart.

Hunger gnawed at his stomach. Looking at his watch, he could see he had walked about two hours, so he should be getting close to his meeting spot. He stopped to drink at a stream. Alert to any noise, he stood to creep back into the shadows, and a gun went off. He gasped. Another shot in the same shoulder. Another blast, and his forearm seared with pain.

Oh, God. Help me!

Chapter 4

Rural Georgia, Near Fleming

James continued to travel and ignored the searing pain. An abandoned building sat to his left sporting a wooden sign. The front door was closed, and the place was dark. That must be the spot. He held back a groan as he pulled a map from his inner pocket, but he couldn't see the printing. Stupid. All this running had dulled his wits, and his memory must not fail now. He eased closer, looking left and right, hoping he'd lost the Redcoats.

He crept up to the bedraggled sign and ran his fingers along the embedded letters. Fox Printing. He had arrived, but he couldn't relax yet. Once he passed along the message, he would find a place to die. Alone.

Three steps and he stood at the door. The rusty metal handle resisted when he squeezed. Surely it wasn't locked. Maybe he was weak from blood loss. He tried again. The door swung open without noise. He held his breath as he slithered inside. Thicker darkness engulfed him. No one greeted him, so he must wait.

Sighing, he settled onto the wooden floor, leaning his back against the wall. The swelling in his left arm made his coat too tight, and his legs ached from running. His eyes drifted closed. He rubbed his face to stay alert, but his body was heavy. A sudden noise jarred him to wakefulness. He squinted into the shadows. A rat. Great. The rodents could devour him after he passed.

Another sound. A footstep? He tensed and reached for his knife as the door opened.

"The ship is afloat."

James almost laughed when he heard the password. A shadowed man with a tri-cornered hat stood above him. He expected at least to see the man's face, but he couldn't in this darkness. "The ship will be safe."

"Did you have any interference?"

"The British chased me and wounded me in the shoulder and arm." He flinched as he pulled the thick package from inside his coat and held it up. "Here's your information. Be wary. Loyalists abound in this area."

"I'll be heading north. Shall I send someone for you? You need medical care."

"No." James sighed. He didn't want to die, but he didn't see an alternative. "I do not wish to endanger others. The Redcoats will keep hunting me."

"You are a brave man."

"No. Determined." Maybe he could place that phrase on his grave marker. A shiver ran through his body.

"I shall pray you find help."

"Thank you." James's heart sank as the man left. His arm and shoulder throbbed more now. Could he make it back to the Moore farm?

Once he stepped outside, he saw a British soldier riding slowly while glancing around. He must encourage the soldier to follow him rather than the courier.

Lord, help me.

Morning Before Sunrise

Sara stood before the small mirror in her bedroom and combed out her hair by lamp light, trying not to wake Anna. Sara's locks curled like her sister's, but she confined them in braids. Her fingers needed to keep moving while she sorted her thoughts.

Sleep evaded her last night after the letter arrived. What would she do now? Despite her many chores, nothing came to mind. Father was dead. If only they could bury him in the church graveyard beside Mama's other babies, Sara could decorate his grave.

Her soldier left too. After supper, she took him food and returned with a hole in her heart. Why should she grieve a man she hardly knew? He *was* handsome.

Forget him.

At least the midwife, Mrs. Baker, came last night with food and stayed with Mama. Mrs. Baker understood Mama's condition and would give Sara directions about her mother. Of course, Sara would feed the animals and cook meals. Benjamin couldn't leave. No.

Sara finished braiding her hair and gazed at her shadowy reflection. She'd made two braids and wound them into a bun. Even though her hair appeared neat; her eyes looked drab, and she had no energy. She had no father either. Tears spilled from her eyes.

When my father and my mother forsake me, then the LORD will take me up.

Once her tears ceased, she recalled the chickens. She must feed them.

As she descended the stairs, they squeaked as usual. How silly. The world should stop. Her life had, why not everything else?

The main room stood empty, so she must be up before Benjamin. A nice walk in the cool morning might feel good.

She strolled along the path to the barn. A boot? Did Benjamin leave that outside last night? She moved closer to the huge holly bush at the back of the house. No. A foot had to be attached. She tugged. "Who are you?"

"Sara?"

Her heart leapt. "James? You came back."

"I thought I was hidden." He scooted out into the open, but his face was shadowed. "I was exhausted."

He had not obeyed. "Where did you go?"

James would not answer her question. But judging from the sound of her voice, she was glad he returned.

"Let me help you to the barn."

"No. I can make it." He tried to get to his feet, but his legs buckled.

"Why do men think they are invincible?" Sara wept.

Uh-oh. His three sisters got upset when something serious happened. He had learned from his older brother to tiptoe around them at such moments. "We are not," he spoke softly, aware she was hurting.

"My father ..." She hiccupped and sniffled.

He gripped his musket, pulled himself up, and wrapped his good arm around her shoulder. "Help me get into the barn before the sun comes up."

Sara grabbed his good hand, and together they inched toward the barn. She had reacted too harshly to his simple statement. What must he think of her? "A few more steps. We are getting closer."

"Thank you." He was breathing hard. "I shall leave as soon as I can."

"No." She stopped and met his gaze. "You left last night, and I worried about you. Do *not* leave again."

He chuckled.

"I did not intend to be humorous." She put a hand over her mouth to hold back tears. He needed a nurse, not a weeping willow.

"Yes, ma'am."

At least he did not resist her now. Once they reached the barn, she waited until he settled himself in the hay. "I will bring breakfast soon."

"Thanks." He looked up at her from the barn floor. "If your brother finds me, what will he do?"

"I cannot be sure." She stepped back. "He wants to join the army too."

James arranged his blanket under his head and allowed his body to relax. "Dear Father, I have imposed on this family at a time of crisis. My presence here could bring danger. Once again, I ask you to guide my steps. Protect this family."

Sleep sucked him into darkness.

Chapter 5

Sara hurried into the house to discover Mrs. Baker, the midwife, working in the kitchen. She wore a white bonnet tied under her chin and an apron covering her green dress.

"There you are, dearie." She stood and nodded toward the bedroom. "I finally got your mother to fall asleep. Anna came downstairs, and I tucked her in with your Mama. I worry how this shock will affect your mother. Dreadful. Let her rest as long as she likes but insist she eat the moment she wakes. The poor dear is so ill."

Sara glanced at the dishes on the table and wondered how she'd slip food to her soldier. "What are in these bowls?"

"I made thick porridge, perfect for your mother." She touched another bowl. "You'll find roast pork in this. Your brother will need some meat on his bones. I know he is plowing right now. The last is corn pudding with lots of milk, perfect for someone ill. I included a bit of sugar, so it goes down easy."

"Thank you. I'm curious how you knew ..." Sara didn't want to say the words.

"The officer stopped in the general store, and news spreads." She patted Sara's cheek. "Now mind you, some won't like your father's choice to fight. Ignore them. He was a good man."

Sara swiped at the tears flooding her cheeks. An insult would suffice for those people. No. No. Even in her sorrow, she would say nothing. "Thank you."

"Of course." Mrs. Baker pressed Sara to her ample bosom. "I shall call again."

Sara sobbed. What responsibility she must face alone.

Sara woke with a start to a darkened room. She was so groggy. Where was Anna? How long had she slept? A glance at her alarm clock told her she should be serving dinner. She groaned as she remembered. Her father. Weeping all night. Her mother and Anna slept downstairs. She heard nothing but silence, even from Benjamin's bedroom, which sat across from hers. The midwife left food. No one needed her.

Except for her soldier ... James. He had not eaten, and he needed medicine. She must find clothing to replace his blood-soaked uniform. With a sigh, she thought of her father's clothes.

She lit a candle and tiptoed downstairs to the bedroom where her mother and sister slept. With trembling hands, she opened the wardrobe and removed the shirt Father had worn for Sunday. Holding the fabric to her face, she could smell the soap he used.

Could she see James wearing this?

She soaked the fabric with her tears.

James shifted his weight, but the barn floor did not feel more comfortable. When he first immersed himself in the straw, exhaustion lured him into a deep slumber despite his pain. Now, however, hunger and constant aching competed for his attention. He tolerated the discomfort when he had a solemn duty. Now he had solitude. And he smelled of dried blood mixed with sweat and dirt. His presence created a problem for the Moore family, and the throbbing spasms in his arm and shoulder made him restless and angry. Is this death?

Father, I need you!

An Hour Later

A bright light woke James, and he gazed up to see Sara carrying both a basket and lantern.

"I apologize." She hung up the lantern and pulled food and supplies from her basket. "Our family didn't sleep last night, so my nap lasted longer than I intended. You must be starved."

He sat up, making his head pound also. "I should not have returned—"

"Fiddlesticks!" She lifted her chin. "This morning you could barely walk. I shall dress your wound before you eat."

"It's obvious I came at a terrible time."

"No." She turned her back and reached into her basket. "You require medication, and I shall have to remove your shirt."

He groaned and tried to pull his jacket off his swollen arm. She came toward him with scissors and slashed his sleeve before he could protest. "You ruined my jacket." As he watched, she hacked his shirt sleeve too, exposing the injury in his forearm.

"You got wounded here too?" Her eyebrows pulled together in a tight line. "This looks terrible."

"Ouch." As she got to his shoulder, the dried blood stuck to his skin sending spasms through his arm. He gritted his teeth against the throbbing.

"Let me dampen this." She splashed whisky on what was left of his shirt and jacket and lifted off the wet cloth.

Unwilling to watch, he covered his face. "That hurts!"

"Sorry. Here." She paused to hand him a damp cloth for his face. "You have more gunshot wounds, and I believe they went all the way through. You said you had *one*, not three."

"That was correct when I said it." He wiped his brow. "I acquired two more last night."

"You should have stayed, like I told you."

"I had a duty." He pulled away from her so he could look into her eyes. "And I *do* keep my word."

"Oh, very well." Her tone softened. "I still do not quite understand why you fight."

"You have *no idea* how the British have treated us?" His pain spoke, and he was too harsh. Given her kindness, he should thank her.

"Yes. You feel strongly." She smeared salve on his wound and applied bandages. "This calendula preparation speeds healing, and I added willow bark powder to relieve pain."

"Thanks. That feels better."

She held a shirt in front of her. "I brought this for you to wear."

"Very nice. That looks too big for your brother."

Her lips trembled and she dropped the garment in his lap. "It belonged to my father, and we just heard he died."

"My deepest condolences." He handed the shirt back to her. "Are you sure you want me to wear this?"

She nodded. However, she grabbed her basket and ran out of the barn sobbing.

Chapter 6

After Dark

When Benjamin retired for the night, Sara slipped outside to the barn. She must overcome her embarrassment about breaking down in front of James. She had important news. Carrying her father's sturdy walking stick, she crept into the barn. Darkness enveloped her and she hoped he'd stayed put. "James?"

"I'm here. Same place."

She stood still until she could see the outline of his body in the straw. "My brother went into the village for provisions. He heard Redcoats had arrived. They are going into homes. Could they be searching for you?"

"Yes." The straw crackled as he sat up. "Now I *must* go."

"I have the perfect place for you."

He chuckled.

Darkness concealed his face, so she couldn't imagine what amused him. "I do not see anything humorous about this situation."

"You are *so* determined." He coughed and cleared his throat. "Where is this *perfect place*?"

"Our property has a small stream beneath a hill. Years ago, my brother and I discovered a cave there while we played. Huge shrubs hide the entrance. There's plenty of room for you, and I can keep you supplied with food."

"How far?"

She took a deep breath, considering how to persuade him. "Less than a mile, maybe half that."

"Tell me how to get there."

"No." What was he thinking? "I will go with you. I brought Father's heavy walking stick, which should be perfect for you. I can carry your gun."

"Never! I keep the musket."

"But you said you had no bullets. What's the danger?"

"Hand me the stick and give me directions."

"You would never find it without me." What an arrogant man. He might fall and need help. "I will not let you go alone."

Using his right arm, James reached for the stick Sara held out. He brushed her soft hand, but he pushed the pleasant sensation aside. His life depended on his stamina. "I have it now. Leave the rest to me."

"Your skin is hot. You must have a fever."

He dropped the stick while he threw the musket strap over his shoulder and reached for his pack. Surely, he could carry everything.

"What are you doing?"

"I have to get my gear. Anything I leave behind will give the Redcoats reason to keep looking."

"I see a bundle. I can carry that. You had a hard enough time just standing this afternoon."

"I am *fine*." His dizziness and nausea said otherwise, but he would never admit that. She moved closer and snatched the pack from him. "Hey, what are you doing?"

"I have your gear. Let's go."

"That's too heavy for you." She moved away so he couldn't reach her. Getting up might be challenge enough. With a mighty groan, he pulled himself up on the stick. The barn spun, but he hung on. His injuries ached more now, but he had to move.

"You are breathing hard. I am glad I took the gear, as you call it."

"I ... am fine." Feeling like cannonballs, his legs held them to the ground; but he would not give up.

Sara laughed. "I do not believe you."

"This will be slow, Sara." She might decide to give up, and he wouldn't blame her.

His heavy breathing and groans stung her heart. At least she had his pack, which was heavy. She could not help her father, but she would hide James even if the job took all night. Finally, James arrived at the door. Moonlight revealed lines of pain on his face.

"I-I need to rest."

"I thought so." She put her arm around his good side, noting his muscular frame. "Let me help you sit."

"Thanks. Tell me about your brother."

"Benjamin is my baby brother. He's fourteen." She sat down beside James and let the gear slide off her shoulder. Knowing what heavy equipment James carried made her admire him. "He just finished plowing the fields."

"Does he know I'm here?"

"No." She imagined him demanding breakfast in the morning after she stayed up all night. "I am not sure how he would respond. The moment we heard Father died, Benjamin said he wanted to join up." She shrugged and gazed up at the stars. "I did not know Father's opinion until he chose to fight."

"Maybe he feared expressing his views."

The horizon sky turned pale pink as James ducked into the musty cave. Sara had told the truth. Vines and bushes hid the entrance so well, he needed her guidance. Once past the small opening, the ceiling rose to about six feet high. Dim light filtered through the leaves. Rocks with a fine coating of dirt made the floor. He collapsed against a wall, panting and hurting.

Sara scooted in beside him. Even though her braids came undone, she was just as beautiful as ever. "I can bring blankets so you can make a bed on the floor."

James felt as if he'd fought all night. His body was already giving way to sleep. "No need. My gear contains everything for camping."

She slumped, as if she was disappointed. "We have a lantern stored in here for evenings. Later, I shall bring food."

He grabbed her small white hand, longing to hold it forever. Instead, he kissed her fingers. "I am grateful. More than I can say."

"I shall go back to the barn and get rid of everything." She slid his pack off her back. "Where is the coat and shirt I cut off?"

"In the pack." He nodded toward the door. "Leave me. You've done all you can. I don't want the Redcoats to attack you."

As he said the words, he longed for her to return.

Sara slid out of the cave on to the ground, but her heart stayed in the cave with James. The touch of his lips on her fingers lingered in her thoughts. She pictured him sagging against the wall with barely enough energy to sit. Fever made his skin feel like fire. He needed her to bathe his brow with water, but she had chores. This afternoon, she could bring water and food.

Right now, she had to shove her way through the thick weeds and head back to the barn. Heaviness in her limbs slowed her pace. How much more pleasant to travel with James. He'd managed to chat even though injured.

When she pulled open the barn door, Benjamin stood inside with his back to her. He turned and stared.

"Where have you been?"

"I could not sleep." That was true, she only left out the part about James.

He pulled a leaf out of her hair "You went to the cave?" He looked into her eyes. "Did you cry all night?"

"I cried, but not *all* night." She pictured James, sitting beside her while she wept. He'd been so kind to listen to her rambling thoughts. If only she could get inside the barn and remove any signs he had been there. "I planned to milk for you."

"I shall take care of that." He rubbed his stomach. "Fix breakfast and check on Mama. She was moaning this morning."

Sara winced.

She urged her exhausted muscles forward toward the house. Smiling, Anna skipped as she came inside.

"I gave Mama water. I did it like you do." She pointed toward the bedroom. "And she stopped crying. See."

Sara's stomach churned at the news, and she hurried to her mother's room. Eyes closed, Mama lay on her side. Droplets of water sparkled in her hair and on her cheeks.

Both Mama's beige nightgown and the sheets felt damp. "Anna, Mama didn't drink everything ... and we need to clean her up. Can you get me a towel from the wardrobe?"

Anna smiled and skipped toward the wardrobe.

Sara eased her mother to a dry spot on the bed.

Someone banged on the door. "In the name of King George! Open up!"

Sara's heart skipped a beat. Would the soldiers search the barn? Her chest tightened as she walked toward the door. "Yes?"

Three soldiers arrayed in red coats and brandishing muskets pushed her aside. "We are conducting a search."

The one who spoke, marched into the bedroom, hurled Anna to the wall, and dumped the contents of the wardrobe on the floor.

Sara froze.

Two other men barged in, and one went upstairs. The other opened the cabinets and pulled out dishes. Anna burst into tears, and Sara hurried to the bedroom to embrace her.

The soldier stomped downstairs, trailing a sheet behind him. "Nothing here." He grimaced as he dropped the fabric on the stairs.

The leader looked under Mama's bed and stalked toward Sara. "This is what happens when colonists harbor contraband."

Anna trembled, and Sara gazed into his cold eyes, her heart racing.

Chapter 7

Taking a deep breath, Sara plopped into the rocking chair James made. She had cared for her Mama and prepared breakfast, but her mind whirled. While Anna nibbled on a slice of fresh bread with blueberry jelly, Sara sought a moment to rest. She needed to sort through her thoughts.

Father had never criticized the British. He probably thought Sara would worry, but he must have agreed the British overstepped their boundaries. He paid with his life. Her mind returned to what James said the first day they met. He believed people had rights, and he referred to the Ten Commandments. Of course, the Bible should guide their opinions. However, she never realized the Continental Congress defended their opinions with God's word.

Reverend Reynolds had formed her opinions with his sermons on obedience. Who was right? If an evil person plotted mischief, shouldn't the government have the right to pursue? Did that include invading the homes of innocent people? Perhaps James could elaborate more on what caused him to join the Continental Army. He worried about inconveniencing the family or getting them into trouble. An honest man. She would also pray for guidance.

James woke with a start and wondered where he was. His entire body throbbed, and his tongue tasted like cotton. A glance around the shady cave brought back memories of stumbling through the fields in darkness. When fatigue overwhelmed him, Sara had put her arm around him and guided him to a resting place. Not many women would stay up all night to help a battered soldier.

He thirsted for water. If only Sara could stroke his brow and moisten his lips.

Enough of that! He groaned as he reached for his canteen. With a gulp, he swallowed its contents—he needed more. He had noticed a stream flowing beneath the cave ... only a short walk.

He sat up, and his head throbbed. Water! Ignoring his discomfort, he pulled himself to a seated position. The cave whirled around him and went black.

Same Day
Late Afternoon

Sara sat on her mother's bed, holding her mama upright. She put a spoon to her mouth. "Another bite. You need strength. Mama!"

Her lips tightened, and she turned her head away.

Sara bit her lip. Her mother appeared to be withering right before her eyes. Tears stung as she recalled her father, so strong and wise. He was gone now. Would she lose Mama too?

Anna danced into the room. "I see Mrs. Baker coming to visit. Maybe she has more pudding."

"Open the door for her." Sara blotted her mother's face with a damp rag, hoping she would wake and eat. "Mama, you have a guest. Take a big bite for the midwife."

Mrs. Baker bustled in. "Hello, Sara ... Mrs. Moore. It's lovely outside today. Sunny and breezy." She wore a yellow dress and beige apron. "I came to take a look at you, dearie."

"She had one bite. A tiny one." Sara looked at the midwife for suggestions and hope.

Mrs. Baker offered a small nod. "Let me look her over."

Sara stood and carried the tray back to the common area. Mama had never been strong, but she never seemed obstinate. *If only I can get her to eat.* While waiting, Sara cleaned the kitchen utensils and wiped down the table. The chores kept her from the cave, but James never left her thoughts.

Mrs. Baker came alongside Sara and encircled her waist. "Your mama is melancholy. I don't think she wants to live."

Sara gasped as pain radiated from her heart to her stomach. "I do not want to be an orphan."

Mrs. Baker squeezed Sara's hands. "Let's pray."

An Hour Later

The Barn

Hay covered the barn floor and appeared undisturbed, but Sara wasn't satisfied. She walked over to the spot where James had lain. Scraping back the hay, she looked for any sign he had been there. The dirt was darker in one area. That might be blood, but the color blended well.

Someone would have to be searching to notice—like she was.

"What are you doing?" She turned to find Benjamin in the doorway. Sweat beaded his face, and she noticed dark fuzz on his chin.

"I am looking for something." She spotted a button, which might belong to James, so she picked it up. Of course, she wanted to tell Benjamin the truth, but she didn't know how he'd react.

"Who stayed in the barn?" His brown eyes bored into hers. When angry, he looked like Father.

She decided not to answer. "Did the Red Coats come in here?"

"Yes." His nostrils flared as he came closer. "But I had already spread the hay evenly. What are you doing? Who went to the cave with you?"

He must think her immoral. She raised her chin at his gaze. "A Continental soldier. He's badly wounded."

"Oh!" He released a sigh. "You may have put us in danger, but I would do the same."

James must be dreaming. A damp cloth bathed his face and neck. "That feels magnificent."

"Would you like some water?" Sara asked.

This wasn't a dream. He opened his eyes. Beautiful Sara sat beside him. Her blue eyes reminded him of sapphires. He had begged God for her to return. "Yes, please."

She placed a cup to his lips, and he drank and drank. Heavenly.

"I refilled your canteen, and I brought food."

"Superb." He thought of King David's words—*I have been young, and now am old; yet have I not seen the righteous forsaken, nor his seed begging bread.* The Lord provided through Sara, and he hoped she'd linger.

"The midwife brought strawberry jam." Sara reached into a basket. "I thought you'd like some with my fresh bread, and I have several ham slices."

His mouth watered. He scooted himself to an upright position and accepted a plate which he wedged in the crease of his left arm. Only able to use one hand, balancing a plate proved to be a challenge. "Thank you, again."

"And I brought a napkin and utensils, so you don't have to eat with your hands."

He threw back his head and laughed. "You want to tame me? I do know my manners. Promise."

The blush creeping up her cheeks made her impossibly more attractive.

"You know a lot about me." Sara settled down on the floor across from him. "May I ask about you?"

He stopped with a bite halfway to his mouth. Sure."

Sara pondered how to start. She wanted to resolve her questions about the war, especially since her father fought. "Why did you join the Continental Army?"

"I saw how unfairly the British ruled." He blotted his mouth with the napkin. "Taxes they imposed crushed us."

She leaned closer. "What about that verse, 'render to Caesar the things that are Caesar's...'?"

"I will pay tax." He shrugged his right arm. "However, when the government takes so much you can't support yourself, that's stealing."

"Wouldn't people complain about any tax?" She folded her arms, waiting for his response.

"Very true." He took a bite and swallowed. "Think about that verse, 'if any would not work, neither should he eat.' Obviously, God intends us to work for a living."

"You make the British sound evil." Magistrates had been so kind to her when she was a child.

"British officials do not respect an individual's person or property. King George believes he has a mandate from God, but he doesn't consider our needs. You saw the passage from Romans. God put governments in place to do good. The implication is they *shouldn't* do evil."

Sara inhaled as she considered his words. Except for the Redcoats coming into her home, she couldn't imagine them doing evil. "I must think and pray over your words. I hesitate to condone rebellion."

"I detest it also." He shook his head.

She pondered his words as she grabbed her basket. "I shall leave bread and dried fruit in case I cannot return in a timely manner. When I come again, I shall check your bandage."

"I shall pray for you, Sara."

Chapter 8

SAME DAY, LATE AFTERNOON

The fragrance of stew filled the house. Sara had cooked pork with canned vegetables from their garden and baked fresh cornbread while Anna napped with her mother.

The front door flew open, and a large-framed British soldier marched in, his sword dragging on the floor. "I come in the name of King George III, and I demand you provide food and a bed."

Sara remembered what James said earlier. The soldier could jail her if she refused. "My bed is upstairs, and I can offer you clean sheets."

He strode to the bedroom where her mother slept. "I prefer this room. Move her."

Sara glared at him. However, she imagined what he might do to her.

"Now! I want a nap before dinner." He moved his hand to his sword.

"She's sick!" Sara spat the words.

"Do as I say." He spread his legs and crossed his arms.

Her heart hammering, Sara ran to the bedroom. "Anna, wake up. You must go upstairs to lie down."

Anna cried but she got up. Rubbing her eyes, they widened when she walked past the Redcoat.

"Mama. Mama! I must move you." Sara put her arm under her mother's shoulder and another under her mother's legs. When she tried to lift, she almost fell backward. Slowly, she got Mama out of bed, though feeling as if her mother would slide to the floor.

"Ouch. You hurt me," Mama moaned.

"Sorry!" Sara whispered.

"Hurry up, girl." The soldier pulled out his sword.

"I can barely carry her," Sara mumbled.

"No complaints, if you please."

Sara trembled with the weight. Her mother's legs dragged on the floor while Sara clung to her upper body. Finally, she moved her mother to the living area, placing her on the floor. She turned and headed back into the bedroom.

"Leave," the soldier shouted.

"I need blankets for my mother." Sara glared at him. The brute. "They are in the wardrobe."

He stood aside. "Carry on ... quickly, girl."

The soldier slammed the bedroom door when she left. She covered her mother with a blanket, folding an additional one under Mama's head to serve as a pillow. Sara hoped moving her mother didn't make her worse.

"What are you doing?" Benjamin stood over Mama, his face red and his lips flattened.

"A British soldier took her room." Sweat poured down Sara's back and her heart raced. Tears burned her eyes.

Benjamin's eyes narrowed. "I shall take her to my bed."

"Thanks." Sara finally felt free to breathe. "I couldn't get her upstairs."

His arms full of Mama, he leaned close to Sara and whispered, "Serve dinner now, so we can eat as much as we want."

THAT NIGHT

Sara was tucking Anna into bed when she heard the soldier roar, "Where is my dinner?"

"Dear Lord, help me to be civil." She threw a house coat over her night clothes and moseyed down to the living area. Her brother lay on a makeshift cot across the room.

The soldier paced. He had removed his coat and hat and wore a loose white shirt, red knickers, and boots.

She tried to keep her voice even as she motioned toward the table. "We were going to bed. On the farm, we rise early and retire early."

"I want dinner." He puffed out his chest, and she noted his round abdomen.

"Very well." She placed cornbread and dried pork on a plate.

He curled his lips. "This is not what I smelled when I entered today."

"We ate while you slept. Four people live here." She pulled wine from the cabinet. "Would you care for wine?"

He arched his brows. "What kind?"

"Blueberry." She held up the bottle. "We made it ourselves."

He frowned and shook his head. "No."

"What about whiskey? We keep some for medicinal use."

"Yes. A tall glass."

Benjamin shook his fist so Sara could see. She guessed his meaning. They paid a high price for whiskey, and their Red Coat wanted a lot.

THE CAVE
THE SAME EVENING

James had to escape the danger, but pain enveloped him. Run! His life depended on getting away and he had to decide which direction. On his left, the water rose faster and faster, so he must travel to his right. His breath came in gasps. If only he could get out of the way before it was too late.

Wait. Where was he? He opened his eyes and saw stone. A building made of rocks? He saw a face. Sara. She beckoned him, but now he couldn't move. No. He saw his lieutenant, and he was frowning.

His back hurt. Was he lying on rocks? A scream sounded in the distance. They must have caught the courier, and he would hang. James should have led the Red Coats further away. He should go to Midway soon. The patriots there knew what to do; but he'd heard they all left.

He tossed. The blankets kept slipping into the river. He should snatch them, but they got beyond his reach. Would someone help him? Please? He couldn't live much longer with this agonizing pain and thirst. He was so hot.

God help me!

THE NEXT MORNING

Sara rose when Benjamin left for the barn and tiptoed downstairs, hoping the Red Coat slept through this meal too.

Benjamin hurried in, wearing a huge smile. "Look what I found. He held out three eggs. The oldest hen finally laid."

Sara clapped, but only in her mind. Their Redcoat had changed her opinion of the British. James would be proud, and she hoped she could get a chance to see him today.

"Fix them for us," Benjamin whispered. "Before our unwelcome company wakes.

The two of them hugged, united against the invader.

After Sara prepared gruel for her mother, she set out three plates of eggs and bread for herself, Anna, and Benjamin. She also placed a half loaf of her fresh bread in the center of the table in case Benjamin wanted more to eat.

Benjamin offered grace, then the three devoured their breakfast.

"What is this?" The soldier strode into the room, without his wig and wearing a loose night shirt. "You did not call me for breakfast."

Benjamin glared at him.

The Redcoat plopped in Father's chair and grabbed all the bread. "I shall eat this." Then he wolfed it down. "Give me whiskey, girl."

Chapter 9

AFTER BREAKFAST

Benjamin left to start planting as Sara washed the dishes while Anna played with her dolls. Meanwhile, the soldier sat at the table, sipping his whisky. Sara had the odd feeling he was watching her. Her muscles remained stiff, aware of everything he did. What did he hope to accomplish? They had little to give.

Plenty of chores awaited her, which included feeding her mother, and taking food to James. Somehow, she must slip out to the cave without attracting his attention. James had been correct all along.

Father, give us freedom from this pesky Britain. Help Mama to get well too.

An idea suddenly popped into Sara's mind. "Come, Anna. I have another grown-up job for you."

Her blue eyes glowed. "Hooray. What is it?"

"I want you to feed Mama." She pointed to the tray she had prepared.

"Feed Mama?" Anna squealed and jumped. "I am very mature."

"Yes, and if she refuses to eat, tell her how much you love her."

"Yes. I love Mama!" She hopped up the stairs. "I shall show her how much I love her *all day*."

As Anna climbed the steps, Sara glanced back toward the soldier. He was staring at her again.

LATE MORNING

Sara's heart raced as she slipped out of the house with a basket of food and medicine for James. Fully dressed, the Redcoat had left the house about three hours ago. While she finished her baking, she had spotted him out the window. He seemed to be following Benjamin, and she planned a covert trip to the cave. She didn't have to worry about Anna since she stayed with Mama.

First, she had to get to the barn. She walked in her normal pace. But instead of going inside, she went to the outside wall where the soldier could not see her. From there she ambled to the clothesline. The sheets she hung out to dry would block his view.

Now, she must face the tricky part. She had to walk ten feet from the clothesline into the wooded area. Sara ran, hoping the soldier had not seen her. She didn't think he had.

The woods consisted of evergreen trees with a smattering of oak and maple, and the deciduous trees sprouted their leaves. Her heart rate slowed as she climbed the hilly area. On the other side of the hill, she looked left and right. Seeing no one, she crept into the greenery that concealed the cave opening.

Would James be okay?

A raucous noise greeted Sara as she climbed into the cave, and her throat tightened. "James?"

He lay on the left side of the cave, limp and pale. His left arm was so swollen, the skin had cracked in places.

If only I could have tended him earlier, but the soldier kept me away

She hurried to him and felt his brow. His skin blazed with heat, and his breathing was strident. What if he died? Her heart constricted. She doused a cloth with water and bathed his face. "James?"

He opened his eyes, gazing into space. "They stole the rice. All of it."

What was James saying? His words made no sense.

She pressed a cup to his lips, and he drank.

A sound at the entrance to the cave startled her. Had the Redcoats found her? Would they shoot her?

Not Redcoats ... Benjamin.

Sara put her hand on her throat. "You scared me."

"I knew you'd come here." He ran his fingers through his dark hair. "When I checked on him this morning, he was delirious. I came back to see if he was better or worse."

"He's very ill." Sara had so many things to tell James. He had captured her heart, and she would not give up. "The fever has reached crisis point. I shall stay and pull him through."

Benjamin nodded. "The Redcoat departed with two of our chickens. I followed him at a distance and heard him tell two other soldiers they should *search* Midway. I do not think he will return."

"Evil man." She should have trusted James.

Benjamin glanced toward James and then met Sara's gaze. "What about Mama?"

"She has responded well to Anna's care. She's eating now." Sara smiled. "I think she will recover. I left bread and meat in the kitchen."

Benjamin held her hand. "I shall pray for you."

"Thanks." Sara had a battle to fight, and the war could last all night.

Once Benjamin left, Sara went to work. She bathed James's face and neck in cool water. Her basket contained several herbal preparations which she mixed and administered.

James moaned and shifted. "Terrible pain."

"I am here." She clenched her jaw hoping she got here in time.

Sara mixed willow bark powder with water and held a spoonful to his lips. "This will dull the pain."

He groaned, then turned his face away.

"You must drink this, James." Her lips were inches from his face, and she imagined what a kiss might feel like. Later. After he healed.

He scowled but drank.

"A little more." She smiled as he complied. "I am Sara, remember. I shall change the bandage and apply salve for the swelling."

He jerked as she unbuttoned his shirt and lifted off the soiled bandage, but he allowed her to nurse his wounds.

"I'm applying ointment. The coolness will feel comfortable." At least she hoped so. The medicine she gave him should reduce both his fever and the swelling.

He nodded.

Dear James. She bathed his brow. He seemed more restful. *Oh, Father, heal this man. I care for him, and I cannot bear to see him so ill.*

As the day wore on, his breathing became smoother—and he slept.

Chapter 10

DAWN THE NEXT DAY

James took a deep breath, opened his eyes, and stretched. A few rays of sunlight brightened the cave, and he glanced around. Sara slept in a huddle on the other side of the cave, a small blanket under her head. Her blonde braids hung past her shoulders, and a large basket sat beside her.

Her eyes popped open. "You are awake."

"Sara, you are beautiful." He sat up.

"That might mean you are close to death, but your color has improved." She reached in her basket and pulled out bread and meat. "Are you hungry?"

"Starved."

She handed him a plate. "Do you recall me coming in?"

"Yes." He took a huge bite of bread and sloshed it down with water from his canteen. "I wanted you to stay away for your safety, but I prayed God would send you back."

"After I left here, a Redcoat demanded to stay at the house." She related how he ordered her to vacate her mother's room. "I felt watched."

"Three of them followed me while I delivered confidential information."

"Yes." She nodded. "The first time the Redcoats searched, three soldiers came in."

"The leader had dark eyes, and he was bald without his wig."

Her eyes got big. "That's the man who stayed."

"I exposed you to danger." He sighed, rubbing his chin. "I apologize."

"No." She came close and touched his right hand. "You made me see truth, and you talked to me about the real world. Father never did that. I am so grateful."

He caressed her hand, then kissed it. "My dearest Sara. You saved my life while risking yours."

"Nonsense." She smiled. "You are my soldier. A good, honest man."

"You did not accept what I said. Instead, you wanted me to prove it." He reached for the Bible in his pocket and realized he wasn't wearing his coat. "I had to use the Bible, and I like that. I do not want a wife who accepts everything I say."

"Wife?" Her mouth gaped.

"Yes. You will make a terrific wife, Sara ... and I covet you to be mine." Her face appeared frozen in shock. "This probably appears sudden, but I have thought about you constantly."

She nodded.

"I love you, and I hope, someday, you can love me as much as I love you." He leaned close to tweak a braid. "After all, you did spend the night with me. I have to marry you to protect your reputation."

Her cheeks turned a charming shade of red. "You cannot tell anyone that."

"Of course, my love." He placed a hand over his heart. "If you will be mine, I shall hold my peace."

Sara giggled. "I fell in love with your wisdom."

"I do not blame you. Reverend Reynolds preached the political stance without anyone to explain or contradict. However, people who speak up can get unwanted attention from the British."

She shrugged. "Perhaps that's why Father said nothing. He did not want to expose us to harassment."

"And I did." He laughed. "You have not given me an answer."

"Yes."

"I need to understand clearly. Yes, meaning you didn't give me an answer? Or yes, you will marry me?"

"Both."

Using his good hand, he pulled her close and kissed her.

Chapter 11

THE NEXT MORNING

Awake before dawn, Sara knelt by her bed to pray. So many things needed to happen. She and James had to decide when to marry and to choose a place to live. Besides. how could they start a life together when Redcoats endangered his life? Mindful of all the issues, she tiptoed downstairs and assembled a basket with medication and food.

Once outside, she reveled in the horizon that grew brighter as she walked. Crocus blooms spilled their perfume into the air, and birds trilled with abandon. God controlled the world. She should not worry.

"Why are you up so early, Sara?"

She gasped, and turned to see Father—and he was dressed in his uniform. His bushy black hair uncovered, he carried his tri-cornered hat under his arm. "Father? I thought ..."

He waved as if to reassure her he was indeed alive. "During battle, information can be confused. As you can see, I am hale and hearty."

"Oh, Father." Sara threw herself into his arms and let happy tears flow. Once she pulled away, her concerns bubbled over. "Father, we must talk at length. Do you recall James Howard—"

Her father's bushy eyebrows sank, and he grabbed her arm. "What do you know of Mr. Howard?"

Her heart sped up as she studied the glint in Father's brown eyes. "He is here—that is, hidden in a cave on our property. He sustained three wounds, all rather nasty; but he has improved. His complete recovery will take some months, I think."

Her father sighed. "I am here on assignment, searching for the Redcoats who have been killing our messengers. The last message Howard delivered gave us vital information, but the courier feared he would not survive his injuries." He held her arm. "Take me to him."

A rustling sound made James wary, but his weary body didn't respond to his internal alarm. He could never forget the sergeant who trained him. Alert and prepared. Right now, James could not brag he had either quality.

"Mr. Howard." A deep voice reverberated inside the cave.

With a gulp James sat up.

"I'm Ezekiel Moore. You may call me Lieutenant Moore." He stood over James. "Obviously, my daughter has you well in hand."

"Yes, sir." James saluted Moore's superior rank and attempted correct posture despite intense discomfort. He still needed a bath, and he wore this man's shirt. "Her nursing skills pulled me through. She is a lovely person. I suppose she told you I have asked for her hand in marriage?"

"No. She did not." Moore threw back his head and laughed. "That explains her intense concern. More about this proposal later. Right now, I need to know how many men pursued you."

"Three." James ran his good hand over his eyes. "At times, I thought there might be four."

"I see." Moore pursed his lips. "My men have apprehended three Redcoats and believe we located a fourth. Did any of them know your name?"

"No, sir. They knew me by sight, and they could have sketched my likeness."

Moore shook his head. "I do not believe they had that much foresight, and I am fairly sure we will have this gang captured today. When we do, that will eliminate any further need for secrecy."

James sighed. "That sounds wonderful."

Lieutenant Moore offered a handshake. "Considering that, I will welcome you as a future son-in-law. I admired your character when you worked with Mr. Barker. Perhaps you would consider making more furniture for my family?"

"Yes, sir." James glanced at his shoulder. "As soon as I recover."

"I suppose you will want to see Sara?" Moore chuckled. "I sent her home to prepare breakfast. But she will see that you don't go hungry."

Chapter 12

THREE MONTHS LATER

Sara stood in her bedroom while her mother fastened the tiny buttons up her back. Her wedding gown had a scooped neck bordered with wide lace and a full skirt gathered into a lace bodice. Her parents wouldn't have had the money for such a lovely dress. However, men in James's regiment bought the fabric when they heard he survived and planned to marry. She and her mother had been sewing for weeks while James recovered. Her joy bubbled over this morning.

"Finished." Her mother backed away and smiled. "All we need is the matching bonnet and veil."

Sara couldn't help grinning as she gazed at her mother's happy face. Mama even had color in her cheeks. "I am getting married today. Do you think I will be a good wife, like you?"

"Of course, Sara. You are terribly dependable." She pulled her toward the mirror. "What a lovely bride you are."

The image in the mirror took Sara's breath away. Mother had fastened up her blonde hair in the latest style. "I appreciate your help, Mama."

Her mother handed her the bonnet. "I am so glad you'll be living nearby so I can see you often."

"Sara," her father called. "It's time to leave for the church."

She hugged her mother and went downstairs.

Lieutenant Jones, the military chaplain, marched with James up to the front of the tiny chapel. He smiled at the crowd. The townspeople filled the building and even stood along the back entrance. Most people considered this a loyalist village, but the people who came to his newly opened shop said they agreed with him. When they won this war, they would have freedom to express their opinions.

His blue military jacket boasted extra fabric to accommodate his shoulder, and he carried his tri-cornered hat under his arm. He wore his freshly washed hair pulled into a neat queue.

The violinist played *Jesu Joy of Men's Desiring* as the back doors opened. Anna danced down the aisle wearing a pretty blue dress. She would be his little sister now, and he would enjoy her energetic antics.

Two of Sara's friends walked forward and then Sara appeared, escorted by her father. The sight of her made James catch his breath. He could hardly believe he would have such a stunning wife. A smile adorned her face as she met his gaze and came toward him.

Once down front, Lieutenant Moore held out her hand. James took it and placed a gentle kiss on her knuckles. How soft, yet how capable. As he looked into her deep blue eyes, his heart swelled with joy.

Lieutenant Jones spoke, "Dearly Beloved, we are gathered here today to join together this man and this woman in Holy Matrimony."

Sara clung to her husband's arm as they descended the chapel steps. Her name was now Sara Howard. She gazed up at James as they walked toward the awaiting carriage where her father held the reins. Her handsome husband was wise and kind.

Her father handed James a sheath of papers. "The military promoted you to private first class and gave you a medical dismissal. Information you delivered will change the course of the war."

"Thank you, sir." James tucked the papers in his coat pocket.

"I had no hand in that." Her father smiled at James. "You served well."

James helped Sara into the carriage, then sat beside her. "Even though I will be fashioning furniture for surrounding villages, I shall continue to work for the military. In fact, I have several wagons behind the shop for the sergeant to pick up now."

"I shall enjoy living in the village." Sara snuggled close to him, tucking her hand under his arm. "Mama and I shall weave fabric and sew uniforms, and Father has engaged Benjamin for the home guard when farm duties aren't pressing."

"Then we shall all participate." He kissed her forehead.

"I'm glad." She stroked his cheek and chin, feeling the stubble of his beard. "I love freedom almost as much as I love you."

"And I love you." James dropped the reins and pulled her into his arms, kissing her deeply.

Cynthia L. Simmons

Cynthia L. Simmons has five grown children and adores her husband. She loves to grow orchids, arrange flowers, and drink tea. Her ragdoll cat, Colonel Brandon, enjoys sitting in her lap while she writes. When she's not writing, she often reads history or researches her family tree. She wrote the Southern Gold Trilogy, mysteries on Civil War money, and hosts *Heart of the Matter Radio* and #Momlife chats offering God's timeless wisdom. https://clsimmons.com.

With Every Step You Take

LANE P. JORDAN

Don't ever let love and loyalty leave you. Tie them around your neck and write them on your heart. Then God will be pleased and think well of you and so will everyone else. Trust the Lord completely, and don't depend on your own knowledge. With every step you take, think about what he wants, and he will help you go the right way.

—Proverbs 3:3–7 (ERV)

Chapter 1

Many, many, years ago there was a kingdom; and despite wars and murmurs of wars it continued thriving through many centuries. It was a very old kingdom.

Some say it thrived because it was situated with mountains on three sides and a great sea on the southern border. Finding a pass big enough to allow an army through was too difficult. So the rest of the world let the kingdom be. Occasionally, some folks who had heard of this beautiful kingdom successfully attempted to come through the pass.

Fresh, clean water flowed from the mountains' snow each spring, bringing forth water for the fertile valley. The land yielded abundant crops of all kinds with rich grass for cattle to graze. Wildflowers grew everywhere as well as flowers planted by the townspeople. Because there was no threat of war, the people lived in peace. The kingdom wasn't huge, but it would take at least one year to ride around the perimeter. There were small towns spread throughout as well as a few larger cities. The castle, built on a mountain in the north, was located in the largest city.

The king, like the generations before him, ruled the kingdom with wisdom. Fortunately, each successor listened well and followed suit. The people of this kingdom loved their king and their country. These kings did not believe in taxing the people. Instead, each family gave a small percentage to keep the ruling family and home operating. The rest of what they earned went to themselves and into their own towns—they repaired their own roads, built schools, hospitals, and other projects.

Now the king had married when he came of age and had twin daughters—Catherine and Elizabeth. They were the darlings of everyone who met them. Their mother, Queen Lily, was a wonderful mother. She taught them every subject—history of the world, math, literature, economics, as well as etiquette and good morals. The girls loved each other and their parents very much.

When the twins were ten, their mother became sick and died. The kingdom mourned for weeks. But the king knew he had to continue raising his daughters, so he hired a governess. Fortunately, the girls loved Miss Francis, and she loved them back, hoping to ease their heartache.

Then of course, as life shows us, the girls grew and became women. On their eighteenth birthday, the king called them into his room. He had decided not to remarry, and so the future of the kingdom would be in the hands of one of his girls. But which one? Who would be the best candidate to continue the traditions of the kingdom and rule with wisdom? How could he decide?

As they walked into his throne room, he felt a burst of pride. They were so beautiful! Each had long, blond, curly hair and skin the color of peaches. Their smile was kind, their walk purposeful, their minds sharp.

"Daughters," the king said, "today is your eighteenth birthday. Before your party begins, there is a serious matter we need to discuss. I won't live forever, and one of you will need to take my place. I know we have talked about this before, and you both have consented to take this hard role. But I believe we need a better way to figure out who should be the next queen."

The girls looked at each other, and their father continued.

"I have decided on a contest. Each of you must fulfill three requirements. The one who does so best will be the next queen."

"But Father," said Catherine, "Elizabeth can have the crown. I don't want to compete with my sister."

"I don't want to compete either," replied Elizabeth.

"You won't be at war with each other, but part of this contest is for each one of you to see if you would even want to rule the kingdom. This is what I propose. First, you have one year to travel around the whole kingdom. The one who does not return in a year will have points taken away. Secondly, you must bring back a journal of what you find—such as types of vegetation, water sources, planting processes, animal stock, and the conditions of the towns and our people. Yes, I have my stewards traveling the kingdom and keeping me informed, but you, my dear ones, need to understand all the difficulties involved in ruling a kingdom. Thirdly, you must bring back something of importance and meaning."

Elizabeth gulped. "This sounds so hard, Father. How on earth are we to accomplish it?"

"You have two weeks to plan. You can take as many horses as you think necessary as well as wagons, carriages, equipment, supplies, and townspeople you think you will need. This is a way for you to discover if leading a country is something you could do, or for that matter, want to do."

"But, Father!" they both protested, looking at each other.

"We don't want to leave for an entire year. We have much to do here. Couldn't we wait on this contest?" Elizabeth asked.

"But, Father, nothing," he said with a smile. "I promise you this adventure will show you what you are made of and what your future should be. And you must start with the most important first step. You must begin to pray for your success and whatever God's will is for your life. Only God knows the right path for you."

Chapter 2

The next two weeks flew by. The whole city knew of the king's plan, and everyone tried to help the girls in any way possible. The thought of these beloved princesses competing seemed like the worst possible plan. But the people trusted their king and hoped the year would seem to pass quickly.

Although the girls were identical twins, their interests were different. Elizabeth loved to be busy—spending time around people, playing with her friends at parties or at the castle, wearing the latest fashions, and enjoying life. Catherine was quieter. She loved to be with her sister and their friends. But after a while, she would slip off to a corner to read. Or in the afternoons, after their lessons, she loved to go down to the kitchen and help Cook roll out dough for bread or cookies. She also enjoyed the outdoors, helping in the garden or feeding the chickens.

These differences of course were not bad ... just the way people are ... but these personality traits led to how the sisters decided on what to take for their journey.

Elizabeth decided on taking the fine carriage with a pair of beautiful horses. She would also take two of her best friends along as well as a separate wagon to hold all her different clothes and accessories. She did take some heavy coats and blankets in case of severe weather, but that was about all she thought important. She didn't feel the need for much food or many tents. "I want to be with the people in their homes," she said, "so I will know them, and they will know me." She did take two men from her father's court for protection and help with physical labor.

Catherine, on the other hand, asked for four wagons along with four men who could repair the wagons if they broke down, plus provide any other manual labor needed. She also brought Cook's daughter, Anna, who could help prepare food when camping away from any town. One wagon was full of vegetables, hams, chickens in crates for morning eggs, plus all types of seed to show the farmers if they were interested in learning new farming methods. She had one wagon full of tools: hammers, nails, ladders, and the like. One wagon would hold all the tents, blankets, bed linens, and personal items for each person. The last wagon would carry everything else she thought would be important as well as carry herself and Anna. Each man would drive a wagon, and the horses she chose were large and used to heavy work.

The week before the departure, Catherine was talking to her foreman and asking who the other three were he had chosen. She was pleased that two of the men were from families who had been living in the kingdom for generations. However, she didn't know who the last man was.

"David? I don't know a David. From what family is he?" she asked her foreman, Jack. "Oh, miss, you wouldn't know him, I don't think. He came over the pass last year and settled down in the town quite nicely. He got a job with the carpenter and is a very fine young man indeed." Jack pointed at the young man. "There he is standing by the well. I think he will be a wonderful addition to our team."

Catherine looked over at the man called David at the same time he looked up from drinking a cup of water. He gave her a warm smile and a nod. She jerked her head back, wondering why her heart was beating so fast and why her cheeks heated.

"I don't know … I'm not sure … if we should take someone we don't quite know," said Catherine in a hushed voice.

"Oh, don't you worry, my young princess. I know good character, and young David there has it. Now, you don't have anything to worry about. We will see you on Monday with all the wagons loaded up and ready for adventure."

Catherine nodded. But as she walked away, she wasn't sure at all how this adventure was going to turn out. And a year was a very long time.

Chapter 3

The morning of the princesses' departure arrived. Catherine was up before dawn, checking and rechecking her list to make sure she had thought of everything they might need.

Elizabeth slept in until Catherine came into her room.

"Sister, you need to get up. Seriously, this is an important event in our lives. I want you to find God's will too."

"Now don't go getting all in a rush. I've already laid out my clothes and have packed the carriage. But you are a sweetheart to worry about me. I'll meet you downstairs by our groups in one hour."

Fortunately, both girls were ready at the same time. Most of the townspeople had walked up to the castle to see the girls off. It was a sight to behold with so many wagons and horses and people saying goodbye to their men and the princesses. The king had tears in his eyes as he said farewell to his beloved girls. He then placed one hand on each head and prayed. "Dear God, we know your will and your path are always the right ones. Help my daughters to trust you each day and to help them go the right way. Bring them back to me safely. In your son's precious name, Amen."

With that, the sisters climbed onto their preferred wagon or carriage. One went East, the other West, waving continually until they were out of sight.

Chapter 4

Now on her own, Elizabeth thought this might be the best idea her father had ever had. *Freedom to do anything I want.* And, she had a wagon full of beautiful new dresses and shoes and two of her best friends. She couldn't wait to get to the first town or city and meet the townspeople, stay in their homes, eat their food, and learn of their ways, certain they'd host a ball or party for her. She had her journal already opened and wrote about the morning's good start.

Around noon, the carriage and wagon stopped for lunch. Elizabeth wanted to know how much longer before they would come to the first town and asked her foreman.

"Mark, can I see the map we brought? And how much further to the first town?"

Mark walked hurriedly over to Elizabeth, spread the map on the back of her carriage, then pointed to a blue line. "Well, here we are at this creek," he said. "It's a good place to rest. And as you can see, the main road continues east for a while before it turns south. Let me see. Yep, here is the first town. I guess it will take about one more day."

"One more day? I thought we would be there tonight? Where will we sleep, and what will we eat?"

"Oh, no worries, my lady. We have some blankets. Perhaps when we get to the first town, we could pick up a few more supplies?"

Elizabeth frowned. The trip had just started, and already there were problems. How frustrating. Why didn't she ask more questions these last two weeks about what they might need? She'd spent more time at the dressmakers than even thinking about supplies. *Well, it's just one night.* Once they get to the town, she believed she'd be able to make things right.

Catherine was sad as they left the castle and her father. How could she be gone from all those she loved for a year? It seemed like an impossible task. She would have to pray every day to have the courage to keep going. She did have faith in God and that he would show her or Elizabeth his will. But this trip just seemed as if it would be too hard and too long.

Fortunately, the wagons and horses were strong. And she felt a peace about bringing Anna for company. She also was mostly pleased with the four men—except she still wasn't so sure about David. He was too new to the kingdom to understand their ways. She would have to stay clear from him.

Soon it was time for a break and the noon meal. As the horses began to eat the grass by the road, she pulled out the map to plot the next step.

Jack was tying up the last horse, and she called to him. "Jack, could you come to check the map with me?"

Jack came to her side. "Yes, I'd like to keep an eye on that map too, Miss Catherine. This was a good place to rest a bit with that stream right here." He gazed at the map. "Let's see. If we continue at this speed, we should reach that peach grove. Do you see it here on the map? 'Course, it's springtime so the peaches aren't ripe yet"—he smiled broadly—"but, oh boy, are those trees beautiful. I guess we'll get there in about six hours. The grass is extra good in that area, and there's plenty of water. Then, the next day we should be at the first town by early afternoon. How does that plan sound?"

"Perfect! Thanks so much, Jack for planning our stops. And I think it will be fun camping out tonight for the first time. Let's build a large campfire and really enjoy the whole experience."

Laughing, Jack said, "We sure will. And you've got a talented team here. We are already friends ... and even the new man, David, gets along with everyone."

Catherine wasn't too sure about David but was happy to know the team members were excited to be on this trip.

When she slipped into her bed roll that evening, there was still enough light for her to write in her journal. She was now feeling good about this trial her father had put her on. As she closed the journal, she looked up at the sky. The stars had come out, and the sight was breathtaking. This adventure would be successful. *I'm sure of it.*

Chapter 5

Dusk arrived, and Elizabeth couldn't get out of the carriage soon enough. She and her friends looked through the wagon and found a few blankets. They would have to sleep in the wagon, and the men would have to figure out for themselves where they would sleep. She was tired and dusty and hungry. Fortunately, the two men had been smart enough to bring some food and caught a rabbit, so they had enough to eat for dinner.

As Elizabeth climbed under one of the blankets, she realized what her father was trying to tell her and Catherine. Running a kingdom was challenging work. More difficult than getting prepared for a year long trip, and she had already failed at that. Starting tomorrow, she would start working harder at this trial test. She wrote in her journal how poorly the day had gone with a promise tomorrow would go better.

The next morning, with the springtime sun streaming into the wagon, Elizabeth felt better and determined she would start this second day of her quest with more thoughtfulness and energy.

After a small breakfast of dried biscuits one of the men had brought, they loaded up and started on to the first town. Hopefully, they would find a family who would take them in. Elizabeth also knew she would have to buy more supplies. She started making a list as the carriage bounced along the rocky road.

Suddenly the carriage jerked to one side and dropped low. The horses screamed, and the girls almost fell out.

"Oh no, what's happened?" exclaimed Elizabeth.

Mark dropped from his wagon and ran over. "Looks like we lost a wheel. Since these carriages are fancier than work-hardy wagons, they are used mainly for driving around town. We'll help you ladies out and see if we can fix it. Sure wish we had more tools."

Elizabeth and her friends walked over to a tree and sat down in the shade. This trip was not starting well for sure. Why hadn't she planned better?

Fixing the wheel took most of the day, and they hurried to reach the first town. Fortunately, all could easily see her royal carriage—the townspeople came out of their homes to welcome her. Elizabeth stepped down, introduced herself, and shared why she had come.

"Is there anyone who could open their home for myself and my two friends plus my two men?"

A tiny women stepped forward and said, "My family and I would be honored if you stayed with us, though our house is not fancy. We promise to give you a delicious meal and lots of companionship."

Elisabeth sighed with relief. "Thank you so much. Please show us where you live."

And with that, the small entourage followed the woman down the main street, then turned down a dusty road to a charming farm. Flowers were beginning to bloom in window boxes. The house looked freshly painted, with a swept porch.

"You can put your carriage and wagon over by the barn. My boys will help with the horses. Come this way, and I'll show you to your rooms. I must say, we are sure excited. Not too much exciting happens this way." She had a sweet smile on her face. Elizabeth felt relieved. This would work. She didn't want to put the townspeople out. But, in her mind, she thought this was the best way to get to know them.

The woman's home was just as nice as the front of the house. Elizabeth and her two friends would share one room—Mark and the other man, Ron, would share another room. The lovely surroundings made them feel at home.

"Dinner will be ready soon. Rest up, and I'll ring the bell. Sure glad you came to our village. Oh, and by the way, my name is Aria. My husband is Eric."

Freshening up and changing into clean clothes felt good. Soon the bell rang. Walking down the stairs to the dining room, the aroma of a freshly cooked dinner wafted toward them. They hurried to a feast of fried chicken, potatoes, greens, rolls, and cobbler. Elizabeth didn't know when she had eaten so well.

When the meal was over, she asked Eric if she could ask questions about their farm and town.

"Be happy to answer any way I can, Princess Elizabeth, though I'm not sure we can help very much."

"Oh, whatever you share will be wonderful. My father, the king, gave my sister and I a journal to record each day as well as each town and family we met. We want to learn as much as we can about how your town and farm are surviving."

"Well, first off, my family and Aria's family have been living in this kingdom for many generations." Eric filled a pipe and sat back in the worn chair. "We pride ourselves on keeping a lovely home, good land for our crops, and being content with all the good Lord has given us. We plant corn, greens, and wheat in the large fields. And close to the house we have a small vegetable garden. So, we have plenty of food. We have a few cows for milk, pigs and cattle for meat. And of course, chickens for eggs and meat. But mostly we live on what we plant. It's a good life. We are grateful to our king that he doesn't tax us to death. I've heard from some who can find this kingdom, how the feudal lords take everything from the people, causing them to live in poverty. Please tell him how grateful we are to live on our own."

They continued talking for a while and then it was time for sleep. Elizabeth couldn't remember a visit she had enjoyed as much. She had a lot to write in her journal.

The next morning, Elizabeth walked the fields with Eric. He explained how they rotated their crops and let the soil rest every seven years. She was busy writing down some of his farming ideas to share with other farmers on the trip. Then she asked where supplies could be bought.

"I realized that one carriage and one wagon is not enough. If you could help us find the right supplies for the year-long trip, I would be appreciative."

"Not to worry, Princess Elizabeth. I've already talked with Mark and his helper. They went into town early this morning and are buying two more wagons and supplies. Looks like you got a great foreman."

"I do. Thank you for helping them know where to go."

As soon as Mark returned with the wagons and four more horses, Elizabeth glanced at the small caravan, packed with all the supplies they would need for the next few months. She breathed relief as she climbed back into the carriage ready for the next stop.

Catherine woke up before anyone else as the springtime sun filtered into her tent. She stretched and smiled as she thought about her arrival in the first town later today.

She woke up Anna. After a quick breakfast of coffee, oatmeal, nuts, and fresh biscuits, the whole group packed up their bedrolls, loaded the wagons, and started on the trail. Her foreman, Jack, had been right the day before. The peach grove he had picked was the perfect stop for setting up camp. Lots of green grass for the horses, and the water nearby was fresh and clean. The sunset last night turned the creek into a kaleidoscope of burgundy, red, orange, and yellow while the slowly fading rays pierced through the tree branches overhead. So far, this part of the kingdom was beautiful.

Jack believed they should be at the first town by afternoon, so they decided to take only one break at noon. As they stepped down from the wagons, the group started preparing lunch and Anna was amazing. She knew how to cook, especially for hungry men.

"Let me get some water for you, Anna," called out Catherine. "I need to move these legs some."

Catherine strolled toward the creek. As she put her bucket into the water, she heard a splash. Looking up she saw David swimming nearby. For some reason, panic came over her, and as she tried to jerk the bucket up fast she slipped on a rock and fell in. Quickly, David was by her side, helping her to her feet. She was dripping wet from head to toe. Though drenched, she was more embarrassed over her clumsiness.

"Here, Princess Catherine, let me help you. As you see, these rocks are very slippery. Are you ok?" David took her hand and helped her up onto the bank, picked up the bucket, then guided her back to camp.

"I'm ... I'm fine. Thank you." Her voice shook. Her whole body was cold except for the hand David still held, and it felt like fire. What was wrong with her? She pulled her hand away and walked stiffly to where Anna was cooking.

"Oh, Miss Catherine what happened?"

Anna glanced accusingly at David, but Catherine shook her head. "I slipped on a rock and fell in. I feel so silly. David helped me out of the water." She glanced at him and said, "Thank you. I don't know how long I'd have been there if you hadn't helped. Now, I need to change into dry clothes."

Catherine felt better in the privacy of her wagon away from everyone. She couldn't believe she had fallen into the creek. She'd been around water all her life. And though she hadn't wanted this stranger, David, to be a part of this group, she was glad he was a part today. In fact, she had been avoiding him as much as possible—although she was not certain as to why she felt uneasy about him. She felt more comfortable with the men who had lived in the kingdom for generations. Maybe she was prejudiced? If so, she needed to overcome this feeling.

After a quick lunch, they hurried the horses to the first town. It was larger than she expected—a wide main street, lots of businesses, a church, and a town hall. As the wagons rolled in, the people came out to see who they were.

Catherine climbed down from her wagon, introduced herself and her team, and asked if they could stay with one of the townspeople.

A woman called out from one of the stalls. "We'd love for you to stay with us. We have a home just around the corner. Let me show you the way. My name is Lettie, and we are so happy you chose our town for your first stop."

Catherine hoped Elizabeth had found as welcoming a family.

The home was clean and well kept. Lettie and her husband were merchants who had a general store in town. After a delicious meal, Catherine asked if she could find out more about the town.

Lettie's husband Tom had been running their store all his life, as had many generations before him. "I'll tell you what. We love living in this town and kingdom. The king knows how to give freedom to his people."

Catherine was thrilled to hear such good news. They talked until late, then went upstairs to their bedrooms. She couldn't wait to write in her journal.

The next morning Catherine decided to walk through the town and meet some of the townspeople. They were accommodating and thrilled to share what made their town unique. She busily wrote down all they said.

Finally, the time had come to continue their journey, and they returned to their wagons. They only had a year to visit the whole kingdom, and the task was beginning to seem hopeless.

Catherine called her team together.

"First, I want to say how thankful I am that each one of you chose to help me on this journey. I've already seen the need for us to work as a team if we are to succeed. A year is a long time, and I'm already homesick. But with Anna cooking, Jack choosing the best time and place to make camp or which towns to visit, and the rest of you men helping set up camp and tend to the horses well … I just can't thank you enough."

Foreman Jack stood up. "It's a real blessing for us, or at least for me, to help one of our kingdom's princesses. This journey will be hard. But all of us want to see you succeed because we think you would make a wonderful queen. But the best thing we can do to help is to pray for you … to see if this is the right path for you."

Everyone nodded in agreement, climbed up on their wagons, and headed for the next town.

The next few months went better than expected. Both sisters and their teams were able to keep to the main road and find other towns and villages to stay. They were learning all the difficulties involved with leading a kingdom. They filled their journals with insights about how people think and how they managed their land or businesses. The only thing neither one of them had figured out was the one meaningful item to bring back to their father.

There was another problem. The twins missed each other dreadfully. There wasn't a way to contact each other, and they hadn't been apart a day in their eighteen years. But the journey had given them insight as to how they might rule the kingdom or how their sister might. And they prayed each night.

Catherine began to be glad David had come on this journey. She was very much against him at the beginning, but no one worked harder or kept the group together better than David. He seemed to have good answers for problems they encountered. He played his musical instrument around the campfire at night and sang beautiful songs. His music gave her peace. He must feel the same way because no matter where she was, she could see him close by. Her heart felt strange whenever he was around. She'd never known a man like him or felt this way before.

Chapter 6

Elizabeth was concerned for her two friends who seemed melancholy. Finally, she asked what troubled them. They looked at each other and then replied, "We want to go home. We thought this trip would be dressing up for balls and parties and meeting new people. We do not wish to offend, but the journey turned out to be difficult. We must make camp, wear old clothes that can get dirty, and sit in the carriage most of the day while we travel between towns. So now we feel we're stuck here!"

Elizabeth sat back and sighed. "I totally understand. I, too, thought this trip would be more like you described. But in essence, it's a work trip—to discover my destiny. I tell you what. At the next town, let's see if anyone is traveling north and perhaps you could find a ride back. Would that help?"

Both girls smiled with joy. "Yes, that would be wonderful, but we can't leave you."

"Do not worry about me. I've become so much stronger these last two months than I ever thought possible. I'm actually enjoying this journey. And I can find a young girl to keep me company and help Mark cook as Catherine did by bringing Anna. My sister is wise. I should have listened more when she shared her plans with me. So, do not be troubled. Okay?"

Both her friends smiled, probably relieved.

Fortunately, the next stop was one of the larger cities. The stone buildings stretched along a wide main street ... lots of shops, even fine inns for meals and lodging.

As soon as they drove to the center of town, Elizabeth stepped out of the carriage to introduce herself to the townspeople.

"Hello, I'm Princess Elizabeth, daughter of King Edward. I'm here to learn about your city, your businesses, your townspeople, and your farmers. We want to be a Royal Court that is current to our people."

A middle-aged man approached Elizabeth from the sidewalk step.

"Good afternoon. I am the mayor for this city and thrilled to be of service. What can we do for you, Princess Elizabeth? I'm assuming you will stay a few days?"

"Yes, and thank you. Myself, my friends, and my team"—she pointed at the men who were standing by the wagons—"would love a place to stay for a couple of nights. I would like someone to talk to me about the city— your needs and what is going well. I especially would like to know how the farmland, crops, and cattle are doing."

The mayor smiled. "Then you came to the right place and person. My wife and I would love to have you stay with us. We have a stable near our city home where you can care for your horses, and we have lots of extra bedrooms. Our children have married and have homes of their own. Now follow me to the stable and then we can walk over to our home. It's not far."

The mayor and his wife outdid themselves in giving Elizabeth and her team a lovely place to rest, freshen up, and enjoy an amazing dinner.

"You must have the best cook in the kingdom. This meal is delicious!"

"Well, you are very welcome. Daria has been with our family for years. Her daughter, Sonya, is now helping her in the kitchen. We love them like family."

When Elizabeth heard the cook had a daughter, she quickly sent up a prayer.

"I have a need I'd like to share with you. My dear friends"—she glanced at where they sat at the table— "have decided to go back to the royal city. They need a way there, and I was wondering if there were any young ladies who could be my companion as well as help with some of the cooking when we are on the road. Do you have any suggestions?"

The mayor and his wife shared a smile and a giggle.

"As a matter of fact, we were planning a trip to your city to share some of our latest building successes with the king. We would be delighted to give these young ladies a ride in our carriage. As for a companion for you? Let us think on the matter."

The rest of the two-day visit went perfectly. The summer heat was not too strong, and everyone wanted to share at least one thing about their city or their business or what they were growing. Elizabeth's journal would make her father proud.

Soon, the time had come to say goodbye to her sweet friends. Elizabeth was grateful for their loyalty to the king and kingdom, and they left each other on good terms ... though not without a few tears. Surprisingly, the mayor said his cook's daughter had begged her mother's permission to let her join this great adventure. To be the companion of the king's daughter would be the highlight of her young life.

Elizabeth and Sonya climbed into the royal carriage, waving goodbye to the mayor, his wife, and her two friends as the mayor's carriage turned and started the long journey north. Elizabeth watched as it rolled out of sight and then her carriage began to journey on towards continuing her quest. And the best part was, she was feeling very content.

So far, Catherine's experiences in all the towns her team visited had been wonderful. Upon studying the map with Jack, they saw a little settlement built a few miles off the main road. They decided to visit the town. They had done well with time—no major storms or carriage breakage had caused delays. By the end of summer, they decided to make the detour.

Surveying the little settlement, Catherine thought this place was small—hardly a town. No one clamored to great them. As Catherine stepped down from the wagon, Jack came quickly by her side. She called out a greeting, hoping someone would come out of the stores. One lone man approached from the direction of a tavern.

"Who did you say you were?"

"I'm Princess Catherine from the king's court, and I am visiting as many towns and cities as possible in a year. Our king wants an update on how the citizens are doing—how their businesses and farms are faring. Would it be possible to talk with you and perhaps find a place where we could stay?"

Without emotion, the man limped over to where they stood.

"I think it best you get back into your wagons and leave. Sickness and fever have come over this village. We lost nearly everyone. We sent a man out for help, but he never came back. We can barely make enough food for the few who have survived because we don't have the strength. The sickness took a lot from us."

Catherine held her hand over her mouth in fear. Looking back at Jack she asked, "What should we do? Perhaps we could go back to the last city and send food, supplies, and men to help these poor people?"

Hearing Catherine's concerns, David jumped off his wagon and walked over to Catherine and Jack.

"Princess Catherine, that's a great idea," said Jack. "Why don't you and Anna stay put? David can stay with you. We can unhitch two horses and ride back faster than with a wagon. We should be back in a day."

"Yes, perfect plan. I'd love to stay and help these people," replied David as he glanced toward Catherine. "We have to help them."

"Anna, do you have enough food for this man's dinner?" asked Jack.

"I sure do and enough for the whole town. Sir, why not spread the word that help has come."

The old man sobbed as he dropped to his knees. Jack carefully lifted him up and walked him back to the building. When Jack helped the old man into a chair, he looked up and said, "I'd been praying for help, but no one believed it would come. You all are an answer from God. That you are."

Jack tipped his hat. "I'm praying I can get to the town and back before anyone else dies," then headed toward the horses.

After the two men left, David joined Catherine and Anna and heard their concerns as to what the first step should be.

"Princess Catherine, may I offer a suggestion?" David met her gaze. "I have a plan of what we could do before the men get back."

Catherine nodded permission.

"Yes. I think you will have to. I'm not sure what to do except start cooking," Anna said.

"Let me help you set up tables and a fire for the cooking. We need to cook for the townspeople first. Princess Catherine, can you start bringing in water from the well?"

While discussing what to do, some people slowly started walking over to them. The old man must have told a few people who then told others. By the time the food was cooking, a table set, and water readied for drinking, a small crowd was there. Catherine saw children, dirty and thin from not having enough to eat. The sight devastated her. She quickly said a prayer and started ladling out water.

When the meal was ready, the girls and David served the townspeople. By the end of the meal, they were smiling. "Thank you! The first delicious meal we have had in many days."

"We're just so thankful we came this way. I guess the Lord was directing us to you," replied Catherine. "We'll have breakfast for you in the morning. Is there anything else you need?"

One woman came over and asked, "If you could help us pull water out of the well, we could start washing our clothes and sheets. With the sickness and fever, we didn't have the strength."

David answered quickly, "We will be happy to. And we have some men who rode to the closest town to ask for help. Hopefully, they will be back tomorrow with plenty of supplies for you. Now rest tonight, and we will see you in the morning."

The people waved goodbye and slowly walked back to their homes. Catherine, Anna, and David dropped down onto chairs, exhausted but smiling. What a blessing to be here and needed.

As they cleaned up from the meal, Catherine realized she and Anna couldn't have completed the work without David's help. He knew exactly what to do and when. She again realized how glad she was he was a part of this team.

They rolled out their bedrolls around the fire. Not until she started to lay down did Catherine realize how close she was to a man. But David was a friend now. And in this situation, no one could criticize her.

David must have understood how uncomfortable this might be. He waited until the girls settled and then pulled out his music piece. His songs kept Catherine from worrying about the people and lolled her to sleep.

The sun was just cresting when Catherine woke. David was already cooking breakfast for the town, the large table set. Anna was still asleep. How did he wake up so early? Whatever the reason, what a blessing that he had. The people were beginning to walk over. Still, in the clothes from the night before, Catherine rose quickly, rolled up her bedroll, and walked over to help David. His smile warmed her heart. This man was special. She said a quiet prayer of thanks to God for David.

As soon as breakfast was over, David asked the group of townspeople, "Where is the best place to start a fire for your laundry? The three of us will wash as much clothing as possible."

The women showed David a large pot for boiling the water, and he built a fire while the girls brought well water to fill the pot. Some of the men who could help did. But most of the townspeople could only sit or go back to their homes to lie down—such a sad situation.

By mid-afternoon, half of the houses had clean sheets on the line—a beautiful sight, a gentle breeze and the warm sun drying them. Soon the men would be bringing back supplies and hopefully, more people to help. These houses needed a thorough cleaning.

While Anna began preparing dinner, the sound of horses and wagons came from the direction of the dirt road. The men were back. As they came closer, Catherine could see many wagons and people. She couldn't believe how many had stopped whatever they were doing to come to help a neighboring village. She looked up. "Thank you, God."

Jack was the first one to dismount. "Princess Catherine, David, Anna. Look at all the supplies we were given." He unrolled the cover from the first wagon revealing hams, live chickens, and bags of grain. "Can you believe this? And we have twenty people to help distribute these supplies."

Catherine and Anna hugged each other and clapped their hands. The town was saved.

The next few days were busy. The helpers started cleaning all the homes, repairing fences, feeding the animals that were still alive plus the new ones, continuing the process of washing clothes, and setting up the general store with the provisions. The owner of the store had died, but his son-in-law would take over.

The time had come for Catherine to leave the town and continue her quest. But as she and Anna and the men packed their wagons, their hearts were full—they had been able to help save a dying town.

Chapter 7

Elizabeth thought she would miss her two friends, but she didn't ... mainly because she now had time to concentrate fully on the trip—the terrain, the people, her thoughts. She was also surprised at how much she had changed. At the start of the journey, her thoughts centered on how much fun she might have. Now, she seriously wanted to learn about the kingdom and if her destiny was to lead it as queen.

Fall arrived with brilliant reds, oranges, and yellow leaves. The air was crisp, and they needed heavier blankets at night. The kingdom did not have an extreme cold in the winters, but sometimes they would have snow in the northern part where the castle was. Now that Elizabeth and her team were almost to the southernmost part of the kingdom, the streams flowing from the ocean warmed the land.

The trip down the western side of the kingdom was complete, and the road began to turn south to the beautiful sea. Gulls filled the sky as they flew and zoomed into the water for fish. Some part of the main road was right by the sandy beach. When the group stopped to rest, they took time to walk on the beach. Although it was late fall, the sun was bright and warm in this part of the kingdom, nor was the breeze too cold.

There were not as many towns on this stretch because the land was too sandy and rocky for farming. Elizabeth and her team had to camp out more often. She was becoming used to the routine, however. She didn't mind helping fill the buckets with water for cooking and cleaning, and she began to enjoy the fresh air and the bright stars at night.

One night as they settled in their bedrolls around the campfire, they heard howling. Not just any howling but the sounds of various animals. And they were not far away. Elizabeth was terrified. She and Sonya quickly grabbed their bedroll and blankets and ran to one of the wagons. The men hurriedly brought in the horses from a nearby field and tied them up to the wagons. Next, they added more logs to the fire. By the time they had reassembled behind the fire and in front of the wagons, a pack of wild wolves circled them.

Everyone was terrified, and no one knew what to do next. The men had rifles and were ready to use them if the animals decided to jump past the fire. One did. Fortunately, Mark took aim and shot him perfectly between the eyes, and the wolf fell onto the sandy ground. The other wolves backed away, but not much, and continued to pace around the encampment.

For the next ten hours, until the sun came up, the wolves kept the group hostage. Elizabeth stayed on her knees praying for deliverance. Finally, one by one the wolves left. The men walked over to where Elizabeth and Sonya had stayed to see if they were unharmed.

"Are you ladies, okay? I know this has been a hard night for you as well as us men. Never seen wolves behave in such a way," said Mark.

Elizabeth looked up as tears filled her eyes. "I don't think I can go on. I've never faced death like this before. What if they follow us? They could pounce on one of the horses in an instant and then jump into a wagon. What should we do?"

Mark looked down at the dead wolf, his face outlined with worry. "I don't really know, Princess, except we got to pack up and head east as quickly as we can. But I do know God is with us. His angels kept that pack from attacking us last night. Those wolves could have jumped us all at one time, and we would be dead right now but for God." Then looking at Elizabeth he added, "We all must remember to trust the Lord completely rather than depend on our own knowledge. And your highness, with every step you take, think about what God wants. He will help you go the right way."

"You're right, Mark. My father wouldn't have sent us on this journey to quit. If all of you want to continue, then I will too. I am, however, very scared."

"And that's to be expected. Let's load up as fast as we can and move along. Hopefully, we can go as far as the next town before dark. We'll push the horses as fast as we possibly can."

The group loaded up and rolled along at a fast pace. But everyone kept their eyes peeled as they prayed continuously. And fortunately, they reached the next town before dark.

Catherine and her team had finished surveying the eastern side of the kingdom and were heading toward the southern part via the main road when the sky darkened. Winter had come, and the team knew they might meet harsh weather. Until now, the air had been balmy and comfortable down by the sea.

Jack trotted next to Catherine's wagon. "We should stop for a break, Princess."

Catherine agreed, and the wagons came to a halt. The team jumped down to stretch their legs, then Jack called them together.

"I don't like the look of those clouds. They are coming fast from the sea. If I didn't know any better, I'd say a bad storm, or even a hurricane, is coming this way. We need to find some rocks off from the main road where we can shelter the wagons and horses. And we need to get on higher ground."

Just then a burst of wind caught them off balance. Without another word, the group started moving the wagons and horses away from the sea. They were able to find an outcropping of trees and rocks about a mile north and hid behind them. Just as the last person moved to shelter, the rain poured. For the rest of the day and into the night, the rain and wind pounded the group. They were all drenched, cold, and scared. The wind became so fierce that two of the wagons toppled over. Trees snapped and the wind howled far into the night.

By daylight, the rain and wind had stopped, and they left their hiding place only to see widespread destruction.

Most of the trees were uprooted, and debris littered their area. They walked toward the main road, now completely washed away.

"Oh, Jack, where is the road? How do we find our way?" cried Catherine.

"Now don't any of you worry. We know the direction we need to go. We'll just head that way until we can find the main road. Let's get something to eat. David, can you find any dry wood for a fire? Anna, can you find something for us to eat? And everyone, change into dry clothes and let's hang our wet garments out to dry. With this warm sun, we should feel better soon."

Everyone went to their tasks. Soon after, with hot coffee, warm biscuits, and dry clothes, the hardship of the previous day and night became more like a bad memory.

Jack, David, and Catherine looked over the map. They could see where they were and where they needed to go to return to the main road. The terrain was rough, but they didn't have a choice—they would have to continue. They were able to lift the fallen wagons, glad the damage was minor—only a few loose boards on the side. David quickly repaired them.

Since no one had slept in over twenty-four hours, Catherine decided everyone should rest before they headed off. After the noon meal, refreshed and feeling better, the men hitched the horses to the wagons and then started towards what they hoped would be the main road.

Hours later, after the men had chopped down tall grasses and scrub bushes to allow the wagons through, they stopped to rest. Everyone could tell this part of the journey was even more difficult than they expected.

Catherine called the team together. "I know this is a hard and rough road we are on. But I don't know what else we can do. We could turn around and head back to the kingdom on the westside, but then we wouldn't have completed our journey. I don't want to put any of you in harm's way."

David spoke up first. "No one forced us to take you on this journey, Princess. I believe I speak for the whole group. Let's keep on. Yes, we will take more time cutting through this back lowland, but we will find the main road. We need to keep going."

All the men nodded in agreement.

Jack added. "I agree completely with David. We will finish this journey. It will just take a little longer."

Catherine smiled and gave a sigh of relief. "Thank you all so much. I know Anna and I aren't strong enough to cut paths. But we'll make sure to cook special meals for you!"

Everyone laughed. After a quick rest, the men cut down the tall grasses to form a path for the wagons. That night they all fell asleep as soon as they hit their bedrolls.

For the next two weeks, time seemed to pass more slowly. Catherine tried to keep the team's spirit up the best she could. Knowing they wanted to help her made the hard trip somewhat easier.

The head wagon stopped suddenly. Everyone hopped down from their wagons to see what had caused the delay. There, on the side of the road, was a small boy. Just sitting in the dirt.

Catherine ran over to him. "Are you all right? Where is your family?" The little boy could only point behind him, and then, he fell over, passing out from what looked like malnutrition.

"Oh no! We have to find his parents and his home."

David quickly unleashed one of the horses and walked over to where Catherine sat holding the child.

"Let me carry him on the horse. I'll ride until I find his family. Let's leave the wagons here for now. Jack, do you want to come with me or stay with the team?"

"I'll stay here and keep watch for any others. Just get back as soon as you can, and let us know what's going on."

With that and cradling the young boy to his chest, David rode off.

The sun was setting when David came racing back to the camp. "Oh, you wouldn't believe what I discovered. The hurricane was worse here. The town where the boy lives is completely gone, and the winds swept away many people. They have no water, no food, no shelter. We need to pack the wagons back up and go right now. The people are starving. The little boy, after seeing his parents die, walked out of his town, looking for help. Praise God we were there!"

Without another word, the group returned to their wagons and followed David to a town that wasn't there anymore.

Chapter 8

Elizabeth and her team drove the entire south end of the kingdom but never saw Catherine. Sand and debris covered portions of the road, but they were able to see enough to stay on the path. Where was her sister? She quickly lifted a prayer for Catherine's safety. Soon, the wagons turned north to the eastern side of the kingdom. They were able to move quickly now that they were away from the coast. The weather was becoming colder as they turned toward the north, and Elizabeth was grateful for the supplies Mark had bought.

Elizabeth was now more than halfway into this journey. She was tired, dirty, and bored from sitting all day in the coach. Yet, for the first time, she felt a real purpose in her life. She was beginning to understand this kingdom, feeling more a part of it, and learning the importance of strong leadership. She realized she loved her kingdom—no amount of discomfort would stop her from doing her best for her subjects. She was not going to let her father down. But what was in store for the rest of the journey?

Catherine and her team finally reached the town or at least the place it once stood. As they stepped from their wagons and looked around, all they could see were a few fabric-covered lean-tos and people just sitting. Children were playing, or rather pushing a ball, in what looked like sewage. One man walked slowly toward them.

"Ma'am, are you an angel?" he asked.

"No, but I am here to help you. We are going to feed you. How many are you?"

He looked confused and then glanced toward where the town once stood. "I think there are about fifty of us, including children. Not really sure. I tell you ... when the storm hit us, the next thing we knew everything was gone. One man left a week ago for help, but I guess he died before finding any. He never returned." The man's eyes filled with tears, then he walked back to where he had been sitting.

"How far is the next town?" asked David.

The man stopped and turned around. "About a day's ride on a fast horse. That place might have been destroyed too."

Quickly, the team jumped into action. David sent one of the men on their fastest horse to go for help. "Do all you can to bring back lumber, food, seed for planting later, and lots of men and women. We need to rebuild this town." Next, David drew water from the nearest well, though there wasn't much in it, and built a fire. Anna started cooking. The other men, after unhooking the horses and tying them up, surveyed the area, making a mental list of what they needed. Food first, shelter next, then medical care.

The next few days were a blur. Catherine realized David was the reason his helpful plans succeeded. He suggested the men build a temporary dwelling with some of the remaining wood beams and tarp they had brought. Then he organized teams—some to clear a new section further up on a hill for the newly built homes. Others hunted for food, and still others assembled a medical shelter. Catherine and Anna helped nurse those who needed care.

By the third day, help had arrived. Not as much as they hoped for ... but ten able men, their wives, and their children. Their town had experienced a strong wind, but nothing like the storm that had demolished this town. They dismounted from their horses and wagons and stood silently, surveying the damage.

"Not sure how long it will take to rebuild this," one declared. "We can stay for a week, but then we need to return to our farms."

"We are thankful for any help you can give us," replied David. "We are mighty thankful."

David split up the new helpers into groups as he did before. Some built homes, some cleared the fields for later planting, and some constructed a road and sewer system.

They found another source of water—a creek dammed by the storm's debris. The men cleaned out the debris and dug a trench to send the stream toward the town, then split it into two sections—one for drinking and cooking and one for waste. They were able to make more drainage pipes from the mud nearby to help with this.

After a week, the helpers needed to leave, though they had done a great deal. However, available labor was now down to just David, Jack, the other two men, Catherine, and Anna.

Jack called a meeting.

"Well, it's just us. We must take a vote. We can leave now and arrive at the castle in time for the contest results. Or we stay here and finish what we started. Princess, it's up to you."

Catherine looked over at the devastated town, still in ruins. She thought about what her father, the king, would do in the same situation. Then she prayed.

"I can't leave these people. We have the tools and materials to help them build back. Some of the men are strong enough to help us now. Many are still too sick to take care of themselves or their family. If any of you need to leave, I understand. But for me, I want to serve these people ... with the Lord's help."

The whole group applauded. She could tell no one wanted to go home ... they wanted to stay.

So, the next month was busy rebuilding the town. Slowly but surely, the people, strengthened by the help they had received, built more houses. The women were able to help Anna with cooking, and the men were able to help make bricks and cut wood into lumber.

The date to be back at the castle came and went. Catherine kept writing in her journal and doing all she could to help the people. She tried not to think how late she would be when she finally returned home.

But one special gift in all of this was the little boy David had scooped up weeks before. His name was William. He never left David or Catherine's side, staying close to them whenever he could, even sleeping next to David every night. And they were becoming very attached to the lad.

And Catherine? Every time she looked at David, she couldn't believe how wonderful he was. Though very handsome—his dark hair, blue eyes, tan skin, and smile was infectious—he, more than Jack, was the one all the men now came to for advice and help. David's patience and kindness were obvious as he interacted with everyone on the team. And he had a smile just for Catherine. She wondered if she might be falling in love with him.

Another month had come and gone.

The construction of more buildings gave hope as more of the townspeople were able to move into new homes. By spring planting, more were healthy enough to help make furniture, pave roads, and build a school as well as other buildings. They even cleared away the rest of the debris from the hurricane, smoothed out the land, and planted grass. Soon the area would be a beautiful park that, hopefully, would help the townspeople forget the death toll from the destruction.

After another month, Catherine, David, Jack, and the other men surveyed the whole town and couldn't believe the beautiful transformation from destruction to hope for a new life. Of course, some families had lost loved ones, but they knew God had sent this team to help them—the salvation of their town, was truly a miracle.

As Catherine and the others finished loading up their wagons to leave, William started to cry.

"What's the matter, William?" asked David as he picked him up.

"I don't want you and Miss Catherine to go and ... I don't know where I'm supposed to live." He sobbed on David's shoulder.

David glanced toward Catherine. She nodded, then offered a smile.

"Why, you are coming with us. We can't do anything without you near us."

With that, William threw his head back and laughed as he hugged his friend, so happy to be able to stay with David.

The townspeople came to see them off with hugs and tears of gratitude, waving until the last wagon was out of sight.

Chapter 9

Elizabeth could hardly contain her excitement. Her team would be arriving at the castle by the next day. Mark had shown her the map while they made camp, and she yelled for everyone to come over.

"We made it, we made it! Mark says we should be arriving at the castle tomorrow. We traveled the whole country and will be home before the deadline."

There was a rounding sound of claps on backs and lots of laughter and happy comments. Elizabeth and Sonya hugged and smiled at the happy group.

Elizabeth walked back to her wagon where she kept her journal and smiled again. She believed she had done an excellent job keeping a record of their adventures. And her one important and meaningful item she was bringing back? She patted her pocket. *I know Father will be pleased.*

Dinner that night tasted extra good, and the group shared special memories from the last year as they sat around the blazing campfire. Knowing she completed this grueling task brought joy to Elizabeth. But even more than that, she felt a new sense of pride in her kingdom. And she wanted to continue to be involved in kingdom matters as much as she could.

The next morning, the spring sun shone warm on the campsite and the group rushed to load the wagons. The men even washed in the creek and put on clean clothes. Hopefully, the townspeople would welcome them home, as well as their families.

One mile from the castle, they spotted a lone horseman. He greeted them with a smile.

"Princess, welcome! I've been waiting to see when one of you would be arriving. I'll let the town and the king know you are here."

Elizabeth clapped her hands with joy. Soon she would see her beloved father and all her friends. And sleep on a feather mattress again.

As soon as her carriage and the wagons came into the capital city, the townspeople had crowded the sidewalks, calling their names and clapping. The king was ready to receive the men with warm handshakes and a special hug for his daughter.

"Come into the castle and tell me all about your journey. A meal is being prepared as we speak. We can help you unload later," said the king.

Elizabeth walked hand in hand with her father. Once in the castle, she noticed the main dining room table was covered with platters of hot food. Her team assembled around the table and began eating as if they had not eaten the entire year they had traveled.

Finally, when they were full, Elizabeth showed some of the highlights of her journal to her father. The whole team also shared some of the happenings from the one-year journey. Later, they would have more time to share everything. At this point, the men wanted to go home to their families and rest. It had been a long and hard trip.

Elizabeth led Sonya to her new room next to the kitchen. She was overjoyed to be able to live in the castle and cook in this amazing kitchen.

That night, as she sat alone with the king, Elizabeth shared the journey with day-to-day descriptions from the journal. Her father couldn't believe some of the hardships and trials they had endured.

"I am so proud of you, Elizabeth. When I saw you leave in that fancy carriage, I thought you'd be home in a month. Now, look at you! You completed the task—you traveled the kingdom, you returned in under a year, and you made the deadline. Now I can't wait to see what memorable item you brought back."

Elizabeth picked up a small bag from her pocket and handed it to her father. He slowly opened it and poured out gold nuggets.

"Did you find gold?"

"Yes!" laughed Elizabeth. "As I was washing in one of the streams, I saw something shiny. When I scooped it out, I realized there were gold pieces in the stream. Can you believe it? Our kingdom doesn't need money like the rest of the world, but in case we are ever invaded, we have gold to negotiate with."

The king stood and pulled Elizabeth into a tight hug.

"I really can't believe all you accomplished, my dear daughter. I am amazed and so happy. And more than proud. But tell me, did you ever see your sister?"

Chapter 10

It was now late spring, way past the contest deadline for Catherine. But as she and David rode together in one of the wagons, they had time to talk and continue to know each other better. In fact, they were inseparable. The only people in the group who didn't know they were in love were Catherine and David.

One evening, David decided to hunt rabbits for their dinner. Catherine kept waiting for him to get back. Something was keeping him ... but what? She had heard a gunshot earlier and asked Jack to help her find David. About a mile past their campsite, they saw David on the ground, knocked out, perhaps from the gun kick-back. Catherine ran to him and fell to the ground next to him.

"Oh, David, please be all right! I couldn't live if something happened to you."

Slowly, David's eyes opened. "Did I hear you say what I hoped you had said?' he asked. "Or was my hurt head imaging it?"

David slowly stood, his hand on his head but looking directly at Catherine.

"Catherine, did you really mean it? I couldn't live if something happened to you either."

She ran into his arms, and they held each other close.

"Well, it's about time you two realized you were in love." exclaimed Jack. "I'll see you back at the camp."

Catherine and David held each other as if they couldn't let go. Then slowly, David leaned her head back and kissed her. Finally, realizing she was in love, she returned David's kiss.

"Well, before we walk back to camp, can we talk?"

"Yes, we need to do that."

Before Catherine could sit, David was on one knee.

"My dearest Catherine, I promise I will love and cherish you the rest of my life. I couldn't live without you by my side. Will you marry me?"

Catherine looked down at his handsome and kind face and smiled. "On one condition."

"Oh no. What?"

"That we adopt William."

"Yes." Then David kissed Catherine again.

Catherine's return was now overdue by two months. The king and Elizabeth were extremely worried—though, if there had been an emergency, one of the men would have reached them by now. All they could do was wait.

Soon the lookout rider galloped up to the castle.

"They are coming," he shouted. "Just a few miles down the road."

Everyone hurried down the castle steps and onto the sidewalk to wait for Catherine and her team. The news carried fast. Soon, all the sidewalks filled with townspeople, just as they had for Elizabeth's return. The peach trees had already bloomed and some of the white and pink blossoms had covered the road and sidewalks, making a beautiful entranceway.

Catherine couldn't believe her eyes when her wagon came through the city gates and saw all the townspeople, her friends, and then her father and sister welcoming them home. As soon as the wagon stopped, she jumped down and ran to her family. They hugged each other tightly, not wanting to let go. But soon the king invited everyone to come in for a meal and share stories about their journey.

As David stepped from the wagon, he reached up for William and then carried him up to the castle.

"Is this where you live, Mr. David?" William asked in awe.

"Not now ... but perhaps one day."

Catherine heard his answer and smiled. She had so much to share with her father and sister about the last year.

After the wonderful meal, the king invited his daughters to his private quarters so they could talk.

"Father, I need to also ask for David to stay with us," said Catherine.

The king peered at David. "So, I'm assuming, young man, that you are more to my Catherine than one of her men?"

"Father, let me answer that," said Catherine. "David has asked me to marry him! I know he needs to talk with you first, but I wanted you and Elizabeth to know David and see how important he and William are to me."

"William?" asked the king.

David answered this time. "The little boy I was holding during the meal. Catherine took him to Cook's room after we dined. It was late, and the boy needed to go to sleep. When we found him, his parents had just died. The three of us became inseparable."

David glanced toward Catherine and smiled.

"Well, David, I think you and I need to stay up and talk. But before the girls leave, where are you from? What work did you do? I want Catherine to know your background too."

David took a deep breath.

"My father was Evan York. I believe you knew him."

"You mean King York of Britany?"

"Yes. Our city and kingdom were overthrown ... burnt to the ground. Before my father died, he begged me to find your kingdom and live there. He said it was the only safe and peaceful kingdom left in the world."

"You mean to say you are Prince David of York?" asked the king.

"Yes, I am. Though now, if I still lived in my kingdom, I would be king."

The king rose to embrace him. Catherine held her hands over her mouth in disbelief.

"I knew your father well. I'm so sorry to hear of his death. But why didn't you contact me sooner?"

"I felt I should get to know your kingdom and its people first before I decided to stay here. When his majesty made the announcement for a contest in order to decide the next queen, I thought this would be the perfect way to see your kingdom." David turned and gave Catherine a smile. "And what a blessing this kingdom is. I could not resist the opportunity to see firsthand how this contest between two sisters to determine who will become queen of this beautiful, ageless kingdom would develop. Trials, heartbreak, and hardship faced them both at every turn of their journey. I wanted to see who would win and if either of them would find true love along the way. Strangely, I became a participant rather than a mere observer. But I never thought I would end up falling in love with your beautiful daughter. I pray with all my heart you will find me worthy enough and give me her hand in marriage."

Catherine ran to David and put her arms around him. "I had no idea you were a prince. But it doesn't matter. I fell in love with the man I met on this journey. Though you did act like a prince to everyone."

"Well, this day just keeps getting better," said the king. "Both my girls are back home safe." The king chuckled. "And I will have a son ... and perhaps a grandson?"

They all laughed and sat back down.

"I would like to show you and Elizabeth my journal," Catherine said. "But that can wait until tomorrow after we rest. We have so much to share about our trips. And of course, I need to show you the one thing I brought back that I felt was important and meaningful."

"Which is?" asked the king.

"Why, it's William, of course. We want to adopt him after we marry."

"Oh yes! What a perfect memorable item to bring back. Catherine, what you did to help that town, its people, and this little boy is amazing. Yes, you missed the deadline but achieved a greater purpose. I'm so proud of you. And what have you decided on about ruling the kingdom and being the queen?"

Catherine looked at David and then her sister.

"I have prayed this entire year about what God would want me to do with my life. I knew this decision was too big for me, so I trusted the Lord completely to show me the way. I could not depend on what I thought I knew. So, throughout the journey, I prayed, and God showed me the right way." Catherine took David's hand in hers. "I want to be a wife and a mother more than anything in the world." And she looked at Elizabeth. "And I believe you would make the best queen. Am I right?"

Elizabeth jumped up and hugged her sister with all her might. "Yes! I do want to be queen. I have come to love this kingdom, and I want to work each day to be as good a queen as Father has been a king—helping the people of this kingdom." She laughed. "Who would have ever thought I would be the one to want this? The girl who loved pretty dresses and parties?"

"Oh, I think God knew all along." Catherine gifted her sister with a wide smile. "To think, after this hard journey we all have a happy ending. Most of all little William."

The End

Lane P. Jordan

Lane P. Jordan loves to oil paint, read, walk, bike, talk with her daughters, play with her granddaughter, and eat chocolate! She also loves to write for women, sharing God's love for women of all ages. She is the best-selling author of six books helping women to become more organized including *12 Steps to Becoming a More Organized Woman* and *12 Steps to Becoming a More Organized Mom,* and her first fiction book, *Evangeline.*

www.LaneJordanMinistries.com
www.PathwaysToOrganization.com

My Favorite Leia

LINDA WOOD RONDEAU

He went to see a movie classic,
but found his future instead.

PROLOGUE

Five-year-old Trisha placed another Lincoln Log on her lopsided church. Why did it have to be a church?

"Daddy, when did you know you loved Mommy and wanted to marry her?"

Trisha always asked deep questions out of the blue ... questions I was often ill prepared to answer. But this answer was written on my heart, even if Shayla and I were separated. There could never be another love like ours.

Then why did you let it end, Dave?

Trisha gazed up at me, her hazel eyes peering, demanding a response. "Well, now. That's quite a grownup question, isn't it?"

She crossed her arms, so much like her mother when miffed at my stalling.

"Don't you know?"

"Yes. I do. I fell in love with her the moment I first saw her."

"Do you still love her?"

"Of course."

"Then why don't you live with us anymore?"

I knew the pain I felt being apart from Shayla, but I hadn't understood my daughter's pain until now. I sat on the carpet and started building my own cabin with the extra Lincoln Logs. This conversation would take some time. How could I explain to a child the danger I posed in my current condition ... that I loved my wife too much to put her at risk? That I could only trust myself for one overnight a month with my own daughter?

"I felt being away was better. Mommy was so unhappy when we were together."

Trisha swiped at the Lincoln Log church, leveling it to scattered pieces. Had my child inherited my disposition? "She's still not happy. She cries all the time. She says we have to pray for you. I do, Daddy, but God doesn't hear me."

How do you explain your own battle with God to a five-year-old ... a battle lasting a lifetime ... a battle causing you to ruin everything good in your life?

Her little eyes filled with tears. "Why can't we all live together like we used to?"

She deserved to know why ... but could her tender heart grasp the truth? Had she forgotten that horrible night?

"I don't like this either, sweetheart. Maybe it's time I tried again. But I've got a lot of work I have to do before I can move back ... if your mother will have me."

Trisha wiped her tears with the back of her small hand as she rushed into my arms. "Will you really try, Daddy? Really, truly try?"

I raised my eyes heavenward. *Can you help me, Lord?*

Yes, I'll help you. But you have to take that first step. Will you?

"I will," I answered to both God and Trisha. "Now it's time for you to get some sleep."

She jumped on to her bed, pulling Mr. Chuckles, her favorite Teddy bear, next to her chest as I positioned her covers. "Tomorrow's Easter, Daddy. Can we go to church?"

Most kids would have asked for an egg hunt and a giant basket filled with assorted chocolates, marshmallow treats, and jelly beans. Not Trisha. So much like her mother ... loving Jesus more than anything else on Earth ... including me.

I closed the door to her room and collapsed into my recliner, thinking about our long Saturday together ... a trip to the zoo, a monopoly game, a dinner at Chuck E. Cheese, and a reading marathon ... a great day until bedtime, when tears and truth grabbed my heart. Two months since her mother and I separated. My fault.

Memory cracked my heart.

Chapter 1

A sharp jab to my ribs pulled me from my fantasy.

Sean grabbed the popcorn bucket from my grasp and offered a disgusted glare. "Earth calling Dave. You've been staring at that girl for fifteen minutes. Stop ogling and talk to her."

Maybe I had been staring a little longer than a good soldier should. Then again, I wasn't a soldier anymore. Anything to take my mind off this sad excuse for a welcome home party. A *Star Wars* Episode IV had to be at the bottom of my How-I-Want-to-Spend-My-First-Night-Back-Home list after three tours in Afghanistan. My hopes for a military career ended by a sniper bullet that shattered my knee. Given the choice of a long furlough or a medical discharge, I'd opted for the second. But as soon as my plane landed, I wished I'd taken the first. How could I possibly adjust to civilian life after fifteen years of being an Army officer? What kind of work would I be suited for now? Especially with a bum leg?

Sean crunched down another handful of popcorn. He meant well. A good friend, one who never failed to email and call when I was on the other side of the world. Time zones never deterred Sean who'd get up at crazy hours just to say hello. He was the first to welcome me home. He stood there with a bouquet of balloons attached to a placard his kids had made. His was more of a family to me than my biological one ... whomever they might be. I'd lost track of them after years in the foster care system, enlisting right after college into OTC.

If nothing else, Sean's company that night was always worth a few laughs. Even if he filled the bulk of his conversation with trivia, like why most of the Stormtroopers are left-handed. "Because of how the weapons were constructed," he explained. "Like real weapons. The magazine is on the left side. When they fire, the weapons hit the troopers in the chest. So they had to switch their grip and that makes them look left-handed."

I cringed at the mention of weapons. At least these weapons were lasers, not rifles. Better to spend time in a rehash of a beloved trilogy than sit alone in my rented room near the VA hospital, worrying even more physical therapy would not give me full mobility, that I'd limp the rest of my life.

Here I sat, a man without a future, late thirties, in Han Solo garb next to Darth Vader. Sean always liked to be the villain at any costume party, a sharp contrast to the man. He was the most valiant human being on the planet, braver than any soldier I'd ever known.

I'd watched the trio of Leias saunter in just after Sean and I had taken our seats, their long white tunics fluttering in the slight breeze from the air conditioning, and sitting in the row in front of us. I immediately honed my glances on my favorite as she leaned toward the Princess Leia on her left as if to share a secret. As her head turned, she caught my stares and smiled.

A special aura hovered around her, though there were at least fifty Princess Leias sprinkled around the theater. And her eyes, like vibrant emeralds, haunted me.

I slumped in my seat. "Sean, I think I see my future."

"Get real, dude. How could you possibly know your future?"

"See those girls in front of us and to the left?"

Sean glanced to where the girls sat, like pretty maids all in a row. "The brunette, the blonde, or the redhead? My money's on the blonde."

"No, Sean. The one in the middle."

"So it's the redhead who's caught your eye? All this time, I've only seen you date blondes, with the exception of Thandiwe, the Nigerian nurse you met at basic."

"Yeah. She was special."

"Name meant beloved ... you only told me like a gazillion times. I thought she was the one."

I chuckled. "Yeah. I did too."

"What happened? I thought you two stayed connected after you went to Afghanistan?"

"We did, until she went back to Nigeria and got married."

"Ouch."

"Ancient history, my friend."

Sean scowled. "Don't know what it is with you and women. She was the only one you dated for more than three weeks."

"Failure to commit some would say. Or maybe I wasn't ready to settle down."

"Dude. Don't you think it's time?"

Could Sean possibly understand my envy? A wife, two kids, and a baby on the way. Settled. Church every Sunday and in-laws for dinner. Faith and Family identified a man, and I had neither—a church dropout, brought up in foster care, and a failure in the romance department.

My only success had been as a soldier. Now what?

I had volunteered for Afghanistan—for men like Sean. Let them stay with their children and let those with no ties fight the good fight. After Thandiwe, I had closed myself off to any serious relationship.

The red-headed Leia laughed at something the blonde had said, catching my attention. A contagious giggle, one I'd like to hear again and again, a call to forever ripping my resistance to shreds.

Sean rapped my head with a knuckle-beanie. "You're drooling. Quit acting like Jabba the Hutt and ask her out."

I thrust a fistful of popcorn into my mouth, and a kernel lodged in my throat. At least I'd stopped drooling. Instead, I would choke to death. I could see the headlines now: *Veteran dies from popcorn kernel after three tours in Afghanistan.*

She turned and looked directly at me. Of course, the whole theater stared at the idiot gagging in the middle of the theater. Sean handed me his soda, then after a few sips the offensive kernel slid down. I wasn't going to die in a theater after all.

This time Sean shoved the sharp end of his light saber into my side. "Well, the movie's about to start. If you're going to grab your future, better do it now."

Chapter 2

Why wouldn't my legs let me stand up and approach my favorite Leia?

The lights dimmed and the coming attractions started. Too late.

I studied the upcoming offerings ... I might be interested in the new action/thriller to be released this summer. Might be a lead in to ask for a date.

No ... still three months away, a long time from April until August.

Why had I let my chance slip? I wiggled my toes on my good leg. No, I wasn't paralyzed. Just scared. Too much uncertainty to ask a girl out right now ... at least a girl I could picture being with forever. Ridiculous fantasy. I didn't even know her name. How could I be in love?

At least within this dark theater, Sean couldn't see me brood.

The movie did not disappoint. *A New Hope* has always been my favorite of the whole Star Wars franchise ... an action-packed space western. I identified with Luke. Who was my father? I'd imagined he'd abandoned me because he had more important things to do with his life—like save the world. While growing up in a succession of foster homes, I made a promise to an unknown father I'd be extra good so when he came back for me, he'd be proud of me. Only he never came back. Neither did my mother. As I grew older, I realized they'd been seduced by the dark side—drugs.

As the lights came back on, I thought maybe all wasn't lost for Princess Leia and me. I could strike up a conversation about the movie, study the waters, see if she'd like to get coffee or something.

Not to be. She was nowhere to be found.

"Let's go to Big Boys Burgers," Sean said.

"Sure. Why not. I start my low cholesterol diet tomorrow."

We laughed as we exited the theater and walked the two blocks to Big Boys, taking a booth in the back. "I don't think we've been here since Senior Skip Day," Sean said. "How did we let so many years go by without coming back?"

"Seems like an eternity ago."

"Big Boys was our home away from home during high school. Remember our church youth group gatherings? Pastor Nick thought this was a good place to learn how to witness to our peers."

"Yeah. We did have some good times."

"What happened to that kid who held a Bible in one hand and his heart in the other? You could recite the four spiritual laws of salvation backward and forward. What got in your way?"

Thankfully, the waiter approached to take our orders. I didn't expect Sean to understand how war sucks Faith out of a person ... made one wonder if they ever truly believed.

We both decided on the Big Boy quarter pounder with extra cheese and a side of onion rings. Sean laughed. "Hope you don't run into Miss Future with that onion breath."

I snickered. Not much chance of ever seeing my favorite Leia again. "He who hesitates is lost," the adage says. I have always been the champion of hesitation, and that night I'd outdone myself.

Sean didn't let the question drop. Once the waiter left, he asked again. "You've changed, Dave. What made you see the world with dark glasses? Afghanistan?"

Partly. Or maybe my former so-called faith was nothing more than platitudes I'd summoned to substitute for a lack of family, a desperate attempt to find purpose for living. How does one reconcile God with war? "Yeah ... war, Sean. Makes one question everything. If God is love, why do the innocent suffer?"

Sean smirked. "You're not the only one to ask this question. As a pediatric nurse, I fight a different war. One against disease. And I've asked God many times why children die from cancer and other horrible illnesses."

Exactly!

"I can't give you an answer because I don't have an answer for myself. Maybe that's what faith requires. Belief in the face of doubt. I believe God cares and weeps. Why he cures some and not others, I can't say. I am not a theologian, nor a philosopher. This much I know, God is Love and where he is, love abounds. I sense him within my very being."

I wondered if I'd ever truly sensed God's presence in my life. "I wish I could be more like you, Sean. I can't accept God without answers. Not anymore. When I was younger, religion was a way of life ... something to feel good about ... a guide. I don't think I ever let it get inside me like you have."

"I'll pray God brings you home, Dave."

Just then our burgers and onions arrived. We gobbled our food like hungry teenagers, paid our bill, and headed for the door just as the trio of Leias entered. I hid my gasp as the redhead looked up to me with a broad smile, her Celtic eyes dancing in the light as she examined me from feet to head.

I checked my face. Did I have a grease smudge or an aura of silliness about me?

Onions! Why did I gorge on onion rings? Another opportunity avoided because I had onions. But did that really matter? I'd never know unless I ...

Before I could stutter so much as an *um ... ah*, the trio whooshed by and grabbed a table in the back. Right next to where Sean and I had eaten.

"Go talk to her." Sean gave me a little push.

"Onions, Sean. Onions."

Chapter 3

I heaved the alarm clock against the wall, gasping as it fell to the floor and stopped ringing.

The alarm clock wasn't to blame. Where did this anger come from?

I'd always been cool and calm under pressure and had the medals to prove I could handle any military crisis. I'd been honored as a leader, and the soldiers under my command could be sure I had their backs.

After my surgery and rehab in Germany, I was still able to joke ... to present myself as strong and in control.

I gazed at my broken alarm. Right now, I was anything but in control.

I showered, dressed, took my pain meds, and wolfed down a Jimmy Dean's microwave breakfast—my last one since I was sure my physical therapist would insist on a more balanced diet.

I checked in at the rehab reception area, then took a seat in the waiting room.

The door opened, and I hitched my breath as my favorite Leia called my name, "Dave Prioux?"

At first, I thought it was a case of mistaken identity. The face looked the same, but without the braided buns I couldn't be sure. I looked up to meet her gaze as she lifted hers from the clipboard bearing all my personal data. "It's you!"

She smiled.

Not mistaken identify. Leia all right, sans the white robe and silver belt. Same red hair and dazzling green eyes. "I'm Shayla. Your therapist. How's your throat?"

The next smile melted my resolve to run and hide. Bad enough she heard me gag and smelled my onion breath. Now she'd see me limp. At least with Leia, maybe this round of therapy wouldn't be so bad. I'd work hard to improve just to see her smile of approval.

"Fine." I pulled myself to a stand, trying not to show the discomfort I experienced just to be upright.

"By the way, Han, I thought yours was the best costume ... looked pretty authentic. Your friend should have dressed like Chewbacca, though. Somehow I can't see Han hanging out with Darth Vader."

"That's Sean for you. He likes to play the villain for some reason. Though he's the greatest guy I know," I said as I limped toward where she led, presumably to the room where my biggest weaknesses could not be hidden by a surly sense of humor.

We walked into a room with rows of various cyclical equipment. "We'll start you out for six minutes on elliptical." She leaned over to adjust the levers, and I glanced at her name tag. Shayla MacGregor. Of course ... Scottish. I imagined her a direct descendant of some Scottish warrior princess or maybe Rob Roy.

I had to know, even if I never got the courage to ask her for a date. Although, asking her out was moot. A therapist-patient relationship beyond these walls probably would be frowned upon by her superiors ... a good excuse. Still, I had to know. "MacGregor, huh? Scottish?"

"The red hair wasn't giveaway enough?"

"That and the green eyes, but the last name sort of erased all doubt." I glanced at her hand. No ring. "Your name or your husband's?"

Her glow ebbed for a second, and the smile vanished. "I'm sorry. Too personal?"

She shook her head. "It's all right. My maiden name was Douglas."

So she is married. Foolish to think she'd be otherwise ... a beauty like her.

"My husband died in a helicopter crash. Five years ago."

What could I say? I met her gaze with as much sympathy as my hardened heart could muster. "I shouldn't have asked. None of my business." I leaned in as if to emphasize the point. "Just so you know, you have an idiot for a patient."

She brightened a little, a slight dip of the head, like a medieval queen. "Not so, oh kind sir." She tapped the clipboard as the machine purred into motion, my feet reluctantly finding the pedals. "Your heroic deeds are all right here."

"Here?"

"This is a VA hospital, so nothing is a secret here. You have a very distinguished record." She leaned in to whisper, close enough for me to catch the flower-scented after-shower mist. "I know tons more about you than you know about me. I'll see you in six minutes." She clicked her tongue and walked away, the same mesmerizing sway of the hips that had caught my attention at the theater.

Chapter 4

I knew I couldn't ask her out. Even if I did, instinct told me she was too dedicated to her job to accept a date. I settled for the sweet moments of our banter during my two-times a week therapy sessions.

We talked about *Star Wars* and how the subsequent movies following the initial three didn't have the same flavor. I asked her how she felt about *Star Trek* enterprises.

"Yeah. I'm a Trekkie too. Although, the new stuff on streaming isn't quite the same."

Was she the type who saw *Close Encounters of the Third Kind* a gazillion times or waited for aliens on top of the Empire State Building? Possibly, but eccentricity seemed inconsequential.

"Don't get me wrong," she said as if reading my mind. "I love all the space stuff to a certain degree. I think I've seen *Close Encounters of the Third Kind* at least a dozen times. But I'm not about to camp out on Devil's Tower to await being carried off in an alien space ship. I'm waiting for the trumpet sound that will take me to be forever with Jesus."

I froze.

I should have known better. I thought there was something ethereal about her ... a spiritual depth I hadn't seen in any woman I'd dated, not even my Nigerian nurse.

I hadn't thought I'd ever marry a religious person. I'd had enough Bible thumping during my teen years. None of it seemed true to me anymore. Yet, my favorite Leia's spirituality only added to her charm.

She stared at my blank face. What could I say? So I said nothing.

"You don't believe? I took it for granted. I can usually spot a believer. Am I mistaken?"

"I used to be," I said, my head bowed as if feeling ashamed.

"Oh. No such thing as used to be. Maybe you're just going through a long desert of doubt. A lot of vets do. There'll come a day when you'll realize what was once will be again. This time, your faith will be stronger than ever having gone through this dry spell."

"So you're a theologian too?" I laughed ... more like a swallowed grunt. Her words struck a chord—like a discordant strum on a guitar.

After that, our banter seemed to stick to therapy and exercise.

I hadn't taken my therapy seriously after surgery. Until now. For once, I did my home exercises faithfully and was amazed at the improvement in my ambulation. I might have a slight limp the rest of my life, but I felt strong enough to start taking walks. I craved my favorite Leia's praises.

After two months, my schedule was inexplicably changed to a later time and a different therapist, Aaron Dubray, a man in his mid-fifties. No sense of humor and couldn't care less if I did my exercises or not. No praises either. Had I done something to offend Shayla?

"Hey, Aaron," I said nonchalantly as possible. "What happened to Shayla?"

Just then, she came into the therapy room, her smile bright enough to smash every corner of darkness in my soul. "Nothing," she said. "Aaron, may I have a few minutes with your patient?"

He nodded, oblivious to the beauty standing next to him. Was he as blind as he was humorless?

"What gives?" I asked.

"Nothing. But I figured if you were ever going to ask me out, I'd have to give you a different therapist. Since I'm the supervisor, guess I had the privilege of changing things up."

I mentally scratched my head.

She swung her long tresses to one side. "I asked to have you assigned as my patient. When I looked at your file, I recognized your photo as the Han Solo I saw at the movie theater. I just had to at least meet you."

"Me? There must have been as many Han Solos as there were Leias. How did you remember me from just a photo?"

"Popcorn. Remember? I turned to see who might be choking to death in case I needed to administer a Heimlich. I saw the way you looked at me. Not like other guys ... ogling. I don't know how to explain it other than I saw a longing for something more than a quick fix to a romantic itch. I'd hoped you'd be at the diner. When I saw you as you walked out, I knew I wasn't mistaken. But you left without saying a word. When I saw your chart, I had to take a chance—to see if that look you gave me was for real."

I was hit-me-in-the-gut stunned. Breathless and speechless.

Her gaze was as fierce as Sean's I-double-dare-you imperative when we were kids. "And?"

She smiled ... and I was hooked.

"Well, was it real?"

I couldn't get words out and bobbled instead.

"I thought so. Well, if we're going to happen, now's the time."

Chapter 5

I never backed away from Sean's dares, and I decided I'd not back away from Shayla's. Sean and I had planned on going to Albany for Comic-Con festival on the weekend. I didn't think he'd mind if I ditched him for a Leia. He'd planned on dressing up as a Romulan, and I was going as Captain Picard. I'd even bought a skull cap.

I gulped and took the plunge. "Ever been to a Comic-Con?"

"Last year. A lot of fun. Why do you ask?"

"There's one here in Albany this weekend … if you're game."

"Game if you are. Let me guess. You want to go as a Starfleet captain."

I bobbled again and tried to mimic a quirky Patrick Stewart smile.

"Actually, I had planned on going with my friend."

"How about going with me instead? Would your friend mind?"

"Will Sean mind?"

She was starting to know me all too well. "No."

"My friend won't mind either … she was the brunette Leia."

"What were you going to wear?"

"Do you think Picard would be intimidated by Janeway?"

"Not in the least." This time my smile was genuine. "What time do you want me to pick you up." I figured Sean would lend me his car in an emergency such as this.

"Has your doctor given you clearance to drive yet?"

My hesitancy gave me away.

"If you're not threatened by a woman driver, I'll pick you up at ten."

So Janeway would chauffeur Picard. "No, not a threat at all. In fact, in Afghanistan, I thought the women were better drivers." But I hadn't driven since the sniper downed me.

She speared me with a questioning stare, her head tilted slightly to the right, her red curls falling over her shoulders.

"Okay ... maybe I haven't been cleared yet. I promise I won't try to drive before the doc says I'm good. So I accept your offer to cart me around until then."

"Fair enough. Tomorrow then."

A day-long date revealed a lot about this girl, though my time with her only confirmed what my instincts had sensed. An officer gets to sum up his troops in a hurry. You can learn a lot from a shrug or salute.

I learned we had almost everything in common except my foster care background and her zealous faith. If I were to win this girl, I had to at least go to church with her ... let her think she had some impact on improving my attitude toward God, at least the God she believed in.

"So how about it," she asked. "Think you might like to make date number two church tomorrow? We have a special singing group coming."

I cringed. I did like the beat to some of the contemporary gospel music; but most of these in-church groups, at least the ones Sean talked about, were so twangy country it hurt my ears. Though I was pretty sure those hard country-type gospel groups weren't Shalya's bag either since we agreed the greatest Rock group of all time was Led Zeppelin and our mutual favorite of theirs was "Stairway to Heaven." She pointed out the interest was waning with the younger set, but she could still hear the song a dozen times a day and not tire of it.

"I suppose there could be two paths in life …" she'd said.

Were Shayla and I on different paths?

"It's never too late to choose the right one, you know," the challenge put forth as I expected.

That's where we differed. I did believe there was a God, that the world didn't just happen. But his creation was so mixed up, I suspected he just sat back and decided to let humankind destroy itself … why he permitted so much tragedy and war. I thought about the Taliban I'd killed. Faceless people—doctrine so harsh my skin crawled. Did God love them too?

I ignored Shayla's challenge and veered our conversation back to her church invitation. "Who's the group?"

I steeled myself for the letdown.

"A new group. They're contemporary Christian Rock— Messiah's Mission. I think you'd like them."

I had no honest excuse since it was music I would probably enjoy if I didn't listen to the lyrics. And I had no plans for Sunday except to sit in my recliner with a six pack. I decided to forego the six pack in exchange for a second date with Shayla. "Sure. I'll go only if you let me buy your lunch after church … at the diner near the movie theater."

Shayla nodded in approval. "Deal. I love Big Boys Burgers."

We spent the day enjoying fantasies of yesteryear, today, and tomorrow. As people paraded around us in their favorite character costumes, we placed the characters with the movie, listed the cast, and compared notes on the good and the bad.

Shayla saw the spiritual in everything. Her way of seeing the world helped me to put on a better pair of glasses. I found my darkness shattering with her insights into matters beyond my capability to understand.

We followed a pair of Trekkies who chatted away in Klingon, dressed like Khan and Worf. Another pair spoke Elfish. They understood one another even if the rest of the world didn't.

The hours passed by like seconds. All too soon, we left the world of make believe and headed home to grim reality. Yet not a minute of that day has left my remembrance. Scenes, smells, and the touch of our hands as we walked hand in hand were forever embedded on my heart.

Chapter 6

Shayla picked me up at the appointed time for church, and I was unusually impressed by the quality of music, though I had come steeled to think Messiah's Mission was just another wanna-be-famous-but-lacking-the-talent performers. They sang with conviction, and I felt convicted. I fought the urge to surrender, a word not in my soldier's vocabulary. I vowed I would not go back to church again, even if my refusal cost me Shayla.

Of course, she asked as we took our seat in Big Boys Burgers. "Well ... what did you think of the service?"

How could I answer truthfully without pushing her away?

"The music was good, and your pastor gave an excellent sermon."

"And?"

I sighed. "I enjoy being with you Shayla, but I don't think church is the place for me."

Unexpectedly, she smiled. "I understand. God has more work to do on you first."

I changed the subject. "So where to next?" Would there be a next? I would understand if she gave me the brushoff.

"How about a driving lesson?"

"I know how to drive."

"Not what I meant. There are ways to drive to minimize your discomfort."

"Sean's taking me tomorrow to get a car. I haven't owned one since my first tour, and that was a long time ago. I figured since I'm stateside for good, I should get a car. Then the next goal is to look for a job. I figure finding one will be easier once I have a car. I see the doctor in a few days and expect to be cleared to drive."

"Well, Mr. Independent, if you don't want driving lessons, how about you take me out for a ride in that new jalopy of yours once you're ready?"

Motivation to endure the pain behind the wheel.

Relief washed over me. She did not intend to cast me aside because I did not share her faith in me finding faith again. "I'll make sure whatever car I buy is fit for a princess."

I hadn't been to Six Flags' Great Escape since high school. Was she the adventurous type? "Do you like amusement parks?"

"Of course. Amusement is my middle name. What are you thinking?"

"When's the last time you went to Great Escape?"

"Been years. Sounds like fun."

"This time, I'm driving!"

She saluted, and we set a date for Saturday.

Chapter 7

The spring I met my favorite Leia and the months that followed turned out to be the best months of my life. The following Christmas, I bought a diamond ring. We married on the anniversary of the day we met.

Spring had always been my favorite time of year ... a time of hope. Like any newlyweds, we thought we'd be together forever.

I expected some ups and downs. Sean's marriage was my role model, and he gave me frequent advice on coupling. "The first years are hard, buddy. Territorial struggles abound. Think of it like getting used to living in a different country. Marriage has its own rules and language."

Made sense, and Sean's predictions were right. Living with a woman wasn't anything like dating. We struggled with the craziness of getting used to sharing space. She monopolized the closet in our tiny one bedroom apartment. Did a woman really need twelve pairs of shoes?

Neither one of us knew anything about cooking, cleaning, or staying on a budget. Since she'd been on the marriage train before, I assumed she was proficient in these areas and was glad to follow her lead. Except ... she knew little more than I did.

I wondered why the subject of her late husband hadn't come up while we dated. "We were only married two years when Chris died, and most of that time he was deployed. I lived with my parents. You've seen my apartment, Dave. That should have been a clue I don't do housework."

Yeah. Big clue. Her messy lifestyle didn't impact me while we dated. But a soldier was taught neatness from the first day of training camp. I tried to ignore the mess. She laughed that I even folded my dirty clothes when I put them in the hamper.

That first year of marriage was clumsy ... like a dance where nobody knows the steps.

Sometimes I wondered if we shouldn't have taken a little longer to truly get to know each other. Yet, in my mind, the unraveling of her foibles and idiosyncrasies made me love her all the more. I thought she must feel the same way because she never complained about my pervasive stupidity on how a relationship should work.

We had lots of spats ... of course. More often than not, though, I deliberately pushed her buttons—she was endearing when her cheeks puffed and her eyes bugged with anger. I knew I wasn't being fair, but the makeup sessions after an argument were my most treasured moments.

Shayla's job kept her pretty busy. She'd come home exhausted, and I hadn't bothered to clean the house or cook anything. We ordered takeout a lot, and the high-caloric diet caused her to gain weight. While she never complained, I figured she would like to eat a little healthier. I tried to be more nutritionally minded, and even studied a few cooking lessons online. But given a choice between salad and a hamburger ... not a choice at all.

Shayla was the bread winner. Though I'd improved physically, trying to get a job proved more frustrating than the treadmill. I wasn't much of a house husband and quickly became bored hanging around the apartment all day. I finally was able to supplement my disability check with work as a security guard at a local department store.

I liked the job. Most of the time, I sat in a small office staring at security footage, drank coffee, and chatted with staff as they came in and out to report anything amiss. Nothing serious ever happened. A few times, I'd catch a couple of teenagers making out in an isolated corner. Sometimes, I had to scare a shoplifter and warn them not to come back to the store for at least a year. The scariest episode was a prank bomb threat on Halloween. I had a bad dream that night. Shayla scowled and said I had been pounding the bed covers.

The fight that night wasn't a spat. Her face turned beet red when I refused to talk about my dream. She screamed something about PTSD and how she knew a lot of soldiers coming back from the Gulf suffered night tremors, drank too much, and became abusive.

I stormed out, came back in half an hour, and downed a few too many beers.

Shayla warned me if I ever got drunk again, she'd leave me. I knew she meant it, so I stopped buying beer and promised her I'd never go out to bars again. If the temptation were not near me, I shouldn't have a problem. I didn't want to think about a life without my favorite Leia.

Chapter 8

After that first year, we did find a rhythm. Life was comfortable, and the night sweats only lasted a few weeks after the bomb threat. Maybe things wouldn't have gotten so bad if I'd stayed at the department store job.

Spring burst early that year. I've always been partial to lilacs. The yard outside the apartment we rented had a few bushes, and Shayla always kept a fresh bouquet on our table. She came home early from work, just before I was due to report for my job. She always had a smile that would brighten the darkest night. That day, her aura was impossibly brighter.

"We're pregnant," she burst before she'd even closed the door.

I thought then this was the most intense joy I'd ever known.

"Great news. We'll celebrate tomorrow night. I'll get the day off, and we can have a nice dinner."

I wished I hadn't had to rush off. I wanted to take her out and buy a crib right away.

As I drove to work, my thoughts began to crowd with worry. Yes, I was thrilled at the prospects of being a dad. Financial worries tore at my euphoria. We'd need more income. Shayla loved her job and planned to keep working, but we barely made ends meet even with my added income over and above my disability check. I didn't want to be a stay-at-home dad. I'd rather lead a battalion into the fiercest battle than the prospect of being alone all day with a baby. Selfish ... macho ... old fashioned ... I knew.

I needed to find a better paying job if we were going to pay for daycare. Then there were savings accounts for extra needs, and our apartment was way too small. We'd wanted to buy a house but weren't quite financially ready yet.

I always walked with Shayla during my supper break every night, before she'd go to bed. She sensed my worry. "God will provide, Dave. Wait and see."

Oh, to have her simple faith in a God who always came through. I had many tough times on tour, but I always managed to get through the worst struggles on my own. I had no one else to depend on.

This new challenge ... parenting ... scared me silly. Could I measure up? Would I fail like my biological mother and father ... long dead from overdoses?

A few weeks later, I got a call from my CO from basic training who retired during my last tour in Afghanistan. He still outranked me though he was only two years older. He bubbled with excitement as we caught up on our lives. "Congrats on the kid, Dave. I envy you. I never did settle down."

The colonel—he'd always be Colonel to me—got really serious. "I'm actually calling with a business proposition."

A few weeks ago, I wouldn't have been interested. Shayla and I were in a good place, even if we struggled a bit for cash flow. That day, I was ready to listen. "Shoot."

"I'm starting a security business. Lots of vets and retired cops looking for work. We're not far from the Adirondacks and Berkshires. Lots of celebrities and politicians have homes in the mountains. I could use a smart man like you as a partner."

"Tell me more."

"Easy work with high pay. Just need to make sure the grounds and property are secure. A lot of the work can be hired out. You'd be more of a manager than a hands-on guy. The only real work is when the celebrity decides to roost for a while. Things can get kind of wild. Mostly fun, though. You get to meet a lot of famous people!"

Deep down, I knew Hector was glossing things over. This wouldn't be the walk in the park he described. But the phrase, "easy work and high pay," caught my attention. I should have checked with Shayla first. She knew me through and through, and she'd have talked me out of it. I could hear her say, "We'll find a different solution, Dave. I don't think this is what God wants."

"I'm in, Hector."

Chapter 9

After I got the job, I made reservations for us at The Grappa 73 Ristorante, a highly rated restaurant in our area. Not as ritzy maybe as a five-star, but fancy enough for a soldier used to desert rations. I wanted to celebrate our good fortune—my new job and our new life to come as parents. I went the extra mile and bought Shayla a dozen roses and gave them to her when I got home from the interview with Hector.

She was excited at the job, or at least I thought so, even resigned to the need for me to be away on occasion as new jobs were set up and to fill in if extra staff were needed for special circumstances.

She'd worn the green dress I liked and had taken my breath away, just as she had done in her Leia costume at the movie theater. I took her in my arms. "You'll always be my favorite Leia."

We were given a table in the rear, and the waiter lit the candle in the center of our table. I thought the ambiance was romantic. But then, I didn't know much more about these things than what I saw in movies.

I couldn't understand her sudden flow of tears. What did I do? Or were hormones to blame?

Sean said whenever his wife cried, he went straight to an apology even if he didn't know what he'd done.

"Chances are, Dave," he'd explained, "I did something stupid so might as well start there."

I followed Sean's advice. "Shayla, talk to me. I don't know what I did to make you unhappy, but I'm sorry."

She squeezed my hand. "You didn't do anything wrong ... this is lovely."

"Then you're crying because ... why?"

"Dave, I had a dream."

"Prophetic or a nightmare?"

Shayla wiped the tears from her eyes, then took a sip from her water glass. I had ordered a bottle of champagne, forgetting she couldn't drink being pregnant. "I guess more of a nightmare, but I hope it wasn't a prophecy."

I grabbed the bottle of champagne. "Do you mind? I think I may need this."

She scowled. But I poured myself a glass anyway.

"I don't want you to take that job. I have a bad feeling about it. Some of those celebrities have pretty wild lifestyles in those mountains. All kind of craziness."

"I won't be partying ... I'll be guarding. A big difference."

She smiled her forgiveness at my thick-headedness. "If I can't talk you out of this job, then promise me you'll be careful."

I nodded. I meant to keep my promise.

Chapter 10

At first, the job was easy enough. Most of the time, we walked the circumference of a client's estate, set up surveillance, and put teams in place. When we finished the job, I'd have a couple of beers with Hector, then head back home the next day.

I had told him about Shayla's dream, mostly making fun of her, though a chill did run the length of my spine.

"No need for worry, Dave. Our job is set up, then the team takes over. Besides, nothing ever happens in these woods, except maybe an errant bear. Sometimes a snake or two gets into the big house. Even squirrels. But nothing dangerous of the human kind."

"Nothing?"

The colonel smirked. "Oh, we get the occasional attempt at a house squat … you know, those bums who think they can break in and get free rooming, take pictures of the celeb's surroundings, and cash in on indiscretion. We catch them pretty fast. They're harmless, though. We bring them in to local law enforcement. Otherwise, things really are pretty calm."

"Yeah? Well if nothing ever happens, why do they want security?"

The colonel laughed. "You know how rich people are."

I didn't know. I'd never been rich.

After a month, I began to believe I happened on the best job in the world. We'd go in for a day or two, scope the territory, and hire out the help we needed—mostly cops looking for extra pay and retired or former military like Hector and me.

The craziness happened two months later.

The colonel sat across from me, his face serious as a briefing before engagement. "Apparently, there's been a bank robbery in North Albany. LEOs are all warning to be on the lookout. They think the perps are headed toward Canada via Adirondack backroads. They'd be stupid, though, to think they could hold up on any of our clients' estates. But our bread and butter people are nervous and want to make sure we have extra coverage. Twila Jones asked for us, you and me, to be on the team we set up"— the colonel grinned as he slapped me on the shoulder— "and is paying big extra bucks."

Shayla and I lived in a quiet, small town just north of Albany, an easy commute to the city via the Interstate. Nothing ever happened in our town. Criminal activity was generally limited to the occasional misdemeanor or domestic violence.

"I don't think Shayla's going to be happy when she finds out."

"Sorry, buddy. We're all hands-on-deck, 24/7 until they catch the bad guys. Nothing like this has ever happened to my knowledge, but our employer insists on maximum coverage for security since she will be at her estate tomorrow and staying for a few weeks."

Shayla was livid when I told her. "How long?"

"Until they catch the perps ... might not even need to go. Troopers do a decent job of tracking these scumbags."

The chill up my back wouldn't leave.

"I warned you about my dream, didn't I? I told you not to take this job."

"Just your hormones, honey."

Our employer settled in the next day, and we instructed all our teams to be on alert at all times, even if it wasn't their shift. We always carried weapons for our protection but were warned to avoid engaging and to call local law enforcement at anything suspicious.

"We're really in no danger there, Shayla"—I kissed her hard so she'd know there was nothing to be afraid of—"just precautions. I promise I won't do anything foolish. In all likelihood the perps are caught already, and I expect I'll just be turning around as soon as the colonel and I get there. Even so, there's slim to no chance the perps are anywhere near Twila Jones's estate."

"Our church is praying, sweetheart."

Why did she have to blab everything to her pastor and ask for prayer? I never minded her praying in front of me, but I didn't want the whole church involved in my affairs. I could take care of myself.

Images of slain Afghans suddenly loomed before me. Our team had run into some urban fighting. No one knows who shot first ... but women and children lay among the dead when the dust settled. The incident was investigated, according to protocol; and no one was charged with wrong doing. For all we knew, the insurgents shot the so-called victims. The Taliban were known to hide behind human shields, then blame the good guys for the death of innocents.

Three weeks later, I was pierced by a sniper bullet that ended my military career. Maybe that bullet was divine punishment for the shedding of innocent blood. And maybe this was why I had fought so hard against giving my life back to God. I didn't deserve forgiveness.

I shook the memory from my mind as the colonel and I traced the perimeter in our ATVs. Maybe we shouldn't have been so cavalier, cracking jokes and slamming each other like we were back in the army, or we might have heard them. The shot was true, and Hector fell from his ATV. I managed to find cover and called for help as ordered. Then, in the cover of darkness, I crawled to Hector. Dead. Senselessly killed.

Tears … silent sobs … chaos … more gunfire … lights … dogs. I don't know how long I lay beside my fallen friend until a trooper found me. He checked the colonel for any sign of life, shook his head, then helped me to a stand. "Sir, are you all right?"

"I am. My friend … no."

"We got them, thanks to your information. They're going away for a very long time. Sorry about your friend."

The next weeks were a blur. After the funeral, the night terrors started again. First, I'd see the slaughtered Afghans, then the colonel's body covered in blood. He rose from the dead, pointed a finger and screamed, "This is your fault. You should have been more alert."

I'd wake drenched in sweat and would grab a beer from my hidden stash under a loose floorboard. One beer became two beers … two became three or more. I didn't bother to hide my stash anymore. I managed to stop drinking before I became punch drunk, trying to keep my promise to Shayla. But the drinking only unleashed the demons I thought had ended when I left Afghanistan.

At Shayla's insistence, I got rid of any booze in the apartment. But without alcohol to tame the demons' hold, the night terrors only got worse. I started sneaking out to bars.

With Hector's death, the business fell apart since I was no manager without his input. I wanted to find other work, but my head was not on straight—anger my constant companion. I slammed walls, even putting a fist-sized hole in our bathroom when I cut myself shaving.

Shayla put up with me for only two months, then came the ultimatum. "Get help or get out."

I gazed at her swollen form. How could I call myself a man and let my pregnant wife go through this alone? I'd promised to be the kind of father I always wanted. The tears of remorse flowed as my love for my favorite Leia turned anger into forward motion. I'd survived three tours and a sniper bullet. I would get past this too. I could rise above the pain of remembrance for her and for our child.

I fell to my knees. "I promise you, I'll not touch another drop. Please, don't make me leave."

She pulled me up and took my hand. "Promise? You'll get help?"

"Promise."

I started AA the very next day and buried my demons so deep, I thought they could never surface again.

Chapter 11

With the help of my AA sponsor, I found another job—produce manager at a local grocery store. Before long, I hated the work. Spraying lettuce was not what I thought life should hand me. I served my country with distinction—a placard of my medals decorated our bedroom wall. My sponsor suggested I use my VA benefit to get my master's degree. But in what? My undergraduate degree was in history, and I had not given any thought to a career after military retirement. I thought I had years to figure out that piece of the puzzle.

What could I do with a BA in history?

I had no patience to be a teacher or even a substitute.

If I did go back to school, what could I study?

I loved action. I was just on the outer edge of qualification for a state trooper, nor could I pass the rigorous physical fitness tests. My limp was hardly noticeable, but I couldn't run without excruciating pain.

As if Shayla could read my mind, she sat me down. "Here's a challenge for you."

"I do like a challenge. What are you thinking?"

"Why not be a stay-at-home dad. A lot more men are taking on that role."

I thought we'd hire a nanny so I could work too. I hadn't been much of a house husband—how could I manage a baby? I'd probably have better success at disarming a bomb.

"We need me to work, don't we?"

Her head drooped. "I didn't want to tell you ... you've been so discouraged about finding work ..."

"So tell me. I can handle it." I braced myself for news like, "I don't want to go back after the baby's born. Why don't you be a man and support your family, even if that means staying in a job you hate."

Instead of scolding, Shayla, my beautiful Leia, just smiled. "I'm getting a promotion to a managerial position at the hospital. A nice boost in salary. It'll still be a little tight, but you can quit the grocery store. I never did like the idea of a stranger taking care of our baby."

My eyes must have bulged as words failed me.

We'd decided not to know the baby's gender. Now I wondered if we'd made a mistake. Shouldn't we be better prepared? "What if we have a girl?"

"You can do this, Dave. I know you can." Green eyes begged for me to take up the challenge.

Shayla laughed. "And you can always call the cavalry."

"The cavalry?"

"Sean. Or did you forget he's a pediatric nurse."

Duh. No his occupation hadn't really been a factor in our friendship ... until now.

I had no viable excuse. "Why not. Maybe I can find work to do at home so I won't be too bored."

Shayla kissed me on the cheek. "Trust me. You won't be bored."

Chapter 12

Trisha greeted the world at eight pounds, four ounces. Mother and child fared the experience well. Can't say the same for me. I put up a brave front with donned gown, mask, and all the coaching stuff I'd learned. As I watched the travail of birth, I knew Shayla's pain had to have been far greater than the sniper's bullet. I thought she was braver than any ten soldiers.

With every contraction, she'd ooze the Lord's Prayer, the Twenty-Third Psalm, or some other Scripture near and dear to her heart. If wishes were prayers, I guess mine were answered. No complications. I knew Shayla's age was a risk factor, but she had done everything in her power to be in good physical shape during the pregnancy. She faced motherhood with joy, confident in her God's ability to see her through any obstacles. I didn't share her optimism that God was in our corner and vowed to myself I'd be there for them both, a leader in my family as much as I'd been a leader in the army.

Shayla's church had given her a baby shower, and I was amazed at their generosity. Our girl would want for nothing ... at least for the immediate future. Sobriety had given me a better perspective on life. I held Trisha's little hand in mine. "I promise you, my little one, your dad will never leave you. Nothing will be more important to me than you and your mother. I will do everything in my power to make you both happy."

I had meant it. And for the next few years, I thought I could be the dad I wanted to be.

Chapter 13

At first, being a stay at-home dad had its rewards. My AA sponsor suggested a parenting support group. Sounded a little Pollyanna to me. Women joined groups. Outside of my AA group, I didn't see the need. The day Trisha rolled off the couch onto the floor, I thought maybe I could use some teaching. Thankfully, she was fine. But after that, I never turned my back. If I forgot the baby powder and changing cloth, I took her with me, got a tote, and carried everything I needed to the couch. We were cramped and had no room for the helpful changing tables—barely room enough for a crib.

The support group did help with care ideas, things I could do to maximize our limited space. I took Trisha for long walks in the park with some of the other stay-at-home dads. Escobar was a vet and struggled with confinement. He found caring for his toddler gave him some action he craved. "A kid can find more trouble than a soldier going AWOL," he said.

Would Trisha give me those challenges when she learned to walk? Would she be as adventurous as her beautiful mom?

Her eyes had turned from blue to brown, though Shayla called them hazel. "They'll change color depending on what she wears."

On Wednesday nights and Sundays, Shayla took Trisha to church with her. On Saturday, we'd take Trisha with us to museums, parks, whatever was inexpensive. But the venue never mattered to me as long as my favorite Leia was by my side.

I was almost happy.

At least, I had every reason to be. I hated that a shallow part of me mourned for something indefinable ... an itch one could not reach to scratch ... a sense of lack. For what? If I couldn't be a soldier anymore, I had everything else I could have hoped for.

At age three, the lessons started. First, gymnastics. I argued with Shayla on that. Why pay for a kid to learn how to do a somersault? Made no sense to me. But Trisha loved seeing her little friends. How could I deny her?

Shayla insisted Trisha start attending nursery school. "Think of the free time you'll have, Dave."

Things were changing again.

I'd developed a very workable regimen with my daughter. I was her major and she'd salute. We played a game—find the Taliban and flush the enemy out. Our days were uncomplicated, for me anyway. Sean laughed at our antics. "Hey, dude. Whatever you have to do to survive being a parent. It's hard, man."

I didn't want this time with Trisha to be different. Nursery school would mean I'd have to be alone with myself again, like when Shayla and I first got married. The idea scared me more than a firing squad.

In matters of parenting, Shayla's will almost always surpassed mine.

I couldn't stay at the house alone. I missed watching Trisha run around, looking under beds for Taliban holdouts. I had to find something to do. Sean, Shayla, and my AA sponsor seemed to think going back to school was the solution. But I needed action ... not academics. I needed work ... a challenge ... a mission.

I fell back to what I knew.

One of our AA members was a cop in the Albany Police Department. I had just turned forty, but he said I could get an age waiver because of my military background. I'd age out at forty-one. So if I wanted to be a cop, now was the time. I wasn't sure about the physical exam. But I discovered the years chasing after Trisha had strengthened my calves. I could run. Maybe not a marathon but enough perhaps to pass the physical exam. I was healthy enough otherwise.

I took the entrance exam and was hired, one of the few living just outside the City of Albany. Perhaps my wall of medals played a part in the waiver. I was proud, but Shayla didn't want police work for me. "The stress, Dave."

I should have listened.

Chapter 14

At first, I thought police work was a good fit for me. I was used to a disciplined lifestyle, and the force was much like the Army. After I graduated from the Academy, I was placed on evening patrol. Shayla hated my hours. But I liked the excitement ... more action in the evening than the morning.

My training officer was tough, and I liked the challenge. But when shift was over, he liked to go bar hopping.

I tried a lot of excuses to weasel out of doing the town with him.

The hours made getting to AA meetings difficult. I should have made them a priority. But I didn't want to seem weak in front of my TO. What would be the harm in going to a bar with him? I could order soft drink ... lots of nonalcoholic options.

I managed to complete the training requirements, and bulged with pride that I'd not only completed training ... the oldest man in my class at the academy ... but was promoted with honors. Maybe I could make detective grade in a few years. A goal ... a challenge.

"Pride goes before a fall," the adage says. Some say it's in the Bible too.

Chapter 15

Life for the Prioux family found another rhythm.

Trisha was happy with nursery school and would start kindergarten in the fall. Shayla didn't like me being a police officer. Yet she felt her faith required her to support me in my decision. Shayla's faith was part of the whole of her. I tried hard not to interfere with her church activities and the exercise of her religion as long as she didn't tell me how to live my life.

She avoided preaching to me, and I avoided talking about my job. On my days off, we were a family. I didn't see how unhappy my wife had become ... how my choices had affected her. We found less and less to talk about ... except for Trisha. "Did you know what her kindergarten teacher said? She's the brightest kid in her class."

"Of course," I said and dug into my pancakes.

We'd grown apart.

I knew this but didn't know how to fix things. Of course, there was still love. But love not exercised can grow into complacency and complacency into indifference. We became two adults and a child in one household, our paths connecting less and less. I wasn't home until after Trisha went to bed, and my contact with my daughter had been relegated to breakfast. I convinced myself I was still a great dad with my five minutes of playtime in the morning before she went to school. I pulled a lot of weekends and volunteered for overtime. My excuse? We could bank the money toward a house.

Would I have yielded to temptation if I'd been more present in my family's life? If I'd noticed my favorite Leia's swollen eyes in the morning or been home to hear her sobs? If only I'd listened to my daughter's warnings ..."Mommy cried hard again last night."

Promises became forgotten memory.

A year on the job, the night tremors returned.

Drink beckoned me. Just one or two before I came home. I tried to hide my alcohol breath, but Shayla knew—her non-verbal disapproval, a sigh as she rolled away from me when I climbed into bed.

My former TO was retiring and the precinct had a party that night. I had to go, right? I had been off for the day and justified going out that night by cooking Shayla's favorite dinner ... Yankee pot roast, one of the few things I'd learned to cook during my stay-at-home-dad days. I read a bedtime story to Trisha and tucked her in.

As I put on my coat, Shayla's eyes begged me to stay home. "Do you really have to go to this thing tonight?" Was it a guilt trip? Premonition? Did she know we'd split up that night?

I was drunk out of my mind when I came home. I only know what happened from Shayla and Sean's accounts. I smashed the door down, kicked a giant hole in the wall while ranting and raving. Shayla called Sean. He coaxed me out of the house and brought me to a hotel room ... even stayed with me until I sobered up the next day.

"This has to end, Dave," he said. "You can't put Shayla through this again. Until you get the help you need, you have to leave. If you love her, move out. You could have hurt her or even Trisha. Did you know she woke up from all the commotion ... terrified ... screaming, 'A monster got inside my daddy.'"

So I did move out, took a leave of absence, and went back to AA because Shayla insisted I couldn't visit Trisha until I received my first AA chip. Then Trisha could stay overnight for Easter weekend. How I missed my favorite Leia. I'd done the unthinkable—the thing I'd promised myself I'd never do. I put the love of my life and the child of that love in danger ... me ... the man who vowed he'd be the best husband and father there ever was.

Chapter 16

They say, "a child shall lead them."

Could I deny my daughter the one thing she hoped for Easter? Daddy taking her to church?

God will bring you home to him, Dave. But he's got work to do first ... Shayla's prophecy when I refused to go to church, when I had dug my heels in like daring God to try and change me. Her words now pulled me to my knees. "I'm done fighting you, God. This was more than messing up. I spurned you ... your grace ... your mercy. You brought me to my favorite Leia, gave me Trisha, and I spoiled these previous gifts with twisted resentment of you. I can only ask forgiveness. I've known all along only you could fill this hollow in my soul ..."

I couldn't get any more words out that night. I simply poured my agony out with moans and groans.

I woke to a soft shake on my shoulder and Trisha's giggle. "Daddy ... why did you go to sleep on the floor?"

I must have fallen asleep while pouring out my heart to God.

"Well, Trisha. I had a long talk with God last night, and I decided I would let Jesus come back into my life again."

Trisha nodded and squeezed my hand.

"Okay, then. Does that mean we're going to church?"

"Yeah. Do you want to see what the Easter Bunny left you?"

"My Easter Bunny is Jesus, and he gave me the best present ever. You."

Chapter 17

"God's got a lot of work to do on you," Shayla said when she came to pick up Trisha Easter afternoon. I'd told her I'd given my life back to God. She simply looked at me, her eyes full of doubt, and said, "I hope you mean it this time."

What did I expect? That she'd tell me to come back home? I'd disappointed her too many times. Maybe she was right to judge me as insincere.

I realized the road ahead wasn't going to be smooth. Rebuilding Shayla's trust would take a miracle. Maybe the Lord had one in his arsenal for me, though I didn't deserve any. For now, I would focus on staying sober and enjoy my one weekend a month with Trisha on the condition I took her to church. Did Shayla think this would be a hardship?

I looked forward to renewing a church life. Remembering the days of youth trips and ministry, I hoped to find a new fellowship.

One day at a time, Dave. Do this for yourself. Not to impress Shayla.

I said another prayer. "Even if Shayla and I are split for good, Lord, I know I have you always."

After Shayla left, I called Sean with the news we were now brothers in Christ once more.

"'Bout time, dude. Did you tell Shayla?"

"Yeah. She doesn't believe me."

"Did you really think she would? With your history, she wants evidence, man. Hard evidence. Can you blame her?"

"Not really."

"You got some work to do, yet, dude. Don't try to convince her with words. Besides, you need to let her go. Let God work on you first. I can't promise you Shayla will ever take you back. But you'll never heal if you put a condition on God's help."

The truth of Sean's words stung. The hardest thing I ever did, more frightening than being ambushed by the Taliban, was to surrender my favorite Leia.

Chapter 18

For the next year, I faithfully attended AA meetings, got my job back, and joined a support group for cops in recovery. I'd done similar things before. Those efforts had been for Shayla's sake ... not mine. This time my higher power was not my self-reliance ... my power now came from the Lord. He told me to take a backseat, and let him do the work. A soldier is used to doing ... not laying low. Taking one day at a time, surrendering that day to God, was not easy for a man used to being in command.

Shayla rarely stayed for more than a few minutes when she dropped Trisha off and when she picked her back up. I wanted to share how well I was doing. But she'd rush off before I could even tell her about my one year chip.

I didn't think I'd go on without my favorite Leia in my life. I did, though. I joined the men's fellowship, even going on a missions trip to Guatemala in February, after taking a carpentry course. I had stopped asking the men to pray for God to heal my marriage. I hadn't given up. I just knew that whatever my future, God would work all things for good—and that brought me peace. Peace I never thought I'd ever feel.

"I'm happy, Sean," I told him when we went to a revival showing of *Lord of the Rings*.

"I can tell, buddy."

I was surprised when Shayla permitted Trisha's daily phone calls after her visit on Christmas. Trisha filled her calls with goings on at school, her Sunday School class projects, gymnastics, and how she'd signed up for T-ball this year. "We need a coach, Daddy. Will you be a coach?"

I checked with Shayla, surprised when she gave her blessing.

Coaching six-year-old girls was, for me, the ultimate test of patience. Yet, the experience proved to be more fun than I thought it would. Trisha was proud to have her daddy lead their team to victory. I enjoyed more time with Trisha, plus the added benefit of seeing Shayla at games and practices, even if our exchanges were limited to Trisha's needs. Shayla told me she'd put her trophy on her dresser along with the team's picture. I hoped the time would come I could see her display for myself.

When Easter came that spring, I asked Trisha my usual question. "What do you want the Easter Bunny to bring this year?"

"All I want is to have dinner with both you and Mommy."

A tall order. What would Shayla say? "Well, then, put Mommy on the phone. I'll ask. But, I can't promise she'll want to do that. She might have something else planned."

"Yes, I'll have dinner with you, as long as we eat later. I sing on the worship team, so I can't miss church."

"Five o'clock?"

"That works." Then she disconnected.

In addition to coaching Trisha's team, except for a burnt ham, Easter dinner was the start of something new for our fragmented family. Shayla approved more frequent overnights with Trisha, and sometimes Shayla would join us on our adventures. I discovered more amazing things about this women God had sent into my life. She was crafty—painted, crocheted, and sowed clothes, not just for herself and Trisha. Her generosity reached to homeless shelters. Why had I never noticed her many talents? Pursuits she hadn't tried until we separated. She seemed happy in her life away from me.

That Christmas, Shayla invited me to dinner. The first time in eighteen months I'd seen our old place. She'd partitioned a portion of the large living room to create a bedroom for Trisha, decorated in full princess theme.

Soon, I was a frequent guest for Sunday dinners and holidays.

We were finding a rhythm in our separated status ... a friendship and closeness absent when we lived together. Had we become better friends than a married couple? Was I being fair to keep Shayla in limbo? Had the time come to divorce? I still loved her with every fiber of my being. "Lord, if giving her the freedom to love someone else is the best way to love her going forward, give me a sign."

Trisha never failed to request a game of dominoes after dinner. We laughed a lot during those times, so I wasn't prepared for her direct question. "Daddy, why can't you stay here all the time like you used to?"

I thought she'd accepted the way her parents now lived—separate but united in their love for her. Apparently, I was mistaken. Shayla and I exchanged glances, then she rescued me from breaking my daughter's heart. "*Right now*, that may not be possible, honey." Shayla squeezed my hand, as if in contradiction. Oh, how I'd missed her touch. "But no one knows what the future can bring."

Hope. Hope I'd not dared to embrace until now.

Chapter 19

I gazed at the lilac buds as I waited for Shayla. Normally, I'd leave when Trisha went to bed, but Shayla had asked me to stay. "I have a question to ask." My fears ran the gamut. Was divorce on her mind? If so, I wouldn't stand in her way. We'd grown closer the last couple of months, even dated ... sort of, more like simply spending time just the two of us. We went for walks, saw a couple of movies, and attended her church couples night on Valentine's Day. I'd bought her a box of chocolates. Nothing physical beyond the occasional hand holding.

We shared a great deal during those moments. I told her how AA was helping me, but my church fellowship helped even more. She'd ask about my police work, concern edged on her brow. "I like my job, Shayla. But it's no longer my passion ... a means to find a purpose."

She'd taken a job as an instructor at Albany Medical for physical therapy. She'd share tidbits about her students and the other faculty. I was proud of her. I loved how her whole aura lit up when she talked about her work. Why hadn't I ever seen how much her job meant to her instead of pushing her to approve of my work?

She handed me a cup of hot chocolate, then sat next to me on the loveseat.

"There's a Comic-Con in Albany next weekend."

"Yeah. I'd planned to go with Sean."

"I figured you might. I rented a Borg costume, thought I'd go as Seven."

"Jeri Ryan's portrayal will pale next to yours," I said. "You're going Saturday?"

"Our worship team has a concert Sunday. So, yeah."

"Interesting, I was thinking about going as Chakotay. I'll look for you."

She set her hot chocolate down, turned toward me, and scowled. "You're as dense as the day we met."

What was I missing? "Are you asking me to go with you?"

She nodded. "If you want to."

I bobbled. Not sure what to say.

"Of course, I haven't totally made up my mind about my costume."

She leaned in and kissed me, a kiss so tender, I mustered all my will power not to take advantage of her. What if she were just lonely? I didn't want to jeopardize our friendship over momentary temptation. I reluctantly pulled away.

"Saturday, then? I'll pick you up at ten. What about Trisha?"

She sighed, then offered a teasing smile. "I hired a sitter."

We'd had a crazy Friday night at the precinct, and I didn't get off duty until four in the morning. Nor could I sleep. I thought I should cancel my date with Shayla ... I wouldn't be very good company. *No. She might be looking forward to the diversion and adult company.* I downed three more cups of coffee, then went to my stash of costumes. I pulled out Chakotay's First Officer's red uniform, then returned it to the closet. On impulse, I pulled out my old Han Solo garb. I hadn't worn the outfit since the night I met Shayla. Did it still fit?

A little snug in the waist, otherwise okay.

I cut a slit on either side of the waistband and found two rubber bands to act like elastic, fastening them with safety pins, assured the repair would at least hold up for the day. Proud of my innovation, I slipped into my costume, invigorated by meeting a challenge, then flipped my keys into the air and caught them on the descent. Too much caffeine? Maybe. But I chose to believe my lifted mood was more about the chance to spend time with Shayla. I felt like a boy on his way to pick up his prom date.

I'd always loved her from the moment she walked down the aisle of that movie theater. Seemed like a century ago, not just a decade. I wasn't that bitter man anymore. Shayla had changed too. Yet, we were still the same somehow in so many ways. We'd lived apart for two years, but I'd grown more deeply in love with her than I had ever imagined possible ... though still uncertain how Shayla felt about me. She'd forgiven me—grace I hadn't deserved. But did she love me ... the new me ... the sober me who loved the Lord?

I gasped as she opened the door. My questions forever answered.

Shayla was never one to be mushy. No romantic poems on the cards she gave. Love, in her way of thinking, was not a bouquet of roses. Love was better demonstrated through effort, through little things. "Love is seen, not spoken," she'd often said.

"I see you finally got the hint, Han." Her red hair was bound in braided buns, her long white tunic, set off with a silver belt—a vision from so many years ago. Her eyes, full of hope, misted as she met my confused gaze. "Time to come home, Dave."

I pulled her into my arms, and she returned my kiss with impossibly more passion than I could hope for. As I held her, so close our hearts beat as one, I whispered in her ear, "You'll always be my favorite Leia."

The End

Linda Wood Rondeau

An award-winning author, Linda Wood Rondeau writes stories that grip the heart, inspired by her nearly thirty years of social work. She enjoys golf and spending time with her best friend, her husband of nearly forty-five years. The couple resides in Hagerstown, Maryland where both are active in their local church. Readers may learn more about the author, read her blog, or sign up for her newsletter by visiting: www.lindarondeau.com

Facebook:https://www.facebook.com/lindawoodrondeau

Instagram:https://www.instagram.com/authorlindawoodrondeau/

Tea for Two

PeggySue Wells

Chapter 1

FEBRUARY

Trina Troyer perched on the stool at the Troyer Elevator check-out counter. Comparing features and price, she checked squares in the business manual's spreadsheet. The February sun reflected across the bright pamphlets, and she inhaled the tangy scent of cedar shavings from the bags stacked on a nearby pallet. Hearing footsteps, she quickly closed and slid the book beneath a catalog of horse tack.

Her father came around the corner and glanced at the pile of product brochures. "What are you doing with those?"

"Reading." She smoothed her homemade dress. "Maybe I can help a customer—"

"Your place is in the home." Her father hitched his suspender. "As soon as your brother can, he will return to farming and helping here at the elevator. At age eighteen, it's time—"

"To be thinking of a home of my own. I know, I know." She spread her hands. "*Dat*, I like business more than cleaning, cooking, and laundry."

"Which is why you are here the days Jonas must be with his wife and the new *boppli*." He settled his reading spectacles over eyes that were so like her own. "Then he will help with the farming and the elevator where he is supposed to be, and you will help at home where you are supposed to be. It is Deitch wege."

The many logical arguments she longed to launch against her father's rigid tendency to compartmentalize the world crowded into her throat. While most people in their Amish community thought twice about arguing with this community elder and his old fashioned adherence to the Dutch ways, Trina didn't feel so hesitant. There were aspects of the Ordnung that no longer made sense to her.

Still, the elevator's store was not the time or place to unleash her opinions. The focus of the workplace centered on the customer and providing an inviting atmosphere for shopping.

But as her father dropped his gaze, Trina knew his thoughts had gone to his grandson. Half a year old, Oliver thrived ... but what would life look like for someone born without feet?

From the rear of the building, the doorbell announced a delivery. "That's the shipment." Caleb pulled the ever-ready pair of work gloves from his pocket. "Come get me when a customer comes in."

"I'll find you if they need more than I can do."

He shook his head. "I'll take care of customers."

When he disappeared to the loading dock, she surveyed the neat shelves, feeling like a store owner from one of the Little House on the Prairie books. But instead of Laura and her Pa, a pretty woman with hair the color of cinnamon came inside. She waved a cheery hello as she walked directly to the paint section.

After a few minutes, Trina went to her. "Can I help you find something?"

In one hand the customer held a quart can, in the other a packet of powder. "I have several pieces of furniture that need to look the same." She raised the can. "Chalk paint gives uniform coverage but requires several coats."

Trina guessed this must be the new neighbor who had been refurbishing the Old Traction Barn. The building had always fascinated Trina, who made up imaginary stories about the property's history and past residents. The place inspired ideas. After sitting vacant for a long time, a new owner arrived last August. Lights remained on late into the night, and a pregnant paint mare came to graze in the corral attached to the pole barn.

At Christmas, Trina had visited the showroom. The transformation of the Old Traction Barn's exterior looked as if the historic structure received a facelift. Inside, the repurposed furniture, the brightly lit Douglas fir tree in the full window, and the aroma of cloves with a hint of furniture polish had charmed her senses. When the mare gave birth in time for Christmas, the local paper ran a touching story about the baby in the Old Traction Barn.

"Milk paint requires fewer coats." Indicating the package, the customer considered. "Fewer coats, less work."

"And the finish lasts longer without a sealant," Trina added.

She nodded. "But milk paint risks spoilage if I don't use it quickly."

Trina agreed. "And mixing smaller batches risks an uneven consistency."

"Exactly." The customer held the two products as if weighing them on a scale. "Hence my dilemma."

Trina recalled her earlier reading. "You may have a third option."

She brightened. "Do tell."

Back at the counter, Trina sorted through her papers until she found the product brochure. "This company produces premixed milk paint in cans like traditional paint."

"Who knew?" She grinned at Trina. "You knew. Do you have some?"

"The information about this new product just arrived. But," she thought for a moment. "Usually there is ..." Searching the shelf that held manufacturer samples, she found the quart and set the paint can on the counter.

The customer studied the ingredients. "This looks worth a try."

"You take our sample, and let us know if this is a product worth stocking."

"Deal." The woman added a package to her order. "And I'll buy a sack of apple horse treats."

Hearing the door at the loading dock slam closed, Trina's muscles tensed. Could she finish this transaction before her father saw what she was doing?

She rang up the purchase and placed the items into a sack. "Let me know what you think of the paint."

From the corner of her eye, she noticed her father come into the room. Disapproval clouded his face, but he quickly changed his expression when the customer turned to him.

"Hello, Mr. Troyer." She pulled the package of horse treats from her bag. "Your recommendation for these apple bites is spot on. The foal pays attention to his training knowing these are in my pocket."

Her father dipped his head, accepting the compliment.

The cheery woman glanced at her watch. "Speaking of which, I gotta get back to the Old Traction Barn to meet the new farrier."

Trina came around the counter and handed the user instructions about the premixed milk paint to the customer.

"By the way"—the customer held out her hand—"I'm Larkin Hammond. From the Old Traction Barn. I appreciate that you know so much about the products. You helped solve my problem."

Trina liked the feel of Larkin's firm business-like handshake. "Trina."

At the door, Larkin turned back. "Better yet, Trina, stop by and see how the paint turns out. I'd like your professional opinion."

Chapter 2

The following week, Trina felt melancholy as she fronted the shelves of her father's store. She added newborn kitten bottles to this week's order, remembering when the Mennonite pastor's children nursed a nest of baby rabbits their dog had carefully carried home from who knew where.

Her older brother, Jonas, had returned to work at the elevator that morning. Jonas and her father quickly settled into their easy routine of running the business. Jonas shouldered the deliveries and pick-ups that were handled through the wide back doors. Her father helped customers find and purchase the products they needed. After spending extra time with the spring chicks and ducklings, Trina switched out the winter horse blankets for fly spray and fly masks, popular spring items.

"Just the girl I want to see."

Trina turned to see Larkin Hammond and realized she had been so self-absorbed she had not heard anyone come inside.

Dat greeted his customer. "Good day, Larkin. What are you looking for today?"

She turned to her father. "I need a halter the next size up for the foal."

"He is growing good, then." Checking the tags, Dat lifted a blue nylon halter. "Here is a size medium. What else can I help you find?"

"Please hold that for me." Larkin then turned to Trina. "Remember the paint you showed me last time I was here?"

"Chalk versus milk paint." Trina glanced at her father who stood awkwardly for a moment before accepting that the continuing conversation did not include him.

"I'll have this waiting at the counter while you shop." He carried the halter to the front of the store.

Trina led the way to the section where cans of paint stood like soldiers ready for duty.

"Did you like the sample?"

Larkin waved a hand to the packets of powder. "It's marvelous stuff. When will you have that brand available here at the elevator?"

Trina considered the shelves. "That's a good question. I'll let you know when I know."

"I'll order a case." Larkin purchased her horse tack. On her way out, she called to Trina, "Be sure to stop by and see how that sample looks on the furniture I painted."

By lunchtime, Trina had worked herself out of a job. Thankfully, the mail arrived with catalogs for cedar shingles and battery powered chainsaws. The catalogs reminded Trina of the order forms tucked inside her business textbook for the milk paint Larkin liked.

As if on cue, her father put a hand on her shoulder. "You did a good job, *dochder.*"

"And I can go home," she finished for him.

"*Jah.*" He inclined his head toward the sun streaming bright through the window. "Plenty of time to be of help at home to your mother as you have been for me."

February in Indiana included the possibility of any kind of weather. Today's brisk and sunny disposition had been inviting enough for Trina to bypass the buggy in favor of her bicycle. Pedaling out of town, she remembered Larkin's invitation to stop in at the Old Traction Barn.

And, okay, she admitted as she parked her bike, the stop delayed her return to household drudgery.

Several cars were parked outside as well as a tour bus. The bell announced her entry, and Trina once again felt the welcome invitation of the faint scent of furniture polish. Larkin busily disassembled an antique wash stand, and packed the basin in layers of bubble wrap within a box. A line of customers stood at the cash register checking their watches. Trina guessed the Old Traction Barn to be a timed stop for the passengers on the tour bus.

"Hey, Trina," Larkin called.

"Hey back." She glanced from Larkin to the people lined up at the counter. The tour guide held her wrist high in the air and tapped the face of her watch. "Fifteen minutes, ladies, until we are back on the bus. Complete your purchases and bring them to the driver to load into the luggage compartment."

Those waiting to make a purchase looked panicked. Trina went to the cash register, relieved the machine operated similar to the one at the elevator. She smiled at the first person in line. "How can I help you?"

In minutes, Trina had rung up and bagged packages for the shoppers. Larkin wrapped several pieces of refinished furniture pieces and rolled them to the bus on a handcart. With a throaty roar, the tour bus departed for their next scheduled stop.

"Nice work." Larkin gave a relieved grin. "You arrived like the proverbial cavalry."

The description reminded Trina of a Zane Grey novel.

Larkin waved her over to a farmhouse dining table. "Look how this is finished with the milk paint you gave me."

A semi-gloss, the country white paint lay smooth. Appreciative of the quality, Trina ran her fingers along the edge. "How did the texture spread?"

"Dreamy. And cleaned up easily with water." Larkin indicated the matching benches that looked as nice as the table. "I have an armoire I'd like to refinish with that brand of paint. How soon will you carry it at the elevator?"

Trina fetched her backpack from behind the counter where she had left it with her coat to help customers. From the main pocket, she produced her business textbook crammed with papers between the pages. She pulled out the order forms and handed them to Larkin. "Actually, my father doesn't plan to expand the paint products. Here is the manufacturer's contact. You can see about carrying this brand at the Old Traction Barn."

Larkin considered the wardrobe. "That would be a two-fer for me."

"Two-fer?"

"Two purposes for one. I could get the paint I prefer to use at cost, and customers who like what they see on display can purchase the same brand for DIY projects."

"DIY?" Mentally, Trina pedaled fast to keep up with the terms this business owner used.

"Do It Yourself. It's trending currently."

Trina shook her head. "In the Amish community, that's always been the way we do things."

"No wonder you are an expert at so many skills. Customer service, cashier, product information, problem solving, business development." Larkin glanced out the window as a vehicle turned in the drive by the barn. She gestured to the surrounding room. "Take a look around and let me know what improvements you recommend."

Halfway out the door, Larkin called back, "Ring up any customers who come in, I'll be back in a few."

Alone in the Old Traction Barn, Trina took a slow tour of the rooms. Applying what she learned in her business books, she admired what Larkin had done to turn the neglected building into a welcoming business. Inside the cover of her book, she made a list of possible additions.

When Larkin returned, Trina sat on a stool at the counter. Bent over her business manual, she cross-referenced several product brochures with her list. Looking up, she noticed someone had come inside with Larkin.

Not much taller than she, the young man wore cowboy boots, a buckle large enough to use for a dinner plate, his muscled arms and shoulders filling his shirt. He looked as if he had walked off the page of Zane Grey's *Knights of the Range.*

Coming around the counter, Larkin opened the cash register and removed several twenty dollar bills. "Trina, this is Bailey Wayne, our farrier. Bailey, this is Trina who is a smart businesswoman."

"Hello." Bailey removed his hat. "A pleasure to meet you."

A single word jumped into Trina's thoughts. *Gorgeous.*

Chapter 3

At home the next day, perpetual tasks kept Trina busy, though her heart longed for something more. She recalled the warmth she felt when Larkin introduced her to Bailey as a smart businesswoman. Replaying the moment over and over in her thoughts led to remembering the handsome cowboy.

Once she had dinner simmering on the stove, she found her mother outdoors folding laundry.

"I have a book at the library I'd like to pick up." Trina removed the clothes pins holding a billowing sheet. Stiff from hanging on the line outdoors, the bedding smelled like the fresh spring breeze that blew the fabric dry.

Her mother added a folded towel to the pile in her basket. "See if the next Jan Karon book is available to read aloud after Scripture this evening. And *Hank the Cowdog*."

With the books to return stacked in her basket, Trina rode her bicycle to town. The cool bite in the air stung her cheeks and affirmed her freedom. She liked to work, and she appreciated the fine art of homemaking. Yet, Trina found the perpetual staying home to be isolating. Being among people in a fashion that made a difference in a larger circle felt like a better fit.

The librarian brightened when Trina arrived. She turned and retrieved a parcel from the shelf behind her desk and handed it to Trina. "I thought this would interest you."

Held together in a rubber band, Trina found the latest Jan Karon book for her mother, two *Hank the Cowdog* titles, and a book about business. "Thank you, these are exactly what I came for."

The librarian beamed. "Sometimes I find a resource that seems exactly right for an exact person."

Trina recalled the paint sample that had been a fit for Larkin's refinishing project. "I feel that way when I have a product at the elevator that solves a customer's problem."

Curious to see if Larkin had decided to stock the paint for DIY projects, Trina stopped at the Old Traction Barn. Inside, Larkin, Tobias, and to Trina's delight, Bailey were talking animatedly at the counter. Larkin smiled her welcome to Trina. The local veterinarian, Tobias gave a casual wave of greeting. Having been alone for a long time after his wife died, Tobias was what Dat called *sweet* on the interior decorator who had taken possession of the Old Traction Barn last summer.

Bailey stood taller. "Hello, Trina, nice to see you again."

Larkin came forward. "As always, your timing is the best." She gestured to the men. "I'd like to go to the barn with them for a short time. Would you watch the store?"

Someone wanted her business skills. "Of course."

"Thank you. And then if you have time after, I'd like to talk. Can you stay for tea?"

"That would be nice." She glanced toward Bailey. Did he like tea?

The bell over the front door announced the arrival of a customer. Larkin mouthed her thanks and disappeared out the side door toward the barn with Tobias and Bailey.

Trina approached the two women who had come into the store. One looked to be in her fifties, and the other appeared to be her mother. Both wore weariness like a sweater. "Is there something I can help you find?"

"We saw a writeup in the newspaper around Christmas about this place." The younger of the two indicated her companion. "Mother is coming to live nearby, and we are furniture shopping."

The older woman ran a hand along an antique hutch. "My grandmother had a piece like this."

"Do you have a style, a color, or a room in mind?" Trina watched tears form in the eyes of both women and wondered what she had said amiss. Apparently the furniture business worked vastly different from the elevator business.

The younger woman fished tissue from her purse and pressed one into her mother's hand. "Please forgive us." She wiped her own tears. "We recently said goodbye to my father. As if that isn't hard enough, now Mama must move from their home to a new address."

"That is a lot." Trina wondered what would be comforting at such a time. "Would you both like a cup of tea?"

The older woman touched Trina's arm. "I drink tea when I'm happy, when I'm sad, and when a kind girl in the furniture shop offers."

Trina patted the woman's blue-veined hand. "Take your time looking around, and I'll make tea."

In the kitchen, Trina found tea fixings that Larkin had together for easy preparation. Apparently, Larkin commonly included tea in her day. From the options, Trina made a pot of lemon ginger, filled two cups, and sweetened them with honey. Placing the tray on an antique tea cart in the showroom, she took a cup to each of her shoppers.

While the women talked, Trina went outside to retrieve the new business book from her bicycle basket. Glancing toward the barn, she spotted Larkin perched on the corral fence while Tobias led the mare, Noel, across the corral. The colt followed his mother as babies do, and Bailey filmed with a camcorder. Back inside, Trina noted the women were talking more than crying which she took to be a good sign.

When Larkin returned without the two men, Trina introduced her to their guests sitting on a loveseat as they contemplated the antique hutch. "Could you match this hutch to my mother's furniture?"

"That should be doable." Larkin looked at the teacups in their hands. "Would you like a refill while you tell me what you are looking for?"

Trina left Larkin to finalize details with her shoppers and returned to the counter and the chapter in her business book about ancillary products.

When the women left, Larkin read over notes Trina had taken during her conversation with the customers. "The tea proved to be soothing."

"From our short conversation, I gathered their hearts are broken."

"Perceptive." Larkin indicated the teapot. "Is there enough for two more?"

Seated at the refinished farm table, Larkin tapped the tabletop. "Thanks to you, the shop will carry the milk paint I like so well. The exact stuff used to give new life to this dining set. I'd like to know what else you recommend for the Old Traction Barn."

"Well ..." Trina glanced around.

Larkin leaned forward. "You've got a strong business head. I'm asking for your best ideas. Don't be shy and don't hold back."

"Well," Trina began again. "Once the paint is in, offer classes where people bring their own pieces and learn how to refinish using your products. For wedding and bridal showers, and birthday parties, provide simple pieces like serving trays, jewelry boxes, or bird feeders. For Christmas, the options are unlimited."

Nodding, Larkin wrote notes. "Go on."

"For employee team building exercises, arrange for companies to redo furniture or signs or something for the community."

"Like refinishing the pews at the Mennonite church." Larkin clicked the pen. "Like your Amish barn raisings except focused on other projects to benefit the community. And I can provide supplies at cost."

Trina relaxed. Far from making fun, this business owner found merit in her suggestions. "What about a Mother's Day drawing for a room redo? Give college students an internship to do your advertising, website, and help with marketing. You could make the flower beds around the building available for experimental gardens and seed observation."

"With the produce going to the community food cupboard."

"At your Black Friday grand opening, you served hot cider. How about a large urn with complimentary hot tea in the cold months and iced tea in the hot?"

"Your offer of tea grounded our shoppers today. Gave them something calming and familiar in the midst of confusing upheaval."

"Tea is a cup of comfort my mother says." Trina indicated an area by the large front window. "What about a tea room? Simple with light fare."

Larkin considered. "I could offer work experience for high schoolers and college students studying hospitality."

"The space could host book clubs and Bible studies which bring in regular customers."

Tobias and Bailey came in the side door. Was his gaze her imagination or was Bailey actually pleased to see her?

Larkin waved them to the table. Tobias brushed a kiss on Larkin's cheek as he took the seat beside her. Bailey removed his hat and sat in the remaining chair near Trina.

"What do you think?" Larkin glanced from Tobias to Bailey.

"You are right, Larkin. The colt has something odd in his gait. What, I'm not sure"—Tobias hooked a thumb toward Bailey—"so I asked this expert for his opinion."

"I have a suspicion," the farrier put in, "but want to look into it more."

"Is that why you used the video camera?" Trina had met a lot of farriers over the years who cared for the farm horses her father and Jonas used in the fields as well as the buggy horses who smoothly got them around town. None of them had recording equipment.

"I'll be able to look at the images in slow motion, even frame by frame. Usually that comparison reveals what I can't see in normal observation." He grinned at Tobias. "And what this experienced vet can't see even with his glasses on."

Tobias leaned back. "I'm eager to see what you and your high tech toys diagnose."

Trina frowned. "A video camera is high tech?"

Tobias laughed heartily. "Precisely."

"Do you have a video camera?" Bailey snapped his fingers. "Oh yeah, that's why you called me."

Chapter 4

On the days Jonas prepared the fields for planting, Trina filled in at the elevator. While men worked, Dat referred to Trina's days in the store as helping out.

Larkin popped by in the morning hours before her own shop opened. "Trina, just the person I'm looking for." She selected a package of apple treats and set the bag on the counter. "The paint and display arrived yesterday. Would you be interested in setting it up."

"Sure." Trina visualized the store and where the new product should go. She thought about Bailey as he observed Noel and her colt.

As if reading her mind, Larkin added, "If you come tomorrow, Bailey is showing Tobias and me what he found about the colt's movement. The day would be a—"

"Two-fer," they said together.

With Jonas at the elevator, the following day Trina biked to the Old Traction Barn. "I think the paint display works near the studio. Easy to access for classes and for customers."

"I'll leave you to it," Larkin said after they moved furniture to make space for the display. In short order,

Trina arranged color charts and samples near rows of paint cans ready for purchase.

Larkin inspected her work. "I knew you would know how to make this fit." She beckoned Trina to a sitting area. "I'd like to offer you a job here at the Old Traction Barn."

Trina sat straighter. Not a request to help out, but a job.

"I know the elevator is a family business so you may have responsibilities there. And I'd like you to set up that tea room you suggested, help me coordinate classes and community projects, and manage the store occasionally." She went to the counter and returned with a file folder. "I put a job description together, so you know what you are getting into. We can make adjustments."

Opening the folder, Trina found a neatly typed outline including monthly salary, holidays, and benefits. Her heart leapt to be recognized as a businesswoman. "I'll consider this and get back to you."

Larkin folded her hands. "There is one more thing."

Was this too good to be true? "What's that?"

"I'd really like to continue to hear and consider your ongoing ideas about making the Old Traction Barn all it can be. Business is always in flux because people and life continually change. To succeed, we have to meet the current needs of our customers."

We. Trina felt eager to read through the offer.

The bell announced visitors as Tobias trooped in with Bailey at his heels. Trina wrinkled her nose. She recognized the smell.

"I told him he's not fit to use the front door." Bailey removed his hat.

"Oh my." As they approached, Larkin put a hand over her nose. "What happened?"

"Well, based on the evidence I'd say Tobias went swimming in the overflow pond or—"

"Never mind." Tobias glanced down at his soiled clothing. "You all go ahead and talk, I'm gonna shower and be back as soon as I can."

"Mighty thoughtful of you," Bailey called as Tobias shut the door behind him.

Larkin stifled a laugh. "What is that smell?"

Bailey shrugged. "I can't wait to find out. We pulled up at the same time. He got out of the truck lookin' huffy as a hen tossed in the horse trough."

"I'd say he got dragged through pig poop," Trina said.

Bailey sniffed the air and considered. "Betcha lunch out, you're right."

The door opened and an oversized bouquet of flowers preceded the town florist. "Larkin, I'm here to talk about cross marketing." She frowned. "Girl, what is that smell?"

"That's gotta be the best timing ever." Bailey glanced toward Larkin.

"Is that?" The florist sniffed. "Girl, you got a pig in here?"

"Just the poop." Bailey placed a tally mark in the air. "Score one for Trina."

Larkin buried her nose in the blooms and inhaled deeply. "You have saved the day. Let's get these in vases around the showroom."

"I'm going to the barn where it smells better." Bailey settled his hat back on his head. "Trina, can you come along while I check a couple things with the horse?"

She grabbed her coat and fell into step beside him. Outdoors, the sun shown on the greening grass.

Bailey took her jacket and held it for her to put on. "I assume you have experience with horses and the like."

"Kinda part of the lifestyle." She gestured to her homemade dress.

"Excellent. If you can lead the colt for me, I have another test to run."

Hearing them approach, Noel nickered a welcome. Inside the barn, Trina placed several miniature candy canes in one pocket and apple treats in her other. Bailey put a halter on Noel and the new blue one from the elevator on the colt.

Following his instructions, Trina led the colt through fast and slow turns, backed up, and stood while the farrier carefully palpated the young horse's legs and hooves. Crossing his arms, he stood and considered the colt who eagerly accepted the apple treats from Trina's pocket. Next, Trina did much of the same movements with Noel.

At the sound of truck tires on the gravel drive outside the barn, Noel nickered a welcome. Minutes later, Tobias strode to the corral looking well-scrubbed and handsome. He gave a candy cane to Noel and her colt.

"You clean up nice," Bailey acknowledged. "Pig?"

Tobias scratched the colt under his chin. "Yep."

Bailey grinned at Trina. "Lunch out."

Chapter 5

March

March brought Trina to work at the Old Traction Barn and the addition of a tea room. Trina sketched a rough design, and she and Larkin began assembly between helping customers and the normal tasks required to keep shop. Tobias stopped by after his veterinary rounds to do the heavy lifting.

According to schedule, Trina was ready to serve her first cup of tea with an Alice in Wonderland theme. She and Larkin had joked that the notion of a tea room would be either good for business or an idea as crazy as the March hare. Opening day, the Garden Club and the Book Club had reservations for lunch, but Trina wanted someone to practice on first. She unlocked the door and turned the sign to open. Minutes later, the bell over the door announced a visitor.

The tall, long-limbed man was not who she envisioned as her first customer. "Hello," she greeted and motioned for him to follow her to a table by the window. She ran down the list of teas as he awkwardly folded himself into the cafe chair. "The opening day special is Savannah Grey with honey and cream. What can I get for you?"

He glanced around the shop. "Excuse me?"

"Would you like something off the menu or the special?"

He shifted and the chair squeaked. "The special?"

In minutes, Trina brought the pot and poured the steeped brew into an Old Albert China cup.

Carrying a clipboard, Larkin came out of her office. She smiled at their guest and tapped the schedule. "Trina, we have a tour bus stopping in the afternoon in addition to the two reservations."

Trina nodded, and felt herself blush as Bailey came in.

"Mornin'." He took off his hat and smiled at the women. "Larkin, I'm meeting a fella from Purdue Veterinary Hospital to check my theory about"—he glanced toward the guest at the table—"Tapeworm! There you are."

Suddenly Trina realized why the man had appeared so out of place. "Poor man, I thought he was my first tea customer."

The cafe chair squeaked as their guest stood, looking sheepish.

The farrier glanced from his friend to Trina. "Of course he's your first customer. That's why I asked him to meet me here."

"Tapeworm?" Larkin shifted the clipboard.

"He outeats Noel and still maintains his girlish figure." Bailey walked to his friend. "Whatever he's having, Trina, I'd like some too. And two cups to go for our heavy-duty consultation at the barn."

"This is pretty good, actually." Tapeworm finished the contents of his cup which appeared comically small in his long fingers.

Tobias came in, and Bailey called, "Make that order for three, Trina. The vet is picking up the tab."

An hour later, the three men were back from the barn. "We have a diagnosis and treatment plan." Tobias pulled two tables together and waved Larkin and Trina to join them.

Bailey played clips on his video camera. The slow motion made the irregularity in the colt's gait easy to spot. "A hereditary condition involving a contracted tendon in his neck and shoulder causes the shorter step when he turns the opposite direction."

"Hereditary?" Larkin frowned. "But Noel doesn't do this."

"Not now, but I suspect we will see signs later." Tobias showed film clips of Noel. "Hormones loosen her ligaments and tendons to stretch for pregnancy and delivery."

Trina thought about the limitations her nephew faced. "Can it be fixed?"

"I think we can equalize the tissue on both sides with a combination of physical therapy ..." the man from Purdue nodded to the farrier.

"And gradual adjustments in the way the hoof is trimmed by yours truly."

Trina stifled an eager grin. She looked forward to seeing Bailey often.

Larkin appeared hopeful. "What about Noel?"

"The timing couldn't be better in both cases." The visitor indicated the video camera. "We can work with the advantage of the hormones in Noel's system to remind the tendons to remain elongated. The colt is young, and his body is responsive."

"First question is always, can we fix it?" Bailey held up one finger and then the second. "Next, if we can't fix it, how can we adapt to make it work."

Tobias tipped his chair back on two legs. "And Tapeworm will document the results to share with the Purdue veterinary school."

"And with the Tennessee farrier school." Bailey clapped the man on the shoulder.

"Is there a name we can call you besides ..." Larkin appeared hesitant to say the word.

"Besides Tapeworm?" He gave a wry smile. "Won't make any difference. To Bailey, I've been Tapeworm since we met in Tennessee."

Trina left the table to prepare tea for customers, and Bailey followed. "I'd like to ask your father if I can take you to lunch."

She turned to study his expression. Was he serious?

"With your permission." The question reflected in his gaze.

If only ... but she knew her father's answer already. "My father—"

"I'll talk to him, but only if you are agreeable."

Gorgeous. She recalled her first thought about Bailey. And the word continued to fit. "Lunch out?"

"You did solve the mystery around that smell."

Chapter 6

The following week, Bailey arrived midday at the Old Traction Barn. "Got time for a picnic?"

Larkin and Trina left the shop in the capable hands of the college intern. Outdoors, Tobias set up four picnic tables. "We just doubled the seating for the Tea Shop."

Bailey waved Trina to a table and unpacked a picnic basket. "Meat sandwiches for the men, and I took a guess Larkin and Trina would want quiche and salad."

Anna, the pretty local midwife, arrived. "Hey, everyone."

Bailey produced a fresh sandwich from the basket. "Thanks for popping by."

"Thanks for bribing me with lunch." Anna sat on the girls' side of the table.

"I owe you lunch out." Bailey said to Trina. "Your dad wasn't fond of the idea, so I brought lunch to you."

"The first time I had take-out from the local diner was the day the colt was born," Larkin said. "Tobias brought extra-large servings of breakfast."

"And extra-large cups of hot chocolate," Anna said. "What a wonder to find a baby in the barn after waiting those months."

Two women exited the shop with iced tea and settled at another table. "These tables are—"

"A two-fer," Larkin and Trina said together.

As they finished lunch, Tobias gathered the food wrappers and tossed them in the trash. "Larkin and Anna, come to the barn and I'll show you the exercises we'll do daily on the horses."

Bailey rested his arms on the table. "Looks like I'll stop in weekly to tend the horses' feet. After two months, we'll reevaluate the colt's gait."

"Using your high-tech video camera."

He grinned. "You gotta admit, the slow motion feature is a diagnostic wonder."

April and May were two of the happiest months for Trina. Weekly, Bailey brought something in the picnic basket from his travels to care for his clients' horses. Sometimes, Larkin and Tobias ate with them, and Anna, when she wasn't delivering a baby. Calling themselves the Lunch Bunch, they played scrabble and Dutch Blitz, told humorous stories and shared books. When the spring rains poured, they ate in the tea shop.

Occasionally, when Larkin had the shop easily in hand, Trina held the horses while Bailey trimmed, then helped with the physical therapy exercises. After lunch, Anna went with Bailey to the barn while Trina returned to the business of the Old Traction Barn.

Anna came inside one afternoon to order iced tea. "How is your nephew?" Her cheeks were flushed from exercising the colt in the spring air.

"He has a tooth coming in." Trina pictured Oliver's grin.

The midwife smiled. "Right on time."

"You were the first to see him." Trina put ice in a tall cup. "That must have been rugged."

Anna stared blankly out the window. "Oliver's birth was the night I met Larkin. The lights were on at the Old Traction Barn so even though it was the middle of the night, I knocked. She invited me inside and made tea."

Trina filled the cup with Earl Grey. "A cup of comfort."

"That's what your mom calls it. I drank a lot of comfort tea at your house when I was growing up."

They were quiet, remembering. Trina recalled the tea parties Anna and Jonas had good naturedly shared with her using her child-size cups. As a girl, Trina expected her older brother and Anna to always be together. Now that she was older she saw the complication of a relationship between the Amish young man and the girl from the chaotic worldly home next door who found welcome and solace with the Troyer family. When Anna went to midwifery school, Jonas married someone else. Someone Amish.

Anna hooked a thumb toward the barn. "The morning after Oliver's birth, Larkin introduced me to Noel. There is something comforting about that horse."

Trina added a lid and gave the cup to the midwife. "And something special about the people the horse draws to her."

"Thanks for the update," Anna said. "I think of him often."

Trina wondered if Anna meant Oliver or Jonas.

As Bailey and Anna spent regular time together, Trina suspected they were becoming fond of one another. And why not? Both were young and adventurous, had lucrative careers, and were not fettered by the constraints of Amish ways. They would make a lovely couple. Despite the laughter they shared and the weekly picnics, a romance with Bailey was impossible for Trina. They lived in different worlds. She would have to learn to squelch the longing that zinged through her every time she saw Bailey.

Chapter 7

JUNE

In early June, Trina rode in the buggy with her parents to the countywide Strawberry Festival. The event took place at the square dance caller's oversized barn. Having given up chicken farming years earlier, he had converted the barn into an event center popular for weddings, family reunions, and civic gatherings.

Today, the barn housed a cake walk, pin the hat on the scarecrow, and tables filled with food. A fiddle player and his band provided toe-tapping music for listening, and the local square dance club served as entertainment.

Outdoors, a maze in the strawberry field was the perfect height for children to follow and not get lost. Folks could go on a hayride, toss water balloons at a target, and play volleyball. Tobias coordinated with several neighbors to supply a petting zoo with a llama, donkey, cow, a pair of Nubian goats, rabbits, a goose, a turtle, and Noel and her colt. Noel's stage debut as part of the cast in last year's Christmas pageant had made her an instant celebrity around town. Shortly after the pageant, she birthed her baby, and the picture of mother and foal became front page news on Christmas day.

In the midst of crowds for events like today's festival, Noel tirelessly received awkward pats and heartfelt hugs from children, and gently received their offerings of apples, carrots, and candy. She had a particular fondness for candy canes. At his mother's side, the colt followed Noel's example and seemed to Trina to pose for photos.

Seeing Jonas arrive with his family, Trina held out her arms for her nephew. "You two enjoy a sit down meal, and I'll take him around to see the animals."

Her sister-in-law smiled her thanks. Jonas put an arm around his wife, and they followed the music inside.

"Hey there, big boy." Trina tousled his blonde head as she carried him to the petting zoo. "Let's pat a horse."

Oliver kicked his legs with glee as the colt nuzzled the boy's pockets in hopes of a treat.

"I'm not sure who likes who best." Tobias stood with his arms crossed, observing the colt's interest in Trina's nephew. Using the colt's ears as handles, Oliver pressed his forehead against the soft fur of the animal's neck.

"He gravitates to animals, and they seem to respond to him." Trina set him on Noel's back and held him secure while he grabbed the thick mane with eager fingers.

At the sound of boys yipping like cowboys, the children who had been petting the friendly animals scampered in that direction.

"That'll be Bailey." Tobias resettled his baseball cap.

Trina's heart leapt. "Bailey?"

"Oh yeah," Tobias drawled. "When he offered to teach kids how to rope, I knew he'd steal the show."

"Rope?" Suddenly she couldn't speak in more than single word sentences.

"Oh, yeah"—Tobias hooked a thumb in the direction of the noise—"Bailey is a skilled farrier. But he wins belt buckles, saddles, and even a horse trailer at ropin' contests. The kids will be throwin' loops around their siblings for the rest of the year."

Would Anna be with Bailey?

Tobias shrugged. "C'mon, let's go watch. No one will be pettin' a bunny when they can watch an expert throw a rope."

As the vet predicted, a crowd had taken seats on hay bales set in rows.

At the front, Bailey twirled a rope over his head. "I need a volunteer."

A boy jumped to his feet and stood where the farrier pointed. Bailey easily tossed a loop over his shoulders and the audience applauded.

Bailey waved away the applause. "Anyone can do that schoolboy trick. The real skill comes in looping a moving target." He looked to his volunteer. "Jump up and down."

But instead of throwing his rope over the boy's head once more, Bailey aimed his rope low and caught the jumper's feet so fast the audience gasped in surprise.

"I need four more volunteers who think they can jump faster than I can rope." Immediately, four bright-eyed boys joined the first. "Make like jumping beans," Bailey instructed, and the five jumped as fast as they could.

Bailey nodded to someone Trina could not see, and Anna stepped into view carrying four more lariats. Anna looked stunning in jeans and boots; her hair fell free under a pert cowboy hat. Trina felt her heart drop. She cared deeply for Bailey and Anna. Having feelings for Bailey would only lead to trouble. Like Anna, he was not Amish.

Her nephew bounced in her arms. "You like the roping?" Seeing his excitement, Trina turned her attention back to the front in time to see Bailey's first throw send his rope under a boy's feet to tighten around his knees. The crowd roared.

Anna passed a fresh rope, and Bailey caught the boy on the right end followed by the boy on the left end. The next swing caught the jumper on the right side of the middle. The last boy hopped out of his spot and around the others. The audience laughed at the unexpected attempt to outmaneuver the roper. Bailey feigned being outwitted; but when the boy looked triumphantly toward the audience, Bailey's final rope zipped forward and captured the fifth volunteer.

Surprised and delighted, the audience cheered.

In moments, Bailey freed the boys and rubbed his knuckles playfully over the last kid's head. "Who wants to learn how to rope?"

The five jumped again, this time with their hands in the air. Shouts of "I do" and "pick me" rang out from kids in the audience.

Anna stuck five plastic cow heads into the ends of hay bales while Bailey gave instructions. "Everyone who wants a turn to rope one of these targets, watch me and do what I do." Step by step, the kids and a few grown-ups followed his directions—the way to hold the rope, the wind up, the throw. "That's all there is to it ... except lots and lots of practice."

When the kids scrambled to form five lines, the farrier whistled loud enough that everyone froze. "If you're cowboy enough to throw a rope, you're cowboy enough to stick to the code."

All eyes were on him. He held up a finger. "Number one—girls can throw a rope." He pointed to Anna who swung the lariat over her head three times and sent the loop forward where the rope neatly wrapped around the plastic cow head. Bailey clapped and everyone joined in.

"Number two"—Bailey held up a second finger—"never rope a girl, or anyone who says no, or anyone your parents tell you not to rope."

Trina imagined the time Anna had spent with Bailey to learn how to rope well. While happy for them, Trina wished she could share such moments with Bailey. She glanced down at her clothes. What cowboy wants to show a girl in a plain dress and sensible shoes how to swing a lariat?

Chapter 8

Trina's arms and back began to ache from standing and holding her nephew. She wondered how her sister-in-law did this carrying day after day. She planted a heartfelt kiss on the top of her nephew's head, and breathed in the soft scent of baby shampoo. The nearly one-year-old patted her cheek with a small hand and signed that he wanted down.

"Down is a good idea for both of us." Trina moved to the second row of hay bales setup for observers and sat where she and her nephew could watch what Tobias called organized chaos. Sitting beside her, the little boy waved his arms in excitement. Rolling onto his belly, he pushed himself legs first from his seat as he did when getting down from furniture or going down stairs. To Trina's amazement, once on the straw covered ground, he reached for the haybale in front of him and pulled himself to stand.

Trina gasped. He stood all by himself. Continuing to clutch the tightly packed bale, he carefully, jerkily made his way around to the front where he could see the children helped by their parents to awkwardly spin and swing the rope, missing their target by a country mile. Mesmerized by the activity, he dropped onto his diapered bottom and clapped those small pudgy hands that only moments ago had patted her face.

"I hoped I would see you." Bailey came over to where Trina sat.

She tried to speak but couldn't.

Bailey squatted down near the boy. "You're getting around, buddy-row."

"Did you see that?" Trina's voice squeaked.

"See what?" Bailey followed her gaze to her nephew who pulled himself up again. Using the haybale for leverage, he balanced on his footless legs and reached for Bailey's hat.

"He's walking." Trina blinked. "He's walking, Bailey."

"Of course he is. It's the natural time to be doing such things." The cowboy took off his hat and balanced it on the toddler's head. "He's a year old, right?"

Her nephew tugged on the hat and laughed when it dropped to the ground.

"In two months." She shook her head. "The doctor said he would never walk."

Bailey put his hat back on the boy's head. "Doctors and others say a lot of things. And usually someone proves what can't be done, actually can be done well." The toddler grabbed at the hat and belly laughed every time it toppled to the ground as the two played the hat game. "In my experience, living things are created to move."

Tobias and Larkin approached, his arm around her shoulders. "Nicely done, Bailey. The hardware store will be completely sold out of rope tomorrow."

Larkin sat down next to Trina. "Hey, look at this little fella."

Bailey held his hat over the boy's head. Looking up, Oliver lost his balance and dropped onto his padded bottom. Tobias signaled to Anna, who left her line of roper hopefuls in the capable hands of a parent.

"Hey, Trina,"—Anna glanced around at the small circle—"what's up?"

"Watch." Tobias nodded toward the toddler.

Bailey set his hat on the hay bale, leaving an enticing amount hanging over the edge where the boy could reach for it. Grasping the hay, Oliver pulled himself up. Bailey moved the hat further down and the small boy followed, stepping with one leg and then the next.

Anna bounced on her toes. "This is wonderful. He will be mobile."

Tears coursed down Trina's cheeks as she laughed and cried at the same time, marveling at each step. The boy the doctor said would never walk made a complete pass around the hay bale in pursuit of a worn cowboy hat.

A sudden scream pierced the air. Everyone turned to see Trina's sister-in-law looking horrified. In a blur of movement, she swept in and scooped up her son. "How dare you." She pressed his body tightly against her own. When he squirmed free, he reached for Bailey's hat. "Don't you ever come near my son again. Any of you."

She spun on her heel and rushed away, leaving Jonas stunned and staring at the adults gathered to wonder at his son's accomplishment.

"Jonas, please." Trina stood and stepped toward her brother, but he backed away from her. "Jonas, he can walk. Your son ..."

He put up his hands to ward off her words. Hope and excitement warred with fear and resignation so much so she thought his heart would burst. He gave a last anguished look at Anna. Then as tears filled his eyes, Jonas turned and went after his wife.

Chapter 9

In the following days, Trina's thoughts returned repeatedly to the wonder of her nephew taking his first steps. Having the ability to walk opened great possibilities for his life. *Thank you, God.*

The one person completely unsurprised that night had been Bailey. While Tobias, Larkin, and Anna calmly welcomed the transition, the farrier anticipated, expected, and encouraged her nephew's development. Her sister-in-law's reaction had continued, and she refused to allow Trina to visit or explain that the boy had taken steps on his own volition.

Good news traveled fast in this town and tea room customers shared Trina's delight. Bailey's roping had been the best fun of the festival, and her nephew had renewed everyone's hope regarding what was possible.

As always, the county fair began in mid-June and culminated six days later with an awards ceremony and silent auction to fund 4-H scholarships. Trina arrived with her parents, and they were seated at the table reserved for sponsors. Larkin and Tobias were already seated, Tobias looking weary after an intense week caring for show animals. Jonas and his wife joined the group, sitting next to Trina's mom.

Bailey came into the event center with a teenage boy and an older couple.

The older man looked dapper in a bowler hat with matching cane as they approached the table. Holding the chair for his wife, he spoke loudly for everyone at the table to hear. "I'm Mr. Wayne and this is my bride. And our son, Marc."

"With that last name"—Trina glanced from Bailey to Mark—"you must be related to Bailey."

"Cousins." Marc took the seat to her right, and Bailey took a seat across from Trina between Mrs. Wayne and Tobias. Next to Trina at the twelve-top table was her father and Trina's mother, Jonas and his wife, Larkin and Tobias.

Going around the table, each guest introduced themselves. Throughout the meal, Mr. Wayne became a student of each person, asking about their ideas, interests, and opinions.

Dinner passed quickly and soon their attention was directed to the front of the room. "And now," the emcee announced, "tonight's entertainment features a dazzling presentation."

Music began and the lights dimmed except for a spotlight which rested on the older couple. Mr. Wayne stood, flipped his hat and settled it at a jaunty tilt over one eyebrow. He bowed low toward his wife. Placing her hand in his, she smiled, and he swept her into his arms. With practiced steps, the two glided to the center of the room, and the spotlight illuminated their graceful movements as they moved in tandem to the ballroom dance music.

Trina didn't think she had seen anything as breathtaking as the easy way these dancers merged with the notes. Though Amish considered dancing too worldly, the community remained tolerant of young people dancing during the Rumspringa season, those late teenage years when youth are given opportunity to consider whether to join the Amish church. Of course, Trina had square danced or joined the youth line-dancing on the rare occasion her father was not at an event. But the beauty of the elderly couple was mesmerizing.

When the music ended, the audience stood and applauded. Still holding hands, the couple bowed and returned to their seats.

"Thank you all for attending tonight's fundraiser," the emcee said from the front of the room. "Be certain to get your bids in for the silent auction that will close in fifteen minutes. A lucky winner will receive ballroom dance lessons from our entertainment this evening, Mr. and Mrs. Wayne."

Several people stopped at their table to shake hands with the dancers. "Your dancing is spectacular," Larkin said.

"As the two-step experts that we are"—Tobias looped an arm around Larkin's shoulders—"we'll see if you have room to teach a couple of old dogs some new steps."

Mr. Wayne inclined his head modestly. "The pleasure will be mine."

Bailey dropped a hand on Mr. Wayne's shoulder as he looked toward her father. "If you'd give Mr. Wayne a moment, I'd like him to show you something beyond his dance steps."

Mr. Wayne nodded. "The dance show is impressive, but wait until you see this magic show." He removed his hat. "With your permission, Mr. Troyer."

When her father frowned at Bailey, Trina spoke up. "Yes, please, Mr. Wayne."

"Every so often, it seems to interest someone to know"—he raised the hems of his trousers—"that I don't have feet." Like her nephew, Mr. Wayne's legs ended just below his knees.

Those at the table gasped. Trina's sister-in-law started to leave the table, but Jonas stopped her with a gentle tug on her arm.

"But how ..." Trina looked questioningly at the humble couple. "How can you ..."

"Dance?" Mrs. Wayne rested a hand on her husband's shoulder. "As with everything, with practice and an attitude of how can we make this happen."

Her father spoke softly. "I thought my grandson was the only one."

"Bailey mentioned you have a similar situation in your family." Mr. Wayne shrugged. "Thankfully, a rare condition. Interestingly, we have more in common than feet—or lack of, to be precise."

Trina had a million questions. "What else, Mr. Wayne, do you have in common?"

"I was born Amish." He hooked a thumb over his shoulder. "Not far from here."

Disapproval clouded her father's face. "And you left the faith."

"Never." Mr. Wayne shook his head. "When I was born, my parents were told I could not walk."

Jonas blinked back tears.

"Of course, he walked at the natural time to be doing such things," Bailey added. Trina recalled how Bailey had been the only one not surprised when her nephew took his first steps. "Usually someone proves what can't be done, actually can be done well."

"You don't just walk," Trina felt the wonder of the couple's waltz, "you dance."

Mr. Wayne continued, "God made me this way to bring him glory. My parents sought options to live our faith and aid my development. You know, appointments for prosthetic fittings, physical therapy"—he elbowed Bailey—"dance lessons."

Her father folded his hands on the table; his knuckles were white.

Mr. Wayne nodded. "Many decisions were difficult, as you can imagine. The challenge is to decide which traditions to keep because they have merit. I'm grateful my parents provided opportunities for me."

Chapter 10

Trina ran the elevator while her parents, along with Jonas and his family, had an appointment with a specialist. Mr. Wayne had made arrangements with his medical team, and Bailey drove them to the meeting to talk about Oliver's options.

Trina's emotions danced between hope for her nephew and melancholy about Bailey being always outside of her world. The farrier's willingness to care about her family even when her father had refused to allow Trina and Bailey to formally spend time together warmed her heart toward him even more. And Bailey encouraged her business interests even though they were outside the traditional roles for women in her community.

If Trina married within the Amish faith, as her father wanted, she would soon be using her skills to run a home instead of running a business. The idea felt constricting, she wanted options in the same way her nephew needed options to live without limits. Could she be involved in something larger than herself, to make a difference with a greater circle?

In the afternoon, Trina answered the phone to hear her father on the other end. "If Larkin can spare you for a couple days, can you keep the elevator open?"

Trina hesitated for a moment before answering. "I'm sure that will work with the intern to help. Why, Dat?"

The hope in her father's voice sounded like music. "The doctors are optimistic they can fit Oliver with a prosthetic so he can walk."

Her heart swelled with gratitude. "I'll run the store while you and Jonas take the time you need."

After a pause, her father added, "It's good, daughter, that you have business skills."

Trina held the phone long after the call ended. Her father had recognized her interests.

Several days later, Trina's heartbeat quickened when she saw Bailey's truck park in front of the elevator. She raced out the door to see her family. Bailey got out of the driver's seat, removed his sunglasses, and winked at her.

Jonas unbuckled Oliver from his car seat and handed the boy to her father. Her father came to Trina and set Oliver down. The boy grinned and confidently took toddling steps in her direction. Trina dropped to her knees as Oliver grinned and threw himself into her arms.

Laughing through tears of joy, Trina glanced at her father, then Jonas and then his wife. "It's a miracle."

"With a little practice, he'll be ready for dance lessons." Jonas picked up his son and swung him in a circle.

Her sister-in-law shyly stepped close. "Thank you." Then, looking embarrassed, she stepped back into her carefully maintained distance. Trina caught her hand and squeezed the slender fingers.

Her father nodded to Bailey who leaned against his truck, allowing the family their shared connections. The farrier tucked his sunglasses into his shirt pocket and joined the circle.

Her father nodded. "Jah. Go ahead."

"Trina," Bailey said, "if you are free on Saturday, I'd like to take you to meet my parents."

Two realities took her by surprise. Her father had used an Amish word to someone outside their Amish circle, and he had given Bailey permission to ask. She looked questioningly at Dat.

"Jah," he said again. "You have my blessing."

"Then, yes." Trina allowed an eager smile. "I'd like to go with you on Saturday."

Chapter 11

Early Saturday morning, Trina heard Bailey's truck come down the Troyer's long drive and park. She opened the door to his confident knock, feeling the butterflies in her stomach.

"Mornin'." He removed his ball cap.

"Do we have time for a cup of tea?"

"Certainly." He stepped inside, and she led him to the kitchen where her mother looked up from kneading bread and smiled.

Trina indicated the farm table, and Bailey took a chair. From the pot on the stove, she poured tea and set the cups on the table. Covering the bread dough with a towel to rise, Trina's mom joined them.

Thumbing the small stack of books on the table, Bailey drew out the *Hank the Cowdog* paperback Trina had borrowed from the library. "This is my favorite series, especially *The Case of the Midnight Rustler.*"

Trina's mom laughed. "The children and the adults like these stories. The boys especially are fond of the burping scene."

"Body sounds are always funny to boys." He stirred cream into his tea. "I think the author knows that."

"How did you become a farrier," her mom asked.

He leaned back. "Always liked the horses, and early on figured out that a lot of important factors go into the ability to walk."

Trina recalled his aunt and uncle waltzing at the 4-H awards banquet. "Because of your uncle?"

He nodded. "I applied to a farrier school in Tennessee. When I didn't hear back, my uncle called to check on my application. 'We thought Bailey's app was a joke,' they told him. My uncle assured them I was serious. 'But he's fourteen,' they said. My uncle replied that we had checked their entrance requirements, and age was not listed."

"Fourteen?" Glancing from Bailey to Trina, her mother's expression seemed to convey a realization that these two young people did things a bit differently than most. "What about school?"

"Farrier school took place in the summer." Bailey absently spun his cup in a lazy circle. "My uncle drove me to Tennessee and picked me up when I finished the course."

"Does he drive as well as he dances?"

"Oh, yeah. When I returned home, I fashioned a box that fit on my bike. After school, I rode to the homes of my clients and took care of their horses."

Trina felt her eyes widen. "You started your business when you were fourteen?"

He grinned. "Yep, and I keep adding to my skills."

"Like how to run a video camera."

"I'm particularly fond of that piece of high tech equipment. That's how I met you and your family."

"And now Trina will meet yours." Her mother collected their empty cups, took them to the sink and then returned with a basket. "Here are some things to take to your parents, Bailey. Tell them we are grateful for their warm hospitality during Oliver's appointments with his medical team."

"Yes, ma'am, I will tell them." He took the basket and looked at Trina. "Ready?"

Outdoors, Bailey placed the basket in the back seat, and held the passenger door to his truck for Trina. Motoring away from her small town, Trina marveled at the vast variety around her. Glancing at Bailey, she never would have thought her father would allow her to spend the day with the farrier and certainly not away from their community circle.

Glancing her way, Bailey grinned. "God surprises me over and over."

"You are so relaxed about whatever happens." She shrugged. "I get impatient for God to do things my way."

"We all do." He pointed to a pasture dotted with white sheep. "I've just given the Lord lots of opportunities to show me that He has a plan, and I've learned to trust His direction—more often than not."

An hour later they drove through rolling hills, and Trina recognized newer Amish homes surrounded by pastures. Each place had a barn, and many housed cottage industries—boutique popcorn, custom furniture, as well as leather, harness, and buggy work and irrigation systems. Bailey turned into a driveway and parked next to a car. "Welcome to the old homeplace."

"This is your home?" She tried to connect his worldly dress and truck to the Amish house.

"While not usual, it will make sense. Sort of." He opened her door. "Come on."

Before they reached the porch, the front door opened. Bailey's uncle and aunt who had danced so beautifully at the 4-H event came to greet her. "Trina, so nice to see you again."

Behind them, another couple smiled their welcome. Bailey swept a hand in their direction. "Trina, you know my aunt and uncle. This is my *Mamm* and *Daed*."

Chapter 12

Over sandwiches made on homemade bread, fruit salad, and chocolate cake from the basket Trina's mother sent, Bailey's family asked about Trina's parents and how Oliver had adjusted to his prosthetics. They laughed to hear that the toddler had become proficient and difficult to corral.

"We get around fine without the help," Bailey's uncle said. "With them, we can be pretty quick."

"You changed our family." Trina glanced around the table. "Thank you."

Mr. Wayne dipped his head, receiving the compliment. "Bailey made it possible by introducing us."

"I knew information that might be helpful"—Bailey pointed his fork towards his uncle—"and seeing is far more convincing than telling."

After lunch, Bailey took Trina on a tour of the property. In the humid weather, the corn in the fields had easily reached knee high before the upcoming Fourth of July. He pointed out his childhood tree fort and the area in the barn where he kept his farrier supplies. He caught her looking at him. "What?"

"I'm picturing you as a boy with an Amish haircut."

"There are some parts I don't miss." He waved a hand to indicate the home where he grew up. "I get the best of both worlds."

"You are Mennonite like your uncle?"

He nodded. "The family tree goes like this. My uncle is the first born. My dad is second. When my grandparents discovered help was available for my uncle to walk, they became Mennonite to pursue those opportunities. It just made sense to transport themselves to the many necessary appointments in distant cities. In the same way a growing child frequently needs new shoes, my uncle needed adjustments to his prosthetics."

She followed him to the pasture fence to watch the big Clydesdale crop grass. "Things must have been less available than for us today."

He gestured toward the house where his parents, aunt, and uncle drank lemonade on the porch. "Unlike Tobias who makes house calls, most specialists require patients to come to them. Medically, my uncle travels for his own needs. He also travels to help others find options."

"Like when he danced in our town." She scratched under the jaw of the soft-eyed horse who had come to the fence. "You arranged for that to happen."

Bailey shrugged. "Just made a suggestion to the decision-makers."

"You knew what was possible for Oliver."

"My dad watched his brother succeed without feet. Dad settled back into his Amish roots to marry Mom."

They walked to the porch and joined the others. "Once I was out of diapers, the men took me along when my uncle tried new developments in artificial limbs."

"He paid pretty good attention," Bailey's dad put in. "He started telling the farrier how to trim our horses."

She thought of how her father dismissed her suggestions for running the elevator. "How was that received?"

Bailey laughed. "The farrier suggested I mind my own business, so I did."

"In addition to his training as a farrier," Bailey's mother said, "he has an instinct for working with horses. Word traveled, and people sought his advice for their equines."

"Riding my bike farther and farther proved exhausting, so my parents and I talked it over. We decided I could be more effective, like my uncle, as part of the Mennonite church."

Chapter 13

On Monday morning, Trina checked her list. The girl who worked in the tea room had plenty of hearty meat sandwiches and gallons of iced tea. The summer intern would oversee the shop. At 9:30, Tobias arrived looking more like he was going to church than to the barn.

He looped an arm around Larkin's shoulder. "Noel is keeping the Old Traction Barn in the spotlight."

"Who would have thought a homeless paint mare would become the Old Traction Barn's best marketing."

"Homeless and pregnant. Because of Noel, I met you." He kissed the top of her head.

Larkin glanced toward Trina. "It all began at your elevator the week I came to Indiana. I went to buy paint, and there was this handsome guy at the counter buying horse grain. He asked your father if he knew of anyone with a barn for the mare."

"Because I was full up at my clinic," Tobias added. "No room in my inn."

"My adult daughter was visiting from California and volunteered my barn."

"I recall a comment about not being able to keep a goldfish alive," Tobias put in.

"My daughter said, 'she's just like Mary. She needs a place to have her baby.'" Larkin frowned. "This arrangement was supposed to be temporary. Somehow, Tobias, you never found another home for her."

He shrugged. "The day the colt was born and Noel invited you to come close I knew she had found her own home."

Bailey came through the door wearing a button down shirt and cowboy hat instead of his usual T-shirt and ballcap. He grinned when he saw Trina. "Big doing's today."

Tobias feigned surprise. "I didn't know you owned anything besides T-shirts." He sniffed the air. "Is that cologne or did you shower?"

"Never had a reason to dress up for you," Bailey returned.

Looking classy in jeans and boots, Anna came in, followed by the photographer from the local newspaper who was already snapping photos.

"Bring your lariat, Annie Oakley?" Bailey hooked a thumb in the direction of the barn. "If we need to rope one of those wild critters, we're counting on you."

"Never leave home without it," she said.

Promptly at ten o'clock, a twelve-passenger van with the Purdue veterinary school logo pulled up. The passengers came inside where Tapeworm introduced two professors and six veterinary students. A car parked next to the van and two representatives from the Tennessee farrier school joined the group.

"Thank you for coming," Bailey spoke to the visitors. "And thank you for considering my case study. You have the history of the symptoms, diagnosis, and treatment that Tobias, Tapeworm"—a collective laugh went around the group to hear the administrator's nickname—"and I carried out. Come out to the barn where you can see the work we've done and examine the results."

When Trina held back to let the others go first, Bailey waved her over to walk with him. At the corral, Noel and the colt came to the fence where Larkin gave them a candy cane. The faint smell of peppermint mingled with the familiar scent of horses. Tobias put a halter on each horse, and the vet and farrier led the horses in a series of movements to show how each part of the body contributed to a balanced alignment. Out of alignment, the imbalance caused a chain reaction of physical issues.

"The key," Bailey summarized, "is not to treat the symptoms but carefully ascertaining the root problem and applying corrective treatment. And corrective treatment means attention to all areas impacted by the problem."

"And the reverse is true." Tobias indicated the colt's shoulder, leg, and hoof. "Bailey's corrective measures to the hoof had a positive impact on the shoulder and neck."

As Anna demonstrated the exercises they had done daily with the horses, Tobias explained, "Physical therapy provided fast results with the soft tissue."

Trina observed the reporter and several students taking notes while Bailey and Tobias answered questions from the group. Wrapping up, Tobias took off the halters, and the horses went back to grazing. The visitors trooped back to the tea shop for sandwiches and iced tea. They were eating and chatting when Oliver arrived with his mother.

Scooping up the bundle of boy, Trina led them to a table. The waitress served tea and brought fruit for Oliver. Spotting Bailey, the boy kicked his legs and Oliver's mother set him on the floor. As he quickly made his way to the farrier, conversations stilled as the visitors noticed the boy's gait. Bailey took his cowboy hat from the ear of his chair and placed the Stetson on the eager boy's head. Oliver pulled off the hat and belly laughed as he and Bailey played their game.

Trina glanced at her sister-in-law. For the first time since Oliver's birth, she appeared relaxed. Her fierce determination to protect and be a barrier between the world and her son had been replaced by pride in her child's ability to adapt. Staying at Bailey's parents and interacting with his aunt and uncle had been a safe place where Oliver's situation was familiar and filled with possibilities. The prosthesis staff addressed her fears, encouraging her questions and hopes.

"This is my friend, Oliver." Bailey spoke to the group. As Mr. Wayne had done the night he danced for them, Bailey lifted the hem of Oliver's pant leg enough to show the prosthesis. "And Oliver is the visual aid of what we talked about at the corral. Mobility for living things is vital for life. Our first question is always, can we fix it?" Bailey held up one finger and then the second. "Next, if we can't fix it, how can we adapt to make it work?"

Chapter 14

JULY

"This will be so much fun." With a wave to the summer intern, Larkin looped her arm through Trina's and steered her out the Old Traction Barn door. At the curb, Anna waited in the driver's seat of her car.

"Where are we going?" Trina got into the backseat and put on her seatbelt as Larkin took the front passenger seat.

"Shopping." Anna put the car in gear and steered toward the larger city.

Larkin turned in her seat to study Trina. "You've had quite the recent weeks. New job and new developments with Oliver which had a significant impact on your family."

"Lots of deep conversations with my parents as well as Jonas and his wife." Trina's eyes filled with tears. "I've pushed my father to bend probably all my life. But watching him actually do it—making way for the best for his family despite his sure beliefs. It's love in a different way."

Anna glanced at her in the rearview mirror. "The Mennonite pastor asked me to help Jonas and his wife settle into our congregation. Thankfully, they are familiar with the church members since being part of the Christmas pageant."

Trina nodded. "Jonas told us he was angry at God for Oliver's condition. He participated in the pageant as a rebellion to his faith."

Larkin's eyes widened. "I wonder how many of us were struggling with big issues during rehearsals and performances. Oliver was a sweet Baby Jesus. They were the stars as the Holy Family."

"With the possible exception of Noel," Anna quipped.

"Jonas said the Mennonites were so welcoming and respectful that they saw God in a new way in a new place." Trina paused. "We have looked at so many possibilities for Oliver's future. Bailey's aunt and uncle, parents, and Oliver's prosthetics team have answered a million questions."

Anna reached back to touch Trina's arm. "This is hard. Your family will be altered from what you've always known."

"Poignant." Trina absently rolled the edge of her apron between her fingers. "Touching with an element of sadness."

They rode in silence for a while. Trina breathed deeply. "With my father's blessing, I'm also joining the Mennonite congregation."

Anna and Larkin exchanged a grin. "That's why we are going shopping."

"The pastor asked me to help you settle in too."

Larkin passed water bottles to each of them. "No one asked for my help."

Anna looked apologetic. "I think the pastor tends to ask those around the same age to become a peer group."

"Foundations first." Larkin announced when they arrived at the outdoor shopping mall and led the way to a store featuring underclothes. "We'd like to have a fitting," she said to the clerk.

"Oh my." Trina felt her cheeks flush. "This is—"

"New." Larkin patted her shoulder. "Precisely why we are doing a girls shopping day. We will help you find some tasteful outfits you feel comfortable in for church and work."

"And find something for ourselves, of course." Anna chose a cami to try on.

Larkin leaned close. "Because I'm old enough to be your mother, what we find for you here is my gift."

Wearing the prettiest and best fitting foundations she had experienced, Trina followed her companions to a clothing store. Passing among the racks, Larkin and Anna helped Trina find several items she liked.

"Try this." Larkin draped a hangar over the top of Trina's dressing room door.

Trina felt thankful that she could explore new styles away from anyone she knew in their small hometown. She slipped the silky fabric over her head and the flowing hem dropped comfortably just below her knees. Examining herself in the full-length mirrors, she could picture herself wearing the modest yet flattering style, which was similar to her traditional clothes for church and work at the Old Traction Barn. Stepping out of the dressing room, she saw approval reflected in Larkin and Anna's eyes.

"Score." Larkin high-fived Anna. "Let's find five outfits you like, one for each day at the shop."

Leaving the clothing store, Trina wore the yellow dress with lavender flowers Larkin had found along with a pair of lake shoes that matched several of her finds. She felt pretty and professional.

"Our next stop is my treat." Anna brought them to a hair salon that smelled of nail polish. Over the hum of hair dryers, Larkin and Anna received a style and trim, while Trina's stylist showed her how to easily do a loose, wavy curl that reached below her shoulders. When she offered to add make-up, Trina agreed to a pale lip gloss.

Staring at herself in the mirror, Trina felt dizzy with the difference in her appearance. "You are lovely, Trina." Larkin smiled at her reflection. "Always have been."

Anna gently squeezed Trina's shoulder. "And this is a lot of change. Give yourself time to take it in. Press into the Lord and let Him lead."

Chapter 15

Larkin looked at her watch. "Anyone else hungry?"

Trina nodded. "Famished."

"Shopping is not for the faint of heart." Anna headed for the door. "And today's success calls for a celebratory lunch."

With their shopping parcels stored in Anna's trunk, they drove to a restaurant. Inside, the aroma of burgers sizzling on the grill and sweet potato fries brought an appreciative grumble from Trina's stomach. The waitress took them to a table where Tobias, Bailey, and Tapeworm were laughing and eating appetizers. Looking up, the men saw the girls and fell silent.

Seeing their attention on her, Trina felt her cheeks color. Quickly, Tobias stood and elbowed Bailey.

The farrier jumped to his feet and came to Trina. "Hey."

"Hey back."

Bailey shifted his weight. "You look sensational."

"Doesn't she?" Larkin took Tobias's hand as he stepped close.

"Yeah," Tobias grinned. "As always."

Then Tapeworm was beside Anna and looking at Trina in that sheepish way he had when she served him her first cup of tea on the opening day of the tea shop.

"Nice to see you, Tapeworm." Trina thought he looked as awkward as she felt.

Tobias indicated the table. "It's the first official off-site meeting of the Lunch Bunch."

"Lunch Bunch plus Tape." Anna took a seat.

Tape? Trina mouthed the word to Bailey who winked.

Sitting girl, boy, girl, boy at the round table, the girls ordered burgers with the works.

"No quiche and salad today," Bailey observed.

Tobias watched Larkin finish her burger and fries. "Shopping must be appetite-building."

"And inspiring." Larkin pushed back her plate. "There is a home decor shop I'd like to look at for trending ideas. Fall is just around the corner ..."

"It's only July." Tapeworm arched his eyebrows.

"Not in the business world," Trina put in. "Retail has to be a season ahead."

"Exactly," Larkin continued, "and I'd like to see what the big city stores are doing before heading back."

Tobias stood. "Let's take a look."

Anna got to her feet. "Tape and I will come along."

Larkin glanced toward Trina. "You look exhausted. Why don't you sit a bit."

Trina nodded. "I don't think I can face another store today."

When the other four had gone, Bailey turned his chair to face her, his gaze studying her face and hair. "This is the first time I've seen you without your covering."

"Not to mention the clothes."

He studied her. "How are you?"

She sorted through the many thoughts and emotions that swirled within. "How did you feel?"

"I was eighteen, like you. So that gives me a couple years' experience. Not exactly an expert by any means."

He rested an elbow on the table. "Going to Tennessee as a teenager felt like being a Yankee in King Author's Court. Expanding beyond our Amish community is kinda like that."

"I've read so many books that take place in settings much different from my life."

He brightened. "Now you will walk in different settings. And not just you ... because your brother's family is taking the same journey."

The waitress collected empty plates from the table.

Bailey waved toward the door where their friends had exited. "You already have a solid collection of friends."

Trina nodded. "And my parents understand and support my decision."

"Encouraged the decision." Bailey stuffed the last of his fries into his mouth. "You and I have the best of both worlds. God is a surprising bridge builder."

She ran her thumb through the condensation on the outside of her water glass. "I was thinking."

He grinned. "I knew that business mind of yours would be turning out ideas."

"What if I opened a shop that brought prosthetics to our area." In her excitement, her words tumbled out. "Oliver and your uncle have to travel for what they need. Surely there are others who would benefit from someone who came weekly to do fittings. And we could provide physical therapy."

"It's a bit of a niche." Bailey signaled the waitress. "If you add orthotics you broaden your customer base to pretty much everyone."

The waitress came to their table. "What can I get you?"

"Tea." Bailey looked at Trina and waited for her nod. "For two."

The End

PeggySue Wells

PeggySue Wells parasails, skydives, snorkels, scuba dives, and has taken (but not passed) pilot training. Solo mom of seven and founder of SingleMomCircle.com, she is the bestselling author of 30 books including *The Ten Best Decisions A Single Mom Can Make*, *Homeless for the Holidays*, and *Chasing Sunrise*. Connect with PeggySue Wells at PeggySueWells.com

Color Me Springtime

A HAMILTON HARBOR SPRING

SALLY JO PITTS

Chapter 1

Raquel Windhelm would have never dreamed the dilapidated houses on Feldman Square could be restored. Of course, she never would have imagined she'd spend thirteen years away from Hamilton Harbor, studying and teaching art in France either. Standing outside the Hamilton House Bed and Breakfast, she scanned the renovated Victorian and Craftsman homes surrounding the park. Too bad she had not been around to sketch the before and after images of the houses.

Claudia Cullen and her husband, Pete, had made her feel welcome in the over-garage apartment of the B & B. She'd opened the window to the crisp spring air, minus the Florida humidity that was sure to follow in the days ahead.

"Don't knock. Just come on in for breakfast. We'll be expecting you," Claudia had told her. Raquel entered the side door of the main house which led down a hall to the dining room, where she was met with rich smells of coffee and yeasty bread.

Claudia entered the dining room from the kitchen. "Ah. You're here. Help yourself to coffee and a fresh bagel. There are toppings of cream cheese, butter, and fruit preserves to choose from. Eggs, bacon, and grits will be ready shortly. We have an agreement. Pete cooks; I put on coffee and order the bagels from the Bagel Bistro on Main Street."

"There's a bagel place downtown? From the looks of Feldman Square, Hamilton Harbor has come a long way since I was here last."

"A lot of work has gone into revitalizing the town. The spring festival committee was elated that you accepted our invitation. To have a home-grown artist of your notoriety is exciting."

Claudia's expressive hand bumped her coffee cup, jostling coffee into the saucer. Claudia grabbed a napkin and plunked it underneath her cup.

"I do hail from here but hanging the word notoriety on me is a stretch."

"That's not what Brad Zimmerman says."

The mention of Brad's name sent an involuntary jolt to her middle.

"What did Brad have to say about me?"

"Brad is on the spring festival planning committee. He said you are multi-talented in various art forms and bragged about you being a French artist."

He bragged on her? They hadn't communicated over the years.

"With you being a Paris artist and having your work displayed at art shows and all, we didn't hold much hope of your coming here."

Ah-ha. Brad must have been on her father's World of Art website where he unashamedly promoted her artwork. "I must tell you from experience, being schooled and instructing art in Paris does not automatically ensure fame." She snickered and added, "but that's the picture my father likes to paint."

She had enjoyed studying in Paris and especially the opportunities she'd had to teach in the surrounding countryside. Special recognition of her art wasn't her concern. However, without some recognition, she feared she would let down her father who had invested money, support, and influence into her career. To make her father proud, she'd spent long, exhausting hours perfecting her skills and creating a style of her own while teaching classes affiliated with the art institute in Paris. Art had been her life since leaving Hamilton Harbor, and there was no way she could have accomplished what she had without her father's help. *Too bad my work didn't rake in thousands, then maybe he wouldn't feel the need to push his daughter's work to gain bragging rights.*

"I hope to be worthy of your expectations. My father has been asking me to return stateside, and I wanted to see my old high school alma mater again. So, the invitation to be a part of the Hamilton Harbor springtime celebration came at a good time. There is no need to pay my airfare or an honorarium." She pulled a check from her pocket.

Claudia held up her hand in protest. "Oh, but the committee wants to cover your expenses and time."

"The funds raised from the festival will contribute to Feldman Park maintenance. Right? You can consider this my donation." Raquel tore the check in half and pushed the pieces to Claudia. "My mother died while I was in college, and Dad lives in New York. So I no longer have a home to return to in Hamilton Harbor. To be a part of the town's rebuilding does my heart good. I can remember when this house and the others around the square were rundown rentals."

Claudia pocketed the torn check. "I thank you, and I know the committee will as well."

Pete pushed through the kitchen door. "Breakfast is served," he said, placing a steaming platter of eggs and bacon and a bowl of grits on the table.

Raquel rubbed her hands together. "Good ol' Southern grits. Grits is an unknown delicacy in France, at least in the parts I've lived."

"Maybe the traditional breakfast staple will inspire your creativity during your stay with us. Are you okay with me praying for the food?"

"Yes, and pray for the children's classes. All my teaching has been with young adults the past several years."

They joined hands while Pete prayed.

Eyes closed, Raquel slumped her shoulders, releasing all cares and tension. Pete's words wrapped her with blessing and encouragement. If nothing else, her trip was worth it to hear his prayer.

Raquel returned to her room after breakfast, gathered her teaching notes and paints, and met Claudia in front of the house.

"This house used to have a sagging porch and peeling paint when I was in high school. I marvel at the transformation of the Hamilton house and all of Feldman Square," Raquel said.

Claudia nodded. "When I arrived in town and purchased the Pampered Pooch on Main Street five years ago, the square was in shambles except for the florist shop. Pete has been the impetus behind the restorations."

"All this and he cooks? You found a prize in him."

Claudia's face lit up, along with her curls, in the morning sunlight. Burnt orange in Raquel's paint box would form the perfect base to replicate her unique hair color. "Prize is a good description of Pete."

They reached the yellow Craftsman cottage surrounded by dog woods, azaleas, and beds of golden daylilies. A metal *Flower Cottage since 1972* sign hung over the trellis gate. Raquel pointed to a bird nest resting in the branches of the rose bush entwining the arbor. "A sure sign of spring."

"If I were a bird, I'd build my home at the Flower Cottage too." Claudia unlatched the gate and motioned for Raquel to enter. "Emme Davenport, the owner, was happy to offer her worktable in the shop for your children's classes today."

"I look forward to meeting her." Raquel's phone buzzed in her pocket, and she checked the screen. "My dad."

"Take the call, I'll let Emme know we're here."

"Hi, Dad."

"I see from my locator app you are back stateside for the spring event in Hamilton Harbor."

"Yes, sir. I arrived late last night. I was going to call you later today. I know Marla isn't an early riser."

"Putting it mildly. One thing we've had to agree to disagree on in married life is the time to greet the new day. I wanted to let you know I approached the art gallery near our New York townhouse with copies of your portfolio and credentials. They are quite impressed."

"That's nice, Dad, but can we talk more later? I'm on my way to have the kiddos in my class make paper flowers."

"Sure. But I don't know why you're wasting time on such a small venue. The metro area is where you'll achieve recognition."

"Yes, sir, but ... I'll call later." How could she get across to her father that his goals and her goals did not coincide?

Her mother and dad had divorced when she was three years old. So, her growing up years consisted of living with her mother in Hamilton Harbor, and a schedule of shared summers and holidays spent with her dad and stepmom who split their time living in homes in New York City and Long Island. Her dad meant well by promoting her artwork whenever and wherever he could. He just had a different set of values that came with dollar signs attached.

Raquel ended the call and climbed the steps to the florist shop. Claudia opened the door for her.

"Everything okay?"

"Yes. My dad. He's … glad to have me back in the States."

Inside, Raquel took in the sweet perfume of hyacinths. In the display window, an electric train meandered through a miniature tree-lined landscape with colorful floral cargo.

"Here she is, Raquel Windhelm." Claudia said.

"Hello and welcome. I'm Emme." The pert blonde, with a broad smile and hair pulled back in a ponytail, came from behind the customer counter and gave her a Southern hospitality neck hug. No air kisses like the French or stodgy nods of the high society circles. Refreshing.

"Thank you for hosting me."

Emme stepped aside, pointing to the worktable. "This is Mellie Tidwell, former florist shop owner who is ever ready to help me when needed."

"Please to meet you." She nodded her head of bright white permed hair. "I'm on my way to make a delivery, but I'll be around to help wherever I can." Mellie scooped up a welcome baby basket of pink nosegays and scurried out the back door.

"I'm expecting a grooming appointment in a few," Claudia said. "Raquel, I'll see you later at the B & B. If you need anything before then, I'm across the street at the Pampered Pooch."

"You have your own little community here. I love the closeness."

"We are blessed."

Raquel followed behind Emme to the work area.

"I set out supplies and the easel you requested for the children's flower project. The committee had over a hundred applicants to participate, and we had to select those applications that were time-dated first. I hated disappointing the children ... but at the same time, you can be encouraged that your attendance has generated enthusiasm. We really appreciate your offer to do extra afternoon sessions, so we were able to serve more."

"I was happy to. I also made a 'how-to' sheet for the project the children will make in case anyone wants a copy. I enjoy teaching, especially those who want to learn."

Emme went to the foot of the steps leading upstairs. "Richie, our guest artist is here."

"Okay, Mom."

A youngster bounded down the steps. "Richie, this is Raquel Windhelm. Richie is in fourth grade and has agreed to be a helper."

"Yes, ma'am. Anything you need, I'll try to be of help."

"Thank you. Richie and Emme, you seem to have thought of everything."

Tires crunching on gravel sounded from the back parking lot. Raquel watched a red van's side doors slide open and several children emerge. A black SUV pulled in beside the van and a tall man dressed in jeans and T-shirt climbed out. The profile, black hair, and strong angular jaw unmistakably belonged to Brad Zimmerman—the guy voted to be Azalea Trail King when she was dubbed Azalea Trail Queen in the spring of their senior year in high school. The sight of her classmate caused her pulse to kick up speed. He opened the rear door of his car and helped a cute little boy unbuckle his seatbelt.

Claudia didn't mention that Brad had a child, but why would she? Seventeen years out of high school, he could have a bevy of children. No such blessing or attachment to produce the blessing had come Raquel's way. She'd dated but always shied away from serious suitors. Romance took a backseat to her art endeavors.

She turned from the window and took a deep breath to calm her quickened pulse. *Focus Raquel, focus.*

Chapter 2

Brad Zimmerman helped his nephew, Aiden, from his car behind the Flower Cottage. A little bird chirped with fervor from a wisteria vine as if announcing Raquel was here. She was now only steps away. His mouth was dry, and his stomach did a somersault. "Ready to learn from a celebrity?"

"What is a celebrity, Uncle Brad?"

"Someone well-known, famous."

"If she's a celebrity, how come I've never heard of her?"

"You're six ... you haven't heard the names of all celebrities. Take my word, she is."

Other children tromped along the wooden walkway leading to the back door of the flower shop where Emme Davenport handled greetings and directed the youngsters on what to do.

"Aiden, hello. Have you had fun spending spring break with your uncle?"

"*Uh-huh*. I outscored Uncle Brad in Mario Kart three days in a row."

"That's okay," Brad said. "I've already warned him there's a rematch coming."

"Sounds fun. Richie is here and will be glad to swap game-winning tips."

"Cool."

Brad shook his head and chuckled. He peered inside and caught his first glimpse of Raquel and *wham*. He felt like Aiden had bopped him unexpectedly in the gut with a ball. They had been high school friends—not boyfriend-girlfriend—but peers, classmates, buddies. Brad put a hand to stomach and took a deep breath. What was happening to him? Years had passed since they'd hugged after her mother's funeral not long before they became college graduates. He'd wished her well with the Paris fellowship she had been awarded. And that was that. They had drifted apart.

He took another deep breath. She was here now. He wanted to reconnect ... but she had built a name for herself. Face it, his pride over her accomplishments was laced with pangs of regret over the thirteen-year chunk of time that left a void where he and Raquel were concerned.

Raquel sat, elbows propped against the worktable, engrossed in conversation with two youngsters. Her chestnut hair fell forward as she nodded with animation. She tugged a long strand behind her ear. The same quirk he'd teased her about in high school.

"I don't call attention to your hairline cowlick," she'd scolded. Then they would both collapse in silly laughter. Theirs had been a comfortable friendship, but time and distance had shoved the comfort into undefined obscurity.

He moved out of the way as Emme ushered in two more children. "I was hoping to speak to Raquel before class started."

"Sure. I'll check with her." Emme turned and scooted behind the children who were taking seats on stools. Raquel went to the easel, her back to him, and flipped the cover of the easel pad to a clean sheet of paper. Brad leaned against the wall at the foot of the stairs. Raquel turned and looked in his direction. She raised her hand, then her hand dropped.

She had seen him, hadn't she? Did he look so different she didn't know him?

Emme stopped to retrieve a paint brush a child dropped then handed another child a tissue. With the children all settled into their seats, Raquel began speaking. Emme looked over at Brad and shrugged.

He nodded and made his exit. How foolish. This was not a good time to get reacquainted. He should have realized she'd be busy. "Shoulda, coulda, woulda is my specialty," he muttered, as he walked toward his car.

He climbed in and sagged against the seat. He should have tried to stay in touch with Raquel. He could have been the one to contact her to be the celebrity guest. He would have called her last night but decided, after all this time, he'd rather see her in person.

Now he was second guessing all his decisions. He glanced at his watch; the class was to last ninety minutes. He'd kill time over coffee.

The bell jangled over the entry door at the Harbor Town Bagel Bistro.

"Brad, just the fellow we need," Dave Burbank said.

Brad was a sometime honorary member of the roosters, a group of male seniors. A group of female seniors, the hens, sat at a separate table. The two factions gathered mornings and afternoons to toss barbs at one another. They hashed out all kinds of issues, ranging from what breed of dog was the smartest to the best brand of tooth floss. Dave was always the most outspoken of the men's gathering.

"Us men think Punxsutawney Phil predicted six more weeks of winter this year 'cause he couldn't see good. With all the news media crowded around his burrow, it's no wonder he went back in. The news media could be what's reshaping our weather systems, standing in the way of poor old Phil's ability to see his shadow and leaving us to wonder how long until spring."

Loretta Huggins, Brad's retired American History teacher, slapped the ladies' table. "You're debating nonsense. Groundhog Day is a legend rooted in astronomy and the seasons. February second marks the midpoint between the winter solstice in December and the spring equinox in March. If the groundhog sees his shadow, there will be six more weeks of winter. If he doesn't, there will be six more weeks until spring. Think about it. Either way we have spring six weeks later. The whole premise is hogwash."

"Nope." Dave popped his fist against the table, then turned to face the ladies, wiggling and blowing on his knuckles. "Us men say it's not hogwash. We say it's groundhog wash."

The men "haw-hawed" at the one up.

Eyes rolled and heads wagged from the ladies' klatch.

"Go place your order," Dave directed Brad, and then addressed the gathering. "As the currently employed up-to-date high school teacher, Brad will set the groundhog matter straight."

Brad shook his head at the good-natured squabbling and spoke to bistro owner Elaine Robinson standing behind the counter. "You have free entertainment every day."

"Yes. And their show generates repeat customers. What can I get for you?"

"I'll try the strawberry bagel advertised on the board out front."

"How about a strawberry smoothie to go with it?"

"No, thanks. Coffee ... plain." He'd stick to what he knew. Unlike adventuresome Raquel who had left Hamilton Harbor to attend college hundreds of miles away and then ventured thousands of miles away to France. Not him. Brad Zimmerman, the play-it-safe, no-risk man, was still in Hamilton Harbor. Still in high school.

Brad swiveled on the stool and faced the tables of men with their coffee mugs and the ladies with their teacups.

"Why am I a source of groundhog information?"

"You're a teacher," Dave said.

"And this teacher was a student of Loretta Huggins and knows that challenging her knowledge would be futile. Besides, the ladies have you outnumbered."

Every one of the women sat taller in their seats.

"Takes two of them to equal one of us."

Scowls replaced the ladies' puffed-up demeanor.

"Oh, boy." Brad tapped his foot on the floor. "I'm looking for the crack that's going to split this floor and swallow you up, Dave. Besides, this industrial tech guy knows next to nothing about groundhogs."

The over-the-door bell jangled. All eyes turned to the sound as Pete Cullen walked in.

"Men, we have reinforcements," Dave said. The men raised their mugs to Pete.

"Do I want to know what I'm reinforcing?" he asked Elaine, wrinkling his forehead.

"Probably not."

"I'll take a bottled water. I've already cooked for and fed our spring festival guest artist."

"Table the groundhog," Dave said. "How did we get a French artist to come to our little hamlet?"

Pete pointed. "Brad."

Brad shrugged. "I knew her in high school."

"Raquel was in my honors American History class," Loretta said. "She was the first and only student from Hamilton Harbor High to be awarded a scholarship to the prestigious Maryland Institute College of Art."

Prestige. Had her status in attending an exclusive school and receiving a coveted fellowship in France changed her? Was her hesitation to acknowledge him this morning because she identified more with those in high society circles?

Pete took the stool next to Brad.

"I've enjoyed meeting your artist friend. She wanted to contribute to the park maintenance fundraiser by gifting back the honorarium we paid her."

His heart warmed at her kind gesture. She hadn't lost an appreciation for her roots. After finishing his bagel and coffee and chatting with Pete about the progress on the hotel being constructed beside the marina, he returned to the Flower Cottage to pick up Aiden. He wanted to talk to Raquel. but she might not hold their old friendship as dear as he did. He wouldn't press.

Other parents had arrived, and excited children emerged holding up their creations. Aiden skipped along the walk carrying a painting and a small pottery container with brightly colored handmade flowers.

"I drew this all by myself." Aiden poked a picture of a beautifully drawn and shaded tulip under his nose. Brad glanced around. The other children were just as excited to show off their drawings.

Emme stood in the doorway, chatting with a couple of parents.

"Uncle Brad, it was so fun. That lady showed us how to draw and mix colors."

But "that lady" was nowhere in sight. Hopefully he'd get a chance to see her and thank her for her contribution.

She'd made Aiden and a lot of other children happy which was a goal of the spring festival. He'd settle for that. He opened the rear car door for Aiden to climb into his booster seat. "I'll place your flowers and picture on the front seat, so they don't get messed up." Circling his car, he opened the passenger door and stooped down to place Aiden's treasures on the seat.

"Brad?" Raquel peered at him through the open driver's door. Her face was flushed, and she was slightly out of breath. "Don't even think about leaving without speaking." She nodded toward Aiden. "You have a talented little boy here."

"Well, thank you. His parents will be happy to hear your assessment."

"Parents? You're not ..." she turned to Aiden. "I thought you said your dad was going to be proud of your work."

Aiden giggled. "No. Uncle Brad ... not Dad, Miss Raquel."

"Oh, I see." She straightened and so did Brad. They locked eyes on one another over the top of the car. "Then I'll tell you that you have a talented nephew, and I'm elated to see Aiden's Uncle Brad again."

Brad held Raquel's gaze. "And Uncle Brad says the same about seeing Miss Raquel."

Her return grin was like spring rain to parched soil.

"You know each other?" Aiden asked.

"From high school," Brad said.

"Cool. You told me she was a celebrity, but you didn't say you knew her."

"It was a long time ago. I didn't know if she'd remember me."

"Your uncle is quite a jokester, Aiden."

Aiden shook his head. "I'm the one who teaches him jokes."

Quirking a brow, Raquel said, "Ah, I see. I have two more classes today and meet with the tri-county art council this evening. But I want to see you and catch up on Hamilton Harbor. Will you be at the Easter sunrise service?"

Emme called to Raquel. "The next group is seated and ready."

Raquel waved and began backing away from the car. "See you tomorrow?"

Brad's heartbeat accelerated, and he gave a thumbs up. "Color me can't wait."

Chapter 3

Easter morning, Raquel poured coffee at the self-service bed and breakfast buffet and smiled to herself. *Color me can't wait.*

The words were the perfect description for not only anticipating seeing Easter morning at sunrise but the notion of celebrating the event with Brad.

Their art teacher, Ms. Hixon had used the expression "Color me happy" like others might say "goodness gracious" or "sake's alive" to express surprise or approval.

Raquel and Brad had modified the saying and created a tradition of their own to let each other know what their day had been like by the time they came to art class the last period of the day their senior year.

"Color me bummed out" ... "Color me upbeat" ... "Color me brainless" ... gave each other a clue as to whether comfort or cheer was needed to make it through class.

Though he seemed happy to see her yesterday, she was puzzled. Why would he say he didn't know if she'd remember him? The fond memories of Hamilton Harbor were because of Brad Zimmerman. He had always been encouraging about her work and a friend she could talk to.

If he was on the planning committee, why hadn't he contacted her? Maybe he was married or had a girlfriend.

If so, Raquel may have put him on the spot suggesting he meet her. So, what if he had another girl in his life? It had been thirteen years since they'd seen each other. He very likely had someone in his life. They were old friends glad to see each other. *Relax. No need to second guess the situation. You will find out soon enough.*

Pete walked in with a dish of preserves.

"These croissants are flaky and wonderful."

"Thanks, but I must give credit to the new bakery on Main. I set out cream cheese and honey but thought you might enjoy this orange marmalade. Mellie, who sometimes works at the florist shop, makes jellies that are sold at the gift shop inside the Violet Feldman house."

"I will have to visit the gift shop and purchase my own supply. I'm looking forward to seeing more of renovated Hamilton Harbor with Brad Zimmerman after the Sunday service."

"Brad is a good man," Pete said. "When I am at a loss on a restoration project, he is my go-to man."

"Really? He used to be interested in construction. Does he have a business?"

"He should. I've tried to convince him to launch out on his own, but he's still teaching industrial tech at the high school."

"Didn't he complete his mechanical engineering degree?"

"Yes, and he knows his stuff. The school is fortunate to have him. He even works alongside students on restoration projects with me which gives the students extra learning experience and community service hours needed for scholarships."

"Sounds like him." He had helped her wield a hammer to earn community service hours during their high school days. Typical Brad. Thinking of others.

"It's nearing six o'clock. You might want to head to the service." Pete said. "I'll be there shortly. Claudia is to meet me after walking her dogs on the trail behind the houses to avoid disturbing the service."

Raquel stepped onto the wrap around porch. The dark sky had turned a deep azure and birds tweeted an Easter greeting. Across the street, several had gathered around the bandstand. Brad moved away from the crowd and waved. He appeared to be alone. Raquel stepped from the curb and met him in the middle of the street.

"Good morning, Miss Celebrity."

"Would you quit with the celebrity thing? No Aiden with you today?"

"His parents picked him up yesterday. They live in Melrose Beach and plan to go to Easter service there. I kept him during spring break so they could take off a few days."

"Nice of you to give up your spring break."

"I enjoyed having a break from teenagers."

"I bet teaching high schoolers is tough these days."

"There are pluses and minuses. Ready for the service? We couldn't have asked for better weather. Clear sky, low humidity and temps in the 70s."

Raquel nodded. Although a small thing, she enjoyed the touch of his hand on her back as he helped guide her across the street. They climbed the slight incline on the walkway leading to the platform where a young man strummed a guitar and led the crowd singing, "In Christ Alone." Raquel hadn't realized how much she had missed Hamilton Harbor.

Pastor Creighton of the downtown community church took the stage and delivered the Easter message with an emphasis on Christ's resurrection and the truth of the Scriptures to help with the everyday decisions of life.

The rays of the rising sun filtered through the oak trees as he spoke. One exceptionally bright ray grew and illuminated a spot on the path next to the bandstand, stirring Raquel's spirit. She expected to see people staring or pointing at the light, but no one else seemed to notice. If only she could press pause to assimilate the moment and ponder its meaning. But the vision had disappeared as quickly as it came.

The service closed with everyone singing, "Christ the Lord is Risen Today." Claudia and Pete joined them as the crowd dispersed. The experience of the light began to fade.

"Pastor Creighton preached an uplifting service," Claudia said, "but it was too early for me to get all my doggie boarders walked. I have more dogs staying with me than usual with families traveling for Easter."

Pete draped his arm on Claudia's shoulder. "I'll help if you want."

"You two make a good team," Raquel said.

"Yup. Pete cooks and restores houses, and I clean and restore dogs."

"Sweet. Do you ever help with Pete's restoration projects?" Brad asked.

Claudia winced. "No, certain places are safer when I'm not around. I've learned where my gifts are. You know the Scripture about each part of the body having a role to play. My role is in pet grooming and care."

"And nothing that requires a ladder," Pete added.

"Right." Claudia giggled and gave Pete's arm a love tap. "We better get going before I have a doggie revolt on my hands."

"Cute couple." Raquel smiled after them.

"Yes, and they are an integral part of the new life being breathed into Hamilton Harbor. Come on. I'll show you some of the changes since you left."

They walked further south. With a touch to her elbow, Brad steered her into an open space where an old building once stood facing Main Street.

"This garden pass-through was created as a part of downtown redevelopment. A deteriorated building too costly to repair was torn down opening a view to Feldman Park and giving quick access to Main Street."

"A creative idea for function and aesthetics. This whole area reminds me of Sceaux, where I've been living in France."

"I thought you lived in Paris."

"My cottage is in a picturesque town about six miles outside Paris." Raquel ran her fingers over the rough exposed walls. "This old brick, climbing vines, and cobblestone walkway duplicates the charm of the French village."

"I doubt a French replication was the intent," Brad said, "but it is cozy place to sit with the benches and pots of flowers provided by Emme from the Flower Cottage."

They continued onto Main Street and turned left toward the marina.

"I see the Top of the Harbor is still there." Raquel gestured toward the high-rise apartment building that brought back bittersweet memories. "After selling our house, Mom had only lived there a short time before she received the cancer diagnosis."

Brad stopped when they reached the front of the apartment complex. "After your mother's funeral and the dinner for family and friends, this is where you told me you'd received a fellowship for Paris."

"You were incredibly kind to take off time from your final exams at UF to come to the funeral." A sacrifice but so like him.

"Just being there for a friend."

He had been a good friend. She walked beside him, and the action was comfortable as if there had been just days instead of years since their parting. "What happened that we didn't stay in touch?"

"Life ... giftedness ... opportunity. You flew away like a baby bird in seek of her destiny, although those close to the little bird hated to see her go."

"You sound philosophical. Did you hate to see me leave?"

"Of course."

"But you never gave me any indication."

"No point. I knew your desire."

"Which was?"

"Go find fame and fortune in France."

She huffed and shook her head. "Why do people make assumptions of what is inside another person's head? People should communicate better. I wish you had told me your thoughts."

His hesitation was slight, but Raquel noticed. "What would that have accomplished? It seemed better for me to step back and be happy for you." Smiling, Brad rubbed his hands together and said, "We are here to see the changes since you've been gone."

The town may have altered but thankfully, not Brad. She had missed his smile. A lock of his hair dropped to the center of his forehead, and she squelched the temptation to straighten it like she used to.

"The marina is a big piece of what has changed and ... oh good, happy days are here again." He pointed toward the end of the street.

Set up in the parking lot behind city hall on the marina was a food truck with a *Happy Days Are Here Again* sign.

Reaching the truck, Brad said, "Henri. Working on Easter?"

"I've got coffee for those who went to sunrise service, then I'll close to go to church and open again for the Easter egg hunt on the marina this afternoon."

"Nice of you. Henri, meet Raquel Windhelm. She is the guest artist for the spring festival." Brad turned to Raquel, "Henri Martin is our resident Frenchman and beloved food truck guy. Kids and teachers flock to him during lunch at school." To Henri, he said, "Raquel has been in your home country a number of years."

"*Bon à entendre.* That is good to hear."

"*Merci,*" Raquel responded.

"Coffee? Cappuccino? Latte? I'll make whatever you two would like. On the house."

"A mocha latte would be wonderful," Raquel said.

Brad ordered a plain coffee. A line began to form behind them, and they walked to a picnic table.

"Did you love Paris every moment of the year like the song says?"

Raquel took a sip of her latte. "There is a lot of mystique about Paris. But when I left, spring had burst forth with cherry blossoms and was drawing visitors to the city just as the cherry blossoms draw people to some of the cities in the United States. But to answer your question, I did enjoy Paris and the surrounding countryside in all the seasons." She twisted around scanning the picnic area. "What happened to the office buildings and shops along here?"

"Demolished. This section is now designated as green space with easy access to city hall and the public library. Plans are in place for upgraded boat slips, and construction has started on a civic auditorium. Part of the redevelopment is to include history with a pirate-themed playground, a hands-on historical museum, and ... you will be happy to hear ... an art gallery. The seawall at the end will provide docking space for a pirate ship and sightseeing dinner cruises."

"Impressive. I understand from Pete that you are his go-to man with construction and restoration questions."

"A well-kept secret. My degree is in mechanical engineering. I enjoy teaching the students, but my secret interest is construction and reconstruction."

"Except not a secret to me. Don't forget I was there when Ms. Hixon taught art sculpture. I sculpted a hand out of pottery clay, and you welded a magnificent structure of copper with a working fountain of water streaming through it. I could see construction design in your future."

He gave her a sheepish grin. "I confess water and walls are a keen interest of mine. Let me show you this new seawall."

He tossed their empty cups into a waste bin, and they strolled side by side along the green space. Wind coming off the bay made the docked boats bob on the choppy water.

At the marina's end, Brad directed her attention to the freshly poured concrete with a four-foot-wide cap and metal railing. "Look on the water side. Those are interlocking vinyl panels and the material will last a long time compared to the old wall of concrete and rebar which is more susceptible to environmental exposure and corrosion."

His eyes brightened with enthusiasm.

"I never knew a seawall could be so fascinating.

"Seawalls are vital to the preservation of waterfront property. I'm taking a marine contractor course online, so I've enjoyed watching the workers strip back the old wall to the anchors and rebuild it."

"Can't seawalls just be repaired?"

"Retention walls will inevitably break down, but maintenance can certainly slow the process. Would you like to see a case in point?"

"Sure. Why not?" She had an idea that for Brad, constructing a seawall equated to her thrill of sweeping a brush on a canvas with the right mix of paint to match the scene she was attempting to produce.

He grabbed her hand, and they walked past more boat slips. Many on the east side of the marina housed boats on lifts in covered sheds.

"The boats that are removed from the water can be maintained with fewer problems from water erosion, but a seawall's whole purpose is withstanding Mother Nature's relentless wear and tear." He spoke with the pride of a coach imparting the importance of the challenge set before his team. Crossing Bay Drive they walked to the property behind the Top of the Harbor apartments. The lot held stacks of construction supplies.

"These are foundation materials for the hotel to be built here. The main building will front the bay. But keep walking." He led her to the right side of the construction site. "This side of the property borders Harbor Bayou with a natural stone seawall."

Raquel stepped up on one of the flat stones edging the shoreline. "This wall is much more pleasing to the eye."

"Yes, and extremely vulnerable to run off erosion as gaps between stones are pathways for soil to move back to the water body. The result is inevitable cracks and joint openings over time. Property owners can try to fill the voids with aggregate"—he stooped and picked up a loose stone—"but this does not solve the root cause of the problem. Eventually the aggregate will work its way back into the water. The hotel will need to deal with this wall or face destabilization and loss of property."

"Sounds like a huge expense."

"If they have to replace it, the expense will be great. But there are new hydrophobic, ecofriendly foams that are not only water impervious, but they also set up in water. There has been great success in injecting foams into failing seawalls. I believe this is the best, most cost effective ... sorry your eyes are glazing over."

"Don't apologize. I'm standing here thinking about what you're saying. The rough-hewn stone seawall is natural and looks better than the concrete or the interlocking wall. Why not talk to the hotel people about your recommendation?"

His shoulders visibly sagged at her suggestion. "I'm no one that a conglomerate like Fairland Hotels with their own engineers would listen to." He tossed the stone he'd picked up, and it rolled between two large rocks.

"I don't know why not. I found your explanation of prevention of land erosion to be riveting."

"Now you're making fun."

"I'm serious." Raquel hopped down from the rock. "You've opened up a whole new world to me."

Brad shoved his hands in his pockets, and they began walking back toward Feldman Park. "Marine construction is a dream, but I'm not sure how or if I'll put it to use."

"Having a dream, I believe, is what powers and empowers us to move forward."

"You're living your dream, aren't you?"

"It would seem so." She snickered. "You want to know the truth?"

Brad cocked his head. "Do I?"

Same old Brad. "Only you would answer me with a question." She steepled her hands together. "I'm living my father's dream. If I was to be an artist, he wanted me to be a specially trained artist. The school I attended and the fellowship in Paris were all his idea, though I did love the opportunity. But staying in a small French town and teaching was not a part of his dream. He wants me back in the States and is looking into art gallery opportunities in New York for my work."

"Returning to the States is not your dream?"

"Oh, I'm ready to return but not sure New York City is the place."

They came to a bench and she sat down, folding her arms across her middle. Brad sat beside her.

"Part of me thinks New York would be exciting but ... "

"But what?"

"The pastor's message this morning goes right to the heart of my prayers of late."

"About the resurrection?"

"No, though the risen Lord is the point of Easter. But he stressed that the truths in Scripture should help guide us in everyday life.

Brad nodded and leaned forward, clasping his hands and resting his arms on his thighs. He was doing what Brad did best, listening. She wanted to tell him what she had seen to get his reaction but was uncertain how to explain the light.

Raquel sucked in a deep breath. "I've been praying for direction and ... I saw something this morning."

Lines creased Brad's brow, but he waited.

"When Pastor Creighton spoke of looking to God for renewal and direction in our daily lives, the sun broke through the trees and lit up that walkway." She pointed to the path next to them. "Not just a little light. I mean like one of those big can stage lights. It was a weird feeling. But even more strange was that no one else seemed to notice, as though the lighted path was just for me to see."

Brad turned and with his hand drew an imaginary line along the walkway's trajectory. "That path leads to the waterfront that we just came from."

Raquel remained silent a long moment, staring at her feet. "Brad, I'm at a crossroads." She turned to face him. "And I believe you are too."

Chapter 4

Brad's gaze ping-ponged off the four walls of his classroom and landed on his marine construction texts and seawall sketches stacked on his desk. Was he at a crossroads and didn't even know it? He leaned back in his chair, propped his ankle over the opposite knee, and jiggled his foot to prod his thinking. In high school, he'd learned to compartmentalize his concerns into ninety-minute slots of the four period day. What did Raquel's vision and comments mean?

Lord, where am I headed, and was Raquel put in my path to tell me I am at a crossroads?

He admired Raquel's fortitude to step into uncharted territory to pursue her career. And if honest, he was a tad envious. Could he ever step out of the comfort of the hallowed halls of Hamilton High? His security. Yet he had sunk a sizable chunk of time and money into the marine construction certification class which enriched his teaching knowledge. But he'd never put what he'd learned to use in the business world. He instructed students with his knowledge and complied with the duties and directives of the school district. There was safety in the confines of these chalky gray walls.

He surveyed his classroom's washable gray cabinets and worktables. The space might not be colorful, but it was functional. He ran a disciplined, orderly classroom, checking all supplies were returned to their proper place at the end of each period. But what would Raquel think of his drab room?

He'd find out soon enough. As part of her spring festival responsibilities, Raquel was the guest speaker in today's art classes. He'd promised to meet her in front of the administration building.

Bam.

Brad jumped out of his chair. Something had slammed against the lockers in the hallway.

Brad yanked his door open.

A soda can flew past him and crashed to the floor, spewing sweet sticky contents on him and the others in the hall.

"You got something to say? Say it to my face!" A red-shirted male student pinned another male student against a locker.

"I just did. And I'm saying it again. You're a liar."

Red Shirt pressed his fist to the boy's throat. "You're takin' that back."

"Break it up." Brad wrestled Red Shirt away at the same time the school resource deputy arrived and held back the other boy, his arms flailing air punches.

Brad recognized one of the onlooking students who was wiping splattered soda off of his book bag. "Jared, what happened here?"

"Sam got mad at Cameron for accusing him of lying about the size of a fish he caught."

"All this over a fish?" The deputy shook his head.

"He's got no right to call me a liar." The student's face matched his shirt color.

"You boys come with me," the deputy said. "Mr. Zimmerman, I'll send the janitor with his mop bucket. You two may be learning to clean floors."

"Is this the right place?"

Brad spun around.

Raquel. More students had gathered in the hall, maneuvering around the drink spill, opening and clanging lockers shut.

"I'm so sorry I didn't meet you, but—"

She grinned. "High school hijinks. I can see you've been busy." She looked around. "This building wasn't here when we were in school."

He brushed his hands together, but sticky doesn't brush off. "It's our new vocational wing, built with grant monies. Come into my room. Mrs. Stafford, the art teacher, should be here shortly."

Brad hurried to the work sink and washed the sticky soda from his hands. "I have first period planning, but her class starts in fifteen minutes in the adjoining room."

The classroom phone on his desk buzzed. He lifted his hands in apology. "Sorry, it's never dull around here." Brad answered the phone. Assistant principal Bill Jenkins was on the other end. "Mrs. Stafford had to go to the hospital with some sort of pregnancy complications. We're having trouble locating a sub. Can you handle her class until we find someone?"

"Will do." Brad hung up the phone. Raquel was studying his safety-first poster. This day was not going as he had hoped. "We have a little snafu ... nothing we can't handle." He explained the situation and walked her through the supply storage space that joined the two rooms together.

Raquel surveyed the bright white cabinets and cream-colored walls that served as a backdrop for colorful drawings and paintings. "Nice. This classroom is more stimulating for the artist in me. I feel I've emerged from a colorless cave to the light."

"Hey, my room features a monochromatic color scheme, if I remember correctly from art class. Battleship gray gets my industrial tech juices flowing."

She chuckled. "Fair enough. Are students allowed to have cell phones on campus?"

"They may have them in their possession but shouldn't use them during class."

"Is it okay for me to have them use the camera function?"

"If it's at your instruction."

"Good." She walked to the teacher's desk. "Okay, crash course in what I need to do. I'm good with talking to the class—but discipline and classroom procedures, I haven't a clue.

He appreciated her unruffled willingness to step in and take on the class. "I'll stay with you first period and show you the ropes. A substitute teacher should be here by then. If not, I'll shuffle between classes. If any student gives you the least bit of trouble send him or her to me."

Brad took roll and introduced Raquel. When she began to speak, he saw that discipline would not be an issue.

"Have any of you ever taken or seen a selfie?" Raquel asked. Hands went up around the room.

"Most of the great artists painted selfies, but they were called self-portraits in Van Gogh's and Rembrandt's time. In a way, their self-portraits were actually the oldest version of the selfie. Why do you suppose artists made self-portraits?"

She called on a student.

"So, we'd know what they looked like years later?"

"Yes, and having the portraits they created gives us not only a glimpse of their physical appearance but tells us something of their mood and emotions in how they saw themselves. The human form is a pretty complex subject to tackle."

"Besides, it was, and still is, common for artists to use hired models which can be pricey. Drawing from life by looking in a mirror is a lot cheaper and more convenient. So artists have experimented with painting themselves for a long, long time. And in this smart phone era, with over ninety-three-million selfies taken daily, self-portraits remain an important source of the creative process. Today, we are going to give it a try."

Raquel took out her phone, snapped a shot of herself and asked the students to do the same.

The class was hooked, and so was Brad.

Beginning with an oval for the face, she led them through a simple basic step-by-step explanation of depicting the neck, shoulders, facial details, and hair. The students were excited to produce some decent likenesses.

"This was so cool." A student in the front row held up his drawing. "This is the first time I've produced more than an emoji face."

Raquel moved about the room, making encouraging comments on the students' work.

Brad pointed to the wall clock. "Five minutes 'til the bell."

"Class, I'll close with this."

Students who normally packed up books and began jockeying to be the first out of the class, sat up and listened. Amazing.

"Creating art is like going on a journey. You have a starting point. But as you move forward, you will make progress. You may hit some obstacles along the way that may be discouraging"—she looked directly at Brad in the back of the room—"but stay with it, whatever your goal, and you'll get past those obstacles."

He didn't know about the rest of the class but her advice struck him like an arrow, prodding him to think outside his gray cubicle.

"I'll leave you with one piece of advice that I have acquired over my years since high school. Always be thankful for every accomplishment, no matter how small. Not to the point of pride, rather to encourage and motivate yourself and others."

"Can you earn a living being an artist?"

"As an artist, I don't claim any profound wisdom nor that my path is the best. My fellowship provided room and board, tuition, and books with a small stipend. And now I teach for the art institute. I earn enough to pay for food and rent. But there are those who create works of art and make six-figure incomes."

"I'm a senior and have no clue what I want to do. I enjoy art, but I don't think it's my calling." He held up his sketch and received some chuckles from those sitting near him.

"I always felt at home with a drawing pencil and sketchpad and have been blessed to turn a hobby into a profession and lifestyle. At least you have found something you enjoy. Art may simply be your hobby."

The bell rang, and Raquel joined Brad at the door. The students filed out, thanking her for coming.

"Well, you were a big hit."

"I don't know about being a hit. They were likely on good behavior because I'm a sub."

"Are you kidding? Have you been out of school so long you've forgotten how unmercifully substitute teachers can be treated? Students will lie about their name when roll is called, swear the teacher allows food and drink in class, and notoriously take advantage."

Raquel laughed. "I remember a certain someone who shot spit balls that stuck to the ceiling when we had a sub in English."

"See? You had these kids enthused and wanting more. As you just advised the class, be thankful for your accomplishment. Here's your next group coming in. I'll leave the doors open between rooms in case you need me, but I'm sure you'll do fine."

And she did do fine. The end of third period, Brad poked his head into the art room.

"Mrs. Stafford has fourth period planning, so you are free to go. I have a class coming in, or I would escort you out."

"No worries. I need to prepare for the sip and draw luncheon tomorrow. Are you busy tonight?"

"Afraid I am. I have a business and finance class which is part of the marine construction certification. But I anxiously await your draw and tell story time at Calico Jack's tomorrow night."

He watched as she gathered her purse and supplies and fantasized what it might be like if she were his permanent teacher neighbor.

"What's so interesting in the storage closet, Mr. Z?" his architectural drawing student asked. "I need help on the three-dimensional program sequence."

Fantasy would have to wait.

Chapter 5

The table in the private dining room at the Gardner Hamilton Boardinghouse Restaurant was cleared of a delicious lunch of strawberry-glazed pork loin and set up with paints and 14" X 18" canvas panels on tabletop easels.

The rich smell of brewing coffee wafted from the kitchen.

Raquel assessed her new batch of pupils. She had considered her age group and interests in her prior presentations. However, for the private luncheon painting party of six, she felt she couldn't go wrong with having them paint azaleas.

"After our lovely luncheon, is everyone ready to create?"

Izzie Harrison to Raquel's left grabbed a paint brush and elbowed her husband, Reed, sitting beside her. "Ready, aren't we, sweet cakes?"

Reed fake-winced, rubbing his arm. "Careful, or I won't be able to lift my painting arm."

Seated next to Reed were the Hamilton sisters. Their flower names and contrast in appearance reminded Raquel of old Mutt and Jeff cartoon characters. Petunia's blue tinted curls bobbled as she replied, "Yes, yes, I'm excited. Aren't you, Marigold?"

Marigold nodded.

Addison Dursema, Fairland Hotels executive, and Vance Padgett, with the firm contracted for redevelopment of downtown Hamilton Harbor, were engaged in quiet conversation and not the picture of enthusiasm. She would try a different tact.

"Mr. Dursema, I heard you say during lunch that the goal of the hotel compact agreement was moving nicely. I've been away from Hamilton Harbor several years, and I'd love to hear more about the agreement."

He shifted in his chair and cleared his throat "Sure. We"—he motioned around the table—"didn't see eye to eye in the beginning. But with a bit of persuasion"—he pointed across the table to Reed and Izzie—"I came to see there was a way to work out the hotel project to everyone's satisfaction. We are building a one-story complex blending into the natural landscape of trees and trails of Feldman Park reaching down to the bay. We have begun the first phase, which is construction of the main hotel guest registration building."

Mr. Padgett spoke up. "The compact is a partnership which provides collaborative landscape design of the property joining Feldman Park and training for the girls in this maternity home that will translate into hotel jobs so they can become self-supporting."

"The hotel will carry literature on the Boarding House Restaurant as a suggested dining option for guests," Petunia said.

"What we first saw as a liability, we now see as an asset," Mr. Dursema said.

Raquel clasped her hands. "My hats off to all of you for working to help each other reach your goals. Government leaders could use your example."

"Amen. You are a French artist but used to live here," Izzie said. "Do you think you will return to the States?"

"My dad who lives in New York City is campaigning for me to move there. Honestly, it is a matter of prayer for me."

"You are very sensible," Marigold said.

As she spoke, Mr. Dursema seemed to zone out. She knew the signs—arms folded and tapping his hands against his elbow. *How do I connect with this group*? She had to try. "Shall we get started?"

"You know what?" Mr. Dursema said, "I've paid, but don't feel obligated to teach me to paint."

He uncrossed his arms and appeared ready to stand. She was losing him. No way she could let that happen.

She clapped her hands, and all eyes went to her. "I had planned to teach you how to draw azaleas and have coffee and dessert served while we work. But I will ask them to put that treat on hold. Bring your cell phones, and let's go on a nature hike first."

Outside, Raquel walked alongside Mr. Dursema onto the hotel property. "Please explain what goes where."

"The Gardner Hamilton house currently adjoins Harbor Lane, but we have obtained a city permit to close off this street so the two properties will flow together with a tree-lined drive and walking trail winding between the properties. With the established azaleas, this landscape will be a showplace for our new, small town classics line of hotels."

"I see the vision. What a lovely solution to blending the old with the new.

Raquel stepped forward and spoke to everyone. "Use your phones and take close-ups of the flowers."

The group fanned out, observing the flowers, except for Mr. Dursema and Padgett, who split off making their way to the stone seawall Brad had shown her.

Raquel joined them. Mr. Dursema was talking.

"... here's what I wanted you to see. There is erosion here that will affect our contracted deadline. Of course, we included a few weeks of extra wiggle room, but we could be looking at an expensive wall replacement which will cause a trickle down of delays. A solid foundation is imperative before we move forward. Water borders two sides of this property. I can't afford to lose any of the land to erosion."

Mr. Padgett stood on one of the large rocks and looked around, rubbing his chin.

"Do you mind if I join the conversation?" Raquel asked.

"No. Please do, especially if you know something about seawalls." Mr. Padgett chuckled.

"As it turns out, I do."

Mr. Padgett hopped down from the rock. Mr. Dursema said, "What can you tell us?"

Raquel related what she remembered of Brad's comments and suggestion of the foam fill to repair the wall which would be far less expensive and an ecofriendly solution.

She finally had their attention. "I can have him contact you, if you like."

Both men agreed and handed her their business cards.

Raquel fingered the plain white stock cards with the identifying information and company logos, then an idea struck.

Chapter 6

Brad pulled into the gravel restaurant parking lot. He'd received Raquel's text.

COME EARLY TO CALICO JACK'S IF YOU CAN. THERE ARE TWO MEN I WANT YOU TO MEET.

He glanced at his watch. Quarter past five. Early didn't happen. Her text had come before the longwinded, after-school parent-teacher meeting. And then, Mr. Jenkins cornered him with a request that might make Brad's fantasy of working alongside Raquel become a reality. Mrs. Stafford had been ordered to bed rest, and Mr. Jenkins wanted Brad to ask if Raquel would sub to the end of the school year. The idea of Raquel working alongside him felt like a coat of fresh paint to his spirit. Brad breathed in the refreshing harbor air, and his shoes clipped a swift cadence along the dock.

The delicious smells of fried grouper and shrimp became stronger, the closer he came to the pirate-themed restaurant at the end of the dock. Seagulls circled and gathered on dock posts over the *do not feed the birds* signs, awaiting morsels to be tossed by customers.

Moored next to the restaurant was Calico Jack's pirate galleon replica. Owner Jack Rudman, who was dressed as the pirate, spoke to a group of enthralled children.

Beside him, Raquel stood next an easel and blank sheet of paper. Customers clustered around. Izzie Harrison with her husband Reed, waved Brad to their table where two men, unfamiliar to him, were seated.

"They've just started. I'll make introductions later," she whispered.

Brad nodded and took a seat.

"Well, blokes. I'll fill you in on the error of me ways. It's like this. I made a career of plundering vessels floating about the Caribbean. But when we started to attack and steal British ships, a kindly Brit offered a royal pardon and general amnesty to us pirates. We become honest men."

Calico leaned to one little boy and whispered, though loud enough for all to hear. "We had well-meaning intentions, but our good behavior didn't last long."

He straightened and adjusted his waistcoat coat and sleeves with frilled cuffs. "Naughty we were. So now is my chance to be better. I traded me side sword for this satchel of coins, and now I give instead of take. You will each receive a gold coin after we hear this maiden's story."

The pirate sat down. The giggling children scooted around to make room for him.

"Thank you, Calico Jack," Raquel said. "I am going to share with you a story about another pirate. We'll call him Captain Scoundrel. He was a foul man with a hook on the end of his arm." She drew a hook in the center of the easel paper. "He carried a sword with a crook at the tip." She drew the sword next to the hook. Continuing to draw, she related the story of a pirate who traveled the globe beneath a skull and crossbones flag. "On windswept seas with islands where tropical flowers grew, the pirate stole gold coins for his treasure chest."

When she finished her story, the strategically drawn objects joined to depict the portrait of a pirate. "Do you think Captain Scoundrel will give up his unseemly ways after seeing the good example of Calico Jack?"

"Yes!" The children shouted and clapped. Others in the restaurant applauded.

Calico Jack thanked Raquel and handed out coins to delighted children who found the coins were gold, foil wrapped chocolates. Raquel acknowledged kind remarks from patrons as she joined their table. Brad greeted her, pulling out her chair.

"Loved your presentation. I dressed for the occasion." Izzie toggled her head, showing off tiny, glittering tricorn pirate hat earrings.

"Thank you. Has everyone been introduced?"

"Not yet. We didn't want to interrupt the show," Izzie said.

After introducing Addison Dursema and Vance Padgett, Raquel added, "Brad is the seawall expert I told you about."

"I wouldn't say expert, but I've worked on seawalls around here and just took a marine contractor's course."

"I hear you have a solution for the eroding seawall bordering the hotel property."

"Replacement is costly. I believe the erosion can be stopped with a new technique … but I don't want to bore everyone."

"Call me with the details." Mr. Dursema reached inside his coat pocket and held up a business card. "I'm pleased to announce this card will be redesigned soon, per Raquel's excellent suggestion."

"Dynamite idea," Izzie said. "Instead of painting on canvas, Raquel modified our art class—we painted designs which can be copied and used on letterheads and such."

"Like business cards?" Brad asked, accepting the card from Mr. Dursema.

Mr. Dursema nodded with enthusiasm. "Yes. I texted a picture of the azaleas I painted to the marketing department. Plans are already underway to create a special logo brand using the floral design to reflect the setting of this hotel."

Brad ran his finger over the raised Fairland Hotel lettering. "An amazing idea." Just as he turned to compliment Raquel, her phone sounded.

"Sorry. It's my dad, I'd better take it." She stood and moved away from the noisy restaurant chatter.

Ideas for the hotel remained in conversation.

"From an interior design viewpoint," Reed said, "our azalea paintings can be transferred and used as designs on curtains, carpet, and bedspreads in the hotel."

"Don't forget gift items," Izzie said. "I envision mugs, shirts and of course earrings with colorful azalea designs to offer at the hotel and Feldman Park gift shops."

"Instead of calling the hotel Fairland at Hamilton Harbor," Mr. Padgett said, "Raquel came up with the specialty hotel brand name—Azalea Place by Fairland. Genius."

"Enough of our excitement," Izzie said, and tapped Brad's arm. "Any excitement at good ol' Hamilton Harbor High today?" Her swinging earrings made sparkles of light dance about the table.

Raquel had generated ideas and enthusiasm. His only excitement was the possibility of having Raquel teaching in the classroom next to him. But he couldn't share about the request for her to substitute teach until he talked to her. "Not a lot to tell other than I had a long parent-teacher conference after school that made me late."

Raquel returned to the table all smiles. "My dad says one of the New York art galleries wants to feature an exhibit of my work, and they have a job opening for an art handler and gallery assistant."

"Sounds like an excellent opportunity." Mr. Padgett said. "Put me down as a reference."

"Me too," Mr. Dursema said. "Your talents are being wasted here."

A waitress arrived with a platter of fried crab claws. Brad bit into one of the crunchy, well-seasoned appetizers but wasn't too sure how well they would sit on his unsettled stomach. Raquel's expertise had scored with big business and a New York art gallery. And he was supposed talk to her about a measly subbing job?

"The next spring festival events on my schedule aren't until Friday, so I'm flying up to see my dad. The exhibit opportunity is huge, but I don't ..."

She turned to Brad with ... what in her eyes? Hope for approval? Brad's heart shrank. He didn't want her to go but telling her so would be selfish. How could a job as a high school fill-in art teacher compare to the opportunity set before her? Quite likely this was the path she'd seen spotlighted at the sunrise service.

His breath caught when he opened his mouth to speak, but he managed to get out, "Congratulations. I know you'll be a hit in New York City."

Chapter 7

"How about coffee and fresh muffins before I take your bags upstairs?" Pete asked.

"You don't have to twist my arm. The stewardess only offered water on the early morning flight."

"How was the trip to New York?"

"Good question." Raquel pressed her lips together, frowning. How was the trip? She wasn't sure how to express her feelings.

She had tried to explain to her father why she wanted time before committing to the art handler position. "I want to find a job that's meant for me."

"Well, of course," her dad had responded. "The place where your talents shine. And what better place than here in this New York art gallery?" Then her father paused and surprised her with words she'd never thought would cross his lips. "But at the end of the day, I claim the words spoken over you at your christening. 'May this child bless others with her talents as she travels through life.' You pray. And I will too."

Pete brought her back. "I didn't mean to pry. I'll set your bags on the utility porch. Come on in the kitchen."

"Your question wasn't out of line. I'm just trying to figure out for myself how the trip went and what I should do next."

"Maybe eggs and bacon added to that muffin will help." He nodded to the coffee pot. "Coffee just finished brewing." Pete pulled an egg carton and a package of bacon from the refrigerator.

"I'd like to help," Raquel said.

Pete pushed the eggs in her direction and handed her a glass bowl. "Stir up six eggs. Claudia will join us after she walks the dogs." Raquel cracked the eggs into the bowl and used the whisk Pete handed her. He took out a skillet and soon the smell of sizzling bacon filled the kitchen.

"Seeing dad and my stepmom was nice. If I go to work in the city, they offered the use of their townhouse they only use on occasion. The art gallery is nearby, and the director was gracious."

"Sounds like a perfect set up."

"But what we're doing right now is what I wouldn't have in New York and didn't have in France. The feeling of ..." She struggled for the word, "belonging, attachment."

"... home?"

"Yes, exactly. Home."

"We ate out every meal. I don't believe the squeaky-clean stove in my stepmom's kitchen has ever been used. And the clientele the gallery serves are rather stiff. No neck huggers."

"Hamilton Harbor is replete with neck huggers." Pete removed the bacon to paper toweling, poured off the grease, and slipped the eggs into the skillet.

"Where did you learn to cook?"

"On the oil rigs. When I wasn't involved in building or maintenance, the cook taught me basic cooking skills, nothing fancy."

"Basic and not fancy is a treat for me."

Footsteps sounded in the hall outside the kitchen, and Claudia walked in. "Hey, all. The dogs are walked and I smell bacon."

They each prepared their plates. Pete blessed the food, and Raquel bit into a moist muffin. "Mmm. My first home-cooked meal in days."

Claudia pointed to Pete with her fork. "Lake said to tell you he delivered the plywood to the park." Then she turned to Raquel. "Pete is creating an outdoor dance floor for the presentation of the Azalea Trail King and Queen, *And*," Claudia said, heavy on the and, "the festival committee conspired after you flew off to New York."

Raquel swallowed a bite of crisp bacon. "Conspired. About what?"

"The mayor suggested you and Brad, as former king and queen, crown the new king and queen tonight. Are you willing?"

"Sure, if Brad doesn't mind."

"He told me"—Claudia tapped her chest—"he'd be delighted to stand as your king again."

"He did?" Raquel grasped her coffee cup, soaking in its warmth. She liked the idea of playing king and queen with Brad again. Returning to Hamilton Harbor and reconnecting with Brad had reintroduced her to her roots and felt ... right. Yet, doors were opening in New York.

"Brad worked on leveling a space at the park, for me to build the dance floor," Pete said.

"When did you realize construction was what you wanted to do?"

"Hmm. I'm not sure. I learned carpentry from my stepfather. I've always gravitated toward construction, and then, I felt called to specialize in restoration."

"I wish I felt called."

"Weren't you called to New York?" Claudia asked.

"Yes, but is New York my calling?"

"Let me ask you," Pete said. "What do you really enjoy doing?"

Raquel took a sip of sweetened coffee, then set down her cup. "I'd have to say teaching. In France, I've been instructing college students. Since I've been here, I've worked with elementary, high school, and adult groups. I enjoy teaching all ages."

"I believe looking at what you enjoy, combined with your giftedness, is a key to unlocking your calling. I see the quest as threefold. Pray for God's will, look at your options, and let him direct the next steps. The opportunities that become available may surprise you."

Pete laid down his fork and folded his hands. "Let's pray right now. Lord, your word tells us to come to you in prayer; and you promise to answer. We stand on your word and pray in accordance to your will for you to show Raquel, in a way she understands, the path you would have her take."

Mayor Brimstead spoke from the dais at Feldman Park.

"Welcome everyone to Spring Festival. On stage with me is this year's Azalea Trail royal court. To crown the new king and queen selected from this group, we are privileged to have former King Brad Zimmerman and Queen Raquel Windhelm. Ms. Windhelm is also this year's visiting artist."

There was polite applause among the spectators, but Izzie Harrison cupped her hands and hooted.

Brad, dressed in a navy suit, squeezed Raquel's hand and winked. "You look lovely."

His compliment made her knees go weak. "Thank you. I borrowed this dress from Emme," she whispered.

"Why celebrate spring?" the mayor asked. "I'm glad you asked." He guffawed at his own joke.

"I didn't hear anyone ask," Brad said in a low voice.

"Would you stop? Don't make me laugh." The easy banter that had existed between them in high school had gained new life.

"For starters," the mayor continued, "spring marks the time when we have equal amounts of daylight and darkness. This year's theme is The Art of Spring ... celebrating nature's painting our fair city with springtime colors. And the celebration began right over there at the city's first garden club." He pointed to the Victorian Violet Feldman house. "The Azalea Trail tradition includes antebellum-dressed young people gracing the lawns of homes that have burst into bloom. The young men and women who make up the court have exhibited exemplary goals, grades, and community service. Let's show our appreciation for their accomplishments." The gathered crowd applauded.

"And now former King Brad and Queen Raquel will announce and crown the new king and queen of our springtime festival."

The mayor, using his cane, stepped back for Brad and Raquel to step forward, then handed each of them an envelope.

After announcing the winners, Raquel was handed a tiara with combs attached to place on the new queen. "Congratulations. The combs on this tiara are a nice addition. When I was crowned, the tiara kept slipping. Hopefully, this one stays put."

The girl wobbled her head back and forth. "Thank you. It feels secure. I was in your self-portrait art class at school, and I tried the technique you taught with the Girl Scouts where I volunteer. The activity was a hit."

The news made Raquel giddy inside. *Was this girl's testimony a nudge for her to concentrate on teaching?*

The mayor returned to the mic. "Now to usher in the season of renewal our new king, queen, and court who will dance to, 'It Might As Well be Spring.'" He motioned to the students to move from the stage. "A special thanks to Pete Cullen and the Helping Hands Ministry from the church downtown for constructing the dance floor. We are a community that works together."

The crowd applauded, and the couples danced through the first stanzas, then Mayor Brimstead shooed Brad and Raquel off the speaker platform to the dance floor.

Brad offered Raquel his hand. "My queen, you look even more lovely tonight than fifteen years ago."

A lock of unruly hair slid onto his forehead, coaxing her to reach up and brush it back into place. But the thick curl was Brad's brand which touched an unforgettable longing and drew sweet memories into the present.

She took his hand and mimicked a curtsy. "The dim light can have that affect, my king."

Brad grinned and tugged her close, gently guiding her along the dance floor. Resting her head against his shoulder, she closed her eyes and breathed in his comfortable scent as they swayed to the springtime lyrics.

Dancing with Brad, the student's remark and song rolled over her like a wave. Was she meant to stay in Hamilton Harbor? Pete had prayed that her direction would be obvious.

"Brad?" Raquel asked. "Where do you see things going from here?"

He leaned back to face her and shrugged. "For you? New York." His answer was matter of fact.

"But I don't know if that's where I should go right now."

"Why not?"

His eyes appeared as dark blue pools, hard to read in the lantern light. Did he want her to leave?

"Hey, you two. The music has stopped."

Brad stepped back. "I ... I guess it has," he stammered. Brad's hand, firm at her waist, steered her from the dance floor closer to Mr. Jenkins. "Raquel, this is my assistant principal, Bill Jenkins. Raquel Windhelm."

"I've heard many good things about you, Ms. Windhelm. Have you made up your mind about joining us?"

"Joining? I'm not sure I know what you mean."

"Uh ... I haven't had a chance to ask her yet."

"Ask me what?"

Mr. Jenkins answered. "Mrs. Stafford, the art teacher you subbed for, has been put on bed rest until she has her baby, and I wanted to know if you'd consider finishing out the school year in her art class."

Raquel wrinkled her forehead. Brad was supposed to ask her, and he hadn't? Why?

A little girl ran over and tugged Mr. Jenkin's shirt. "Daddy. The bouncy house. Come on."

"Let me know. Excuse me. Duty calls." He winked and followed the little girl.

"You're probably wondering why I didn't—"

"Of all people, I thought I could count on you to be open and honest. I was ready to pour my heart out to you about my quandary over where I should go next, but I guess I have my answer. You don't want me here."

"That's not true."

A pang took hold of her spirit. "Really? We seem to be back where we left off years ago, with you encouraging me to leave. Don't worry. When my commitment to the festival is over, I'll will be leaving ... for New York."

Chapter 8

Brad sat at the foot of the stairs that Raquel had marched up to enter the garage apartment at the B & B. She ignored his knocks. He stared at a sprig of grass that had managed to sprout up in the pavement.

From the park, line dancers had taken over the dance floor. Instructions blared on the PA system to "slide left, slide right, and boom, boom, clap." Scents from the fried funnel cake booth wafted across the street, smelling sickeningly sweet.

Brad rested his head in his hands. How had things gotten so messed up? Stupid. He should have told Raquel right away about Mr. Jenkins request for her to sub and let her make up her mind on what to do.

"Mind if I join you?"

Brad lifted his head. Pete stood beside the stairs.

"Please do." Brad slid over to make room.

"I don't mean to meddle, but I saw that Raquel left in a flurry."

Brad sniffed. "Yes, she did. She is not pleased with me at present. I failed to tell her that she had a substitute teacher job offer."

"Her reaction fits," Pete said.

"Fits what?"

"I hope this is not a betrayal of her trust, but she requested prayer about the direction for her career and told me her real interest was teaching."

Brad's stomach knotted. "Great." Brad slapped the wood railing. He winced and shook his hand. "I held back the teaching offer and got in God's way. No wonder she's upset with me."

"The way I see it, you might be interfering not only with what God wants in her life but also what God may be doing in your life."

Brad stood and raked his hand through his hair. "I thought I was being helpful by supporting her New York opportunity. Especially since she promoted me for a seawall job."

"The teaching and seawall jobs may both be providential." Pete, hands on his thighs, pushed himself up from the stairstep. "I'm no love expert. So, take this advice or leave it. But I believe Raquel would like to stay here ... if she knew you wanted her to."

"The only thing she wants from me is the opportunity to spit in my eye."

"Sleep on it," Pete said. "Morning may paint a different picture."

Pete left Brad to stew alone. Raquel had told him about the lighted path vision and the belief she was at a crossroads. She wanted direction, and he'd parroted what he thought she wanted to hear when the New York prospect came up. He'd decided Hamilton Harbor was not the best place for her. Who was he to make that determination? Now she thought he wanted her to leave. The truth was the opposite. But how could he let her know?

Cloggers stomped and pounded the dance floor at the park while Brad eyed the valiant grass sprig. If that tiny plant could break through concrete, he'd find a way to show Raquel his true colors.

Chapter 9

She might as well get this over with.

Raquel climbed the steps to the historical society carrying a satchel of art supplies for painting birdhouses. The project was her last obligation and unfortunately included Brad. He'd been the collector of milk cartons for the event. Maybe he'd be working in a separate room.

Inside, Petunia spoke and gestured with her hands. "We have the procedure all worked out. There are four groups of eight signed up. In the exhibit room, Marigold and I will tell the story of Feldman Square and how it began. We'll send the children to Brad to prep their birdhouse. Then you will instruct them on decorating. There is plenty of space on the porch for the birdhouses to dry before the children take them home." Petunia stopped to catch her breath. "Does that work?"

"Your plan sounds fine."

"Brad is already here with the birdhouses," Marigold said. "You two will be in the kitchen. The festival has been a great success thanks to you. This is the last event, but I do hope you will stay for the afternoon festivities."

"Thank you but I have a flight out this afternoon at five."

A plop sounded followed by clatter coming from the kitchen.

"Oh, dear." Petunia's hand went to her throat.

The three hurried to the kitchen, which was a large room in the rear, stretching the width of the house. Brad stood surrounded by a sea of empty milk containers.

He grimaced. "Evidence of the domino effect. Lining these cartons up was a bad idea. I'll put them back in the bag." He motioned to the large, plastic bag lying on the floor.

His ears had flushed red. Was he as uncomfortable as she was?

"We'll use the grab bag approach for the kids to select their birdhouse."

Raquel gave him a curt nod. "I'll set up opposite you."

She opened her case, holding paint supplies, slipped on her art smock, and pushed up the sleeves. Behind her, the containers clunked together as Brad bagged them.

This was not their first Spring Art Festival project. She and Brad had worked on a canvas banner in Ms. Hixon's art class, senior year. After a bit of haggling and compromising on the lettering, creativity abounded on the rest of the banner with all class members contributing springtime drawings of flowers, butterflies, birdhouses, and watering cans. Her contribution had been two cuddling lovebirds.

Working with Brad had been fun, but now ... she gave Brad a sideward glance as he gathered the scattered milk cartons. Two had skidded to her side of the room. She picked up the plastic containers and handed them to him.

"Here ya go."

He made eye contact. "Appreciate it." He opened the bag for her to add them.

"Izzie sent over decorating supplies in case you need them," Brad said, and handed her a paper bag. Inside were Popsicle sticks, bamboo plates, buttons, yarn, and pieces of trim.

"Thank you."

"You're welcome."

Brad made no other comment. After holding out on telling her about the local job offer and encouraging her to leave, what was there to say?

Petunia poked her head into the kitchen and spoke in a singsong voice. "The first group is here."

Raquel busied herself sorting tubes of color into various shades and tints. She had cups for water and went to the sink to fill them.

"You need eight cups of water?"

She nodded.

"Let me help."

Raquel filled two cups and carried them to her space. Brad brought the rest.

"Thank you."

"You're welcome."

His response was stoic, but she caught the twinkle in his eye. How do you stay upset with a twinkle?

Marigold's strong voice reverberated down the hall. She gave the origin of the Hamilton name of the town—however, the Feldman story, related by Petunia, was new to Raquel.

"Albert and Edith Feldman have a magical story. Edith was eighteen years old when her father died. She was one of five sisters, and her mother had no means of support. They lost their home. The sisters and their mother depended on other family members for help. At the same time, Albert Feldman needed a wife. He placed an ad for a woman of reasonable appearance, tolerably well-educated and well-versed in housekeeping. Edith boarded a train and entered into a marriage with a man she'd never met."

"A marriage of convenience started Feldman Park?" Raquel asked.

"News to me," Brad said.

Petunia went on. "In Edith's diary on display here, she wrote: *Marrying someone I'd never met was unthinkable. But I didn't want to worry my mother; so I stepped out in faith trusting that God had my future in his hands.*"

Raquel thought of Pete's prayer.

"Edith and Albert were married in the winter but come springtime," Petunia giggled, "according to her diary, they had fallen very much in love."

Raquel glanced at Brad. He said nothing, but his dark eyes were trained on her. "Friends to lovers. A sweet story, don't you think?"

"I do."

The oh-so-sweet look he gave her, melted her stupid pride. "Brad, I'm sorry I got mad at you."

"Don't apologize. It's me who was wrong. I shouldn't have assumed what you would want to do. It was not my place. Truce?"

"Agreed."

Marigold's voice boomed from the classroom. "Speaking of springtime, it's time for you children to begin work on your birdhouses."

"Show time." Brad grinned, the forelock of hair sprung loose and hung on his forehead. Raquel's friend was back.

Chapter 10

Brad watched Raquel twirl about on the front porch of the historical society where the children's projects were drying.

"Aren't these birdhouses the most beautiful sight?"

No. She was the most beautiful sight. He smiled rather than voicing his thought and enjoyed observing her exuberance over the colorful designs.

Raquel lifted a bright red birdhouse with a picket fence made of popsicle sticks. "Jared, the adorable boy missing his two front teeth, told me this house would hold an entire hummingbird family because hummingbirds like red."

"Birds are sure to want to pack their belongings and move in."

"What's funny is my stepmother collects birdhouses with high price tags. The cute houses provide decorations for their sunroom, but birds never get to enjoy them."

"I see your point. These birdhouses may not be as fancy but provide a place for the birds to hang out."

"And teach a way to recycle materials and have fun."

"A win-win."

Raquel held up her hand and they high-fived.

Her spirited view highlighted the crux of the matter that had caused the rift between them. Brad had placed Raquel on a high society pedestal out of his reach, believing he should encourage her success. He had decided she was an unattainable, big deal French artist. But underneath, Raquel had been and still proved to be, down to earth Raquel—his friend. And if he could convince her to stay, he'd like nothing better than to become a friends-to-lovers story, like Edith and Albert.

Smells of caramel corn, sizzling burgers, and corndogs came from the festival vendors at Feldman Park. A few runners from the early morning 5K race with numbers pinned to their shirts milled in the festival crowd. Small children giggled and squealed, bouncing inside a ball-filled inflatable pool.

"Everything smells yummy."

Brad glanced at his watch. She said her flight left at five o'clock. Add loading her bags, travel to the airport, baggage check-in and security, he didn't have much time.

"I'll treat you to lunch shortly." He sucked in a risk-taking breath. "But first, I have a surprise for you."

She stopped and did a double take. "Surprise?"

He jangled his car keys. "It requires taking a ride."

"I love surprises."

He opened the passenger door of his Jeep Cherokee. "Hop in."

Leaving Feldman Square, he turned onto Main Street headed north.

"Every time I go past the old theater where the community church is now, I think of the giant snow flake we made in art class for the Christmas parade float."

"Uh-huh. The snowflake fell off, barely missing a baby carriage," Brad said. "I had to jump off, quiet the baby, grab the snowflake and hold onto it the rest of the parade route. My arms were sore for days."

"Hey, you had offers to help."

"Still no sympathy for my sacrifice?"

"Nope. And I'm getting over my mad about you keeping the teaching job offer from me, but not completely. Why didn't you tell me?"

"Truth?"

"Truth is always a good idea."

"I was going to tell you that night at Calico Jack's. But you got that call about the New York art gallery, and Mr. Dursema said your gifts were being wasted here. I chickened out."

"But you knew teaching interested me."

"Yes, but you've been teaching in a Paris art institute."

"That's no reason not to tell me about the sub job."

Brad pulled into the high school parking lot. "I'm making the offer official."

"You had to bring me here to tell me?"

"Yep. Follow me."

Brad unlocked the main door to the arts wing of the school. He flicked on the lights in his gray industrial tech classroom.

"Okay you have my curiosity up. What is going on?"

"Azalea Trail Queen Raquel Windhelm, King Brad Zimmerman admits to the folly of making assumptions about the queen's desires. He humbly admits to being stupid, presumptuous, and rash and formally invites you, per the suggestion of Assistant Principal Jenkins, to be the substitute high school art teacher through the end of the school year at Hamilton Harbor High."

He stepped through the adjoining storage space, moved aside for Raquel to enter, and flipped on the lights in the art room. Extending across the board in front of the room was the spring festival banner created by their art class seventeen years ago.

Raquel's eyes widened, and she spoke in a disbelieving whisper. "You saved our banner all these years?"

"I couldn't part with it."

Raquel walked to the front of the room and stared at the *Celebrate the Colors of Spring* banner. She ran her fingers across the painted drawings of spring flowers, garden implements and birdhouses until her hand came to rest on the lovebirds. A heart drawn above their heads had B + R written inside.

"I always wondered who wrote the B + R in that heart, didn't you?"

"No." He turned to face her and gently grasped her shoulders. "I didn't wonder because I wrote our initials in the heart. I had hoped Brad plus Raquel had a chance. The hope still remains"—he tapped his chest—"right here."

"You never told me."

"I didn't have the nerve. But a sprig of grass encouraged me to take a risk."

"A sprig of grass? I have no idea what that means." Raquel moved closer and stroked his chin, sending a sweet sensation through him. "Pete prayed with me about career decisions and said opportunities might be surprising."

"He was right." Brad wrapped his arms around her middle, leaned down, and kissed her cheek.

"The invitation to spring festival and the spotlight on the path must have been leading me back here ... and to you." Raquel reached up and brushed the pesky tuft of hair from his forehead.

He laughed softly and cupped her face in both of his hands. "Color me springtime," he whispered, and lifted her chin.

"Color me weak-kneed."

Her words were barely audible. And under the *Celebrate the Colors of Spring* banner, Brad sealed the hope of B + R with a lingering kiss.

The End

Sally Jo Pitts

Sally Jo Pitts brings a career as a private investigator, high school guidance counselor and teacher of family and consumer sciences to the fiction page. Tapping into her real-world experiences she writes what she likes to read, faith-based stories, steeped in the mysteries of life's relationships. She is author of the Hamilton Harbor Legacy romance series and the Seasons of Mystery series. You can connect with her at www.sallyjopitts.com.

Welcome Home to Redbird Falls

SHELIA STOVALL

Chapter 1

Jen Bennett picked up the pen to renew her lease. *Why stay in New York?* After ten years of building her reputation as one of the top pastry chefs in the city, she was unemployed. She was an artist, or she had been—food her medium. A misstep on an icy sidewalk had shattered her wrist and her career. Her boss replaced her in less time than it took to temper chocolate. Meanwhile, her savings and her dream to open her own shop were dwindling.

Outside her apartment window, cars honked and a siren blared as Jen scrolled through her phone contacts. Her spirits lifted when Aunt Queenie's name came up. Jen pictured Aunt Queenie in her old farmhouse kneading dough and hit the call button.

Aunt Queenie sputtered. "Jen, is everything all right?"

"What makes you think something's wrong?"

"A call on a Tuesday when your habit is to phone on Sundays."

"Everything is fine. But since the doctor removed my cast, I thought it might be a good time to visit."

"I'd love that." Aunt Queenie's voice now sounded cheerful.

"Can I stay for a few weeks? I need to start physical therapy, but I can do that anywhere." Jen bit her lip. "Maybe, time with you will help me figure out my new career plan."

"This is an answer to prayer. I'd love to have the chance to spend some time with you before ..."

Silence. Did the call drop? "Aunt Queenie?"

"There will be no hiding my condition when you get here."

"What condition?"

Aunt Queenie sighed. "I have cancer."

"What type of ...?" Jen couldn't say the word.

"Pancreatic." Aunt Queenie's voice was matter-of-fact.

"Is it ... terminal?" Jen's chest squeezed.

"Honey, we're all terminal. I've had radiation and chemotherapy. There's naught else to be done but to live each day with joy and thankfulness."

"Why didn't you tell me?"

"You've had your own troubles."

"I love you. I would have come."

"Friends have helped me."

"But I'm your family. You should have told me."

"I'm sorry, Hon. I hope you'll forgive me."

"Of course. And like it or not, I'm headed your way."

"I like it. Just let me know when to have someone pick you up at the airport."

"I'll hire a taxi."

"That will cost more than a fat hog. I have friends wearing me out trying to do for me."

No use arguing. "I'll be there as soon as I get things settled."

After asking questions, Jen disconnected and made a list of things to do. A heaviness pushed down on her. She'd missed holidays and family birthdays due to her ambition. No wonder Aunt Queenie hadn't told her about having ... cancer.

Monday morning came, and Jen was on her way to the airport. Her landlord agreed to keep her Ikea furniture. She had shipped her cookbook collection and a few mementos to Aunt Queenie's address. Everything else she owned was in her rolling bag.

Jen swallowed hard. She wouldn't be returning to New York. Ten years. Wasted. She'd never taken to city life, but she'd been determined to impress her mother. Too bad nothing short of a six-figure salary would accomplish that goal.

Thank goodness Jen had Aunt Queenie. Her love and support had given Jen the fortitude to go to culinary school instead of an Ivy League college. If not for her, Jen would probably be miserable ... practicing law in a big ten firm.

Jen squared her shoulders. Aunt Queenie needed her. Time to pour herself into something other than trying to make her mother proud. Jen was not going to give up on her aunt or her dream to open her own bakery without a fight.

A flock of migrating robins covered the field next to Chase Wilkins's greenhouses. It was time to leave to collect Miss Queenie's niece, Jen Bennett, from the airport. Though the drive was one hour to Nashville, he'd still lose half a day's work.

Every breath in the greenhouse was a different mixture of soil, herbs, and leafy plants. He pinched a lemon-basil leaf and tucked it into his shirt pocket. When he inhaled the scent, just a touch sweeter than lemon, he started humming.

Though today was the first day of spring and his to-do list was longer than his driveway, he didn't hesitate when Ms. Queenie asked him to collect Jen. He'd do just about anything for his favorite neighbor. Without her help, he'd never have achieved his dream of running his own operation instead of working for his dad like his older brother Liam.

The hillside covered in yellow daffodils made him smile. Spring in Kentucky was a feast for all the senses.

Folks in Redbird Falls liked to claim Jen Bennett as one of their own as she'd spent her childhood summers with Miss Queenie. Last year, the Cooking Network had featured Jen in a television show, and everyone in their small community gathered at the church to watch the program.

Chase rubbed his jaw. He'd been ten years old when Jen had lost her dad, Miss Queenie's brother, in Afghanistan. He didn't know much about Jen's mom other than she was a high-powered attorney. Annually, she had dropped Jen off at Ms. Queenie's place on Memorial Day weekend, then would leave town after visiting the cemetery, returning to collect Jen on Labor Day weekend.

Chase remembered coming home from college to discover the gangly girl had transformed into a knockout. Jen had just graduated high school, too young for him to date, but now … No. He shook his head. Jen was out of his league; and even if she wasn't, her life was in the city. Besides, when she learned what Ms. Queenie had asked of him, Jen would see him as an enemy.

Jen strode into the baggage claim area, looking like a tall glass of lemonade. Her blonde hair was loose and unstyled, and she wore an oversized, powder-blue sweatshirt—a shade lighter than her eyes. A sling held her left arm. This was a different image than the woman featured in *Bon Appétit*.

Chase removed his Stetson. "Hey, Jen. I'm your ride."

Jen halted, and her lush lips parted; but she didn't speak.

Chase extended his hand. "You probably don't remember me. I'm Chase Wilkins."

"Of course, I remember you." She gave a half-smile. "I expected one of the church ladies." When Jen clasped his hand, a current of energy traveled up Chase's arm, and warmth flooded him.

The light above the baggage carousel lit, and Jen jerked her hand away.

"Point out your bags to me, and I'll grab them." He closed his eyes as he savored a faint floral scent. *Lovely.*

"There's just the one." Jen's cheeks flushed. "It's an ugly green thing."

"One bag? But Miss Queenie said you'd be staying for a while."

"I had a tiny closet in my apartment, so I have a minimal wardrobe."

So this wasn't just a quick visit. "Had?" Does that mean you're not returning to New York?"

She lifted the arm wrapped in a sling. "I'll never be able to perform at the same level. Even if I could, I'm tired of making fancy desserts for food snobs."

"But you're a famous chef."

Jen shrugged. "I'm an unemployed pastry chef, but that's the least of my concerns with Aunt Queenie being sick."

"The chemo was hard on her." Chase dreaded for Jen to see how fragile Miss Queenie's health had become.

"She said there's nothing else to be done, but I will not let her give up."

Chase liked the sound of Jen's words. But sometimes, all one could do was to turn the situation over to God. He was confident Miss Queenie would be healed, but he didn't know if it would happen in heaven or on earth.

Jen followed Chase's broad shoulders and placed her palm over her warm cheek. He filled out a pair of Levi's better than any man she'd ever met. Oh, those dark curls, his chiseled jawline. She'd not let history repeat itself—her once silly schoolgirl crush was history. Hopefully, Chase had forgotten how she'd stalked him. When he'd touched her hand a few minutes ago, she felt vacuumed back to her awkward teen years. No other man's touch had ever made her heart race like this. Thank goodness, he seemed oblivious to her reaction to him just now.

Chase stopped in front of a black truck and started securing Jen's case in the back, while she waited by the tailgate.

"This truck is huge."

"A dually offers more stability when pulling a load." He caressed the side of the vehicle. Jen imagined him gazing at her with such appreciation. *Stop it.* He opened the passenger side door. When Jen stepped up, she wobbled, and Chase placed his hands on her waist. "Careful."

She thought her heart might beat out of her chest as she fumbled with the safety belt.

Chase reached across. "Let me help you."

His face was so close to hers, the scent of fresh-cut grass and citrus made Jen's breath catch. The old yearning intensified. She steeled herself against the tug on her heartstrings.

When they pulled onto the interstate highway, traffic came to a stop. As they waited for the road to clear, Chase sent a text message. "I'm letting Miss Queenie know we'll be late."

"That's thoughtful of you." Jen watched the clouds build. "Looks like rain."

"Hope so. Rain makes grain." Chase rolled down his window but exhaust fumes filled the cab, and he hit the switch again. "I don't know how people stand living like this. You can't get a breath of fresh air."

"You sound like Aunt Queenie."

"I'd take that as a compliment." Chase stared straight ahead, as if oblivious to her presence. Chase Wilkins definitely wasn't interested in her. Not then ... not now.

The tension in Jen's shoulders relaxed the moment Chase turned into Aunt Queenie's long drive. The white plank fence seemed to glow against the emerald pasture in the background. Buds sprouted from the limbs of the sugar maples lining the drive. The front door of the white gabled house opened, and Jen's spirits lifted. A woman with salt and pepper hair waved as she stood on the front porch.

"Is that Lee Ann?" Jen asked.

"Yes. Mom and some of the church ladies take turns visiting."

Worry crept up Jen's spine when Aunt Queenie didn't join Lee Ann on the porch.

As soon as Chase parked, Jen opened the truck door.

"Careful." He unbuckled his safety belt.

"I'm not an old woman."

"You're right about that," he muttered.

Lee Ann opened her arms. "Welcome home."

Jen skittered up the steps. "It's good to be here. Where's Aunt Queenie."

"She's resting." Lee Ann smiled tightly. "Waiting wore her out. The traffic must have been awful."

"We were stuck for over an hour." Chase removed his hat and held open the front door.

Jen walked inside and inhaled the aroma of something cooking—something with tomatoes. "Thank you for picking me up."

"You're welcome." He placed her case by the stairs. "Enjoy your visit," he said, his tone flat with politeness.

Lee Ann frowned. "You're not staying for lunch?"

"No, ma'am." Chase put his hat on. "The crew is waiting on me."

"Suit yourself." Lee Ann said.

Chase pecked his mother's cheek and walked toward the front door.

Jen couldn't resist watching him leave.

Lee Ann grabbed the rolling bag. "I'll put this in the bedroom."

Jen reached for the handle. "I can get it."

"Nonsense. Not with that arm. You look almost as feeble as Queenie."

"I wish she'd told me about her illness sooner."

"Me too, hon. But don't fuss at her. Just make the most of this time with her."

Jen swallowed the lump in her throat.

"I have tomato basil soup on the stove, and there's Gouda cheese from Bobbie Jo's dairy in the refrigerator for grilled cheese sandwiches."

"I knew something wonderful was going on in the kitchen."

Lee Ann smiled. "Why don't you wake Queenie, and I'll toast the sandwiches."

"Okay." Jen ambled to the bedroom and knocked. "Aunt Queenie."

"You're finally here." Aunt Queenie picked up her glasses from the bedside table.

Jen's breath caught. Aunt Queenie's long gray braid had been replaced by short white fuzz.

Jen turned on the bedside lamp and sat on the bed.

Aunt Queenie stroked Jen's face. "You are a sight for this old spinster."

"Lee Ann is finishing up lunch." Jen hugged her aunt's skeletal-like frame.

Aunt Queenie hugged her back, then flung the blue and white log cabin quilt aside to reveal black sweatpants. "I'll bet you're starved. We can catch up while we eat."

They settled in at the table, and Jen lifted a spoon to her lips but dribbled soup on the red and white checkered tablecloth. Embarrassed, she placed a napkin over the spill. "I'm sorry."

"Don't worry about it." Lee Ann gave her a fresh napkin.

"I'm left-handed, and I'm still clumsy using my right hand for everything." Jen swallowed. "Your soup tastes heavenly."

Aunt Queenie grinned. "She uses Chase's heirloom tomatoes."

Lee Ann brushed a crumb off the table. "I was a little nervous about feeding a chef."

"The best dishes of my life have come from this kitchen." Jen bit into her sandwich. "This Gouda tastes wonderful with your sourdough bread."

Lee Ann pushed up the sleeves of her pink cardigan and blushed. "Thank you."

Jen licked her lips. "Mm. Roasted mushrooms would make this spectacular."

"I think it's perfect as is." Aunt Queenie's tone was curt as she gazed over the top of her glasses.

"Of course. I'm sorry. It's a bad habit of mine to analyze and try to improve everything I eat."

"No need to apologize." Lee Ann's face softened. "Chase does the same thing with his vegetables."

"What type of tomatoes did you use for the soup?"

"Last year's canned Black Krims."

"So that's the reason for the odd color."

Lee Ann shrugged. "Some folks find the plum-color off-putting."

"What else does Chase grow?"

"Name a vegetable, and he probably has several varieties. His heirloom produce is in high demand."

"So he has a big garden?"

"It's more than a garden. Chase leased Queenie's place and started a Community-Supported Agriculture program."

"A CSA? Is that where people sign up to get fresh produce each week?"

"Yes. Customers pay up-front for a weekly basket of vegetables, and he sells heirloom seeds and plants in the spring."

"I hope I'm still here to sample his products this summer."

"You won't have to wait that long." Lee Ann sat up straight. "He has cabbages, kale, collard greens, broccoli and Brussel sprouts almost ready to harvest in the greenhouses."

Aunt Queenie's eyes twinkled. "I'm sure he'd enjoy giving you a tour."

"I'd love that."

After they cleaned up the kitchen, Lee Ann left, and Aunt Queenie went to her room to rest. Jen didn't hesitate to pull on Aunt Queenie's green rubber boots in the mudroom. After snatching a red jacket, Jen scurried down the back porch steps. She stood under an ancient white oak tree and inhaled. The fresh air exhilarated her as she walked with purpose. Moments later, she stopped by Redbird Falls, soaking in the surrounding beauty. Even through the gray sky, the wild redbuds' blooms were still vibrant. She breathed in the loamy earth while savoring the sound of water hitting the limestone rocks.

Across the creek, a deer snorted and leaped from the bank into the brush. A cardinal landed on the twig above and chirped as if to say, "Welcome home." Jen wished she could stay here forever—her happy place—to have a life filled with joy and thankfulness, just like Aunt Queenie.

Jen savored the moment. If only she could stay in Redbird Falls.

Chapter Two

Jen scheduled her physical therapy appointments to start a week after her arrival. Chase's habit of visiting daily both thrilled and irritated her. If only he'd give a girl a warning before he knocked on the back door and strode in—time enough at least to make sure she looked presentable.

Yesterday, she'd scorched scrambled eggs while pretending to ignore the easy rapport between Chase and Aunt Queenie. Some chef.

Most mornings, Jen and Aunt Queenie took rambling walks on the farm—heaven on earth.

Members of the church's Casserole, Cake, and Company Committee also visited. Even though Aunt Queenie lived in a tiny community, she had many friends. Their chatter made Jen realize how lonely she'd been in the city.

Jen spent her afternoons exploring Chase's greenhouses, dreaming of dishes she'd like to try. A few of the young men working for him wore straw hats, and Jen surmised they were Mennonites. They would tip their hats and blush when she'd pass them.

The days flew by just as they had during her childhood summers. Saturday arrived before Jen was ready to face it. Her hands shook as she started Aunt Queenie's old blue Buick to drive to town to buy groceries. She hadn't driven in years and needed practice before tackling the Nashville traffic for her PT appointments. As she slowly drove through the rural landscape, she passed Chase's black truck. He honked, causing her to almost drive into the green wheatfield.

After picking up groceries in Weldon, Jen turned toward home. At the crossroads, she passed the post office and the old Redbird Roost General Store. The rust-colored barn-shaped building sat empty. A wave of nostalgia assailed her as Jen remembered Miss Louise, the owner. The place had been a community gathering place, filled with joy and laughter.

The snooty atmosphere of the restaurant where Jen had worked left her longing to open her own shop where she hoped to replicate the same feeling of comfort and the sense of belonging that was missing from her life. It would be a long time before that dream became a reality since her weeks of convalescing had gouged her saving.

Jen rubbed her aching hand. For now, she'd take Lee Ann's advice and enjoy this time with Aunt Queenie and her friends. She pictured Chase's crooked smile, and her heart fluttered. *Stop thinking about him.* But she couldn't.

Aunt Queenie never missed a church service, and this Sunday would be no exception. Jen looped her arm through Aunt Queenie's elbow. "Please keep your mask on in the church. We don't want you to catch a cold."

Aunt Queenie lifted her chin. "Fine, but I'll not forfeit hugs."

When they entered the front door, people swarmed them. Jen recognized some of the women who had visited with food. Leta Evans and her bouncy white curls stood next to Jolene Pitchford, whose red hair was pulled back in a tight bun, a little girl hugging her hip.

Aunt Queenie led the way to her usual seat. "This is my pew."

Chase strode toward them. "Hey, good lookin," he said as he gave Aunt Queenie a hug.

Heat flooded Jen's face. She hoped no one else thought he had been talking to her.

Aunt Queenie patted Chase's cheek. "Hello, sweetie."

He turned toward Jen and offered a handshake. "Welcome to Crossroads Church."

Jen shook his callused hand, and his dark eyes seemed to drink her in. "Thank you." Her chest tightened.

He left them to greet others, and every little old lady received a hug and a playful comment. *The big flirt.* Still, Jen thought the way their faces lit up was sweet. Chase seemed to hug everyone except her.

When the organist began to play, he returned to the pew in front of Jen, where his family sat. Chase's brother, Liam, and his wife, Holly, were stationed next to the center aisle. On the other end, Lee Ann and her husband, Sam, held hands. Chase sat between the couples and rested his elbows on the top of the pew.

The Wilkins men wore similar Chinos and starched shirts. Liam and Sam were clean-shaven and sported classic buzz cuts, but dark curls touched the cobalt collar of Chase's shirt.

Jen tried to focus on the minister as he explained the Parable of the Sower, but she was distracted by Chase's nearness.

After the service, Jen and Aunt Queenie exited the church. Chase stood next to a beautiful young woman with a long crimson ponytail, who held a basket.

Chase grinned. "Jen, this Bobbie Jo Lyle. She's been looking forward to meeting you."

"It's an honor to meet a famous chef." Bobby Jo extended a basket. "I wanted to give you a sampling of my cheeses."

Jen smiled. "It's nice to meet you, and it's a pleasure to discover a fromager in Redbird Falls. I loved your Gouda. I had some for lunch the other day."

"Thank you. Let me know what you think of the rest."

"I will. Thank you."

"Chase said you're staying for a while?" Bobbie Joe bit her lip. "I wish we could talk *you* into opening a restaurant."

Jen shrugged. "It's a lovely idea."

"Jen's cooking is a bit fancy for Redbird Falls." Chase winked at her.

She held up her bum wrist. "I'm not sure what I'm going to do, but I can guarantee you it won't be fancy."

"We like to keep it simple around here." Bobbie Jo elbowed Chase. "You could use his vegetables, my cheeses, and his dad's beef."

Jen poked around in the basket. There was Asiago, Colby, Habanero Cheddar, and more. "If this sampling is as good as your Gouda, I'll be happy to recommend your products to other chefs."

Bobbie Jo beamed a smile. "That would be awesome."

Aunt Queenie asked, "Why don't you two join us for lunch?"

"Thank you, but Mom's expecting us," Chase said.

So Bobbie Jo must be Chase's girlfriend. Jen's spirits sagged as she looped her good hand through Aunt Queenie's elbow. "Enjoy your lunch."

When Jen and Aunt Queenie reached the Buick, Jen struggled with the basket while helping Aunt Queenie into the seat. If only she had two good hands.

"Let me help you." Chase reached for the basket.

"I've got it." Miffed, she let the door close harder than she should.

Chase furrowed his dark brows. "What's wrong?"

"Nothing," Jen snapped as she put the basket on the back seat. She rubbed her throbbing hand.

Chase leaned in close. "If your hand is hurting, I can drive you home."

Today he smelled of Sandalwood. Jen tore her gaze away. "Your girlfriend is waiting."

"Oh, she's—"

Jen didn't hear the rest because she slammed her car door. As Jen drove away, she glanced back to see Chase opening the passenger-side truck door for Bobbie Jo. They looked like they belonged on the cover of *Farm Today*. The dark clouds in the sky matched her mood. She should have known Chase had a girlfriend.

When they passed the old general store, Jen asked, "Is Miss Louise still around?"

"Bless her. The good Lord called her home while she slept." Aunt Queenie frowned. "I could have sworn I'd told you."

"No. I don't think so." Jen had been so wrapped up in her New York life, she'd probably zoned out during that phone call.

"The store's been empty for over a year," Aunt Queenie's tone was mournful.

Miss Louise's place had been an oasis in the rural landscape, well-watered with her conversation, and kindness. Her absence left a dismal void in the community.

If they lost Aunt Queenie, there would be another gaping hole. Jen swallowed hard. She couldn't lose Aunt Queenie too.

Chapter 3

Early on Monday morning, pink hues lit the gray horizon as Jen removed the clay bowl from the warm oven. There was nothing like kneading dough to work out your problems. Even though her left hand was almost useless, it felt good to plunge her fingers into the gooey mass. Jen hummed under her breath and inhaled a waft of cinnamon. The rolls would be ready to bake in an hour, which would give her time to take a walk.

Birdsong filled the air, and Jen's breath fogged as she crested the hill. Six large greenhouses lay in the valley, but the mist hovering over the creek obscured her view of the cascading water.

When she reached the bank, Jen could just make out the shape of a man sitting on an old bench. His head was bowed, but Jen recognized the broad shoulders. *Chase.* Was he praying? Jen retreated. She didn't want to appear to be stalking him again.

By the time she returned to the house, it was time to put the cinnamon rolls into the oven. While they baked, she sat in the quiet of the kitchen, picturing Chase with his head bowed. With her busy schedule in New York, she'd rarely taken the time to pray. Jen closed her eyes. *Father, Forgive me ...*

A few minutes later, Aunt Queenie, wearing a belted pink chenille robe, entered the kitchen and sniffed. "Something smells wonderful."

"I rose and started baking before your rooster crowed."

Aunt Queenie sat down at the table, and Jen filled a mug with coffee.

"Thank you. Are you making Ovaleta's cinnamon rolls?"

"Yes. I've experimented with your cousin's recipe for years, but she's bested me." Jen smoothed icing over the warm buns.

Aunt Queenie shook her head. "That's something I've never understood about you."

"What?"

"You feel like nothing you bake is ever good enough."

"Not settling for good enough is how you become the best." Jen placed the platter of pastries on the table. "But I've given up on trying to make these better."

A knock came from the back door. "That will be Chase," Aunt Queenie said with a lilt. "Come in. We're in the kitchen."

Jen cringed. She hadn't bothered to run a brush through her hair yet today. When would she learn to be ready for any possibility where Chase was concerned?

"Good morning." Chase squeezed Aunt Queenie's shoulder. "How do you feel today?"

"Finer than I look. Sit down and have one of Jen's cinnamon rolls."

Chase pulled out a chair. "I smelled them the moment I opened the door."

Jen poured him a cup of coffee.

"Thank you." He took a bite and mumbled, "These are almost as good as Miss Queenie's."

Aunt Queenie smirked. "We use the same recipe."

"Yes. But everything you make has a little bit of your sweetness." Chase winked.

Jen rolled her eyes. "I should put my boots on. It's getting pretty deep in here."

"Have another roll." Aunt Queenie pushed the platter toward Chase. "Then we can get down to business."

"I'll leave you two to talk." Jen wiped her hands with a towel.

Aunt Queenie reached for Jen's hand. "Please stay. The business Chase is here to discuss involves you."

"O ... kay." *What business, I wonder?* Jen pulled out a chair and sat.

Aunt Queenie clasped her hands together. "I'll get right to the point."

Jen sipped her coffee. "Please do."

"I've asked Chase to buy my farm."

Jen sloshed coffee on her hand and winced. "But it's been in our family for generations." She couldn't be serious. "You always said it would be my responsibility to protect the land."

Aunt Queenie swallowed hard. "I trust Chase to do so."

"If you need money, I still have a little in my savings." *But not enough ...*

"This is not about money, and you've shown no interest in the farm since you left for culinary school."

Jen's heart hurt. "But I love this place."

Aunt Queenie's face softened. "I will not burden you with this responsibility."

Chase shifted in his seat. "Miss Queenie mentioned this a couple of weeks ago, but I asked her to speak with her family first."

Aunt Queenie's sympathetic gaze melted Jen's resistance.

"I'll keep the house. And Jen, when the time comes, it will be yours. But I need to ensure the waterfall and the land are safe from developers. They've hounded me for years."

Chase blew out a long breath. "I don't have enough capital to buy your farm."

"I'm sure you have enough for a down payment. We could probably make some sort of arrangement for the balance."

"I probably had enough cash at one time, but I bought the old Redbird Roost last month. I need a market place for my extra produce, and Bobbie Jo wants me to carry her cheeses there too. Dad plans to lease a section to sell his beef."

Aunt Queenie's mouth hung open. "I had no idea."

"And I had no idea you would ever sell this place." Chase sipped his coffee. "I'm not saying no, but I need to speak with my banker." He patted her hand. "Don't worry. We'll figure out something."

Aunt Queenie fiddled with her napkin. "It's time for me to get my affairs in order."

"Don't talk like that," Jen said almost in a whisper.

Chase's dark eyes were somber. "Your land is worth at least half a million, maybe more. I won't take advantage of your situation."

Jen's eyes filled with tears. The farm was Aunt Queenie's. She'd paid Mom a hefty sum for Dad's share of the homestead. That money had paid for law school. With no other heirs, Jen and her mother had assumed the farm would be hers someday.

Chase gave a wry smile. "You've given us a lot to think about."

"I want this settled so I can stop worrying. Maybe"— Aunt Queenie stared into space—"we can figure out something that works for everyone."

Chase arched a brow. "I can't see Jen giving up her career to be a farmer."

Aunt Queenie sat up straight. "But she wanted to open a bakery in New York."

"That's not going to happen." Jen crossed her arms.

"These cinnamon rolls would be a hit anywhere, as well as the scones and the fresh-baked bread like you made yesterday."

Jen leaned forward. "So where do you think I should sell them?"

"You could buy the Redbird from Chase, then he would have the money to buy the land."

Jen held out her hand. "Whoa!"

"Louise made a good living at the Redbird Roost."

"But she ran a store. It's not the same as a bakery." Jen shook her head.

"You can be diversified." Aunt Queenie squeezed Jen's hand.

"I don't know." Jen's stomach ached.

"How will you manage to grow your produce and run the Redbird?" Aunt Queenie asked Chase.

"I plan to hire someone to manage the store."

Jen massaged her temple. "My head is spinning."

Chase leaned back in his chair. "Let's leave it for now. Maybe, the two of us can go for a walk this afternoon and talk."

Jen shook her head. "Can't do it. I have a PT appointment in Nashville this afternoon. Maybe, another day."

Chase gave her a long look. "I'm not sure you're ready to handle the Nashville Speedway. Why not let me drive you, and we can talk?"

Jen frowned. "Don't you have work to do?"

"The perks of being self-employed is that I can take off when I have other priorities."

Jen dreaded driving in traffic, though she'd never admit to her fear. "Fine. Pick me up at one o'clock."

Chase stood and grabbed his denim jacket. "See you then."

Jen sighed. No man that good-looking could be trusted. When she turned, Aunt Queenie's eyes sparkled.

"What?"

"I think everything is going to work out better than I ever imagined."

"I don't want your home or your farm. I only want you to get well."

"That's probably not going to happen, but having your future settled and my affairs in order will make me feel better." Aunt Queenie gave her a hug. "It's probably selfish of me to want you to stay. But, more importantly, I want you to be happy."

The farm was Jen's happy place, though earning a living here would be impossible. The population wouldn't support a bakery. Some dreams were just that. Impossible dreams.

Chapter 4

Chase spent the morning methodically cutting and grafting tomato plants. He hoped to produce a red tomato with the flavor of the purple heirloom varieties. The look Jen had given him this morning had made his heart pinch.

Chase wished he wasn't attracted to Jen. He wished she would trust him. He wished ... she'd decide to stay in Redbird Falls.

Chase had watched her work in the kitchen all week, humming while she baked, her hair messy and face untouched by makeup, so different than the image of the New York chef. He pictured her in his kitchen, cooking his vegetables, sharing a meal together. He groaned. Someone like Jen wouldn't want to spend the rest of her life living in his little cottage.

Jen's ambitions had taken her to the top of her field in New York City. Running a place like the Redbird Roost was beneath her abilities, even with an injured hand.

Chase was torn. He would love to buy Miss Queenie's farm, but he didn't want to upset Jen. Still, if Ms. Queenie didn't trust Jen to protect the land, then he shouldn't either. Chase couldn't let Miss Queenie down.

When Chase picked Jen up that afternoon, her hair was brushed for a change and hung loosely at her shoulders. She wore a bluish polo-shirt and khaki slacks.

"You look nice."

"Thanks." Jen pushed her long hair behind her shoulder. "I'm still not used to wearing my hair down."

"Why the change?"

"I need two hands to make a ponytail or a bun."

"Oh." Chase drummed his hands on the steering wheel. "How long will you have to suffer through PT?"

"Weeks, months." Jen shrugged. "I don't know." My doctor in New York thinks I'll be able to do basic things like hold a hairbrush soon but not a pastry bag."

"Tough break." Chase winced. "Sorry. That was the wrong thing to say."

"Don't worry about it." Jen admired the herd of Black Angus cattle grazing in the green pasture.

"Miss Queenie is looking better."

"I think so too."

"I've noticed you walking every day, plus the bread you've been baking must be good for her."

Jen smiled. "Did your parents like the zucchini Asiago tomato scones I sent over?"

"Dad and I arm wrestled for the last one. They sort of reminded me of pizza."

"It's the sun-dried tomatoes."

Chase told Jen about the different heirloom varieties of tomatoes he was experimenting with. He hoped Jen would be around in a few weeks to help him decide which varieties were the best. Before he knew it, they were in Nashville. When Chase parked in front of the medical complex, Jen turned to him. "This will take a while, so if you have any errands—"

"I brought my laptop." Chase reached behind the seat. "I have plenty of work to keep me busy."

"At least one of us won't be wasting our time."

Jen trudged inside the dull gray building. She'd been warned the physical therapy sessions would leave her hurting. At the end of the appointment, Dr. Gerald placed an ice pack on Jen's aching hand.

Jen winced. "That didn't go so well."

Dr. Gerald gave her a sympathetic look. "The body amazes me with its ability to heal, but it's going to be a while for this hand to be useful. In the meantime, use your right hand."

Jen's jaw hardened. "I can't even write my name with my right hand. How can I do anything else?"

"My grandmother lost an arm when she was a teenager." Dr. Gerald pushed his glasses to the top of his bald head. "Later, she married and raised six kids."

"I'm not even dating, so I'm not going to worry about that today."

Dr. Gerald frowned. "You still have one good hand, and left-handed people have experience in making accommodations. Focus on what you can do."

Jen grimaced. "I can knead dough with one hand."

"That's more like it. You need to work hard and be patient. I'm going to give you an exercise regime, and try to knead the dough with your left hand to help your muscles regain strength."

"Okay."

"And don't give up." He handed her a sheet of paper. "Exercise morning and evenings. When I see you next week, I expect to see improvement."

Jen nodded.

When she exited the medical complex, Chase immediately opened his truck door and stepped out to help her get in. "How did it go?"

"Awful."

"I'm sorry." Chase hugged her.

Jen leaned into him and savored the feel of his strong arms. "Don't be. If not for the accident, I'd still be in New York, missing this time with Aunt Queenie. I've been pretty selfish."

"Don't be so hard on yourself. You've worked hard, and she's very proud of you."

Jen lifted her head ... his lips were so close. Time seemed to stand still as they stared at each other. Remembering Bobbie Jo, Jen inhaled sharply and stepped out of the embrace. "Let's get out of here."

Jen concentrated on controlling her breathing as Chase weaved through the traffic. Why was she so attracted to this man? The guy was a natural hugger and was probably just being compassionate. Goodness, she'd almost made a fool of herself.

Jen remained mute and stared at the countryside for the rest of the drive home.

When Chase parked the truck in front of Aunt Queenie's house, he squeezed her shoulder. "It's been a tough day for you."

Jen shrugged away from his touch. "I thought we were supposed to talk about the farm and the Redbird."

"We both need more time to think."

Jen closed her eyes and leaned back on the headrest. "I can't imagine making enough money to support myself in Redbird Falls. And you don't have to worry about having a down payment because I'm sure Aunt Queenie will sell the farm to you at a price you can afford."

Chase stiffened. "I won't take advantage of her."

"Why would I think that?" Sarcasm dripped from Jen's tone. "Just because you flirt with all the ladies at church."

Chase harrumphed. "You can blame Mom for that."

Jen rolled her eyes. "It's pretty wimpy to blame your mom for your behavior."

"It's the truth." Chase lifted a shoulder. "When I was a kid, Mom asked me to give all the widows extra attention. Everyone needs a hug now and then."

"Aunt Queenie's not a widow."

"She's like a favorite aunt."

"Well, she's *my* favorite aunt." Jen crossed her arms. "So, I'd like to see the Redbird tomorrow?"

"Surely, you're not considering ..." Chase pursed his lips.

"Not really. But out of respect for Aunt Queenie, I'm going to go look at the property."

Chase scratched his jaw. "If you're sure, I can give you a tour tomorrow morning."

"I'm not sure about anything." Jen opened the truck door and jumped out. A rainbow painted the sky and disappeared into a field of daffodils. *This place was so beautiful.* If only she could call it home. Jen shook her head. *Don't get your hopes up.*

Chapter 5

Jen tossed and turned through the night. The next morning, when she stood inside the deli section of the old General Story, it seemed a dream. A bad dream. Dust covered everything. "I wonder if the commercial oven still works."

"It was functioning when the store closed." Chase opened the oven door and a spider crawled out.

Jen wiped the pine counter with a tissue. "This needs a good scrub. Still, I love the vintage display cases."

Chase squatted down and wiped away dirt. "I think the floor is oak."

Jen glanced out the dirty window. "If there were more people in Redbird Falls, this place would have potential."

"You've been gone a long time. Nashville is bursting with growth. Most of my CSA customers live on the fringes of the metropolitan area. Plus, the farm-to-table movement is growing." Chase pinched his chin. "Maybe, we can be partners."

"No. If I'm in this deal, I want complete control."

"So, are you interested in buying the place?" Chase removed a blue bandanna from his pocket and wiped his hands.

Jen bit her lip. "I need to think about it?"

"And I need to decide whether or not I want to sell." Chase reached for her hand. "Let's pray about it together."

Jen's breath caught. "I don't—"

Chase lowered his head. "Father, thank you for every blessing, every opportunity ..."

Jen could hardly think for the feel of his callused hands. When he said, "Amen," Jen's eyes popped open to discover Chase's face much too close to hers.

Chase cleared his throat and stepped back. "I need ..." His voice was husky. "I need to get to work."

They stared at each other ... until a scraggly black cat padded across the floor and yowled."

Chase smiled. "Hey, Roscoe. I wondered where you were."

"He lives here?" Jen's mouth hung open.

"Yes. I took him home with me twice and he returned. So, I leave food for him."

Jen picked up the cat. "Poor baby. All alone in the world."

"I guess whoever ends up with the store gets Roscoe."

Roscoe rubbed his chin against Jen's. "I've always wanted a cat. *A bakery with a cat. Mom really will have a conniption.* Jen smirked. If she got to keep Roscoe, it might just be worth the drama.

As Jen kneaded dough that evening, her thoughts swirled. She respected her mom too much not to tell her about the Redbird. Waiting would only make it worse.

After putting the dough in the refrigerator, Jen checked on Aunt Queenie. She discovered her snoring in front of the television while *Wheel of Fortune* played.

Jen called her mother and returned to the kitchen.

"Are you enjoying the wilderness?" Her mother's voice was crisp.

"It's wonderful."

"How's Queenie doing?"

"Her color is better, and she's not complained about pain. But she sleeps a lot."

After small talk, Jen blurted, "I'm thinking about buying the old Redbird General Store."

"What?"

Words tumbled from Jen's lips. "Miss Louise died, and the place would make the perfect bakery."

"Redbird Falls isn't even a town, just a crossroads."

Jen's stomach knotted. "I feel at home here. When I walk into the post office, they know my name. People wave at me."

"The pool of eligible men is very slim there. You'll probably wind up being an old maid, just like Queenie if you stay. Is that what you want?"

Jen pictured Chase's crooked smile. "No, but finding the perfect husband seems pure serendipitous luck to me. It can happen here, or anywhere.

"You've gotten me off the topic. Everyone needs to be able to take care of themselves. I learned that when I lost your dad. Queenie and I won't always be around to be your safety net."

"But Redbird Falls is where I'm happy. And right now, Aunt Queenie needs me."

"I'm glad you are able to be there for her, but buying a rundown building is a mistake."

Jen fumed. "You haven't even seen the place."

"I don't need to see it. Be patient. I'm working on a plan that might make all your dreams come true."

A feeling of dread washed over Jen. *This can't be good.*

"I have another call coming through." Her mother's tone was curt.

"Okay. Take care." Jen disconnected and thought about Dr. Gerald's words. *Don't give up.*

Chapter 6

On Wednesday morning, Chase sat on the old bench at the creek and lifted a petition. *Father, give me wisdom. Not my will, but your will be done. Amen.*

A sense of peace filled him. The idea of Jen staying in Redbird falls lifted his heart, but he was afraid to hope. Too many questions. Could he trust her with his business? Would Jen get along with his dad and Bobbie Jo? He'd been Bobbie Jo's mentor since she'd started making cheese in 4-H at the age of twelve. Now she was twenty and pursuing her dream, just like he had.

Jen had looked so sad when she'd exited the medical clinic. He shouldn't have hugged her. Even though she'd leaned into him for a brief instant, she'd pushed away. He longed to see her smile, to laugh, and to be at ease in his company. Too bad everything he did had the opposite effect.

Thank goodness he hadn't yielded to his impulse to kiss her yesterday while in the Redbird ... and after praying, of all things. Her lips had looked so soft. An inch more, and ...

He was in trouble. Big trouble. He lifted his petition again. *Father, help me do the right thing for Jen and Miss Queenie and the others counting on me.*

When Chase saw Jen again an hour later, he handed her a manila envelope.

"What's this?" Jen lifted her face to him.

"The paperwork that goes with my purchase of the Redbird and the receipts from my CSA customers. I'll sell the place to you for the same price I paid for it if my CSA customers can pick up their weekly orders at the Redbird. I'll pay you a fee for each box of produce you handle."

Jen removed a sheaf of papers and scanned the first page. The purchase price was doable. Her heartbeat increased. Property was much more reasonable in Kentucky than New York. "Will your dad be upset?"

"Not if you're willing to lease him a section so he can sell his beef."

She nodded. "So, you're also asking me to sell your excess vegetables."

"And Bobbie Jo's cheeses."

Sweat beaded on Jen's forehead. "I'll need to hire help."

Chase lifted a shoulder. "I can recommend some people."

"I need to run the numbers." Jen bit her lip. "The building might just sit there for a while."

"From the bread I've tasted, you could open as soon as you get everything cleaned up and people hired.

"It depends on Aunt Queenie's health."

"I wouldn't have it any other way."

If she bought the Redbird, her mom would throw a hissy fit. *Not the first time ... nor the last.*

The real barrier was her infatuation with Chase. Could she keep everything professional? Plus, she liked Bobbie

Jo. The idea of watching her relationship with Chase advance to the next level made Jen's heart hurt.

Still, Redbird Falls was the place she wanted to be. That's what her heart desired above all else. But would it be worth the risk? She might end up broke, with a crushed heart as well as a crushed hand.

Chapter 7

The next two weeks sped by as Jen made preparations for a new business. "I'll need to buy a van soon," she said to Aunt Queenie while loading cleaning supplies into the Buick. Even though the sale of the Redbird wouldn't be final for another two weeks, Chase had given her the keys to the place.

"I don't mind sharing my old car." Aunt Queenie handed her a basket of lemon-blueberry scones.

"Why are we taking these?"

"We'll need a snack and you never know who might stop by." Aunt Queenie giggled. "Let's go."

Jen picked up a bag of cat food and put it next to her supplies. "Fine. You can watch me clean; but if I see you wipe off a table, I'm bringing you home."

She finished loading the car and headed to the Redbird, gasping when she pulled in to park. "Why are all these cars here?"

Aunt Queenie beamed. "You'll see."

Lee Ann held the door to the Redbird open. "Surprise."

"What's going on?" Jen looped her arm through Aunt Queenie's.

"We came to help." Lee Ann gushed. "Leta Evans and Jolene Pitchford have already started on the windows, and

I started scrubbing in the old deli area. More neighbors are coming."

Jen swallowed the lump in her throat. "I don't know what to say."

Aunt Queenie elbowed her. "I'd suggest you say, 'Thank you.'"

Jen nodded. "Thank you, everyone."

Roscoe curled around her legs and mewed.

Chase walked in carrying a tray of sandwiches wrapped in cellophane. "Where do you want this, Mom?"

Lee Ann pointed to two crockpots on the counter. "Over there."

"I have a cooler of drinks in the truck." He set down the tray, cupped his hands like a megaphone, and shouted, "It's time to raise the Redbird Roost."

Jen smiled at the new name.

Bobbie Jo arrived with her hair pulled back in a high ponytail looking like a schoolgirl. She hugged Jen. "Thank you for this."

"I should be thanking you for letting me sell your cheeses."

Later in the day, they settled in for delightful lunch. As the pastor blessed the food, Jen thought her heart might burst with thankfulness. Then by early evening, the antique wooden countertop shone like new. Jen couldn't believe the transformation. One by one, everyone left except Chase.

She threw a paper towel in the trash. "Do you mind giving me a ride home? Aunt Queenie left to take a nap. Guess all the excitement tired her out."

"Happy to." Chase wiped his forehead with the back of his hand. "Why don't you join me tonight at my place for a bowl of chili, and we can work on the floorplan."

"I'm a mess."

Chase looked at his watch. "I'll give you an hour to change if you'd like, then I'll come back for you."

"Is Bobbie Jo coming?" Butterflies fluttered in Jen's stomach.

Chase frowned. "I don't think so. She doesn't really care where you place the coolers for her cheese, but I'm very interested in the floorplan."

Jen studied her scuffed tennis shoe. "Okay, but I can drive the Buick over and bring a pan of jalapeno cornbread."

"Now you're talking." Chase pointed to his cheek. "You've got a smudge of dirt there."

Jen's breath caught. "Umm. And you have grease on your face."

Chase grinned. "We're a matching pair."

She wet a paper towel and dabbed at her cheek.

"The other side." Chase took the paper towel from her hand, then gently wiped the smudge away.

Jen's heart thundered, and she stepped back. "If I'm going to bake cornbread, we should go."

"Sounds good to me." Chase's voice sounded husky.

On the drive home, she thought about Chase's closeness and scrambled out of his truck as soon as he parked in the driveway. She rushed inside and found Aunt Queenie sitting at the kitchen table drinking a cup of tea, her face flushed.

"I was about to call you."

Jen washed her hands. "We accomplished a lot today. It was so nice of everyone to pitch in."

"That's the way we do things around here." Aunt Queenie beamed.

"It was fun." Jen turned on the oven. "I'm going to put in a pan of cornbread and join Chase for a bowl of chili at his house. Do you want to join us?"

Aunt Queenie smirked. "And get in the way of romance?"

"It's not a date. Chase already has a girlfriend."

"Who?"

"Bobbie Jo."

Aunt Queenie tsked. "Nonsense. She's far too young for him."

"Tell him that."

"It's not necessary."

Jen added oil to an iron skillet and placed it in the oven. "We're going to talk about how to organize the different sections of the Redbird."

"Well, then, you and Chase will work better if you're alone."

"Okay. Can I fix something for you?"

"I had a huge lunch. Enjoy your evening." Aunt Queenie stood. "Besides, it's almost time for *Wheel of Fortune*."

While the cornbread baked, Jen showered and slipped into a pair of jeans and a new T-shirt featuring a cardinal. She grimaced at the pain in her left hand but was thankful for all she'd accomplished today.

She couldn't stop thinking about Aunt Queenie discounting Bobbie Jo as Chase's girlfriend. Had she made a mistake? She didn't think so. To assume otherwise, was just wishful thinking.

Chase opened his front door when headlights lit up his drive. His hair was still damp, and the cool spring air made him shiver. He stood in front of the robin's egg blue arched door that had charmed him three years ago when the real estate agent first showed him the home.

Jen's hair was pulled back with a large clip, and she wore dangling gold earrings. Her worn denim jacket fit snug across her shoulders.

Chase cleared his throat. "Did you have any trouble finding the house?"

"Your directions were easy to follow. I hadn't pictured you in an English cottage."

"What did you imagine?" Chase took the platter of cornbread.

"A cabin in the woods. Something rustic."

Chase shrugged. "I fell for the ivy growing up the chimney."

Jen followed him inside and stuck her face in a vase filled with forsythia. "These are breathtaking."

"Just wait until the roses bloom in a few weeks."

"I'll look forward to it."

After Chase blessed the food, they ate greedily.

Jen closed her eyes. "This is delicious."

"Thanks. Everything in the chili, except the beef, is from my produce."

"What kind of beans did you use?"

"Cherokee Trail of Tears beans. The seeds are very rare, but I hope to change that."

"I've already ordered special shelving for the seed display."

Chase refilled Jen's glass with sweet tea. "Do you think you'll be able to open the Redbird in time for the Dogwood Festival?"

Jen bit her lip. "That's only two weeks. Pretty iffy. I might wait until after Easter."

"Maybe just give out samples of your bread at the festival, then."

"I'm not even the owner yet."

"A small technicality."

Jen held her index finger in the air. "First, I need to experiment with the different flours that are being delivered tomorrow by the Amish mill. "Second"—she held up two fingers—"I need to train Hannah."

"I'm glad you hired her. Her brothers Levi and Jacob work for me."

"I didn't know that." Jen now held up three fingers. "Third. I need to hire someone to run the register."

"I'll think about who might be a good fit. Maybe you could consider the Dogwood Festival as a trial run. That's the first week the CSA customers resume their weekly vegetable orders."

"I like the idea of a trial run."

After dinner, they sat on Chase's leather sofa. He turned on his laptop. "Look at this, and tell me what you think."

Chase clicked on his 3D-virtual tour of the new Redbird, pleased at Jen's squeals of delight "I love it"

"I've been playing with this design software for a few weeks. I tweaked my original version for your bakery.

"It's not going to be a full-blown bakery. I'm just going to start out with basic bread and rolls, scones, and cookies. I've a lot of recipes to test. Tomorrow I'm baking a sourdough sweet potato crunch, a multigrain sandwich loaf, and an olive and rosemary loaf."

Chase leaned back and clasped his hands around his neck. "That doesn't sound like basic bread to me."

Jen closed her eyes. "I envision simple signs. *Bread, Cheese, Vegetables, Seeds, Plants and Beef.* Do you think the mill will let me sell bags of their flour and cornmeal?"

"I don't know why not?"

Chase adjusted the design on the screen. "Dad only wants to sell beef on Fridays and Saturdays. That's the normal pickup days for my CSA customers. If you can be ready by the Dogwood Festival, you might consider offering my customers a free sample with an order form attached. Bobbie Jo is going to try that with her cheeses."

Jen clasped her hands together. "If your CSA clients sign up for a weekly bread order, it will help me with inventory control and reduce waste. I like the idea of a shortened work week."

"The locals are pretty excited about you being open all the time," he said. "Still, it's your operation."

Jen shrugged. "Rebecca and another person can probably take care of the locals who gather for coffee. I might add deli meats and close after lunch. I refuse to work seventy-hours a week again."

"I've never had any problem hiring when I need help, but it might be a challenge to find someone with bakery experience."

"That might be a good thing. I can train people to do things the way I want."

When the mantel clock chimed ten bells, Jen stood. "Goodness. Look at the time. I need to go."

"Should I stop tomorrow and sample your experiments?"

"Please do."

"Let me get your jacket."

Chase couldn't remember when he'd enjoyed someone's company as much as Jen's. He inhaled her soft floral scent as she ran her hand into the denim sleeve. When she turned to him, it seemed natural to wrap his arms around her and lower his head. At her quick intake of breath, he froze. Instead of kissing her, he gave her a brief hug. "Goodnight." His heart hammered. He'd almost ruined everything. Maybe someday, Jen would feel the same way about him as he felt about her. A guy could only hope.

Jen fretted most of the night. She'd almost kissed Chase when he'd only meant to give her a friendly hug. She couldn't think straight with him so close to her. As he'd worked on the design of the Redbird, she could hardly concentrate for the thrum of electricity flowing through her veins. When he'd scooted in close to her on the sofa, her muscles had tensed.

Too bad she didn't have the same effect on him. This was going to be torture. This was too complicated. And there was Bobbie Jo's feelings to consider. Jen's fixation on Chase could ruin everything. Anyone with a lick of sense knew romance and business didn't go together. The problem was, around Chase, she didn't have a lick of sense.

Chapter 8

On the day of the Dogwood Festival, Jen hit the alarm at four o'clock in the morning. The papers had been signed and filed, and The Redbird was all hers.

When she arrived at the store, Chase was standing in the parking lot, his hands behind his back.

"What are you doing here?"

"Waiting for you."

Jen unlocked the door. "I have a million things to do."

"Let me handle a few of them for you, but first"—Chase handed her a package wrapped in white paper with a huge red ribbon taped in the middle—"open this."

"You shouldn't have." Jen tore through the paper. Inside, wrapped in tissue, was a black chef's apron with her name embroidered next to a beautiful cardinal. "I love it."

"And there's a matching headband like the one you've been wearing when you bake."

"That's so thoughtful."

Chase shrugged. "It's nothing. I noticed you'd ordered white aprons with redbirds on them, but I thought yours should be different. After all, you're the boss."

"Thank you."

"What can I do to help you?"

"I have loaves ready to bake as soon as the oven heats. You can help me transfer them to the racks."

"Before we start, let's say a prayer."

Jen gulped. "Okay."

He gently lifted Jen's two hands to his chest. "Father ..."

As he prayed, calmness washed over her. When finished, she opened her eyes and lost herself in Chase's dark eyes. He leaned down and gently touched his lips to hers. He was so tender. His was more perfect than any kiss she'd ever experienced. She wrapped her arms around his neck and he deepened the kiss, feeling the strength in his arms as she clung to him.

When the back door opened, Chase pushed away, leaving Jen feeling bereft. She blinked, came to her senses, and whirled around, her cheeks on fire. "Good morning, Rebecca." Thank goodness that hadn't been Bobbie Jo.

"Good morning." The young teenager wore jeans and a crisp red shirt that matched the color of Chase's cheeks. She was digging through her purse, then brought out a piece of paper. "Mom sent a list of heirloom seeds she wants to purchase before the crowd descends on us." The girl handed the list to Chase. "Here."

"I'll be glad to put this together for you." Chase strode away.

At seven o'clock, the new cashier, Winnie Riley, an elderly matron with a cheerful smile, arrived. Next, Sam and Liam started filling the beef cooler. They both wore new black and white striped butcher's aprons. Rebecca's older brothers, Levi and Jacob, were in charge of the produce section. Their white aprons with cardinals matched Rebecca's. Chase stayed nearby so he could introduce his CSA customers.

At eight o'clock, Jen unlocked the front door. Vendors were busy setting up tents in front of the post office and alongside the road. The official festival didn't start for another hour, but people poured into the Redbird Roost.

Jen had scripted the prices on the blackboard. She'd opted to keep it simple with traditional baguettes, a variety of loaves and, cinnamon rolls, a selection of sweet and savory scones, and cookies.

Aunt Queenie walked into the Redbird with Lee Ann who lifted her nose in the air. "It smells amazing in here."

Aunt Queenie spoke under her breath. "Brace yourself."

Jen's mother entered wearing pearls and a light blue cashmere sweater.

"Mom!" Jen shouted.

"You didn't think I'd miss your grand opening." She hugged Jen and fluffed her sleek blond bob.

"It's just a trial run for the festival."

A handsome fellow with a yellow cashmere sweater looped around his neck stood behind her mother. His dark hair was slicked back with gel. "This is Walter Stale." Her mother leaned in close to Jen and whispered, "He's the producer of the show *Best Barbecue in the South*."

Walter offered a handshake. "I watched your segment on the Cooking Network. The camera loves you."

Heat flooded Jen's face. "Thank you. It's nice to meet you."

Mr. Stale pointed to a man behind him with a camera on his shoulder. "We wanted to get a few shots of your place."

"Why?"

"I'm planning to produce a Southern baking show. Your mom hasn't stopped bragging about your awards. After watching you on television, I knew I'd found my next star."

Jen crossed her arms. "Maybe you should sample some of my baked goods first."

He shrugged. "That's not important. It's all about the image."

Jen's tone was curt. "If you'll excuse me, it's a big day for the Redbird."

Her mother gripped Jen's elbow and whispered. "This is the chance of a lifetime." She straightened and brushed her hand over her sweater. "I'll make dinner reservations so you and Walter can get to know each other."

Jen rolled her eyes. *Leave it to my mother to derail all my carefully laid plans.*

The day had brought more than a few surprises. Exhausted by the rush and excitement, Jen locked the door and thanked her new staff. She had sold every baked item, and Sam was down to a few packages of ground beef. Chase had signed up over a hundred new CSA customers. Most of his returning customers had added baked goods, cheese, and beef to their weekly orders.

Bobbie Jo hugged her. "It's been a great day."

Jen's insides had twisted every time she'd thought about Chase's kiss, unable to meet Bobbie Jo's gazes. Jen was so disappointed in Chase. He'd seemed so honorable. So good. The man prayed more often than a rooster crowed. He had no business kissing another woman senseless.

Chase wiped his hands on a handkerchief. "Are you too tired to celebrate tonight? Mom's grilling steaks."

Jen's heart skipped a beat. "I'm sorry, but my mom arrived with a guest."

"I met him and his cameraman." Chase's jaw hardened.

"Have you heard of the show, *Best Barbecue in Memphis*?"

"Sure."

"Mr. Stale, mom's guest, is the show's producer. He's thinking about doing a baking show."

Chase's face blanched. "That ... sounds like an amazing opportunity." His tone was cold.

"Mom thinks so too."

Chase stepped back. "We'll miss having you and Miss Queenie tonight."

"I'm sorry."

Bobbie Jo bounced on her heels. "If you get your own television show, will you use my cheeses?"

Jen held her palms up. "I just met the man today. This is all my mom's scheming. She's very .... ambitious."

"Nothing wrong with that." Bobbie Jo winked. "Maybe, you can suggest a cheese show?"

Yeah, right! "I should send you to dinner with them tonight."

"I'd go." Bobbie Jo raised her delicate brows.

Jen shook her head. "Sorry, but Mom would kill me. She's made reservations in Nashville at one of her favorite restaurants."

"You can't blame a girl for trying." Bobbie Jo looped her arms through Chase's elbow. "I guess I'll have to settle for dinner with you, old man."

Jen watched them leave with mixed emotions. The day had been a success and her heart should be soaring. Instead, it was heavy with guilt. And ... she closed her eyes ... jealousy. *Lord, help me.*

Jen yawned as Walter talked nonstop of his success and her mother lapped up every word. She sipped from her water glass. "If I agree to this arrangement, how many days of the week will you film in the Redbird?"

Walter grinned. "Oh, honey, we'll film in Memphis. That's why the cameraman was here. We'll create a set that looks like the Redbird."

Jen's stomach tightened. "I can't run the store from Memphis."

"Just hire someone." Walter winked. "You just have to show up every now and then to meet your fans. Think about the Gain's magnolia empire."

Jen's mother squeezed her daughter's knee. "I heard you telling Queenie you might only work a few days each week. Maybe you can film the show in Memphis, and then return to your bakery on Saturdays to meet your fans.

Jen's temple throbbed, and she forced a smile. "Thank you for dinner. I'll give you my answer in a few days." As for now, she had no answers for anyone.

Chapter 9

After an almost sleepless night, Jen rose early and watched the sunrise from the old bench at the waterfall. The wild Dogwood trees were in full bloom. She rested her elbows on her knees and dropped her head. "Father, help me." The water from the creek gurgled. Usually, the sound calmed her, but today, her insides churned.

So many people were counting on her. Chase, Sam and Liam, Bobbie Jo, and Rebecca, as well as the other people she'd hired. Her mother had paced in Jen's bedroom last night and listed all the reasons Jen should sign a contract with Walter. Every time Jen had closed her eyes, she relived Chase's kiss, and guilt assuaged her. Maybe leaving Redbird Falls would be best for everyone ... everyone except her and Aunt Queenie.

If the show was a hit, Redbird Falls might turn into a dining destination. Aunt Queenie would hate that. *Father, give me wisdom.*

Someone plopped down next to Jen, and she jumped.

"Good morning." Chase's deep baritone made Jen's heart skip a beat.

"Hey."

"What's wrong?" Chase wrapped his arm around her shoulder. She shrugged out of his embrace. "Don't you have a hint of guilt for kissing me yesterday?"

"Nope. Not since you kissed me back." He gave her a sad smile.

Jen planted her fist on her hip. "What about your girlfriend?"

"I don't have a girlfriend." He leaned into her, "Unless you're volunteering for the job."

"What about Bobbie Jo?"

"Whoa." Chase turned to face her. "That gal is not my girlfriend."

Jen narrowed her eyes. "You're always hugging her."

"She's always hugging me, and she just turned twenty. This conversation is making me mighty uncomfortable." Chase whispered in her ear, "And I wouldn't be kissing you if I had a girlfriend." He lifted Jen's chin with his finger. When their lips touched, it seemed a dream. Nothing could be this perfect.

When Chase released her and walked away, she felt stunned. "This is a bad idea." He stared at the falls, his shoulders rigid. "You'll probably be leaving soon."

But I don't want to leave.

"I knew all along your talents were too big for Redbird falls." He ran his hand through his dark curls.

"No, they're not." Jen stood up and planted her fists on her hips. "I'm finished with trying to create magical experiences for spoiled foodies."

Chase gave her a serious look. "What about the show?"

Jen shrugged. "That was never in my plans."

"But your Mom—"

"Mom's definition of success will always be different than mine."

Chase swallowed hard. "I can manage the Redbird for you, if you want to do the show."

"Would you really do that for me?"

He came to her side and tweaked her cheek, as if she were a kid. "If that would make you happy."

Jen leaned into him. "It's been a long time since I've been this happy. I'm not going anywhere."

Chase squeezed her hard. "Do you really think you could be happy in Redbird Falls?"

"I *am* happy in Redbird Falls. This is where my hearts always longed to be, but I had to leave to realize it."

"What about your mother and her plans for you?"

Jen's heart pinched a bit. "I love and respect her, but I'm going to follow my heart. Redbird Falls has always felt like home to me. I'm staying."

Chase owned her lips, and Jen thought it wondrous. Then he nuzzled her neck and whispered, "Welcome home, Jen Bennett."

A cardinal landed on a dogwood branch and chirped as Chase nibbled on her ear. Jen sighed and rested her head on his shoulder. *It's so good to be home.*

Shelia Stovall

Shelia Stovall is the director of a small-town library in southern Kentucky, and the children call her Miss Shelia. She is the author of the acclaimed *Weldon Series*. Shelia and her husband Michael live on a farm, and she enjoys taking daily rambles with their two dogs to the creek. Spending time with family, especially her grandchildren, is her all-time favorite thing. The only hobby Shelia loves more than reading uplifting stories of hope is writing them.

Website: www.sheliastovall.com
Facebook: https://www.facebook.com/writerSheliaStovall
Twitter: https://twitter.com/Sheliastovall1
Instagram: https://www.instagram.com/stovallshelia/

Charity's Shadow

TRAVIS W. INMAN

Chapter One

A young lady glided among the plants and balloons lining the walls of Edna's Flower Shop. Her fingers tenderly brushed the crimson petals of a long stemmed rose and paused while she leaned forward and sniffed gently, closing her eyes as the fragrance teased her. While other girls saw the flowers in the case and appreciated their beauty, she saw the allure of romance and the adventure of love. She smiled deeply and suggested a subtle curtsy as she longingly made her way to the door and out into the street.

An elderly woman wearing a long apron stepped aside as she swept the sidewalk and glanced at her with a frown, forcing the lines in her forehead to wrinkle. "Charity, you'll be late for work again if you don't mind the time," she admonished, and her face softened.

Charity gently tucked a strand of Edna's hair behind her ear. "Oh, Edna, you're so sweet to worry about me."

Edna didn't try to hide her affection. "Nonsense, child. Now run along. I'll see you tomorrow."

With a deep sigh, Charity turned and made her way down the sidewalk and around the corner, seeming to float along as she glanced back for one final glimpse of the roses before they were out of sight, leaving her fleeting shadow as the only evidence she had been there.

Edna, long familiar with Charity's morning routine, now turned to witness the next act of the play. A young man, unaware of Edna's gaze, was leaning from his second story apartment window, staring wistfully after Charity's shadow as she floated into the sunrise glowing around the corner.

For months, the young man had silently watched Charity but never developed the courage to chance meeting her. So, he watched from the safety of his window, secure in knowing that he would never have to face this unnamed beauty.

While the boy watched the girl, Edna watched the boy with an understanding gleam in her heart. She once walked through fields of flowers in search of the very thing that surrounded her, never managing to wrap her heart around her elusive love. *But,* Edna decided, *this time it will be different. Maybe it's too late for me, but perhaps I can help make it happen for them.* She swept for a moment, then paused, examining the broom closely. *And all it will take is a push in the right direction ...*

The young man straightened, walked away from the window, and grabbed his jacket. "I'm leaving now, Ma."

A tight-faced, narrow-eyed woman bent through the bathroom door and spoke over her cigarette, several of her hastily rolled curlers dangling lower than they should. "Benny, don't you leave without kissing your mother."

He sighed and walked across the room. "It's Ben, Mom. My name is Ben."

His mother squeezed his cheek. "But you'll always be Little Benny to me."

He exhaled with resignation, pecked his mother's cheek, and disappeared down the hall, wincing at the voice following him. "Don't be late, Benny! Dinner's at six. We're having a brisket."

"Bye, Ma," he shouted over his shoulder as the door shut behind him. "I'm a college grad, for Heaven's sake. I'm not Benny," he mumbled.

Once in the street, Ben stopped and inhaled deeply, as if the air outside tasted cleaner than the air in his apartment. He crossed the street and stepped over the broom lying in front of the flower shop. Thinking it odd for Edna to leave her broom on the sidewalk, he retrieved it and leaned it against the door frame. He peered through the window and saw Edna lying on the floor just inside the shop. He hesitated, glanced around as if looking for help, and then cautiously opened the door and crouched beside her. "Ma'am?" he called. "Miss Edna? Are you okay?"

Edna stirred and stared at Ben as he extended his hand to her. She grasped his hand firmly and sat up, causing him to recoil. "Oh, my. I must have fallen."

He blinked and swallowed, as if restraining his panic. "Ah … well? Um, are you … okay?"

She smiled sweetly. "I'm fine. Really. Could you help me to my feet?"

He nodded and hesitantly pulled her to a stand.

"My, you're a strong one," Edna beamed and squeezed his biceps.

"Well, I, uh …" Ben had no idea how to respond. "Thank you. Are you okay?" he repeated and let go of her firm grip, almost having to pry her fingers apart.

Edna wobbled for a moment and started to lean forward.

Ben couldn't hide his concern as he steadied her. "Why don't you sit down for a moment?" he asked, tilting his head toward a stool.

"You're nice," her smile broadened as she observed him. "And caring, also."

"I'd better call an ambulance," Ben offered.

"That won't be necessary. I only tripped." She tried to take a step, and groaned with pain. "Gah!" she gasped and sank to the floor. "I think I twisted my ankle."

Ben blinked rapidly, and peeked at the door, as if wishing someone would come help him. "It's a good thing you're sitting down. Where does it hurt?"

"And compassionate," she noted.

"I beg your pardon?"

"And polite."

Ben blinked again.

Edna smiled innocently. "Don't mind me. I'm only an old woman who talks to herself. What's your name?"

"Ben Greene."

"Oh, yes. I knew Beulah Greene, who lives just a block down the street."

He nodded. "She's my mother."

"Please call me Edna."

"Okay." He hesitated. "Hi, Edna." He looked at the window toward the corner beyond. "If you're okay, then I'll be on my way."

"Oh? Where are you off to?"

He sighed. "I have to go to the pharmacy. Then I need to go by the Workforce Commission."

Edna stretched for his arm and inhaled sharply. "Dear boy, did you get fired?"

He blushed. "No, nothing like that. I got laid off from my last job," he confessed slyly. "I have a job coming in a few weeks ... at the museum ... but I need some work to tide me over until then."

Edna's eyes brightened. "So, you're looking for work?"

He looked at the floor. "Yes, ma'am. Sort of."

"What a stroke of luck. I need to hire some help. How about it?"

His eyes narrowed, and his nose wrinkled. "In a flower shop?"

She crossed her arms. "Is there something wrong with a flower shop?"

Ben's face flushed crimson. "No!" He responded, too quickly. "It's just that—I don't know anything about plants. Or flowers. Or ..." he swallowed. "Balloons."

"Well, I'll teach you."

He hesitated. "About flowers?"

She glared at him. "Of course, about flowers!" she snapped, and then paused to change her tone. "But what I really need, is someone to make deliveries for me." She patted her legs. "I'm getting too old to run all over the block and make my deliveries." Sadness mirrored in her eyes. "My tired old feet swell, and I shouldn't get too far from the shop."

"Oh." He didn't know what to say. Finally, he settled on, "So. Um. How much does the job pay?"

Edna blinked and scratched her chin. "I haven't thought of that." She shook her head as if disagreeing with herself. "Never mind the cost. How much should I pay?"

"Well, my last job was for twelve dollars an hour."

She coughed and her eyes grew large. "Twelve dollars? Why that's more than ..." Again she shook her head. "And there are some things worth more than money." She smiled and inhaled sharply. "It's a deal. You'll just have to get it done quickly."

"Get what done?"

She waved dismissively. "What you have to do." She pressed imaginary wrinkles from her apron. "Oh, there's one thing I need to know first. Do you have a girlfriend?"

He was startled. "Does it matter?"

"Of course not." A silly laugh escaped while she studied his quizzical expression. "Well?"

"Well, what?"

Her smile narrowed. "Don't be coy with me. Do you have a girlfriend or not?"

He squirmed a moment as he considered his response. "I, uh, don't date ... uh, older—um ..." his voice faded as he saw Edna's stern look. He sighed and looked beyond the window as if he could still see Charity's shadow. "No, I'm afraid not."

Her smile returned. "Good! Now, can you start in the morning?"

He shrugged. "I suppose so."

"Great. I'll see you at seven o'clock."

He shifted, and then shrugged. "But ... I can't be here until eight."

"Eight?" Edna scowled and shook her finger back and forth. "That won't do at all. You must be here before eight for it to work."

He pressed his fingers into his forehead, as if pushing away a headache. "For what to work?"

She smirked. "For work to work. What else could I mean?"

"I'm really not certain."

"Then you must be here earlier than eight."

He hesitated. "Well, it's just that I—can't leave my mother before eight. She needs me to help with the house."

"Oh! You also wash windows?"

He pursed his lips. "I can, if you need me to do them."

"What? These windows?" She pointed. "Don't worry about these windows. I'll take care of them." And then she leaned forward. "Say, what about dishes?"

He winced. "Dishes?"

Edna glowered at him. "You just said you helped your mother with the house. Do you wash dishes?"

"Uh…" He lifted his watch. "I have an appointment with the Workforce Commission for my scheduled job search. I need to be going."

With hands on her hips, she leaned forward. "You don't need to keep that appointment. You have a job. Right here with me."

Ben swallowed. "Well, I … I don't know much about washing dishes at a flower shop."

Edna rolled her eyes. "Whatever are you talking about, Ben? We don't wash dishes here."

"But you said …"

"I said nothing about such things. You're the one who said you washed dishes."

"But I didn't! I said I helped my mom with the house."

"Of course, that's what you said." Her look of approval radiated warmth. "You'll work out just fine."

He couldn't hide his concern. "Miss Edna, are you certain you're feeling well? Did you hit your head when you fell?"

"Now don't worry about me. You just be here before eight o'clock in the morning."

He gazed wantonly toward the long-gone shadow. "It's just that … I can't leave before eight." He winced when he saw Edna's glare. "I sorta … I have to meet a friend."

"Oh, don't I know!"

His eyes grew large. "You do?"

"Never mind that. You just show up before eight, and I promise everything will work out." When he hesitated, she responded, "Trust an old lady. I know what I'm doing."

She winked. "Well, I don't know …"

"Listen to me, Ben. I need you to be here at seven o'clock. For things to work out, you must be here early."

He sighed with resignation. "What needs to work out?"

Edna pressed her face into her hands with a sigh. "Dear me. You worry about the details, don't you?"

He smiled anemically. "I'm just confused. I thought you said something about …"

Edna stopped him short. "Ben, I need you here early. We have stems to cut, baby's breath to arrange, and leaves to pull, and it all must be done before eight. If we get the work done early, then you can take a break around eight and go tend to your mother."

He blinked. "Tend to my mother?"

"I'm beginning to think you're a scatter-brained boy. You said your mother needs your help in the morning."

"I did?" He nodded. "I did, didn't I? Well, if you need me here at seven, then I'll be here at seven. But I have to take a break before eight. Good bye, now."

The next morning, Edna and Ben busied themselves cutting stems and posing leaves for their morning deliveries. While Ben filled balloons with helium, Edna prepared several vases for their mid-morning orders to the hospital down the street. She glanced at her clipboard and sighed. "I feel like all I do is send flowers to the hospital, and then send identical arrangements to the funeral home a few days later." She looked up from the clipboard. "Life seems so short, doesn't it?"

Ben shrugged. "Oh, I dunno, I haven't noticed." He studied his watch.

"Men," Edna tsked. "Never paying attention to what's important. All you know is that it's spring. You didn't pay any attention to the fact that it was just winter. And the flowers were sleeping in the cold ground, waiting for the warmth of the sun to coax them back to life. Men just seem to be surprised that the sun is warm and that it's a good day to play golf." As she talked, her clippers snapped loudly. "While us women are busy keeping the world moving forward and watering our romances, trying to keep them alive. Well, it's up to you to help with the watering, you know. We can't plant *all* the seeds and do *all* the watering." She exhaled loudly. "It goes much smoother if you help out, you know." She frowned when he glanced at his watch again and gazed out the window. "And you really are a man, aren't you? Haven't heard a word I said."

"Huh?" he glanced at Edna and blinked several times. "Did you need me to water something?"

She threw her hands into the air and pointed. "Just fill those balloons. You seem suited for hot air."

Soon, their first hour of work was complete, and Ben gathered the cuttings and stuffed them into a trash bag. He peeked at his watch. If he hurried, he could still watch his mystery woman walk down the street.

Edna, sensing that eight o'clock was drawing nigh, announced to Ben she was going to sweep the walk, not realizing Ben had already dashed through the back door and was making his way to the dumpster in the alley, trying to get to the corner before Charity made the turn.

When Charity approached, she started to greet Edna as usual but was quickly ushered into the shop without a warning, "You need to hurry, or you'll run out of time. Quickly, child. Now, take your time and smell the roses." She waved her on. "And hurry up!"

Somewhat disoriented, Charity found herself shoved through the door and standing in the small shop, which was void of people, save herself. Uncertain of what was happening, she stood for a moment and glanced through the store for a moment and then exited the building with a shrug. Edna, alarmed at Charity's sudden re-emergence, quickly scolded her. "What are you doing out here? I sent you inside the store to smell the flowers."

Charity stared at her blankly and leaned closer. "Edna? Are you all right?"

"Heavens to Betsy, I'm okay. Why are you out here?"

Concerned, she replied, "Edna? It's me, Charity. Are you well?"

"Never mind that, child. Why aren't you in the store? It's costing me twelve dollars an hour, and I want you to smell the roses."

"I beg your pardon?"

Edna's eyes widened. "Oh, dear. Didn't you like him?"

"Who?"

"That boy."

"What boy?"

"Ben, that's who. What's wrong with him?"

Charity tentatively glanced through the window. "Ben? ... er?"

"No, not Ben Hur. Ben, a boy."

Charity's concern for Edna was increasing each second as she leaned forward to peer into her eyes. "No, Edna. I've never been a boy. What's wrong? You look flushed."

"Charity! I want you to go into the store and meet Ben."

"But I was in the store. There's no one in there." Her eyes scanned Edna's face. "Are you certain you're okay? Have you been sleeping well?"

"Balderdash! I'm fine. And what do you mean that no one's in the store?"

"Just that, Edna. No one's in there. It's just the two of us. Maybe you should let me walk you to the hospital."

"Never mind the hospital." Edna grabbed Charity by the shoulders. "Come with me, there's someone I want you to meet."

"Okay." She surrendered to Edna's pulling arms and followed her into the store, where she was wandering through the room calling, "Ben? Ben?"

Charity was getting scared. "Edna? Who is Ben?"

"The boy who works here. I want you to meet him."

"But, there's no boy here. It's just you and me. And you've never had an employee in all the time I've known you." Edna frantically searched the room. "Let me walk you to the hospital where I work. It's only a couple of blocks down the street."

Edna's lips pressed together until they turned white. "I need no doctors. I need to find Ben."

Charity saw the clock and gasped. "Oh, look at the time. I have to run. Are you certain you're okay?"

"I'm fine. Perhaps I'll see you tomorrow?"

"I promise to check on you in the morning. Oh, I'm late. I must hurry." With that, she turned and trotted from the store and down the street.

Ben stood on the corner as Charity rushed past, sighing with resignation when her shadow disappeared around the corner. Dejected, he returned to the store, only to find Edna glaring at him, her arms crossed.

"Where have you been?"

"I took the clippings to the dumpster."

"Why on Earth would you do that?"

He glanced at the open door and the street beyond. "Are you asking me why I would take out the trash?"

Rubbing her temples with both hands, Edna collapsed into a chair, pressing her hands against her temples. "The best laid plans of mice and men ..."

"I beg your pardon?"

Her smile returned. "And you have such good manners too. But it won't mean anything if I can't get you two to meet, will it?"

"I don't follow you, Edna."

She shook her head and emitted a deep sigh. "I wanted to introduce you to a young lady I know. She's so sweet, and she comes by here every morning. She's very pretty and has a lovely smile. But, for some reason, she hasn't found love." She smiled warmly. "I wanted you to meet. You seem like a perfect match."

A crimson streak burned around Ben's ears as he stared at the floor. "I don't know what to say."

"Tell me that you'll meet her tomorrow."

"Well, to be honest, there's a girl that I want to meet, but ..."

Edna's face softened. "But what?"

"But she's just too pretty to meet a guy like me. So, I just watch her walk by, not even knowing her name."

Her smile returned. "Ah. Well now, I think we can solve this problem. I want you to be here bright and early in the morning. Try to be here as close to seven as you can be. This young lady comes by every morning, but only stays a moment. She's the sweetest thing, and I know you'll just love her. Won't you try to be here on time?"

"I'll be here. I promise," he said, shyly.

The sun was barely peeking over the horizon when Edna turned the key in the lock and saw Ben cross the street, his hand lifted in greeting. "Good morning," she called.

He shoved his hands in his pockets. "Good morning, Edna. Are you having a good day?"

"Absolutely lovely. I work with flowers. How can anything go wrong for me? Oh, I'm glad you're here a few minutes early. I need to run to the corner market and make some change for the register. Will you accept the morning delivery for me?"

"Of course."

Edna flitted through the store a moment, then stepped into the street and around the corner. After a moment, the bell rang, and Ben gasped when he saw the delivery girl. She was tall and slender, with shoulder-length brown hair, and a tempting smile. Her eyes sparkled when she laughed, and she laughed when she saw his awkward wave. She was every bit as lovely as Edna described.

"Hi, my name is Ben."

She evaluated him when he extended a hand toward her. "How are ya, Ben? My name is Chastity. Are you new here?"

Ben smiled, as if he'd never breathed fresh air. "It's my second day." He was motivated by her smile and shapely figure, so he dug deep into his heart for courage and commented, "Edna said she hired me so I could meet the pretty girl who came by every morning. That has to be you, right?"

Chastity returned his smile. "How sweet of Edna. She's the greatest. So, she wanted us to meet? Wow. I wonder how she knew I wasn't dating anyone?"

Ben seized her words and stepped closer. "So, you're currently single?"

She shrugged with ambivalence. "Single? If you mean not married, then absolutely. If you mean not dating, then unfortunately, I mean absolutely. A week or so ago I told my boyfriend to take a hike."

"That's too bad. So, he's only been gone a week?"

"Yep." She flipped her hair across her shoulder. "He was such a bore. Always talking about himself. Always snapping selfies, posting pictures of his shoes. He was a know-it-all too."

"I hate that type."

Her smirk faded. "I wonder how Edna knew I lost my boyfriend. Or that I even had one, for that matter."

"I dunno. But somehow she did."

Chastity reached into her pocket and placed a receipt on the counter. "So, what about you? Dating anyone?"

Ben flashed red again. "Me? Not a chance. I—uh, haven't had a date in several years."

"Oh?"

Her interest made him feel as if he should explain. "Well, it's just that, well ... I only just graduated from college a few months ago. I was so busy with my studies. And, I had little time for other things." His face flushed again, and he glanced out the window. "I even still live with my mother," he confessed.

She began to twist a curl of her long hair in her fingers. "Well, that's okay. Especially if you were going to school. It's not as if you're some dead-head bleeding his parents dry. Right?" She winked. "So, what were you studying?"

"Museology."

"Come again?"

"Museum Curation."

She slightly cocked her head sideways. "I'm sorry. Like, try again."

Ben smiled softly. "Museum administration."

"Like, with mummies and books?" Chastity eyed him warily. "I didn't realize such a degree existed."

He shrugged. "Well, it's the nerd option most people don't take."

She stifled a yawn. "Well, at least you have a plan. Right?"

Did he? He hoped so. "That's right. How about you?"

She put her hands on her hips. "Me? *Pshhh.* I don't have a plan. I live for the weekend."

Ben's eyes widened. "Ah, a weekender? That doesn't get you into trouble?"

"As often as possible!" She considered him as if he were a purse that might match her shoes. After a few seconds, she said, "You and I aren't a perfect match, but do you want to go out this weekend?" She reached for his hand and wrote her phone number on his palm. "Call me this afternoon."

"Uh, sure. Why not? I'm pretty sure I can change my plans. Besides, it'll make Edna happy."

She winked at him and collected her empty delivery cartons. "Making Edna happy is what it's all about." She turned and began to walk away. "Until it's time to make *me* happy, that is." As she left, she waggled her hips, causing him to blush.

When Edna returned from her errands, she grabbed her broom and smiled. "Oh, it's almost time, Ben. Are you ready?" She closed her eyes and looked up at the ceiling. "This time I won't play games. I'm simply going to introduce you to each other. How does that sound?"

Ben placed his cuttings in a trash pile. "Oh, you're back!" He came to her side. "We already met. In fact, she just left."

That surprised her. "Oh? You met Charity?"

"She was awesome!" He was excited. "I can't thank you enough for all your efforts. But her name is Chastity."

She waved dismissively. "No, Charity. But no matter. I knew you'd like her."

"Well," he reasoned and suppressed a thin smile. "I don't know if we're a perfect match, but we're going to get together this weekend."

"A date?" She clapped her hands in short bursts. "I'm so happy. Everything is working out."

"A date?" He repeated and then nodded slowly and shrugged. "I guess it's a date."

Edna wrung her hands as if they were wet. "For a little while, I thought you two would never meet."

"Well, I'm surprised she's interested in me; but I can't wait until tomorrow."

"Tomorrow? Heavens to Betsy. It's Friday, isn't it?" She turned to her appointment calendar. "I have the Pippin's wedding delivery this afternoon. We'd better get after it."

They busied themselves preparing the delivery and failed to notice when Charity glanced through the windows for a fleeting moment. When she noticed that Edna was busy, she shrugged and continued down the sidewalk.

When Saturday afternoon arrived, punctuated by beautiful spring weather, Ben found himself standing on the pier overlooking the Atlantic Ocean, searching for his date. He found her on the beach a few yards away playing volleyball with a handful of girls. When Chastity saw him, she yelled and waved, "Hey, Ben!"

He waved awkwardly, and then blushed when her friends turned and smiled at him. He'd never seen such a collection of girls. There was no doubt they were beach bunnies, and all could have passed for bikini models. He had no idea how to be around these girls. But what concerned him even more was the fact that they weren't making fun of him.

Suddenly questioning whether he should be there at all, he found a place near a sandcastle where he could watch them as they bounced and jumped on the sand. For the first time in his life, he was able to watch the girls without feeling like a pervert. When their game was finished, Chastity approached him. "You found us! You have perfect timing. We were about to go to the Cove and hang out. You wanna come?"

Having no intention of leaving early, he readily agreed. As the group walked to the Cove, the girls took turns introducing themselves to Ben. He tried valiantly to learn their names; but they came at him so quickly, the only ones he remembered for certain was Portia and Marla. And probably only because they flirted with him a moment before Portia asked, "Where do you go to college?"

His heart raced, and he struggled to breathe. Never had he received so much attention—and from such a group of women. "I, uh, graduated last semester."

Portia nodded. "From where?"

He flushed red. "Northcorn University."

Her face brightened, and she gasped. "Northcorn?" She pushed him playfully. "No way! My best friend in high school went to Northcorn." She nodded in appreciation. "So, whaddya study?"

"Museum administration." Again, he blushed. He expected that at any minute they would start laughing at him. But quite the opposite occurred. Marla turned, her eyebrows raised. "Museology? There's good money in that."

He blinked rapidly. "You've heard of it?" A thin smile spread across his lips. "Yeah. I'll do pretty well."

"I'll say," she responded, her lips twisting as she examined him closer. "You could make close to five figures." She leaned closer and placed a finger on his shoulder. "You might be looking for a different figure in the meantime, eh?"

Chastity leaned on him as they walked. "Easy, girls. He's with me." To his horror, she grabbed his hand and interlaced their fingers. "Ben is all mine."

Portia huffed. "And what about Rocky?"

Chastity glowered. "What about Rocky?"

Portia flipped her hair. "He's only your boyfriend."

Chastity shrugged. "We broke up."

"No, you didn't," Portia corrected. "You had a fight. There's a difference."

"I caught him with someone else. We're done."

"Whatever."

Chastity stopped walking and turned to face Portia, jerking Ben closer. "What's that supposed to mean?"

"Like you were faithful to him. You cheated first."

Chastity leaned into Portia's face. "He was asking for it. I saw him checking out other girls."

Portia made a point of rolling her eyes. "Like that matters! Every guy checks out girls. That's what they do, right, Ben?"

Ben, caught completely off guard, had no response. "I, uh, don't know."

"Ben is different." Chastity placed her arms around his shoulder. "He's smart, not tough."

Marla butted in. "But once you've had tough, it's hard to go back to average." She glanced at Ben. "No offense."

He swallowed anemically. "Uh, none taken." Ben wondered how he could get out of this conversation but was conflicted with being surrounded by beautiful women and didn't want to accidently mess up. Maybe he could just enjoy the moment and forget what they were saying?

Chastity rubbed her hand on his chest. "Don't be mean to Ben. He's the kind of guy you marry."

Portia jumped in again. "Really? You're going to marry?"

Chastity rolled her eyes again. "Who, me? Yeah, right! I'll never be a slave to some piece of paper."

"Whatever." Portia turned and continued walking. The rest of the group followed her lead. The fight seemed to be over for the moment. "What are you going to tell Rocky?"

"Nothing. It's not his business."

"He'll notice Ben is here. He's not blind you know."

"Let me worry about Rocky." Her grip on Ben's hand grew stronger. He was along for the ride, and he was holding hands with an insanely hot girl. What did he care?

When they arrived at The Cove, Ben discovered it was a hang out he would never have explored on his own. Couples were scattered along the boardwalk surrounding it, and many were making out—more than should be allowed in public. Despite his surroundings, Ben held fast to Chastity's hand, and they entered the club together.

He immediately hated it. The music was loud, and he felt the beat as it pulsed through the air. He also smelled marijuana smoke as they moved closer to the bar. He resisted the urge to scan the room, almost expecting to see his old youth pastor checking up on him, fully expecting to be caught doing something wrong. The girls made a beeline for the bar and each ordered a Cosmopolitan and then turned to Ben, who was expected to order also. "I'll have a Coke."

Portia smirked. "Definitely the marrying type. Come on, Ben. This is a bar. Live a little."

Ben's stomach sank when he saw her expression. He shrugged. "I don't drink, and I don't know what to order."

Portia placed a hand on his chest. "Well, then. Let me take care of you. I know what you need." She turned to the man behind the counter. "Long Island Iced Tea for Ben." She smiled. "You drink tea, right?"

"Yeah." He drank tea with almost every meal, so what could go wrong?

"Well, you'll love this. It's just like tea, only it has a little bite." When she said *bite*, she snapped her teeth together.

He shrugged. "Okay, thanks." He couldn't stop himself from continually scanning the crowd to see if anyone was going to recognize him and accuse him of indulging in immoral behavior.

While they waited on their drinks, Chastity began to dance to the music and started moving in a circle around Ben, who had no sense of rhythm. She leaned close to him and whispered, "Let's hit the floor."

For the hundredth time that afternoon, he was embarrassed. "I, uh—don't know how. To dance," he stammered.

"Come on, it's easy. I'll show you." She pulled him to the dance floor and began to tease, as if delighted in his innocence. "You can do it ... just follow me."

As she danced, Ben felt sensations he'd never imagined possible. There was an unexpected tugging in his stomach that made him want to join her with complete abandon. Watching her dance around him was intoxicating, and he desperately wanted to allow himself to indulge; but something was holding him back. To both his relief and dismay, the bartender motioned their drinks were ready. She grabbed his hand and pulled him to the bar. Uncertain what his drink was, he tasted it, half expecting it to explode in his face. "This is iced tea?" he asked Portia.

She tasted her Cosmopolitan and smacked her lips. "What does it taste like?" she asked without looking at him.

He sipped a second taste. "Well, like iced tea."

"Then it's iced tea."

He blinked several times, not sure how to proceed. Was he supposed to sip it? Was he supposed to down it in a few gulps? He glanced around the bar to ensure no one was watching him, and then nipped at it again. He liked the flavor and began to sip on his straw. In a few minutes, the drink was disappearing. Chastity was nodding at him with a devilish grin as she finished her first drink and lifted her hand for another. She motioned for him to order another drink.

Suddenly, he felt both flushed and comfortable, as if drawing strength and courage from the drink itself. He even found enough rhythm to join Chastity on the dance floor. Only, a few minutes later, the room started to spin; and he reached for her arms to steady himself.

Chastity giggled at him. "Wow, this really is your first time, isn't it?"

They made their way back to the bar, where he grabbed the wooden rail with both hands. "Do you want another Long Island?" The bartender peered at Ben, his eyebrows slightly raised.

He swallowed but couldn't find his voice. He looked at Chastity, who replied, "I think he does. It's going to be a fun night, and it starts right here! Woo hoo!" The rest of the girls lifted their glasses in salute and joined her with loud cheers.

The bartender must have had the drink ready to pour, and he placed glass number two in front of Ben. He blinked at it several times, trying to make his eyes focus. He knew in his heart he shouldn't drink it, but his mind told him to enjoy himself, as if saying, *you've come this far, why not go all the way?*

Chastity ordered her third drink and then focused her attention on Ben. She ran her finger along his arm and winked at him while her lips puckered. "You need to finish that drink," she encouraged. "There's something I want to show you." She opened her hand and revealed a small vial, then grinned again.

After a few blurry seconds watching her run her fingers over his hand, she exhaled loudly and grabbed his arm. "Come on, Benny Boy. Let's find a private place out back." She pulled on his arm until he wobbled to his feet and stumbled behind her. On the boardwalk, they found an isolated corner near the beach. She wrapped her arms around him and began to kiss him furiously. He had lost his ability to think rationally, and he began to return her affections with complete abandon.

He felt a hand grab his hair, and he was furiously flung backwards where he landed with a thud and rolled in the sand. A large, burly man pointed his finger at Ben. "What are you doing with my girlfriend?"

Rocky had found them.

Chapter Two

On Monday morning, Ben arrived at the flower shop early. Edna was busy sweeping and failed to notice when he walked in. When she saw him, she screeched and clutched her chest. "Sweet Moses in the river, you gave me a start."

Ben was standing taller than before. "Sorry, Edna. Are you okay?"

She pressed imaginary wrinkles from her apron. "That's a question everyone seems to be asking me these last few days. So, how was your date? Don't make me beg for an update."

On cue, he turned and let her see his right cheek and the shiner he sported.

Her hands went to her mouth. "Merciful Heaven. What happened?"

Ben gave a Reader's Digest version of events, politely eliminating any references to their acts of osculation. He emphasized how Rocky attacked him and then proceeded to pummel him until Chastity could get between them.

Edna frowned and seemed to be searching for the right words. "Ben, I'm old fashioned. I don't understand. Why didn't you try to defend yourself?"

It was Ben's turn to frown, followed by an exhale. When he spoke, his voice was small. "It's because I drank that stupid New York iced tea." His shoulders fell. "They must have put something in it that affected me. I mean, I was feeling pretty good—but I had almost no control over what I was doing." He sat on a stool near a refrigerator filled with roses and slowly shook his head. "I was in way over my head. I didn't belong to such a fast crowd. Honestly, I feel as though I'm lucky to be standing here." His lips curled in distress, and he shoved his hands in his pockets. "It was exciting. And I almost got swept away with the excitement, but I didn't belong there. My mother raised me better than to go drinking and carousing."

"And fighting," Edna pointed out with a mischievous smile.

"And fighting." Ben stood and stretched. "Man, Rocky was a south paw—he could hit like a pro. I must have looked like a fool laying there getting beaten."

Edna shook her head and walked to the window with her hands on her hips. "I just can't imagine Charity behaving like that. She seems like such a sweet girl. I'd never have guessed she was so—racy."

Ben shrugged and rubbed his jaw. "Well, I'm done with women. They're just too painful."

The grandmother in her smiled warmly. "Now, now. Let's not throw the baby out with the bath water. We misjudged the qualities of this particular woman. We'll find you another." She reached for her clipboard and checked the time. "We have a delivery at the hospital. Could you run this order over to room 549?" She inhaled deeply and then sighed. "It's for a friend who has cancer."

He reached for the potted plant and held it thoughtfully. "I'll be right back."

"And tell him ... he's in my thoughts and prayers."

"Will do," he replied and darted out the back door.

At that moment, Charity glided through the front door and lingered over the daffodils on the counter. "These are so pretty," she mused.

Edna looked up when she heard Charity's voice and her face clouded. "Had a good time this weekend, did you?"

Charity smiled and didn't seem to notice Edna's icy tone . "I did! We had a wonderful time." She quizzically glanced at her. "How did you know?"

Edna shrugged. "Ben told me."

Charity cocked her head. "Ben? I didn't know you knew Ben."

"Of course, I do, you daft girl." Edna moved to the counter and picked at some yellow leaves on an ivy. "Don't you feel bad about what happened?"

"With Ben?" She was almost sarcastic. "Well, he deserved to get beaten like that. Did him some good, you know."

Edna's eyes narrowed, and she leaned forward. "*Deserved*?" she enunciated carefully. "He *deserved* it?"

Charity chuckled softly. "Why, he was strutting around, telling everyone that he was the king of the hill. I had to put him back in his place." She laughed at the memory. "You should have seen him a few minutes later. That boy never saw it coming, bless his heart."

"That's the truth. But? Did he deserve to be humiliated?"

Again, a silly smile brightened Charity's face. "Oh, you wouldn't ask if you heard him bragging about how good he was. Why, when I delivered that first ringer, he was shocked." She demonstrated throwing a horseshoe with a careful toss. "And he knew then it was over. You should have seen his expression. Priceless!"

Edna faced her and crossed her arms. "What? It was *you* who beat him?"

"Of course, it was me! That's what's funny about the whole thing. It's not my first time throwing shoes, you know."

"But," Edna stopped to think. "But Ben said it was your boyfriend who beat him."

"Edna," Charity said patiently. "You know I don't have a boyfriend." Her eyebrow lifted. "What made you think it was my boyfriend?"

Edna stopped to consider her question. "Well, it's what he said. Ben told me it was ..." She lifted her hand to her mouth and then sorrow washed over her. "Oh. I can imagine how embarrassing that must have been. He was beaten by a girl."

Charity playfully flexed a muscle. "And severely beaten, I might add. It's not the first time I was the ringer." She glanced at her watch. "Oops, look at the time. I better get to work." She stepped onto the sidewalk and yelled over her shoulder. "I'll see you in the morning!"

Edna sat on her stool and leaned into her knees in deep thought. "Why would Ben lie to me about what happened? Was he ashamed he was beaten up by a girl? Or, was he simply being a gentleman and refused to strike a woman?" She heard his shoes shuffle on the sidewalk as Ben returned from his delivery.

He glanced over his shoulder and lingered by the door, as if waiting for a falling star. He seemed lost in the moment, unaware he was being observed. "Are you okay, Ben?"

Her question brought him back to himself. "Yes. I was just—watching the shadow." He turned his focus to Edna. "So, your friend said to say hello to you."

Sadness washed over her face. "Bill James and I grew up together. I'm sorry to see him suffer so."

"He had a positive attitude about his condition and said he got a good report. I sat with him a few minutes." He smiled meekly. "I hope it was okay."

"Of course." She waved him off as if his concerns were unfounded.

Ben rubbed his jaw and smiled. "I had no idea you were so close."

Edna paused. "Why, what do you mean?"

He grinned widely. "He's a man in love with you, and he didn't try to hide it."

Her lips pressed thin. "That old goat. What does he know?"

"Apparently, he's been in love with you for years."

Edna's face relaxed and her hand touched her hair. "He—told you that?"

"He made no bones about it," Ben's eyes were as bright as his smile. "He said you went out several times. And got pretty serious."

She shook her head vigorously. "Bah! Back in high school. And that was a long time ago." She folded her arms. "And then he went and married *Martha*."

"Who apparently left him almost twenty years ago."

She shrugged. "Well, who's counting?"

"He is," Ben said softly. "He asked me to invite you to come visit." His voice altered with his imitation. "You make sure she understands. Life is too short to live with regret. None of us knows how long we got left, why waste it? Let's make the most of what precious time remains." Ben shrugged, and his cheeks turned pink. "Well, that's more or less how he said it."

Edna chuckled. "That's a good imitation. You sounded just like him."

Ben nodded and then hesitated. "He also asked me to tell you that he was—sorry. And a fool. He said you'd know what he meant."

Edna inhaled for several seconds and then grimaced. "And he should be. Sorry, that is."

"He said he was wrong. And it cost both of you."

She turned to face the window. "More than either of us could know," she said, her voice growing weak. "He hurt me so much. I never tried to love again." She smiled meekly. "Which is why I'm trying so hard to get you and Charity together. I don't want you to live the lonely life I've lived."

"Chastity," Ben replied casually. "She's not Charity."

"No, I suppose she's not at all charitable."

Ben waited for Edna to speak again, but she simply stared at the floor while her face processed several emotions. "You want to talk about it?"

She hesitated and picked at a dark spot on her apron before sighing deeply. "Nothing to talk about, really. I laid it on the line for him, and he rejected me."

"What happened?"

"Oh, you don't want to hear my sad story." She shifted her weight and almost smiled. "We were getting married. He bought the ring, and I bought a dress. He bought me a single daffodil—my favorite flower. He said he'd give me the rest of the bouquet on our honeymoon. Oh, it was all very romantic. And then we had an argument."

"What about?"

She pressed imaginary wrinkles from her apron before continuing. "I wanted a church wedding. And he didn't."

"So?"

She inhaled and seemed to hold the breath. "It was our only fight. He said he wanted nothing to do with God or religion, and if I wanted a church wedding, we were done." She shook her head. "What was I supposed to do? My family insisted on a traditional wedding at our church. And they wouldn't hear of it. I was barely out of high school and couldn't imagine defying my parents. Not for something so serious. And I let him walk away."

Ben shrugged. "Maybe it was for the best? I mean, if he didn't want to serve God, what kind of marriage would you have? Isn't there a verse about being unequally yoked?"

Edna smiled warmly. "That's what my mother said. And it's easy to say, when you're not the one who's heart is broken."

"Fair enough. I guess you could quote that old phrase, the one about walking in someone else's shoes."

Edna's sad eyes studied her fingers. "Well, it's all in the past now. And it can't be undone. And Martha left him. Not that I'm surprised to hear it." She lifted a hand to her temple. "I wonder what happened?"

Ben cleared his throat. "He said he was bull-headed, and she had all of him she could stand." He shrugged. "Which is why I said it might have been best for you to part ways."

"Bull-headed. That fits," she agreed.

"He said their separation brought him to his knees. Literally. He said to tell you he found God and forgiveness. And it was too late for Martha, but it's not too late for you. Apparently, he's a changed man. And he has twenty years of proof."

Edna's shoulders fell. "Well. Enough of that. I'm sure he's a fine man, and all. But I'm not so sure I'm ready to just jump back in." She stared out the window. "You can't paste petals back on a flower and expect it to win the blue ribbon at the county fair."

"Maybe," Ben agreed. "But sometimes the flowers that bloom late have the sweetest fragrance."

Edna turned and looked at him with raised brows. "Meaning what?"

He shrugged. "Look, who am I to talk? I've never found love. And I'm too afraid to meet the girl of my dreams. But if I've learned anything over the last few days, it's that love takes effort. It doesn't just happen." His hand lifted to his jaw again. "And mistakes are painful." He grinned. "I can only imagine how much Rocky's hands hurt. I hope he's learned his lesson."

Edna closed her eyes and then chuckled. "Oh, Ben. What miserable people we've turned out to be."

He smirked, and his mouth opened several times ... as if he was trying to speak, but the words wouldn't form. "Maybe," he finally agreed. "But, if it's okay with you, I'm going to take a chance. The next time I see her walk by, I'm going to say something."

Edna considered his words. "Something? Like what?"

"I dunno ..." he hesitated and blushed. "She casts a really nice shadow. Maybe I could tell her that?"

Edna shook her head and waved him off. "I have no idea what you're talking about. But, it doesn't really matter. It's important that you try and not give up."

"Is this true for both of us?"

Edna looked out the window again and inhaled deeply. "We'll see." She turned back to him. "For what it's worth, I'm sorry about your date. I heard the truth about what happened."

He was silent a moment. "So, she came by again?"

"Just as she does each morning. Why didn't you tell me that she was the one who hurt you?"

He considered her question. Was it Rocky who hurt him, or the fact that Chastity and Rocky reunited while he lay on the ground with a bloody nose? Perhaps it was the humiliation of being left lying in the sand while his date affectionately greeted his tormentor. Either way, he couldn't think about Chastity without recalling some level of pain. "Well, some women are mean," he said dismissively. "Either way, I'm through with her." He smiled weakly. "My museum job will offer better company, so long as it's full of mummies."

The phone rang. Edna took another delivery order, which she handed to Ben. "This is going to the hospital for a young lady admitted over the weekend." She hesitated and then closed her eyes and inhaled sharply. "Before you go, I must make a confession. Would you sit for a moment?" She waited until he was settled on a stool, and she had his attention. "When I hired you, it was only so you could meet my friend. I'm sorry it didn't work out. I had a good feeling about you two, but I've learned my lesson. Unfortunately, I can't afford to keep you on at twelve dollars an hour. My profits are already small, and I simply can't afford you. I'm sorry to do this while you're down, but I have to let you go." She reached for his hand and affectionately patted it. "You can finish the week and then that will be the end."

He gave his best crooked grin. "Well, I understood that this was a temp job when I agreed to work for you. And I won't need to stay on all week. I'm okay finishing today." He squeezed her hand in return. "I appreciate your trying to fix us up. I know you meant well."

A tear glistened in her eye. "I did. And I'm sorry."

He stood and finger combed his hair. "Well, if it's okay with you, I'm going to make this delivery, and then, I'll clock out." His smile was miserable. "I just don't have the heart to be here any longer."

"I know." She watched him make his way out the door and onto the sidewalk. "Yes, I've learned my lesson. I'll never interfere with matters of love again. I'm not good at it." She picked up a package of baby's breath. "Some things weren't meant to be." She opened the package and then her gaze lifted to the ceiling. "Is it possible that bull-headed goat has really changed?"

She placed the package on the counter and reached for her broom. She could concentrate on her thoughts when she held a broom. She began sweeping with small strokes, but as her face turned red, the strokes became long and began to create a dust cloud. And then she stopped moving, her shoulders fell, and her hand loosely held the broom. "There are days I wish I could use the language that I'm thinking. But it just isn't Christian to do so." She pressed her fingers into the bridge of her nose. "Lord, is it possible you have actually changed that man? Could he ... did you ... is he?"

She exhaled and began to sweep again with small brushing strokes. "Well. If it's true, then the Christian thing to do is forgive him. Lord knows I've tried to forgive him. So many times. But maybe now I can really let it go." She stopped sweeping and leaned against the broom. "Perhaps it would be easier if I actually saw him? Heard him? If I hear it from his own lips. But—only so I can forgive him. If he thinks we're going to start up again— well he has another thing coming."

She glanced at her reflection in the window and tugged at a loose strand of hair, gently placing it behind her ear. She placed the broom in the corner and flipped the *BACK SOON* sign and stepped into the street.

Ben made his way into the hospital and stopped by the information desk to ask for directions. "Pardon me? I'm looking for C. Wilson. Could you tell me which room?"

The gray-haired lady paused a moment, and her fingers pressed several buttons on her computer. "Let's see. There are two Wilsons. Both have an initial of C. One man and one woman. Do you know which one?"

His forehead wrinkled as he tried to remember what Edna said about the delivery. "I think it was for a young lady who just arrived a day or two ago."

The woman nodded and said, "The young lady was admitted Sunday morning."

"Has to be her." He reached for the sticky note as she handed it to him and examined the number. "This will be the elevator in the west tower?"

"Yes." She pointed across the lobby. "The west tower."

When he arrived at the second floor, he realized he was heading for the intensive care unit. He walked to the end of the hall and double checked the sticky note. "Room 232. This must be it." He knocked on the door. Since no one answered, so he cautiously pressed against the large frame until the door opened slightly. From where he stood, the room seemed empty except for the lifeless form lying on the bed. He tiptoed around the bed and placed the vase on the windowsill and then turned to leave. He stole a glance at the young lady and stopped cold in his tracks.

Chastity!

He was forced into a double take as he considered the girl lying before him. Examining her closely, he was certain she was his former date. Chastity appeared to be sleeping. Afraid he might wake her, he tiptoed out of the room and almost tripped over the nurse carrying a tray of bandages. The woman asked him, "Are you one of Miss Wilson's family members?"

He shook his head. "No. But I did know her. We sort of dated. Once. What happened?"

The nurse shook her head. "Sorry. I can't tell you if you're not family." She pointed at a woman sitting in the corner. She's her sister. Maybe she could help."

"Thank you." He hesitantly approached the young woman. "Excuse me? Do you know Chastity?"

The woman didn't seem to hear him and didn't respond for several seconds. Finally, refusing to look at him, she said, "Chastity is my sister. What about it?"

"Well … I, uh, was with her at the party. I was sort of her date."

The woman looked at him; and he could see the familial resemblance beyond her tired, puffy eyes. "Sort of?"

Ben was certain his face was flushed from embarrassment. "She was kind of using me to make her boyfriend jealous."

The woman smirked and studied his face. "I guess that explains your bruises."

His hand involuntarily touched his cheek. "Yeah. Lesson learned."

The woman looked away. "Chastity has always been reckless. And a user. You're lucky you didn't get caught up in her drama and got away with only a few bruises." Anger clouded her face. "She was brought into the ER yesterday from an overdose of crystal meth. She and a friend of hers."

"A man or a woman?"

"A woman. There were three of them, and they were doing drugs late Saturday night … or early Sunday morning. One of them noticed that the other guy wasn't moving. They checked on him, and he didn't respond. At least they called 911. By the time the ambulance arrived, all three of them were unconscious. The boy who was unresponsive died last night. The other two were very sick, but they will probably recover. With brain damage, though." Her lips twisted and she closed her eyes. "Chastity bought a bad batch of meth. It was laced with fentanyl … and, well, they're lucky to be alive. The guy who died certainly wishes he was."

Ben felt his face flush at the thought how Chastity was throwing her life away. Was the guy who died Rocky? "Thanks," he mumbled. "I hope everything goes okay." He nodded and began to make his way down the hall, but he stopped moving because his hands began shaking, and his knees felt as though they were buckling. When he saw the waiting room on the right, he faltered a moment and then collapsed into a chair. His eyes were blurry and his breaths labored.

The enormity of what happened to Chastity was overwhelming. The longer he considered how he could have been in a hospital bed near her, the more distress he felt. Would he have done the drugs with her? Who knows? He hadn't said no to them at any point. By the time they got the drugs out, he might have been so drunk that he would have tried anything. After a moment, he collected himself and stood on shaky feet. "Lord forgive me, I was not being the person you made me to be. And I'm sorry. Thank you for saving me from this"—he glanced down the hall—"life, and please help Chastity. Let this accident be an act of redemption for her. And her friend. And, if possible, let me be a good witness to her." He shook his head and scowled. "I know. I've tainted my witness with her. But if I can, I will tell her about you and how you can offer her a new life." He sat silent for a moment, and then whispered, "And so help me, I'll never dishonor you again in exchange for a girl's attention. Oh, what was I thinking?"

The room started to spin again, and he reached out to find something to support him. Next thing he knew, a pleasant and friendly voice was directing him to sit back down. From his chair, he looked up and gasped to see she was the girl from the street, the one he watched walk past his apartment every morning.

She observed his reaction and must have thought it odd. "Are you okay? You look as though you saw a ghost."

"More like a shadow." He smiled. "My name is Ben."

She returned his smile. "Pleased to meet you, Ben. My name is Charity. I like the name Ben—it's my brother's name."

He hesitated a moment. "Listen, I don't want to seem like a weirdo, but I've seen you before."

"Where?" Her eyes were friendly. And inviting.

"I live just down the street, kind of across from a little flower shop on the corner."

Her face brightened. "Do you mean Edna's shop? I stop in there every morning and smell the flowers on my way to the hospital."

He blinked rapidly a moment. "Every day?"

"Practically." She laughed to herself and then her cheeks turned pink. "That sounds a little strange, doesn't it?"

He shook his head. "Not at all." He hesitated and concentrated on building the courage he needed to take the leap. "I've wanted to meet you for a long time, but I never had the opportunity."

"Well," she pushed a stray hair behind her ear while her cheeks turned pink. "Hi."

"Charity?"

"Yes?"

"Would you join me for a cup of coffee?"

"I'd love to."

Edna was sweeping her sidewalk when she saw a shadow on the wall and turned to see a stately man with gray hair grinning at her. He didn't say anything for several seconds but simply stared at her. His hand reached for his fedora, which he pulled from his head and held across his chest.

"I've heard this is the best place to buy flowers."

Edna stiffened and exhaled loudly. "It depends. What's your occasion?"

The man shrugged. "I'm looking to make an apology." He stepped closer and leaned toward her. "But it's not just any apology. This is my last chance to make things right." He rubbed his chin. "Years ago, I hurt my best friend. And I've been haunted by it all this time. Do you have any flowers that say, 'I was a bull-headed fool, and I don't deserve a second chance … but I'm really sorry for hurting you and dearly wish I could start over?' And these flowers also need to demonstrate how beautiful my friend is. I mean, do you have any flowers that reflect the sunset, as it settles into the sea, surrounded by the clouds of heaven and caressed by the gentle sea breeze as its rays brush gracefully across her captivating smile?" He shrugged innocently. "Or would that be best said with a balloon?"

Edna began brushing the sidewalk again for several strokes and then looked up. "I don't have any potted plants that say those words, but I think a daffodil might do the trick."

He reached for the door and held it open. "I'd like a single daffodil, if you have a moment to spare."

She leaned the broom against the wall. "I think I can spare a few minutes to make a new arrangement."

Travis W. Inman

Travis W. Inman grew up in the West Texas ranch country, spending his first twenty years cowboying with different ranches. He had a desire to enter the ministry but could never find the proper fit. After serving for a year as a traveling missionary throughout South America and Mexico, he finally found his place—and it required a uniform! The Army was his next adventure, although short-lived. After a year in the infantry, he sustained a life-changing injury and received a medical discharge. He then found his way into civilian service, where he became a field agent with the Department of Homeland Security, working along the northern and southern borders. During his twenty years with DHS, Travis volunteered as a police chaplain, and served on the Traumatic Incident Event

Response team, responding to such events as active shooter incidents and deaths of his fellow employees. Travis is now retired from law enforcement and is concentrating on his writing, being a grandfather, and traveling with his wife of almost thirty years. If you're looking hard enough, you can find him roaming the world, searching for hidden treasures, sampling local cuisines, and typing feverishly on his next novel.

Made in the USA
Columbia, SC
09 May 2022

60001867R00289